ORACLE CITY

THE MAKARIOS

ORACLE CITY

THE MAKARIOS

KAIT WATERHOUSE

Published in the United States of America February 2026 by Kait Waterhouse.

Cataloging-in-Publication Data is on file with the Library of Congress.

ISBN Paperback 979-8-9930112-0-2

Ebook 979-8-9930112-3-3

Author website: http://www.kaitwaterhousewrites.com/

Editor: K. Morton

Cover Design: Laura Sampaio

Formatting: Jade Nioma

For Ashlee—
You made me feel cool even when I wasn't.
I wish you were around to read this.

Dear Reader,

It is my greatest wish for you to enjoy Oracle City: The Makarios, and so I must inform you of some possibly triggering content found in this novel. At the risk of spoiling details, I'll list the content here: drug abuse/addiction, depictions of overdosing, depictions of seizures, graphic violence, murder, cursing, alcohol use, gambling, sexual harassment, misogyny, and sexual content.
I believe this list is complete, but if you feel I have missed something, please reach out to me.

Sincerely,
Kait Waterhouse

Characters (In order of appearance)

Lilith Lawson— *Styx's younger sister, serving Cronus Othonos*

Styx Lawson— *Lilith's older sister, right hand to Cronus Othonos*

Cronus Othonos— *Number One Titan in Arcadia*

Ares— *God of Discord*

Jason— *The surly bar owner*

Eve Raptis— *Unofficial graphic designer for The Titans*

Ivan Diamantis—*Nephew of Cronus, jack of all trades*

Nick— *Second best at everything, aside from annoying Styx*

Chester—*Forger, thief*

Tam Pappas— *Front Gate Security at Olympus*

Cap— *Official King of the Street Urchins*

Gertrude "Gerty" Galantis—*MMA fighter, The Amazon of Arcadia*

Marge Cirillo— *Rival Boss of the Othonos Family*

Sylvia Kouris—*Delos Park resident, Merchant*

Adrian Kordos—*Local celebrity, Prince of Arcadia*

Hyperion Othonos—*Arrogant brother of Cronus, Titan*

Crius Othonos—*Pervert brother of Cronus, Titan*

Tobias Diamantis—*Owner of Old World Diesel Service, Father to Ivan*

Leon Soto— *Spanish Syndicate Leader*

Antony Maldonado— *Bodyguard to Leon*

CHAPTER 1

The gods hated me.

My sister struggled to pry her arms from the greasy piece of meat whose hands were all over her. I rolled my shoulders and pleaded once more, "Just—let her go. How much does she owe?" I tongued the inside of my cheek, tasting blood from that last hit.

The temptation to spit washed over me then faded away in an instant when the beefy man holding Lil started chuckling. "More than anyone can hold in their pockets, little lady. She's not leaving with you today." He sized me up, but this time I knew he wasn't contemplating hitting me. No, he was imagining his hands around my throat. I glared at him a second before glancing at my sister. Her eyes were wide, almost totally blank with shock, but in them I could see a flicker of shame. At least she had some humility.

My stomach seized into a tight little knot. We'd never make it out of here. I jerked when the crowd on the other side of the cement wall roared to life as the horses left their gates in a mad rush.

I knew this was all going to end; I knew that Lil and

I were both goners. And yet, I couldn't stop myself. The desire to live, to get the hell out of here overpowered all my senses. I said, "She can't pay you back if she's dead. I can help her get the money. Give us two weeks. Two weeks." My nails were cutting moons into my palms.

The gods *really* hated me today.

The human scab who'd decided to hit me not long after I'd arrived, sniffed and flicked his cigarette butt at my feet. He sneered, "Her two weeks were up two weeks ago. It's over." Lil started crying in earnest, her long legs visibly trembling. The race announcer's voice echoed through the empty corridor. His words a blur of long-winded names and nonsense expletives. It was just us, everyone else was glued to the track.

No witnesses. A shuddering breath racked my lungs. I wasn't ready for this.

Lil started blubbering, "I'm sorry, I'm so so sorry. It was a mistake! I can get the money back, I promise I can get it back. Oh gods, please, please—" My sister's wails ricocheted through my brain until they were nothing more than a dull ring, leaving me deaf to everything else. The scab walked towards me, and I crouched down, fists raised, ready to fight to the end.

He smirked at me, his chapped lips curving into a saccharine smile. "Time to pay." His voice was murky, like he was speaking from deep underwater. My knees threatened to buckle beneath me, but I held, willing the fear in my blood to boil away. Fear wouldn't save us. It was no good. I was a statue.

He was too close to me. He kept leaning forward and his breath soured the air around us. My heart stuttered and he grabbed a fistful of my hair, yanking me closer to him. In his other hand was a butterfly knife. Cold and silver and ready to cut me to ribbons.

Then, the knife skittered out of his fingers. I watched as it fell to the ground, clattering to my feet. The man's eyes bulged in his skull, a thick vein popping out of his neck like a little snake was going to slither free of his skin. The hand that once held onto his knife became a claw, and he groped at the air. I shrieked as his body crashed to the floor bringing me with him. The human scab let out a groan, and then I felt his fingers release my hair. He convulsed as though run through with pure electricity. Then he stopped. I choked on my disbelief.

Did he just die?

Lil's sobs grew more frantic, her breath coming out in wheezes like someone was squeezing her to death. I twisted up from the ground to see the beef stick had wrapped his forearm around her neck, crushing her windpipe. He was on his own now, and he knew he had to make a move, had to make a choice.

He chose wrong.

Without a coherent thought, I snatched the butterfly knife, cutting my fingers in the process as I fought for a better grip on the handle. I shot forward like one of the horses on the track, my heels pushing into the floor, propelling me towards my sister, racing upwards like I might break through the ceiling.

So fast. It all happened *so fast*. Clumsy with the knife in my hand, it felt wrong, so horribly wrong as I pushed it hard into the side of the hulk's neck. The cut was deep. His eyes went blank. He released his grip on Lil, then toppled to the concrete floor like a felled tree, dragging my sister down with him.

I went to my knees clawing at the man's still warm body in order to give Lil a way to escape from under him. I shoved at his shoulder, and then I was staring into Lilith's watery eyes. The next thing I knew, I was dragging her away from a bleeding mountain of a man, squeezing the steel handle of the butterfly blade as we raced down the corridors of the arena. My grip was less sure now with all the blood making its way between my fingers. There was a ringing in my ears and above it was the warbled roar of the crowd echoing down the chamber, screaming for whichever horse had crossed the finish line first. Any minute now these halls would be crammed with people, witnesses who would definitely notice the blood that coated my skin.

My mind screamed one thought at me, over and over, with every pounding footfall of my sneakers. *Survive. Survive. Survive.*

Lil's perfume was a mixture of roses and stale prosecco, her voice was raw from being choked. "Where are we going?" It came out slurred from fear and booze. She'd never been able to do anything in moderation, and that meant *anything*. I never thought she'd go this far. She'd fallen off the cliff of all bad decisions this time.

My eyes shot around us, the rising echoes of footsteps sending alarm bells ringing in my skull. "Home. We have to go home. We can't stay here." People began oozing out of every exit from the stands, swiftly blocking our path. Someone would see us if we didn't get out of here, someone who knew Lil and knew that she was supposed to be dead by the end of this race.

Lil whined, "Home? But what about Mom and Dad? Won't they—"

Of all the times to argue. I wanted to throttle her with every word out of her mouth. This was her mess that I was risking *my* ass to fix, and all she cared about was hurting Mom's feelings. Typical. I glared back at her and said, "That's the least of your worries, you moron. Now shut up and run!"

Her fingers dug into my arm as I allowed my adrenaline to propel us through the crowd. I pushed and shoved, kicked and spouted obscenities, anything to make people get out of our way. Lil limped along, huffing and crying at the same time.

We were two steps from the wide staircase that led to the stadium exit. I wrenched Lil forward, bringing her up to my side when two frightening looking men in black suits came barreling out of a side door that had the word SECURITY stamped on the back of it. I tucked the knife into my jacket pocket.

Shit. Lil cast a horrified glance my way, and that's when I knew we were screwed.

One of them shouted, "Lilith Lawson. Stop right there unless you want a bullet between your eyes." Both men drew their pieces and aimed at us. This was it. This was the end.

My sister would be the death of me.

Lil was begging and pleading for our lives, and I was trying not to break into a million pieces. The two men rushed us, shoving their guns into our backs, heavy hands gripping the napes of our necks like we were a couple of misbehaving kittens needing to be scruffed. There was no way we were getting out of this. *Goodbye future. Goodbye dreams. Goodbye Mom. Goodbye Dad.*

They pushed us down the stairs one step at a time. With each subsequent stair, my heart sank lower and lower into my gut.

The man shoving Lil snarled at her, "Shut the hell up, Lilith. You've had every opportunity to make things right. Now you've done it. You're fucked."

I should have bitten my tongue. Should have let my sister take all the blame. This was her fault anyway. But I couldn't. "She didn't do it. I did."

The muscle man holding his gun on me raised an eyebrow and *tsked*. Like I was an eight-year-old who'd been caught stealing candy. "Then you're both fucked." We stepped out of the stadium. At the curb were two black cars, engines running. The back doors were opened, ready to take us to our deaths.

The goon forcing me towards the car pulled something out of his pocket and whispered, "Say goodbye." Lil cried even harder as he stuffed my head into a black sack, then handcuffed me. I could only assume they did the same to her. Her cries became muffled, then distant. I was shoved into the backseat, landing on my side. The door slammed behind me.

I couldn't hear Lil crying anymore.

The driver was a maniac on the road, and I slid all over the leather seats, unable to find any kind of traction. We hit a bump and I took a chunk out of my tongue. I started crying. And howling. I was giving Lil's meltdown a run for its money. I was on a different planet, in a different galaxy, dreaming maybe. This couldn't be real. I had too many plans. Too much on my to do list for this to be the end. I told Mom we would be home for dinner, dessert at the latest. Now I was going to be a liar, just like Lil.

I couldn't tell how long I'd been in the backseat by the time the car stopped. After several moments of panicked silence, someone ripped me out of the backseat by my arm. They didn't give me a chance to find my footing, instead opting to drag me behind them, only holding on to me by my shirt.

My feet bounced uselessly against the pavement as I tried to find my footing. "Lil? Lil, can you hear me? Are you there?" I sobbed as I yelled, needing to hear her voice at least once more before the end.

"I'm here! I'm here." *Oh, thank the gods.* At least we'd be together. Someone ripped the black bag from my head, and I was momentarily blinded by the bright daylight around us.

Lil gasped, "Oh gods, I'm so sorry. He's going to kill us."

We stood in front of a palatial mansion. Massive marble columns ensconced with ridiculous carved filigree stood towering on either side of the grand entryway. Before it was an immaculate lawn, sprinkled with statues of satyrs and goddesses. Mature trees and shrubs lined the driveway, and a fountain with leaping mermaids curving up into the sky stood central to it all. Whoever lived here—they had deep pockets and a very healthy ego. This was getting worse with every minute.

The man who had my shirt in a death grip continued dragging me along. "Cronus is waiting for you."

My mouth ran dry.

I knew that name. I wish I didn't, but I did. Everyone knew it. *Of course,* Lil would be involved with him. One of the most terrifying Titans in Arcadia wanted us dead.

The two grunts herded us into the front room, which was more like a royal chamber than a place for a family to come together for a game of pinochle. There were golden cherubs posted as tiny guards on pedestals scattered around the room. The ceiling was in the classic fresco style, and paintings lined the walls. A wingback chair covered in ivory velvet sat in front of a bay of windows. On either side of the chair were angry looking dogs, with arguably more muscles than the men pushing us around. Gold chains dangled from their necks. My stomach rolled. I would much rather be shot to death than eaten by a rabid mutt.

I sniffled and it echoed off the shiny floors, bounced downwards from the domed ceiling and back in my face. I didn't want to die like this. I didn't want to die at all.

A broad-shouldered man in a white suit and a blue tie, with curling white hair, walked in from another room. His leather shoes clicked loudly against the floor, every step sure. Everything about him oozed opulence, power. He swaggered towards us, one eyebrow raised impatiently as he pulled his hands from his pockets.

His voice boomed and he gestured to Lil with a casual flick of the wrist. "Well, well, well. You always have to make things more difficult, don't you?" He adjusted the lapels on his jacket and rolled his head from side to side, sending a loud *click* into the air as his spine cracked. His fingers were decorated with gaudy rings, each one twinkling beneath the chandelier's lights. I bet one of those was worth Lil's weight in gold. I looked over to see her hunched forward, staring down blankly at her peep toe heels. Lil was beyond tears and groveling at this point. She had given up. I wasn't so resigned.

I tried to reason with him, daring to look the Titan in the face as he strode closer towards us. "If this is just about money, why the need to kill? Doesn't it make more sense to force her to earn the money back somehow?" Cronus turned his gaze toward me. Narrow blue eyes, creased around the edges with age, pinned me to the spot. His stare, icy and filled with ire, made me want to slink away and hide until this was all over. But there was no escaping.

He took a white handkerchief out of his back pocket and dabbed at my cheek. It came away red. He held it up in my face and whispered, "I'd ask the same thing. You've got blood on your hands. The blood of my men. This is personal now. What to do with you…" The butterfly blade felt instantly heavier in my pocket. There had been no time to accept what I'd done, but now… my pulse skyrocketed, and then went double-time as he continued to assess me, jaw tight as he tried to make up his mind. Then Cronus reached for something hidden in his jacket.

He held a tiny packet in his hand, dangled it out before us like he was ringing a dinner bell. "I think I like this idea. See this? It's something we've been developing. You're going to test it out for me. If I like what I see, then maybe. *Maybe* we can work something out."

I swallowed. "And if you don't?" I ignored Lil as her head shot up, panicked. One minute ago, we were goners for sure, and now there was a chance at life—but I wasn't sure I could do anything to sway the odds in my favor.

"You're already supposed to be dead, so it's a small matter to me." If it wasn't my life on the line, I would scoff, maybe spit on his shoes. This was not the time for spitting. "Bring them here." Cronus turned away from us, heading towards the big white armchair. The man holding Lil began to push her forward. She stumbled, turning an ankle in those clunky shoes, but she didn't fall. Then I too was lovingly nudged to where Cronus sat. He snapped his fingers. Heavy hands pushed me down to my knees, and Lil along with me.

Cronus taunted her, "Do you remember this, sweet Lily? This divine substance and what it gave you?" He dangled the baggie in her face, and she flinched away from it, unwilling to look him in the eye. "You didn't nearly have the reaction I wanted from you. But maybe your sister might prove more useful. Take her cuffs off."

One of his goons came up behind me, releasing me from my bondage with the snick of a key in its lock. Then, quick as lightning, Cronus' hands were clamped on my face, hard.

His fingers wiggled between my teeth to force my jaw open as if I were one of his guard dogs. His man stopped me from struggling free and Cronus dumped a teaspoon of powdered something onto my tongue. He forced my mouth closed while I tried to cough. I choked on the substance. It was sweet, so sweet it made my jaw ache. I squeezed my eyes shut then the convulsions started. My neck lost the ability to hold up my head, and I rocked back and forth like a rag doll.

Lil squealed as I flailed. I couldn't keep my balance and slowly plummeted to the ground. My cheek slammed into the marble floor. My tremors turned to seizing, muscles so tense they felt like they might tear.

Fire filled me, burned me from my fingers to the ends of my hair. My throat was nothing but cinders, my skin charcoal. I was consumed with it from within. I tried to look at Lil, but it was so bright, too bright to see her. Everything was burning. A fire of brilliant orange and white ate the tables and cherubs and curtains, climbed the walls and danced on the painted ceiling. The world was ending.

Then there was darkness. And a voice.

"Get the knife."

So, I did. Pulled it from my pocket while I still laid face down on the floor.

"Now stand."

So, I did, gripping the crusted blade in my right hand. I was fast. Faster than I'd ever been. Faster than Cronus had anticipated. He leaned back in his chair. A strange look on his face, like he was preparing to witness a grand performance.

"Kill them."

So, I did.

THREE YEARS LATER

CHAPTER 2

I checked my phone for the millionth time. The ice cube in my highball clinked against the glass as it melted. It was my second whiskey in the last hour, and I was losing interest by the minute. Eve was late, as usual, but I had things to do while the night was still young. Things I *actually* wanted to do for once. I couldn't wait much longer for her ass.

I eyed the bartender, an old man named Jason who'd decided instantly that he didn't like me, but he liked my sister even less. This was one of her favorite places to stop after she was way past three sheets to the wind. For good reason I guessed. It was a quiet little spot. Dingy lighting, pilled velveteen barstools, and a pool table that had seen better days made Jason's bar a perfect place to drink and forget the world. Or, if you were Lil, a great bar to try your luck dancing on the counter and dry heaving your cocktails on the carpet.

I sighed when the next person to walk through the door was *not* Eve for the umpteenth time. Jason scowled my way and grumbled, "Your shitty attitude is stinking up the atmosphere." He ran a white towel along the inside of a glass as I smiled and gave him my middle finger. I knew he was too scared to do anything more than talk. He continued to glower while I sipped my watered-down drink.

I hardly registered the liquid roll down my throat as I watched sweaty wrestlers grapple with one another on the TV. Eve had ten more minutes. Jason flipped the channel, landing on a news station. The subtitles flashed across the bottom of the screen. Something about job shortages, the economy on shaky legs. "Come on, Jay, put the fights back on." He rolled his eyes at me, but silently obliged.

When my glass was mostly warm water, Eve finally made her entrance. An obscenely curvaceous person, tight jeans hugged every inch of Eve's lower half. She wore her dark curls down tonight; her wavy hair had been the envy of all the girls when we were in school. Her eyeliner was impeccable as always, sharp enough to cut. Underneath her coat she wore a simple long sleeve buttoned all the way up to the starched collar around her neck. It gave the false impression that she was actually somewhat respectable. She scanned the bar, her eyes passing over me once before she doubled back.

"You cut your hair? Why, *why* would you do such a thing?" She strutted over to me, big hips swinging, arm already reaching out to run fingers through my freshly shorn hair.

I let Eve get one good ruffle in before ducking away from her. "I was sick of people grabbing my ponytail. No ponytail, no problem."

Eve rolled her eyes before bellying up to the bar. "Hi Jason! Can I have a tequila sunrise? You know how I like it." She batted her eyes at him, and Jason lit up like a firework. Everyone liked Eve. She eyed my empty glass and added, "Make that two, Styx is all empty."

I shook my head to stop Jason from making mine. I stood up, pulling my bag from its hook under the bar.

"*You're* late. I gotta run. Did you bring them?" Eve took off her coat, throwing it across the seat of her stool before sitting on it. She lived in an alternate reality where there were no clocks or alarms or deadlines. Any time she did a job for me I started sweating bullets that maybe this time she would slip up, forget the timeline I was working with and leave me high and dry, but it hadn't happened yet.

She smiled reassuringly at me. "I have the goods right here in my satchel. They will keep for five minutes. Stay, you can have a few sips of mine." Eve patted the stool next to her and waited expectantly. "You know, now that I'm looking at you, I'd say short hair suits you. Totally completes the whole *untouchable badass* vibe you've got going on." I smiled at her, and I meant it. I was always genuine with Eve. We'd known each other too long for there to be any sort of pretenses between us.

I tucked a strand behind my ear. "Thanks. Where's Gerty?"

Eve's lips flapped as she sighed through them. That didn't sound good. "She picked up another shift at the club. *Another* one. Can you believe that? She's been working double overtime for almost a month now. It's driving me nuts." Jason slid a glass in the shape of a cowboy boot across the bar and Eve caught it without spilling a drop. She hadn't even glanced away from me. Eve was magic like that.

Gerty, Eve's girlfriend, was pure badass—golden and terrifying in every way. The two had been hot and cold for a few months now, and it was getting a tad annoying hearing both of them complaining to me about the other one any chance they got.

I sighed and said, "You know how Gerty is, she loves the fight. And it's good money. Don't hold it against her." I patted Eve on the back while I glanced at my phone again. I was cutting it close. Eve raised an eyebrow at me and pushed her drink my way.

Her tone was set. "Uh-uh. You can't leave without having at least one drink with me. Do not make me drink alone." My head dropped back in dramatic fashion.

I hated when she got needy like this. "You know I would love to. In fact, as soon as I'm done with my runs, I'll meet up with you." I gave her my best I'm-good-for-it grin, hoping she'd decide to believe me. I never knew when Cronus would call, which made me a pretty flakey date.

Eve replied, "You're a liar. A big fat liar. But I know I can't stop you." She took back her glass and sipped gingerly at it, choosing to stare me down the entire time. Her round brown eyes burned a hole into my heart, but I didn't let on. I wished I could stay. I really did.

I held my hand out, knowing full well that Eve had already forgotten why she was here to meet me in the first place. "Invites?"

"Oh shit, right. Invites. Here." She slapped a fat yellow envelope into my palm, and I immediately stashed it in the inside pocket of my leather jacket. Eve watched my every move. "Hey. I know you always are, but…be careful, will ya?"

I smiled but it felt more like a grimace. Eve knew too much. I might as well be standing naked in front of her. "Give Gerty a big kiss for me." I planted my lips on Eve's forehead. Then I called out to Jason, "Put it on my tab, Jay!" who grunted in return. Eve swatted my ass as I walked past her towards the door. The night was young and there was work to do.

The air smelled like cold sugar as it wafted from the candy shop down the street, sweet and cloying with ripe undertones of refuse. There was no amount of perfume or booze that could hide the grime of this city. It permeated every corner and back alley, seeped into everything and everyone. It didn't matter how hard you tried to stay clean, stay safe. Sooner or later, something would taint you.

The streetlights in this part of town were shoddy at

best, and tonight only about half on this street were willing to glow, however faintly. I used to get nervous wandering around a place like this. Not anymore. No one would ever think to mess with someone working for a Titan. And if someone was idiotic enough to try, it would be their first and final attempt…at anything.

Steam billowed out from a vent in the damp sidewalk, sending hot air into my face, stinging my eyes. The lights ahead of me flickered, threatening to go out entirely. Not many people were out, just a few guys, smoking their cigarettes and chattering with one another as they wandered down the street on their way to someplace else.

The envelope set the shoulder seam of my jacket off, and it was beginning to get to me. The fabric rested too far to the right. I shrugged again and again to readjust it, but to no avail. The world was beginning to get too tight around me, the buildings leaning downward, the sidewalk rising up under my feet.

Breathe. Just breathe. In and out. Stay present. Breathe.

I forced air into my lungs and out my nostrils in slow, calculated breaths, until my skin stopped crawling. I didn't stop walking. I could deal. There were more important things to do right now. My heart still pounded in my chest as I sauntered up the street, pausing only to stop for a red muscle car that honked as it flew past, nearly side swiping me. I held my hand up, middle finger on display as I cursed their gods-damned mother. They were long gone by the time I'd had the presence of mind enough to shout at the imbecile.

I readjusted my jacket again, looking both ways before crossing the street. A neon sign flared vermillion from its mount on a slimy brick wall. *The Siren's Lair.* My second stop. The windows were painted black, disguising the bar as a dilapidated warehouse. The magic only happened once you pulled the door open. A wall of sticky warm air greeted me as I made my descent into tiki madness.

Grass skirts hung over everything— the counter, the tables, even the stall doors in the bathroom, swear to gods. Carved statuettes of deities from the other side of the world adorned the walls. Fake palm fronds hung from the ceiling, and the tackiest bamboo wallpaper adorned every inch of wall space. The bartender mixed a mai tai and poured it into a wooden cup with the very same deity etched into its front. I had to squint to see who it was, dim red lights hanging from the ceiling were the only form of illumination.

He was a handsome enough guy, if he'd push the shaggy hair out of his hazel eyes and stop being such an idiot all the time. I waved at him as I called, "Ivan. Didn't know you'd be working tonight." I rested my forearms against the countertop, leaning towards the surprised brunette on the other side. He proceeded to shake whatever cocktail he was mixing and ignored me, so I flicked a discarded cherry stem at him. Things had been shaky between us for a while. I'd done my best to avoid him, but the fates had other plans it seemed.

He scowled when the stem hit his chest. "I'm still not talking to you." He poured the mixture into a coconut and then popped open a tiny pink umbrella, stabbed a wedge of pineapple with it, and stuck it in the drink. Ivan sighed dramatically and took the beverages to a table in the corner where two ridiculously busty women sat, eyeing him like he was the daily special. A twinge of jealousy burned in my gut, but I let it go. I had to let him go.

I rolled my eyes. "Oh, come on. You don't get to be mad, it's got nothing to do with you anyway." Ivan circled back and collected some spent glasses scattered across the other side of the counter. He wiggled his way between the barstool next to me. Close enough that I could feel the heat of his skin radiating from him.

Ivan looked at me like I'd just stabbed him in the heart, puppy dog eyes gleaming with feigned distress. "Don't say that to me. You don't get to say that to me." He reached in front of me, swiping a half-empty cocktail glass while somehow managing to further close the gap between us.

I ran my tongue over my teeth, trying to ignore his proximity. "It's a haircut for gods' sake."

Ivan scoffed, "But it was so *pretty*."

I pushed him, and he nearly toppled over the stool beside him. A couple walked in holding hands, ready for a night on the town. Their entrance diverted Ivan's attention long enough for me to skirt away from him. Ivan didn't know what personal space was. If it was personal, it was his space as far as he was concerned. Especially when it came to me. The first time we met, it was like he decided instantly that he and I were meant to be, and I'd been fighting back my growing agreement ever since. I had to get out of there.

I reached into my pocket and tugged the envelope free. I slapped it against Ivan's arm impatiently. "Here. These are for—"

"My uncle. I know, I know." One of the men who'd just walked in flagged Ivan down to get drinks ordered, and Ivan tucked the envelope into his back pocket. He glanced back at me, genuine adoration shining in his hazel eyes. "I got work to do. See you later maybe?"

I didn't like when he looked at me like that. I tried to believe that anyway. I reached over the bar and snagged a pineapple wedge, popped it in my mouth, and waved goodbye before turning to leave. The door of the Siren's Lair shut behind me when my phone started buzzing in my jeans.

You're needed. Now. Car's en route to you.

I took slow deliberate breaths, tried to hone my mind, forget all the noise buzzing around in my skull. I didn't want to guess what I was needed for. It was never good. Sometimes it was downright awful. But that didn't matter. I would do whatever I was told. A loyal little monster to the very end.

Ambrosia had changed everything for me. For Arcadia. Since its creation three years ago, it had exploded in popularity. Definitely illegal, and definitely addictive, it quickly became Cronus' ticket to his title as *Number One Titan*. There had been a few cults to pop up here and there, using Ambrosia like a sacred substance. The feds really hated that. There was a rumor that the stuff was made from the bones of the gods, and that each person who ingested it could channel the god that most connected with their spirit, or whatever. Long story short—it was a drug that gave people short term magic of a specific nature— but that was it.

The gods were long gone, having tired of lowly mortals many years ago. They existed now only in movies and our imaginations, though plenty of people still prayed to them. The followers of the old Pantheon called themselves *Epoptai,* and they were still holding out for the return of the gods. The rest of us knew the truth: we were on our own.

A black sedan rolled up along the curb, engine idling like a purring tiger. My heart thudded against my breastbone as I pulled the back door open and sidled in.

"Here." Nick, who was driving, didn't even look back at me as he tossed a tiny bag into my lap. My jaw tightened. My fingers started twitching; I had to fight them to get my seatbelt on, keep them from what they really wanted.

I fought the terrible urge to open the bag and down its contents without any regard. I was so starved for it, for the power. The way it filled me with fearless disregard, endless strength. When Ambrosia coursed through my veins I was free, limitless.

My voice was faraway when I asked, "Where are

we going?" Nick had a major chip on his shoulder when it came to me. He never liked how fast I became an asset. That made two of us. He made a point of being an asshole every moment we were together. Nick was a human wall, thick like one too. He'd decided that I'd purposely gotten in his way, even though that was absurd.

He turned a hard right and I slid to the door but he eventually replied, his words more of a grunt than anything else. "About five minutes from here. Disloyal customer. Gotta show 'em who's on top."

I fisted my hands into my pockets, avoiding that little baggie like it was poisonous to the touch. How long could I hold out? "So, what does Cronus want me to do? Maim, permanently disable, or kill?"

Nick glared at me from the rear-view mirror. I returned his sour stare with my very own. He didn't know what it was like. No one did. "He said, *make sure he can't steal from me ever again.*" I sighed. So, it was to be a bloody night after all. I zoned in on the bag in my lap, its powdered contents singing to me, threatening me, promising me all that I could have if I just opened it up and tasted a little magic.

I caved. Just like I was supposed to. The zip seal snapped open between my fingers and in a rush I dumped the contents into my palm. A tiny, beautiful mountain of crystalline mana rested in my hand, until I shoved it against my mouth, unceremoniously licking my skin to claim every tiny fleck of Ambrosia.

The fire started in my limbs, always my limbs, then to my fingers and toes. It filled my lungs and my chest and my gut and then every single inch of me was burning like I was an effigy to the gods themselves. My pulse raced, my heart thundered, and all the world slowed as we pulled up to our destination.

"Hello again."

My life became a series of photographs. My mind

was too slow to keep up with my reflexes. Nick led me to a man, who saw me and began to beg and plead like they always do. He went to his knees, holding his hands up in prayer.

It was me but it wasn't, when my hands raised up, took his face between them.

"Break his neck."

No. Cronus just wants him hurt.

"Where's the fun in that?"

I purred, disgusted and invigorated at the same time. "You look like you've seen a ghost. Don't worry. You won't be journeying to Hades just yet. Only your thumbs will." I didn't see my hands as they moved from the man's ruddy, horrified face. Only when I grabbed his right thumb, I watched it fall to the floor after my blade had already slid through his muscle and bone. And again, with his other hand. The disloyal customer fell to the ground, trying pathetically to collect his discarded digits. I stared down at him, utterly numb. "You can keep them as souvenirs. Next time though, next time you see me, that will be it for you."

"More? Let there be more."

Nick sneered at the de-thumbed man before he jerked his head in the direction of the car. "Let's go. You've got one more stop." Adrenaline raged inside me, had me bouncing on my toes like I was a boxer in the ring. I felt tough enough to take Gerty down. Nick rolled his eyes in my direction, but I didn't care. I didn't care about anything. "I could cut some idiot's thumbs off, don't know why it's *you* that's got to do it."

My voice wasn't entirely my own when I spoke, "You know why. He likes the ego trip." If I'd said that in any other state of being, my head would already be splattered against the pavement. Nick at least knew well enough to stay clear of me when I was under the influence.

I couldn't help the taunt as it slithered out of my mouth, "And besides, we all know what happens to *you* when you take Ambrosia. Having a knack for *gardening* doesn't exactly make you a hot commodity in Cronus' eyes." Nick's eyes flashed red, and that perceived threat was enough to bring hell out of me.

"He dies. Now."

Ambrosia held me in its grip and in a second my still bloody knife was pressing into Nick's throat. My knee shoved down on his chest as he heaved in terror from the ground where I'd dropped him. I could feel his fear, his malice, all of it inside him. I wanted to extinguish every ounce of it. My fingers loved the feeling of my knife in my hand. My eyes longed to see his bright red blood ooze from him. But I pushed back against that nasty voice inside.

No. This isn't me.

I stood up and turned away from Nick, wiping my blade against my leg. "Let's go."

CHAPTER 3

I am the enforcer of Cronus' law. No one can piss
unless it's done in a way that pleases the self-proclaimed
Titan. Time and time again I have to prove this point to the
people of Arcadia. In this life there are only two choices:
break or do the breaking. I've chosen the latter. I don't get
to play fair and no matter how much it pains me, I will do
what it takes to survive. Sometimes saving my own life
means I take someone else's.

Yes, it hurts. Yes, I am broken to pieces about
it. When I can, I look the other way. If someone's going
to steal from Cronus, they better be smart enough to do
it without getting caught. If someone's going to lie to
Cronus, they better be the best damn liar in the universe.
If someone's going to kill one of Cronus' own, they better
make it look like an accident. Because if they don't, it's
over. I'll make sure of that.

I vibrated in the backseat of the car as the drug ran
laps through my nervous system. Nick drove like a demon
through the darkened streets of Arcadia. He was afraid of
me now. I could smell it on him. "Who's next?" I wished

I didn't like how sensual my question sounded. I wished I didn't love this feeling of raw power and rage.

"Cronus wants to see you." Those five words sent a chill down my spine, but the voice in my head had a different opinion.

"Perhaps you can stab him to death tonight."

I didn't respond. Instead, I tried my damndest to sober up. But maybe it was good I was high, that way he couldn't get to me. Maybe he just wanted to discuss another job for me in person, or maybe he wanted to gloat some more about how much of our debt I still owed. You never could tell with mob-boss types like him. With every mile, I felt the pull on the invisible leash he'd strung around my neck, yanking my collar tighter and tighter. I was beginning to doubt that we'd ever be free of him. The dreams I'd once had of seeing the world had grown more dim by the day and I was getting reckless with the need to be anywhere but here. I checked the time on my phone. I was definitely going to be late for that meeting.

We arrived at Cronus' compound and the iron gates opened wide for us, closing immediately behind the vehicle. Cronus had his own village that he lovingly referred to as Olympus. *Very* modest. He liked to keep his own close, including me. I had an apartment unit at the other end. Technically Lil lived with me, but she didn't come home much. Even though I lived on the same sprawling property, it was rare to see Cronus. He preferred to work behind the curtain, pulling strings like a deadly puppet master.

When he wanted an audience, usually it wasn't good. My guts momentarily liquified when I thought it might have something to do with my sister. She'd promised me she was staying out of trouble, but I knew well enough that keeping promises was not her strong suit.

Nick pulled up to Cronus' palace. I got out, slammed the door shut, and Nick sped back down the drive, tires spinning on the gravel. His red taillights flared once before he faded from view. *Scaredy cat.* I smirked. Part of me wanted to be scared too. The other part, the part ruled by that nasty voice inside, was hungry for battle, for blood. I smacked my cheeks lightly with both hands, hoping to look at least somewhat sane for this meeting.

The butler, whose name I didn't know, opened the door after one knock. He only briefly glanced at me, not deigning to give me any more attention than was required of him before turning and leading me towards the throne room. I could already see Cronus' velvet chair, but it was turned towards the bay windows now. He sat in it, and I could make out that he held a glass of amber liquid in one hand, resting it on the arm of his seat. The memory of my first visit to this room slammed into me, fueling my drug induced state of ire.

Cronus watched as I slaughtered the men in the room. I twisted limbs and cracked bones. Thrust my knife into fleshy bodies again and again and again until blood rained down over me like a glorious fountain. All the while the voice in my head urged me on with unbridled glee. Soon my skin was slick with gore, and I was ready to destroy the man himself, but when I turned my attention to Cronus, he held my sister, my sweet, idiotic sister, with a gun to her head. "You make one more move and she dies…"

The memory dissolved as quickly as it came on when Lil walked into the throne room, holding a tray with a fresh drink and a cigar on it. Her presence reminded me why I needed to keep my shit together. I had someplace to be, for her. She kept her eyes averted as she made her way to the front of his chair. "Your drink, sir." Cronus nodded and took it from her, the cigar too. He placed his spent glass on her tray and waved her away. Lil gave me some serious side eye. Whatever was about to go down, I knew it wasn't going to be pleasant.

Cronus began speaking to me. His words came out of the side of his mouth around the cigar clamped between his teeth. "How is my little *hoplite* this evening?"

"Swine. Kill him now. You are no mere foot soldier."

I gritted my teeth. Fought the will of the voice in my head. Held myself in place though my fingers itched for a weapon. "Fine." I never knew what to say or how to act in his presence. Should I bow? Call him *master?* Nothing seemed right. I was always terrified he could see right into my mind with those eyes, read all my secrets and fears.

A plume of purple smoke drifted into the air above him. "Come here."

My legs moved mechanically towards his chair. Each step closer ratcheted the pace of my pulse. The hunger for violence spurred on by Ambrosia welled up in me. A craving that repulsed and excited me all at once.

I stopped when I came around to face Cronus. Tonight, he wore a red suit, with a matching silk ascot tied around his neck. He chose to accessorize with a pair of thick-rimmed glasses that formed perfect circles around his pale eyes. If I didn't hate him, I would say he looked dapper, classic even.

Pompous bastard.

Cold eyes stared into me. "My nephew tells me you've been working too hard lately. He tells me you need a break." I swallowed down my hope. I could feel the potency of the drug waning, soon I would feel worse than a deflated balloon in a rainstorm. I needed to stay strong for just a little longer, just until I could get away. This was not how I envisioned my night going at all.

Cronus puffed his cigar twice more, then stubbed it out in a crystal ashtray on the table beside him. "Here, pull up a chair, stay a while." His offer was deeply confusing, especially because there were no other chairs in sight. He offered me the glass Lil had served, and I took it, suddenly aware of how much taller I was while Cronus remained seated. Maybe I was unsettling him.

He raised his white eyebrows and commanded, "Sit."

I held his eye contact while I knelt to the floor and crossed my legs in front of me. I downed the scotch in one gulp, never once looking away. I was still powerful enough to glare at the King of Titans, at least for a few more minutes. He wasn't really all that anyway. Cronus and his brothers had decided on the moniker knowing that everyone in Mycenae would know what kind of power was behind them. They were just greedy men; if the gods were real, they would sneer at such hubris. Sometimes I liked to imagine that Cronus' real name was something like *Gene*, or *Phil*.

He cleared his throat in consternation. "But you see, it doesn't matter what Ivan thinks. Because you owe me. And I will work you until every single cent your worthless sister stole is earned back. With interest." I didn't understand why this conversation was necessary. I was fully aware of my status. There was no way out—I'd tried everything already, well almost everything.

"*Kill…*"

The voice was becoming more distant by the second, leaving me with nothing but my apprehension. I started feeling cold, my heart didn't want to beat quite right.

Cronus eyed me, appraising his attack dog. His Killer Bee. "*You* don't get to ruin yourself. That's my call. I *own* you."

My face scrunched up, hating that phrase with all my being. "Cronus, I don't know what you're—"

He sighed, lacing his fingers together in his lap. "*Don't* be an idiot. Ambrosia. It's starting to get to you. You're no good to me if you overdose, and it sounds like you might be one foot in the grave already." I really wanted to roll my eyes, give him the middle finger and stroll away, but I was on thin ice. I could feel it shifting under me as he stared me down. It wasn't my fault he kept throwing Ambrosia at me every time *he* needed me.

"You're the only person with the gift of Ares.

Ambrosia's a crap shoot like that. You are valuable, precious even. But not if you're dead." He leaned forward in his chair, mock concern painting his features. "If you die, who's going to watch out for your silly Lily? She gets prettier and prettier by the day…maybe one of my brothers would like to have her for a trophy of their own?" Bile rose up into my throat. If I burned out, he'd pawn my sister off to another Titan in an instant, especially if it meant he'd profit. Cronus reached a giant hand out then patted my cheek with a heavy palm. I forced myself not to flinch away from the contact.

"You keep walking that line for me, Styx. That's a good girl. I need you sharp for the upcoming festivities." Cronus eyed me for another horrible moment before he stood up and left the room, leaving me alone on the marble floor with an empty glass. In a week's time, Cronus was planning on opening up the compound for what he called an *Expo of excellence*. The guest list was terrifying to look at. I was supposed to be heading up the protection detail for Cronus and his near and dear ones.

Ambrosia's magic seeped out of me, leaving behind an exhausted and angry husk of a human, hungry to blame my problems on someone else. *Ivan, that little snitch*. He was always putting his nose in other peoples' business. Especially mine. I thought about pulling my phone from my pocket and scream-texting him all of the meanest things I could come up with, but I relented. He was just trying to help. Ivan was right, every time I took Ambrosia, that voice inside got a little louder, and more of me, the *real* me, was chipped away.

I heard someone sigh from the perimeter of the room. I looked up to see Lil leaning against the entryway, a tray tucked under her arm. I raised my empty glass to her in silent salute. Lil's eyes were distant, veiled with sadness. I knew she felt guilty. Over the last few years, I'd tried to convince her it was okay, that I would make the same choice again and again…but she never believed me. Instead, she drowned her feelings with booze and partying when she wasn't busy serving Cronus as his personal barmaid.

We were alive. Not resting at the bottom of the lake behind Cronus' house. For that, I was grateful. I wished things were different. Every gods-damned day I wished for that. But they weren't, and this was our life. Mom and Dad thought we were living our dreams in the city, but we knew the truth. Cronus was our master, and we were his little pets. No more art school for Lil, no worldly adventures for me. Just this never-ending hell.

Lil spoke, her voice dancing across the room to my ears, "Got more errands to run tonight?" The way she said *errands*, it was hard and clumsy like it barely escaped her mouth. I stood, dusting off my ass with one hand as I walked over to her.

I checked my phone, five missed calls. "I was supposed to pick something up from someone, but we were going to meet an hour ago now. He's probably pissed and drunk somewhere. Not sure I want to risk it. Eve invited me out too…Are you off soon?"

Lil took my glass from me, her lips pursed as she noted my shaking hand. "Sounds like Cronus is going to have Hyperion and Crius over…it's going to be a long night." The way her shoulders sagged, shrinking her into a smaller version of herself, I knew she'd rather eat hot coals than to stay and serve the arrogant pig brothers. But she had no choice. I nodded, understanding what she didn't want to say. Lil shrugged it off. "Well, see ya around." She turned and stalked off to the kitchen, her heels clacking loudly against the floor.

We were less like sisters by the day. The bond we'd had as girls was thin, near to breaking. Maybe it would never be strong again. Maybe we were too broken and afraid to ever be free like we were as kids, without all of this bullshit weighing us down.

I zipped up my jacket and headed towards the door, redialing the number from all those missed calls on my phone. "Chester."

A nasally voice piped in through the speaker, "Oh, so the *mighty* Styx finally decides I'm worthy of her time. Where were you?"

There was something about Chester I didn't like. Maybe it was the fact that he's a shifty little rat. Maybe it's his annoying attitude. I growled into the phone, "I got called up to Olympus. Can you meet me at the docks? Twenty minutes?"

Chester sighed in exasperation. "Fine." I pocketed my phone and started my walk to the other side of the property. Some fresh air would do me good.

CHAPTER 4

The night air licked my fevered skin. I tried my best
to hold my spine straight, put one foot in front of the other
like a sober adult not about to go through a brutal come-
down. The massive willow trees lining the paved residential
street swayed in the chilly breeze. The last few yellowed
leaves broke free of their branches and skittered across the
ground at my feet.

I felt like a sponge that had been rung completely
dry. Every time I took Ambrosia the aftermath worsened.
Cold sweats, chills, and a general hit-by-a-bus nastiness
deep in my bones. Cronus was right. It was owning me.

My stomach muscles spasmed, and I clenched my
fists inside my jacket pockets to keep from groaning out
loud. It would pass. It always did. I focused on my breath,
the way my chest rose and fell too fast to match my pace.
Calm down. Breathe. A bead of sweat slid from my forehead
down to the corner of my jaw. Dripped down the lapel of
my jacket. Ivan would freak out if he saw me like this. One
of the last blowouts we'd had before I officially closed that
door was about me and Ambrosia. Yes, I was an addict, but

did I have a choice? He didn't understand.

I walked past the indoor pool; its lights already dim for the night. Weekends were usually pretty quiet in Olympus. Cronus had all his minions out running his bars and brothels or peddling his designer drug. The rest were busy collecting dues like the loyal dogs we were. Only Cronus had time to host his brothers on a Friday evening. Everyone else was hustling for a cut of that caviar, even though we knew we'd never even get a taste. The only time Cronus shared was when he wanted you to know that he could take it away from you, no problem.

I thought about Lil, serving those little finger sandwiches with colorful toothpicks stuck in them to the Titans as they gloated to one another about the latest deals they made. If Ivan was invited to this soirée, he might be able to shield Lil from the worst of them. He was good like that—always looking out for her, for me. The further up the ladder he climbed, the more sway he held with Cronus. Sometimes that was a good thing, and other times…He understood what it was like to be under Cronus' constant surveillance. Different circumstances to be sure of course, but still. That commonality was a comfort to the both of us.

The ten-foot-tall perimeter fence came into view. Foreboding black iron tipped with the sharpest spikes, warning any would-be intruders to keep out. This section of the compound was heavily monitored, with routine muscle doing rounds, and security cameras constantly scanning every angle. Even though the dock was public access, Cronus didn't want anyone tampering with his shipments and he used his property's proximity to the bay to his full advantage. Ships came and went at all hours. It was impossible to tell if they were bringing things in or sending them out, but all I knew was that Cronus was getting richer by the day, while the rest of Arcadia withered, like he was sucking the very life from the city with his avarice.

I checked my phone again—just after midnight. Someone would be coming by any minute now to check the docks for any riff raff. I had nothing to worry about since I was one of Cronus' pets. If anyone happened upon Chester and I, they would simply think I was doing what I always did—*errands* for the big man. There was no way in hell anyone would think to question me. I used my key to unlock the gate and made my way towards the pier.

The rhythmic shushing of waves filled the air as they smacked against pilings. A bank of fog obscured the tiny islands that peppered the rim of the False Sea. Chester's lanky figure paced up and down the pier, underneath a yellow spotlight. A cargo ship anchored behind him, piled high with massive containers filled with all kinds of contraband that Cronus would make a killing selling overseas. I rolled my shoulders, pulling myself together as much as I could. Chester had the ability to smell weakness—like a rat with cheese. I wasn't about to falter in front of the likes of him. This was too important.

I continued towards Chester silently, until I was near enough to speak without shouting. "Hey."

He whirled around, hand going for his piece instinctively. "Holy shit, you scared me. Don't sneak up on people like that, it's messed up. Especially you. It's like being stalked by a lion or something."

I smirked. "Lioness."

Chester pushed his narrow frames up his nose, eyeing the blood staining my thigh. "Busy night putting the fear of the gods in your enemies?" I bit my tongue. I commissioned him only when it was absolutely necessary for me to do so. He held no love for me, and I felt the same about him.

Without replying, I pulled out a wad of cash, wrapped three times around with a rubber band from the very bottom of my bag. My fingers curled around the money possessively. Nearly everything I made went to Cronus, for Lil. This was worth it. I'd made a good choice for once in my life.

Chester nearly started drooling at the sight of the fortune in my hand. "Is that all of it?"

Not one to be toyed with, I tucked it in my jacket pocket. "That depends. Do you have what I asked for?"

He rolled his eyes. "Why else would I come here after you so rudely stood me up earlier? Just for you to beat my ass? No. I don't think so."

My heart jumped up into my throat. "Well let's not draw this out. Give me what I asked for, and the money's yours." I held out my hand, waiting. I was losing my nerve by the minute.

I was out of my mind. A masochistic maniac. If I was found out—

Chester planted a wrapped parcel into my palm which immediately went into my satchel. After I'd zipped my bag shut, I tossed the wad of money to him. He snatched it out of the air and ripped the rubber band off. His gaze went all hazy as he immediately began counting it out once, twice. His brows arched upwards in confusion and his eyes shot up to mine with the question reflecting clearly back at me.

I sighed, finding a tiny sliver of relief in my new possession. "There's extra in there. Insurance. So you don't blab." I stared Chester down, allowing my eyes to tell the story instead of my words. He swallowed, his mouth parting slightly in trepidation.

"Cross my heart and hope to die." The bundle of money formed a conspicuous bulge in his skinny jeans pocket. He patted it once for good measure before a slimy smile spread across his face. "Don't you want to know how it went? Aren't you curious to hear about my skills?"

I turned away from him, walking back towards Olympus. "Nope. And I'm not going to hear it from

anyone else, either. Got it? So long, Chester." I didn't
bother waving or looking back once. Chester would have
to be a fool to do anything so stupid as to go talking about
what he did for me. It wouldn't just be my head on the
chopping block, but his too. To cross me meant to cross
death itself. Chester was too much of a coward to take that
risk. I was too desperate to let him.

The night was quickly becoming frigid. Sweating
so profusely during my come down had left me feeling
damp and chilled. I wrapped my arms around my body
as I hustled my way home. My shoes smacked against the
pavement as I walked like a zombie through the dark.
Every inch of me was beginning to hurt. Like someone had
decided to ram their pointer finger up and down my body,
leaving behind tiny pulsating sores. A gust of autumn wind
thrust itself in my face, stealing the breath from my lungs
in an instant. Any hope of socializing tonight quickly fled
from my mind. It was time to hide. Rest. Recover. Then
later I could start thinking about the next stages of my
plan, when I could actually think again.

When I made it to my front door, my hands
were frozen in pain. My fingers curled together as if I'd
been clenching them for so long, they no longer knew
how to unfurl. Trying to fit my key into the lock was
embarrassingly difficult. Thankfully I had no audience. The
place was totally dark inside, except for the hallway night
light—a little moon glowing pale yellow from just above
the baseboard. If Lil ever came home, it was usually late.
It helped her not to stumble so much as she made her way
to bed. I couldn't remember the last time I'd heard her trip
down the hall.

I wasted no time in locking the door and lurching
to my room at the end of the house. I stumbled over a pile
of laundry on the floor obscured in the darkness. Luckily, I
found just enough balance to make a safe slow landing. My
knees barked as they made contact with the laminate floor.

It was at this moment my muscles decided that sitting up, standing, all of that, was now off the table.

I was toast.

I pulled myself to my closet, inching my way along like a pathetic little slug. The door was open thankfully. There was no way I could haul my ass up enough to reach that handle. I wiggled in far enough to reach my secret spot. I pried up the loose floorboard in the corner with my middle finger. The board came away without much fuss. My hands plunged into my bag, searching for the package. Once found, I placed it in my tiny hiding spot.

I dropped the slat back down, shuffled backwards on my knees, and slammed the closet door shut. Exhaustion and relief overtook me, and I slumped over. My whole body shivered like a leaf in a windstorm. My eyelids grew heavier, hazy darkness started crowding into the corners of my vision.

Someone nudged me, tapping my folded legs with their boot. Helpless panic laced itself through my aching body. There was nothing I could do to protect myself from an intruder. My head rolled back on my shoulder so I could get a look at who had let themself into my house as I prayed silently that it was someone safe. I could barely open my eyes wide enough to see who it was, terror doing nothing to dull the agony of coming down.

His honey smooth voice told me before I could make out his face. "What happened to you? I thought we were going to meet up." *Ivan.* He sighed as he knelt down next to me. "You look like hell."

I laughed. "It's just a haircut. You'll get over it."

I felt Ivan's hand, cool and slender as he brushed the hair away from my forehead. "That's not what I'm talking about, and you know it." If I could have opened my eyes, I would have rolled them at him. He slid one arm under my knees and the other around my shoulders. Without speaking he lifted me up and carried me to the doorway. "You've got a fever. Let me run you a bath."

Ivan. Oh Ivan. Always trying to take care of me. The first time we'd met, he'd been put in charge of my supervision. "Babysitting duty," Cronus had called it. He didn't trust me to stick around, so Ivan had been saddled with me while Lil was put right to work in the palace. Ivan didn't understand why I was there, and I didn't understand why Ivan was so willing to lick Cronus' boots. While I was busy raging at myself and the world, Ivan was falling head over heels for me. The next thing I knew we were…But that's over and done with.

I scowled. "You snitched on me. Your uncle thinks I'm going to burn out. You think I'm a junkie." My words were all jumbled and slurred. I'd used every ounce of stability and strength during my meeting with Chester. Now I was just a mess. My cheeks grew hotter with shame. I just might burn a hole through Ivan's shirt.

Ivan's tone was plainly hurt. "I never called you that. I said you needed some time off. A break. Cronus said…forget what he said. Let's pretend he doesn't exist right now."

I sighed through my muscle spasms. I was too tired to argue anymore. Ivan set me on the toilet, and with one hand still supporting me, reached over and turned the bathtub faucet. I leaned forward, resting my elbows on my thighs and my chin in my hands. My eyelids closed and I drifted in and out of awareness while the sound of water filled my ears and steam began to billow out from the tub.

He let go of me for a very wobbly moment, then I felt Ivan drape something warm and scratchy around my shoulders. I cracked my eyes open—just a peek—to see if he had a shirt underneath the flannel he just draped over me. Much to my disappointment, he was wearing a plain white tee. It seemed to glow in the darkness of the bathroom against his olive skin. His ash brown hair had flopped into his eyes, and his gorgeous, stupid smile was nowhere to be found. Instead, his mouth was set with concern. I pouted. "I hate when you get like this."

Ivan's hand twitched against my side, warm and painfully enticing. He scoffed. "Like what? Like I actually care? Tough."

I needed to hang on to my anger. No matter how stupid it made me. "You are so arrogant." I didn't know what I was saying. He was too close. He was always getting too close. There was no reason to be found when I could feel his body heat against my legs.

He held his free hand under the water, testing the temperature as he said, "Arrogant, huh? I'm not sure an arrogant person would go out of his way to help someone who treats him as shittily as you treat me sometimes. Just shut up and let me do this for you." I clamped my teeth together. I was clearly determined to make an ass of myself tonight. Ivan pulled the shower curtain aside, and continued, "It's full. Do you need help taking your clothes off?"

My eyes snapped open, all kinds of heat flaring to life inside me. He'd seen me naked before, but never again, no matter how much I wanted it. There were too many risks, too many things hanging over our heads that might come crashing down. I glared at him, knowing full well which one of us always caved in to the other first. "I think I can manage. Turn around."

Ivan inched away from the tub and turned towards the door. I shrugged out of my jacket and tugged off my shirt and jeans, letting them fall in a pile on the floor. I braced myself against the wall with one hand while I gingerly stepped over the rim of the tub and into the hot water. Before I sat down, I pulled the shower curtain shut, sealing myself away from Ivan. "You can turn around now." The water felt boiling hot against my fevered skin, but I took it, every second of it, as I sank beneath the surface.

There was a long silence between us. I rested my

head against the wall, trying to sink as low into the tub as possible. The bits of me that were out of the water felt like they were made of ice. Every time I moved, the water sloshed around my shoulders, and I grew increasingly self-conscious as I sobered up.

Ivan cleared his throat. "Doing alright in there?"

"Mmhmm."

He sighed. "I hate seeing you like this."

I knew he wanted to talk about things I didn't have the capacity to hear. "What are you talking about? You can't see me at all right now."

The shower curtain swayed as he wrapped a knuckle against it. "Ha-ha. You know what I'm saying. I miss you. I worry about you." *Damn Ivan.* Damn him for always speaking his mind. For always knowing how to get at me. When I felt all alone in this new dark world, he'd been the one to take my hand, showing me that I could find a way to walk this path, as terrifying as it seemed.

I pursed my lips before snapping, "It's not your job to worry about me. I'm fine." I pretended to ignore his scoff. I wished I was dumb enough to give in to him. But even I have my limits.

Ivan peeled the curtain away with a finger and I gawked up at him, shocked at his boldness. His eyebrow was raised, anger rolling off him so thick I was afraid he might melt the plastic liner. "Yeah, right. You're just *fine.* You're *Styx.* Untouchable. Why worry about someone who's immortal?" His words stung. I averted my eyes, too ashamed to look at him anymore. He dropped his hand and the curtain slid back into place.

He left the bathroom, quietly shutting the door behind him and I knew he wouldn't be around when I finally got out of the bath.

I stayed there until the water turned cold.

CHAPTER 5

I hauled my shivering, pathetic ass over the side of the tub after too much time had passed. Lil's fluffy pink bathrobe was hanging on the back of the door, so I snagged it, wrapping it so far around myself the flap went under my armpit. I tugged the tie into a squishy knot around my middle. My bones clanged against my other bones, matching the perfect rhythm of my chattering teeth.

I opted to avoid my room, instead turning back towards the front of the house where a pile of blankets had been turned into a nest of sorts on our hand-me-down couch. I wasted no time burrowing beneath them, anything to get warm when something angular jabbed me in the side.

I fished out what was poking me. It was one of my books stuffed halfway in the cushion. I still clung to the tiny hope that someday I might get to hop on a plane and get out of this place. The bag stuffed in my closet flashed across my mind, but what was inside wasn't for me. I allowed myself a moment to imagine what it would feel like to breathe in the air from another place. I looked down at the book cover. It was an old road atlas of São

Sebastião, one of the top five destinations on my list. It was practically on the other side of the world, might as well be on another planet at this point.

When Lil and I had "moved in" all of this stuff was already here. Kitchen appliances, furniture, and way too many paintings of silhouetted palm trees hung from the walls. Whoever lived here really had a thing for the tropics. Every knick-knack and tiny bit of kitschy decor was beach themed some way or another. They taunted me with the dream of escape. If only. I would burrow my toes into the hot sand. Feel the lingering heat of the sun on my skin. Fall asleep to the sound of waves crashing against the beach.

Instead, I was here in a frigid hell with only the whisper of a plan.

The warmth from my breath slowly started filling the void within my cocoon of blankets, and my shoulders began to ease away from my ears. Everything ached.

Everything.

From my ankles to my eyelashes. I was the living embodiment of hurt. And I'd hardly lifted a finger tonight. Ambrosia was going to burn me sooner or later if I didn't learn to pace myself a little better. I'd seen that toadie OD when he was getting ready to kill Lil, and I'd heard plenty of stories since. If you were to partake in a little too much, the drug burned you up from the inside out. Burst capillaries, heart attack, aneurism—all of it. Instantly. There was no time to get your stomach pumped, to get an I.V., nope. Too much Ambrosia, and you were dead. Completely. The ferryman called your number then and there.

And even though I knew that, I couldn't stop myself from gorging on the stuff as if it were candy whenever it was handed to me. I was a suicidal glutton. There was *nothing* compared to the feeling of invincibility that came with the high. I would never admit that to anyone, but it was true. To be completely free of fear? Who wouldn't pay the ultimate price for that? If I didn't use

Ambrosia, I was no good to Cronus. And if I was useless to Cronus, Lil and I were both dead women.

I buried my face in the blanket, trying to warm up the end of my nose. Curling into a ball, I pushed every single one of my stupid thoughts into the imaginary box that lived in my head. Then I shoved it *way* into the back of my brain. Then added a few imaginary bricks to the lid, just in case. Just like every night. There was no other way for me to get any shut eye.

Pretending I was in control of my thoughts enough to keep them at bay for a few hours was sad, I know. But it helped. Sometimes though, sometimes the box began to shrink and the ideas, the dreams, the worries exploded out of their bindings and torpedoed across my psyche so violently that I couldn't stop them for a single moment. Those nights I ended up wandering the compound, too pumped up to sit still. Not tonight though. I was too spent to give a shit about anything but the warm weight of the blankets and my heavy eyelids. And the things whining at me from the back of my subconscious, begging to let me give them some room to run.

I heard the door catch and burrowed further into my nest to avoid any glimpse of sunlight. The sound of clunky heels smacking the floor was muted by the worn rugs strewn about the room. Lil probably didn't realize I was there. If she did, she wouldn't be keen on sticking around.

I couldn't remember the last time we'd hung out together, let alone have more than a twelve-word conversation. I kept extending the invitation, kept holding my breath, waiting for my stubborn sister to come around but she usually flaked on me. I was torn between staying hidden in the blankets to stop Lil from rushing out or springing myself on her to force her to stay. I groaned, choosing the latter. I needed to tell her about what I'd gotten for her.

I sat upright, allowing my covers to fall away from me in a tangle at my waist. "Morning? It's still morning, right?" My mouth tasted like an ashtray. I needed water.

Lil's glossy blond head popped around the side of the kitchen, eyes narrowed and locked on me. "Oh. Didn't know you were under there. Yeah. Morning." She disappeared around the corner. I heard the suction of the fridge door opening then bottles clinking around as Lil searched for whatever it was she was looking for. She re-emerged with a beer in one hand and a bruised banana in the other.

She started to head towards her room, and I found myself blurting out, "Breakfast of champions."

Lil snorted, holding her beer up in the air as if she was cheers-ing me. "Yeah well, you know what they say. You want one?" Lil tossed her hair over her shoulder, eyeing me with one perfectly shaped eyebrow arched. "You look like you need it."

I smacked my lips and nodded. Without another word, she turned for the kitchen and retrieved another beer. When she came back, she handed the bottle over before kicking her shoes from her feet and crawling onto the couch cushion beside me. She took a deep swig as she sunk lower into her seat. "Long night? Cronus has been keeping you pretty busy."

I nodded, allowing her to fill in the details for herself. I struggled to find the words to tell her. Instead I deflected. "What about you? Are you just getting off or did you hit the town last night?" Lil turned her head still sucking on the mouth of her bottle, and I could see—just for a moment—how bone tired she was. I took a sip from my beer; the carbonation burned all the way down my scorched throat.

She licked her lips. "Cronus kept me on until two. Then I went out with some of the kitchen crew, and we ended up at the pool hall downtown." My eyes widened in shock. Anywhere there might be gambling was where Lil should not be. She noticed my change of expression and rolled her eyes. "Chill out. I didn't even play. I just watched and drank. When I swore off betting, I was serious. You should know."

The urge to smack my sister rippled through my body. I *would* know better than anyone. I was still paying off the mountain of debt she owed Cronus, among other things. We had to get out of here. Every day we stayed we both sank further into the depths of our own darkness. She continued, "How many appendages are now floating in the bay, thanks to you?"

I nearly spat my beer all over Lil. "*Excuse me*? I don't throw limbs into the bay…I let them keep them. As souvenirs." The laugh that peeled out of Lil's mouth was cold, brutal. I leaned into it, choosing rather to be the version of me that never hurt and never bled. "I would, however, dump an entire corpse. Burying stiffs takes way too much effort." Lil's stare could have cut me if I cared to let it. Instead, I wrinkled my nose at her, daring her to push me. I was beginning to regret not staying under my blankets. The beer was hardly a consolation for fighting with my sister first thing in the morning.

Lil sighed and we continued drinking in silence. My mind tripped over possible conversation starters, each one dumber and shallower than the last. How did I tell her that I'd gotten her a forged passport? What would she say? How would she react? Better to just stay quiet. Enjoy the simple nearness of my sister. It was never easy between us, not even when we were little girls living a wholesome life with our parents outside of town. She always had a talent for getting herself into shit and finding a way to rope me in along with her.

Lil began to pull the peel free of her brown banana with one hand as she tugged one of my blankets over her lap with the other. "Mom messaged me. She wants us to come visit for dinner soon." Dread began pooling in my guts. Over the last three years we had successfully managed to keep our parents in the dark about our new career paths. But it was getting harder and harder to manage the lie. Lil was supposed to be graduating with an art degree soon. What would they do when there was no ceremony or diploma to be had? I didn't want to think about that. Not now, not ever.

I groaned, "Didn't we just see them for their anniversary?" Shame at my own petulance burned the ends of my ears. "I hate lying to them."

Lil nodded, not bothering to look my way. "I'll see if I can put her off a while longer. You know Mom. She'll get suspicious if we push it." Mom thought we were both living our best lives in Arcadia. Enjoying our twenties to the fullest. Lil was supposed to be finishing her studies, and I was working, taking care of Lil, and saving up for my trip overseas, which had been long delayed at this point. Her and Dad had no clue what our situation really was.

I set my empty beer bottle down on the coffee table in front of us. "Just tell her we can be there after next week. I want to get the stupid Expo thing out of the way. It's going to be nuts, and I don't need to deal with the added headache of being a fake daughter." The Expo was unavoidable. Cronus invited everyone and their brother to this massive event in which he planned to gloat about his success as the biggest monster in town.

We could see Mom and Dad, tell them we were taking a trip, and then…run. Run as fast and as far as we could go.

Lil had leaned back against the couch, her head resting on the cushions. Her eyes were closed, brow furrowed. "Don't remind me. I'm *so* not looking forward to next week either. Cronus wants me to be "party hostess" which sounds like a fancy way of saying "eye candy." I'm just hoping everyone minds their manners." Her voice started drifting, growing quieter as sleep began to take hold. Meanwhile my blood began thrumming through my body. The mere idea of some drugged out, power hungry asshole trying to grope Lilith made me want to punch something. Hard.

"Don't worry, babe. I'll make sure they know who your sister is." I reached out and took the half-eaten banana as it began to fall from her grip. Lil started snoring while I finished it for her. She would take the passport, I knew she would. At least one of us would get to experience freedom.

CHAPTER 6

I fell asleep beside Lil for a few more hours, and then decided waking up was the best plan when my neck started barking after being bent for so long. I threw my blanket over Lil's head and went to clean myself up. I had to dig through the mounds of laundry on my floor in order to find a pair of pants without any blood stains and then threw on a black sweater, my trench coat, and an old pair of boots. I smoothed out my bedhead with a wet brush and dabbed some dark brown eyeshadow across my lids. As I finished brushing my teeth, Eve and Gerty texted asking me to breakfast with them. There was no coffee to be found anywhere in the house and I felt bad about bailing on Eve last night, so I agreed.

When I stepped outside, rays of sunlight nearly burned my eyeballs out of my skull. I shielded my eyes with a pair of scratched-to-shit sunglasses and headed towards the compound gate. Though it was bright, the wind bit at my skin. I flipped up the collars of my coat to shield my neck and ears from the chill and gritted my teeth. Currently, we were enjoying the depths of Hades' asshole that was

January. I just wanted flowers and rainbows and golden sunshine that was actually warm.

Tam was running the gate this morning. Ivan didn't want to hire him at first, worried about exposing Tam who was fresh out of high school to a mob environment, but he caved when Tam explained he needed the money for college. Honest work was hard to come by in Arcadia, especially for the low ranking members of society. No degree? No money? No opportunity. Running the gate for Cronus was probably the cleanest job Tam could find.

He grinned at me, cheeks rounding up to his eyes. His gaze caught on my freshly shorn pixie-bob. "Hey, Styx, nice haircut. Got the morning off? Where you headed?" He was so scrawny. He reminded me of a daisy flopping around on its leggy stem. Cheerful. Weak.

I gave him a quick smile. "Yep. I need caffeine." Tam activated the mechanism that slowly hauled the gates apart. The machine whined as I stepped past the threshold. "Hey, Tam?" I swallowed, hating what I had to say, what I needed to say.

He raised his brows, waiting for me to speak. "Yeah?"

"If you see Ivan, tell him to call me." I didn't look back to see his reaction. I didn't want to care that he was probably grinning so hard his face was going to split.

"You got it!"

Fuck.

As I made my way through the gate, trying my best to save the small scrap of dignity I clung to, Tam called me back to him. "Can I ask you something?" I wanted to snarl, but Tam didn't deserve it.

I turned on my heel. "What is it?"

The eighteen year old wrapped his hand around the back of his neck as a tinge of pink spread across his round cheeks. "I'm just wondering, how do I get in? Like, how do I get in with Cronus? Working the gate is fine and all, but I really need money. My mom's got high hopes for me, and this paycheck isn't going to cover tuition at U of M."

I sighed, understanding and dread coiling together like hungry snakes inside me. "Trust me Tam, it's best to keep your nose out of the Othonos family's dealings. You've got too much going for you. It's not worth it." Tam frowned, the sting of rejection plain on his face. I didn't say any more. I grimaced and walked away.

Crunchy leaves skittered over the sidewalk, snapping beneath my boots as I wandered toward my destination. The sunlight was absorbed by the grime caked on the lower half of the buildings lining the street. Stucco walls adorned with neoclassical columns, sun bleached statues of Zeus and other gods peppered the corners of the town. Only a few were actually remnants of the old world. The rest had been rebuilt after ancient wars. Modern skyscrapers shone on the south end where the wealthy lived and worked. This part of the city was a hodgepodge of businesses and residences all squished into one area. Small brick apartment buildings sprinkled between shops and restaurants painted in a mosaic of different shades of white and pale blue.

Arcadia could be described as two different cities. The morning Arcadia was a welcoming place for tourists and shoppers, eager to spend their hard-earned money. Ambrosia wasn't a threat in this sunlit version, and no one walking the streets now recognized me as Cronus' murderous right hand.

The café Eve suggested was bustling with people who had everything handed to them. They most likely always had time off to run around and take the dog on a long walk around the park. They lived up in the hills, away from the darkness that lingered between the allies and cracks in the walls. I wanted to be like them, and it pissed me off. It wasn't in my stars, at least not as long as I stayed here.

Sitting at the entrance, in a throne of his own possessions was a familiar urchin. His wispy white hair peeked out from under his wool beanie. He cocked his head up when he saw my boots. Cap jingled the cup in his hand, dark eyes flashing at me as a few coins clinked together. "Killer Bee! Killer Bee! Got any honey for me?"

I smiled while I fished a couple bills out of my back pocket. "Just for you, Cap." The gesture was returned with a subtle grin and a nod of appreciation. There were so many people in Arcadia, and most of them were too worried about their own bullshit to notice a guy like Cap. Like me. But that didn't mean we didn't exist. Cap and I were a part of the night Arcadia. The version of the city that was dark, dangerous, full of things, and people, to fear. Night Arcadia was where we thrived.

There was a line to the door when I tried to make my way inside the cafe. Hungry customers tapped their toes in impatience while they waited for a table. The walls were shades of yellow and orange, adorned with local art made by painters with too much time on their hands. The air smelled like cinnamon and coffee. My mouth watered.

I spotted the girls quickly enough; they were sitting with their backs to me. Gerty was bundled in a parka, her high ponytail looking like it had already consumed its own cup of coffee. Eve was leaning against her, arm linked through Gerty's, curly head on her girlfriend's shoulder. The perfect couple.

I flipped Gerty's ponytail before sliding into the seat across from them. "Hey, cuties." My body jerked as I recoiled from their haggard-as-hell expressions. Eve had blue smudges staining the flesh below her eyes and Gerty's skin was barely a shade warmer than that of a corpse. "Holy shit, you two. What happened last night?"

Gerty swallowed, stirring her coffee with a straw. "We had a lot of fun. Isn't that right Eve?" Eve kept her eyes closed and nodded while grunting her agreement. I wanted to laugh, but after scowling at my own reflection this morning, I knew I wasn't much better off. A cup of coffee would help, maybe.

Eve sounded like she was still half-asleep or maybe half-drunk. "Gerty's boss gave us endless free drinks at the club since she's been working so much. Who can say no to endless drinks?"

The server navigated his way towards us, clearly noting the state of my two companions. He took our orders and promptly returned with a fresh pot of coffee for our table. The aroma of nearly perfect french roast went straight to my brain when I sipped from my scalding cup. One addiction to dampen the sting of another.

The mere thought of Ambrosia kindled an ache in my bones. Even my baby toe longed for the surge of power that came from a taste of it. I started talking to distract myself from the want. "Are you going to take some time off now, Gerty, or is there more overtime in your future?" Eve perked up, more curious than I was at her response.

Gerty set her mug down and I realized I may have set a trap for her. She cleared her throat. "That depends. It's hard to stay away, especially when they need someone to work the door...or fight in the ring."

I didn't have time to respond. Eve was already jumping all over her. She put her cup down hard enough for it to echo against the table. "I thought we agreed—no more fighting?" Eve pulled her arm from Gerty's in order to look her square in the face. "It's one thing to bounce the door and swing when they swing first, but *intentionally* getting into the ring?" She sipped her coffee with a sour smirk. "Don't come crawling to me for sympathy when you've got broken knuckles and black eyes."

Gerty was already prepared with her next move.

Her blue irises sparkled as she tried to charm Eve. "Baby, you know me. I'm *The Amazon of Arcadia*. Don't you have any faith in me? What about the prize money? I'll buy you all the software and hardware and tech you could ever want. I promise." Gerty leaned over and planted a kiss on Eve's cheek, who couldn't keep her lips from twitching into a smile. I smiled too.

"You better. I've been needing a new monitor." Gerty wrinkled her nose and nuzzled against Eve. The PDA was getting to be a bit much for me. I cleared my throat, not wanting to ruin the moment but very much wanting the touching to stop.

Thankfully, Eve got the hint. She straightened up and then perked up even more when she saw our server returning with steaming plates heaping with scrambled eggs, hashbrowns, and toast. Silence fell over the table as we all leaned forward and shoveled food into our faces.

I'd just stuffed a corner of sourdough in my mouth when a shadow appeared over our table and stood there, looming. I continued chewing, not daring to look up from my meal. I wasn't ready to have my day ruined just yet. The shadow rumbled, "Madame Cirillo wants to have a word with you."

Gerty dropped her fork and Eve froze mid-bite. I forced myself to push it. To make this guy wait for me. I took another hunk of toast between my teeth and swigged out of my coffee cup. Stupid, I know. Still, I couldn't let up. I had a reputation to maintain. It didn't matter how terrified I was on the inside.

He leaned over me, his bad breath severely tainting my meal as he said, "Now, *please*." That *please* was anything but a request. All the same, I rose, dropping my napkin on the table by my plate.

I sighed as I took stock of the seven-foot-tall hunk of muscle that had summoned me. "Let's make this quick. My eggs are getting cold." The hulk grunted and placed a heavy hand on my back, right between my shoulder blades. Eve and Gerty stared after us, faces flushed as he ushered me out of the restaurant.

I tried to focus on my breathing, tried to take even paced steps, kept my chin up, my eyes bored. Everything I needed to portray the part of badass enforcer. M. Cirillo was one of the rival bosses in town that was hot on Cronus' tail. He hated her, and she hated him. We'd had several bloody run-ins this last year alone. I'd taken out my fair share of her lackeys. Things were not good between our people. Whatever she needed to say to me, it couldn't be sunshine and rainbows. The urge to escape rose up in me. I could bolt, turn the opposite way, race home and grab my shit and get the hell out of here. I sighed, letting the fantasy evaporate.

Mr. Meathead continued guiding me like a marionette through the doors and around the corner where a maroon sedan was running. I scanned the area, checking for familiar faces. If word got out that I'd been seen with any of Cirillo's crew, well, it wouldn't help my case much. Lucky enough for me, daytime Arcadia really was a different beast and all the creeps I usually dealt with were tucked into their slimy little beds for the time being.

M's muscle man opened the car door for me, and I slid into the seat. On the other side was Madame Cirillo herself. If she wasn't sitting in this scary car, she could easily be described as a sweet middle-aged lady—only she wasn't. She had honey colored curls that looked like they'd been set in a salon, makeup from three decades ago, and a sense of style that my mother would also appreciate. Her kindly appearance was a strange, off-putting disguise for the cutthroat businesswoman she really was. At least Cronus embraced his role. There was no mistaking him for anything other than a monster.

She nodded my way, "Styx. Adam, take us to the office."

I swallowed. "That's not going to work for me, Cirillo. I'm in the middle of a meal."

M smiled, her eyes veiled behind sunglasses. "I don't give two shits about your meal. But…why not. Let's keep this discreet. Adam, around the block please. Put up the partition." Adam silently did as she requested, and the partition slid into place while he put the car in gear. I leaned back, trying to maintain my cool facade. Without Ambrosia I was weak, afraid. She didn't need to know that.

She crossed her legs, angling her body towards me like a school counselor about to give a wayward student some meaningful advice. "Styx. We've had some problems between us. Despite this fact, I'd like to start fresh. Give our working relationship a new start." Panicky little snakes started to uncoil inside me.

My palms grew damp. "I already have a job, Madame. I think you know that."

Cirillo tapped a set of squarely filed acrylics on her knee. "I do know. And I've recently learned a little more about your work situation. It seems you're not just a hired employee, but more of an indentured servant. Is that right?"

My heart started a jack hammer rhythm. It wasn't that big of surprise that she'd learned of my agreement with Cronus. What worried me was *why*. "That's right. So what?" The urge to squirm in my seat became overwhelming. I didn't like where this was going.

M smiled, and it was the smile of a snake about to open her jaws wide enough to swallow her prey in one gulp. "I also know that before you were *Styx*, you were Calliope Lawson. The very same who committed a double homicide that took place three years ago. Before that, and I'm guessing still, you are also the eldest daughter of Theo and Andrea Lawson."

A wave crashed between my ears with a roar that blotted out all coherent thought. She knew she had me now. Part of the deal with Cronus was to protect me, give me an alias so the cops wouldn't come looking for me. To protect my family too. When the police started sniffing around my parents three years ago, I'd been able to convince Mom and Dad that it was all a terrible mix up. Cronus had paid those cops off to keep their mouths shut.

Cirillo pulled something out of the front seat pocket and tossed them on the middle seat between us. Photos. Of my mom and dad. At the grocery store, outside their house, even one of my dad walking their tiny dog, Pivo, around the neighborhood park.

Helpless fury burned up and down my limbs. I wanted to tear the interior apart. Slap that smirk clean off Cirillo's face. And then light the car on fire. "What do you want?"

She became a viper then, leaning forward, her breath hissed out of her with every word. "I want what Cronus has. All of it. I want his customers. His money. His power. I want everything. And you will get it for me."

She cocked her head to the side, feigning sympathy. "But don't look so upset, sweetie. If you pull this off, I'll swear to square up with you. I know how much you and that trampy sister of yours owe. I'll pay your debts. And then some. Because with your assistance, I'll have that much and more. Right? What do you say?"

The roaring in my ears had only gotten louder with every subsequent statement out of her mouth. It was too much, all of it. "Look, you don't get it, M. I'm just muscle. I don't know shit. I tell the goons where to go, and I hurt the people who get in Cronus' way. That's it. I wouldn't even know where to begin to get the intel you want." It was true. Cronus had countless moving parts going all at once, and he liked it that way. With so many people doing his bidding, his network was like a human labyrinth—impossible to navigate or decode.

M took my chin into her hands, squeezing my

cheeks the way a loving granny might. "I don't buy it. This is the deal. Take it, or don't." She released me from her claws. "Do you *really* want to go to prison? Do you really want your sweet mama and papa to get hurt because you can't do this for me?" She knocked on the partition, alerting Adam to roll it down again. "Take us back to that shabby hole in the wall they call a café. Styx wants to finish her breakfast."

CHAPTER 7

I didn't know how much time had passed. Each step felt mechanical and distant. My mind was still back in that car with M, still listening to her spill my secrets, each syllable a link in the chain around my throat. The world was muted, hazy.

Cirillo and her shady crew had been trailing behind Cronus and his brothers since they'd brought Ambrosia to Arcadia. She'd sunk her claws into every other addictive substance she could, dealing them for cheap in order to one-up her rivals whenever she could. She and her gang of ghouls were constantly under the Othonos family's scrutiny, though Cronus and M were cordial enough face to face. They made their goons do the dirty work for them, tearing each other to pieces like pawns in a game of chess. Cronus pretended not to care about Cirillo. But she was like a tick, sucking up *his* precious money for her own gains.

When I walked back into the restaurant, it seemed like I had only turned away for a second. My cup had a curl of steam rising from it while Gerty and Eve were hunched together, whispering up a storm. I didn't need to guess who they were gossiping about. How had this become my life?

I plopped down into my seat, sending Eve out of hers in a flurry of nerves. "What. The. Fuck. Was that? Styx?" She leaned forward, tapping gently on my shoulder as if to wake me. Even three years later, it still felt strange to have someone from my old life call me that. My alias was a shield, but when Eve said it, I felt…pathetic.

I was going to vomit. The aroma of my lukewarm breakfast wasn't helping much in that department. I shook my head as I picked up my fork, pretending to be interested in my eggs. "Not here."

Eve wouldn't let it go. "Styx, what did Madame Cirillo want? Is everything okay? Are you—"

"Not here, gods-damn it—just drink your coffee." It came out harder than I wanted it to, but my point was clear. Eve's eyebrows wrinkled, then cool understanding replaced her worried expression. She stretched against the seat of her chair, nodding at me before shooting a very pointed glance at Gerty. This wasn't over.

My arms felt too heavy, and my head was throbbing like I'd just smacked it against some concrete. Withdrawal was upon me, and I was beginning to ache, like my whole body was a sore tooth. In the end, all that helped was Ambrosia. And that was terrible because after I'd gotten high as a kite, the crash down to earth hurt all the more. This was the reason I never carried it or bought it for myself. It would be way too easy to burn up in a moment of furious, blind need.

Instead, I'd drink coffee and feel miserable. It was better than the alternative.

Gerty's plate was polished, every single crumb consumed. She delicately wiped her mouth with her napkin then dug into her back pocket. She brandished a worn-out wallet and pulled her credit card from the inside. "Breakfast is on me. Let's get out of here, shall we?" I couldn't handle taking another bite, hating M even more for ruining my appetite and my mood. Today wasn't supposed to be like this.

I downed what was left of my coffee. "Yeah. Your place?"

Eve was still watching me, trying to gauge the severity of the meeting through my eyes. She should have realized that my poker face had improved far too much for her to read me that easily. She said, "Yeah, Gerty bought a new record she's obsessed with, I'm sure she wants you to hear it too."

Gerty grinned at the server who took her card, and then at me. "I totally forgot about that! Good reminder, baby. Styx, you're going to love this band. It's four chicks, all of them are amazingly talented. Punk rock meets folk. It's right up your alley." Gerty had introduced me to about a million other artists, so I was confident she knew what she was talking about. It had been a long time since our schedules had synched up for us to exchange music and listen together. At the moment though, not a number one priority for me.

I tied my coat belt around my waist, preparing for our exit. "Awesome, can't wait." The lack of enthusiasm in my voice triggered some serious side-eye from Eve. Gerty signed the bill and the two of them followed me as I made my way around customers waiting for a table. I tried to swallow the burning lump of ash in my throat, but it was lodged in place.

There was art on every surface of the girls' apartment. From Gerty's framed comic book covers to Eve's paintings, the place was a mosaic of patterns and colors. Nothing matched and that's why it all worked so well. Eve was obsessed with design, and it showed. Gerty was happy to supply her with all the tools and tech she could want so she could continue to create.

I sat in the wicker chair in a corner of their living room, staring at an orange and purple lava lamp as its contents undulated. Silence still permeated the room after I'd spilled my guts about the conversation with M. They knew I was in deep shit. They knew there was no way out.

Eve was the first to speak, like usual. "Well then, there's no good way around it. How are you going to do this?"

I groaned, grabbing the sequin pillow that was wedged between my back and the chair, and shoved it against my face. "Are you serious? I'm going to die." My mind drifted to Lil's forged passport. At least she could escape this disaster. Me on the other hand? Toast.

Eve grumbled, "You are *not* going to die. You're going to do this for M, and then you're going to be free, your family will be safe. Isn't that what you've been wanting all this time?"

She knew that was all I'd wanted since the minute I'd signed that contract with Cronus. Sandy shores, warm sunsets…a mai tai made by someone *other* than Ivan. But this was impossible. No one made it past Cronus. Because—

I dropped my pillow. "Holy fucking shit, you two. What if I do this? Like, really. What if I can pull this off?"

Gerty's mouth flopped open, the pupils in her blue eyes down to the size of pinpoints. "No, really? Styx—I know you've had it rough and all after your sister's gambling, but do you realize what you're saying?" She started whispering, as if the very walls were against us. "Cronus is *the* Titan. You're essentially committing treason against the most powerful man in the country."

Gritting my teeth, I held Gerty's gaze, daring her to believe me when I said, "He's nothing more than an asshole in a nice suit. Besides, who's going to stop his Number

One Enforcer?" I pointed to myself as Eve and Gerty exchanged looks, Eve's bordering on the unhinged. Gerty's was a mixture of shock and terrified awe. I nodded, licking my lips. "That's right. Nobody. Because I'm unstoppable."

Gerty put her head in her hands while Eve stood and began pacing back and forth, her hips swaying like she was dancing. "Okay, so say you were actually—" she paused, exhaling like she was about to say a bad word, "going to do this—where do you begin? What's the first step?"

I scrunched up my eyes as I zhuzhed my hair at the scalp. "I guess I need to figure out what kind of intel would be worth it for M to pay such a gargantuan amount of money to Cronus." My eyes tracked between my two friends and my heart sank at their matching expressions. "I'm in way over my head, aren't I?" *This is impossible.* "What do I do? I'm just a junkie bodyguard. I'm not a spy or whatever it is M thinks I am."

Eve came to my side, kneeling on the carpet in front of me. "Do not *ever* call yourself that. Ever. You hear me?" She glared at me, waiting silently until my head bobbed. "It's going to be okay. You are going to figure this out. We're going to help you."

I held Eve's gaze with my own fierce stare. "No, I think you need to stay away from this. Keep your nose clean. If word gets out that *I'm* doing this, I'm dead. You don't need to be dead too. It's one thing to know what I'm doing, but to actually get mixed up in all this—I'd never forgive myself if something happened to you because of me. Either of you." I reached out and grabbed Eve's hand, letting my heart soften just long enough to send some love down my arm into her palm.

"What about Ivan?" Gerty was leaning forward with her forearms resting on her thighs. Her ponytail dangled over her shoulder. Ivan no doubt knew every little detail about the inner workings of Cronus' empire. He was next in line to take charge, and Cronus was busy as can be getting Ivan in shape to lead. But I couldn't do that to him. Put him at risk like that? I was cold, but I wasn't a monster. Not all the time anyway.

Not yet.

"No. I've got to find another lead. If Ivan gets involved, it would spell disaster. He's too…He's just…"

In perfect unison they both cut me off, "You love him. We get it."

My face burned scarlet. "No— *no* that's not what I said! You don't…Forget it. Dicks. He stays out of this. Please? I can take care of it, I just need a starting point. An in." I gave my best impression of Lil's puppy dog eyes.

Eve stood up and went to the kitchen table. She scrounged around looking for something amongst the mess of papers and paint brushes, pretending she didn't notice the red hue of my cheeks. "You know what I do when I'm in need of some clarity? I make a list. And on that list I write down all the things I think might be helpful." She kicked out the chair next to hers and patted the seat. "Get over here. Let's write down all the helpful things."

I squinted at her, trying to see if she was being honest or not. When I confirmed it, I couldn't help it, I laughed. I laughed hard. When I had enough breath to talk, I asked, "Are you serious? You want to make a paper trail of my deceit to the baddest Titan in Arcadia? *Are you nuts?*"

Eve's bronze skin darkened in embarrassment. "Well, no. When you put it like that, no. Shit."

My laughter diffused the situation just enough to make both women smile. "I need to think about my connections and their connections. And I don't know, wing it—I guess. But I think I know what Cirillo wants. What could be my ticket out of this hell hole."

Gerty asked first, "What? What's your idea?"

I sighed, stretching my legs out in front of me while I locked my hands together behind my head. "She wants ultimate power, right? What's given Cronus the edge on all his competitors?"

I watched as Eve swallowed. "Ambrosia. That's what Cirillo needs in order to best Cronus. It's her ace in the hole."

I crossed one boot over the other, silently hoping I looked more confident than I felt. "Should be a piece of cake, right?"

Gerty shook her head, shock and anger was painted in a mixture across her pretty, angular features. "Oh yeah, the stuff that makes people into super freaks? The stuff that Cronus readily kills people for? The stuff that has you wrapped around its little finger? The stuff that's—"

I rolled my eyes. "Oh my gods. We get it already. Yes, that stuff. If I can figure out how it's made, or where the supplier is…I don't know. I'll figure it out, okay? I always do."

Gerty pinched the bridge of her pert little nose as a vein throbbed in her forehead. "If you get caught Styx… He'll kill you this time. And it will hurt."

My phone started buzzing in my back pocket as I responded, "Either way, I'm dead meat." I stood up, pulling my phone out. "I'd rather be dead out here in the streets than dead in a cell somewhere. Duty calls."

It was Nick. I let his call go to voicemail. I wasn't in the talking mood. I used the moment as an excuse to get out of this suddenly tight feeling space. The shock of Cirillo's visit was waning, and in its place was the stale ache of withdrawal and disappointment. It was like the sensation of thirst, always present, sometimes more pronounced, but never truly gone or sated.

Nick calling meant I would get my hands on some Ambrosia, and as much as it sickened me to admit—I wanted it. Eve and Gerty both stood and came together making a human barricade in front of their door. Gerty's arms were crossed in front of her. The instinct to control traffic out of any exit must really go deep. Eve was busy wringing her hands, looking more like a mother hen than my friend.

I sighed, rolling my shoulders in an effort to shake off the twitching spasms that were beginning to ricochet through my body. Each cell was ready for a hit of Ambrosia.

I hated the flare of irritation that pricked my skin when I realized they intended to delay me. "It's going to be alright, you two. It's not like I'm running out there to go find Cronus himself and ask him to hand over all his secrets. I'm not that stupid. I promise I'll be careful. I've got a job to do now, so I gotta go. I'll keep you both updated."

I tried my best to look earnest as I glanced at each of their faces. Eve's brown eyes were still round and unconvinced, and Gerty was so busy watching Eve's assessment that she didn't look back at me. I'd already given them too much. It was risky to share all of this with them. Eve only ever did contract work for Cronus; she didn't need to get in deep with him like I was. I swore to myself then that I wouldn't let it happen.

Gerty broke her tough girl facade first and wrapped her arms around me in a bear hug that pulled me off the ground. The next sensation was Eve's warm embrace piled on top of Gerty's.

"Okay, that's enough touchy-feely crap! Let me go. You're always making me late."

Gerty smacked a kiss on my head and let me down. "You promised. Don't go back on your word now. We'll be expecting your call." A chill ran down my spine when I saw the ice coating Gerty's eyes. She could be downright terrifying when she wanted to be. I nodded silently while saluting them both, then ducked between them through the door.

CHAPTER 8

I had to clear my head, and fast. I shot a text to Lil, seeing if she was awake. I needed to tell her about the passport right away. She had to get out of here. There was so much shit rolling around in my brain, I was barely keeping it together. But I couldn't be caught unawares when Ambrosia kicked in.

That side of me, that dark, blood thirsty side of me that only whispered when I was high, became especially cruel if I was caught off-guard. It was starting to feel like I was of two minds, literally. And lately, that other, nasty mind was wearing out its welcome. I smacked at my cheeks as I hustled down the flight of stairs that lead out onto the sidewalk.

I am *in control. I am* not *a junkie.*
I am *in control. I am* not *a junkie*
I am *in control. I am* not *a junkie.*

The mantra had a nice beat to it, and I found myself bobbing my head as I made my way north towards Olympus. I had to cut through Delos Park to get there. Delos was built over the ruins of Old Arcadia's *agora;* it was less of a park and more of a vendor's market. There were crumbling pillars and dusty remnants of walls eroded by centuries of weather scattered randomly between stalls. It was in the heart of the city, a place people had traveled to for hundreds if not thousands of years. The path was ancient brick, laid by the founding members of Mycenae, pounded smooth by millions of steps.

Ever since I was just a kid coming to visit Arcadia to watch the wrestling matches with my dad, it had been a bustling place where anyone could buy anything if they knew how to find it and who to ask. Dad didn't like walking through the narrow rows between open trucks and rickety stands—said it made him feel claustrophobic. I never minded it. In fact, I liked the mismatched array of shoddy structures, the smiling faces of each person eager to sell their wares. It never felt scary to me. When I got older, I realized I had been too dumb to notice the dangers lurking behind the shadowy corners of every alley and intersection in the park. My dad would die of shame if he knew that I'd become just another scary figure haunting the dark crevices of the city.

I had a few hours before Nick showed up to ensure I was able to enforce Cronus' rule. I needed to start formulating a plan to get the goods for Cirillo, and getting Lil safely away. Skulking around Olympus was risky—too many eyes. I could wander Delos easily without garnering suspicion. Admittedly, I wasn't the best strategist. I hoped I would have a light bulb moment or find something at a stall that would set me on the right course to getting my ass out of this mess alive.

Against my will, thoughts of tropical breezes and the scent of a clean ocean wafted through me like a seductive phantom, pulling me to that unknown paradise I had been dreaming of, caressing me with its warmth and beauty. It was cruel, but I relished the sensation while it lasted. Dreams were nasty things that only made reality sting all the more. I needed to set that dream aside.

My fantasy was pulverized by the ever-present odor of burnt popcorn and stale beer as I casually meandered through the tourists who were too afraid to step close enough to any of the vendors to actually see what was for purchase. Cherubic grannies and their young grandchildren milled about, debating whether or not to explore Delos more deeply. Most would inevitably turn away and opt for a slice of pizza instead.

Me, on the other hand? Delos Park was like a playground for those doing business under Titan orders. We were treated like royalty here. The vendors knew our bosses and knew how deep those pockets were. The wind bit at the back of my neck, reminding me of my newly shorn hair. It was a good enough temporary disguise. Not many of my *colleagues* had seen me since I cut it. Paired with my sunglasses and coat, I was practically spy worthy.

My breath clouded around me as I exhaled slowly. I mentally gripped the reins on my cravings and yanked hard. *I am* not *a junkie*. It made it a little easier knowing I would see Nick sooner than later, and therefore would have Ambrosia on my tongue before the day was done.

The first row of stalls was a mix of jewelry claiming to be real sterling silver and beach blankets that were supposedly hand-stitched. The real seedy stuff was hidden behind the more tourist-friendly businesses. I weaved through people, eyeing the storefronts of each little shack and cart, waiting for my instincts to shout *Ahah!* But my instincts appeared to be asleep on the job.

I meandered towards Sylvia's stall. Her skin was rich brown. Her ancient face was so wrinkled she had to raise her eyebrows up to her hairline in order to get a good look around. Her bony wrists were adorned with an assortment of gold cuffs that jingled when she reached for her customer's tender.

She glanced at me while she bagged whatever it

was she had just sold. "You look older with that new cut of yours. I like it." Sylvia was one of the few people in Arcadia who wasn't completely terrified of me *or* hated my guts. At first, her blatant disregard for my reputation and clout was uncomfortable. She made me feel like a fake.

But I *was* a fake. The version of me that was *Styx* was a drug-addled killer who was addicted to chaos and violence. That version hadn't existed until I'd run into Cronus. The real me, the one and only Calliope Lawson, who liked playing sports and spending time with her family had all but disappeared. She showed up when it was time to go home and eat dinner with the folks, but that was beginning to feel more like acting. I didn't know what bothered me more.

I chose to ignore the hair comment. "How's business today, Sylvia?" I started poking around the few tables arranged beneath her sun-bleached canopy. Each item was unique, staged to entice the customer. Delicate bottles of handmade perfume lined one table, and on another was a colorful tower of Sylvia's handmade soaps. She'd stamped each wrapper and handwritten tag with her family seal. It told the world she had the confidence to stake her family's glory on the quality of her craft. Most people treated that like it was a vow. Politicians were the only ones who liked to throw theirs around as if they were bits of confetti.

Sylvia shrugged. "Not too shabby. Lots of visitors came in with the sun. Lots of husbands and girlfriends buying special scents for their special people. Is that why you're here? Did you and that lovely young man of yours see reason at last?" Sylvia's eyebrows were raised to high heaven, right up there with her hopes, until one look at my face told her the truth. Sylvia had firmly been on Ivan's side throughout our turbulent relationship. Everyone had been, actually.

I rolled my eyes. "*No* perfume for me today.

Anything else that might be of interest to anyone I know?" Maybe she had something, something I could sink my teeth into that could help with my predicament. I patted my jacket pocket as if there might actually be a healthy wad of cash tucked inside waiting for Sylvia to take it all off my hands with Cronus' blessing. She was a great lady, but she was also a very greedy lady. The temptation of wealth was enough to get her to put aside the tourist wares and show me the *real* goods. The illegal goods.

She turned around, pulling drawers open on the stand behind her. She stepped to the side so that I could look over the counter and see what kinds of treasures she was peddling today. Several fake looking watches and thick gold chains lay inside one. Another drawer was filled to the brim with wallets that had a slightly skewed although very familiar label painted over the leather.

"Come on Sylvia... *This* is not what I was talking about. Is there anything in those drawers that isn't a knock off? If that's all you've got, I'm gonna have to look elsewhere."

I slid my hand into my pocket, pretending to reach for my wallet, and Sylvia's eyebrows launched sky high. "Alright, alright. Yes. I have something. Just because it's you, and I know you'll appreciate this." Instead of opening another drawer, Sylvia ripped a bit of receipt paper and pulled a pen from behind her ear. She scrawled out three words.

Ambrosia bust, Docks, 2:00 a.m.

Then she pushed it toward me, that smug smile of hers showing off the bold gap between her front teeth. "How much is that worth to you, Missy?"

I raised an eyebrow back at her *Missy* comment. "That depends on what this is. Come on, spill it." Sylvia looked left and right, then waggled her bony hand back and forth in silent command to come closer. Her bracelets tinkled as she rested her hand on the countertop before her. I leaned over it, inhaling the strong scent of cardamom perfume Sylvia was wearing.

The peddler's voice caressed my cheek as she whispered, "Word around here is some idiot hotshot is planning to skim from Cronus' next shipment of…you know."

I snorted, "Does this kid have a death wish? He must not be from around here."

Sylvia shrugged, then held her hand out and rubbed her fingers together. "That's none of my business. I just thought you might appreciate the information and thank me generously for being such a help to you and yours."

Something in my psyche needled at me to trust her intel. I winked at Sylvia and turned back towards the busy path that led towards other vendors. "Oh, absolutely. I'll be back to pay up once I've confirmed you aren't full of shit. Thanks." She gave me two middle fingers, proud and knobby with a smile that was a nice combination of pissed and pleased. We worked well together. Not exactly helpful to my cause with Cirillo, but it could give me some insight into Cronus' shipping operation. I was grasping at straws and I knew it.

People were always trying to get in on Cronus' action. They were desperate fools who usually ended up face to face with me when their plans didn't work out. The lucky ones escaped, sans a limb or two. This guy was going to be just another notch in my very long, very holey belt.

I started making my way towards the seedier section of Delos Park, when a force from behind crashed into the back of my head, sending me sprawling face-first into the cement below. I barely had time to get my hands under me before needing a new nose.

I looked up to find the asshole who was going to get murdered and got an eyeful of some idiot *flying* through the throngs of people, his body still tumbling through the air after our collision. Whistles and shouts surged from the entrance to the park. Several winded police hustled by as I dusted sticky debris from my knees. Even though most of Arcadia's cops were on Cronus' payroll, it was a felony to possess or use Ambrosia. If you were like this guy, who had no hope of hiding the special side effects, it was only a matter of time before you found yourself locked up, if it didn't kill you first. Having monstrous fighting skills and a lack of empathy was much more inconspicuous than being airborne after a taste of Ambrosia. Though maybe not as fun.

Someone held a hand out to me. "I wish I could fly," Ivan said. I scowled up at him as I took his hand, allowing him to pull me up from the street. Ivan jerked his chin at the cops. "Do you think they'll catch him?"

I stared after the flying man, now a speck at the far side of Delos Park, far away from his pursuers. "I think he's free for another day." I glanced over at Ivan, instantly annoyed at his cuteness. It was wrong for someone like him to be so damned charming. And nice. It made apologizing even worse than it already was. "How did you find me?"

Ivan's lips split into a square mouthed grin. "I was going to ask you the same thing. I was just cutting through Delos on my way back from my dad's place." I noted a smudge of grease along the side of his neck and reached a sleeved hand out to wipe it away before thinking anything of it. When my hand made contact with Ivan's warm skin, his eyes locked onto mine. He stared into me; without speaking he asked so many questions. There had never been hesitation between us. The connection I'd made with him was instant, and no matter how hard I tried to sever it, I was always reaching for him before I knew what I was doing.

I swallowed, breaking eye contact and focusing very closely on getting every last iota of grease wiped up. "Did he pay you for the work you did?"

Ivan laughed, short and chopped—more like a

cough than anything. "Yeah right. As far as he's concerned, I'm a lost cause. He still can't get over the fact that Cronus has me at the table. My dad wants me to be straight and narrow. Not messing around with, you know. All of it— The Othonos family." His shoulders rose in a defeated shrug. He was the rock in a hard place. Once Cronus wanted you, there was no escaping. We both knew that. His dad was just trying to protect his only son, keep him from a life full of crime and death, but his brother-in-law had other plans. The first time I met Tobias, he was in the middle of a long, expletive filled rant about how cruel and manipulative Cronus was. How Ivan was better than all that. It reminded me of something my own father would have said if he knew my situation.

We started heading out of Delos together, walking in step like a matching set. It brought me back to my first days in the city, when Ivan was ordered to stay at my side day and night, making sure I didn't do anything against Cronus' wishes. I wasn't very pleasant to say the least, but Ivan hung in there, dishing it back at me when he'd had his fill. Until neither one of us could deny that the sparks between us were more than just those of anger.

My cheeks flushed as I remembered our first time, on impulse. Then I realized Ivan's hand was in my coat pocket, his fingers tangled with mine. I leaned into him as I squeezed them, delaying the end of this moment for as long as I could. Cronus had never publicly claimed any knowledge of our relationship, but all the same, it was a risk. I was just another member of the goon squad. Not suited for an upcoming prince. We were leaning towards a raging fire with complete disregard for the flames.

I started to pry my hand out of my pocket. Self-loathing roiled inside me while I tried to force space between us, but Ivan merely tightened his grip, holding my fingers in place between his. "Just let me have this. Please? I know everything you're about to say. And I don't care."

I swallowed the sudden urge to cry or to shout at him for making me feel so torn up in public. Instead, I nodded and kept my eyes ahead. I wanted to look at him, to soak up every second of closeness, and so I refused. I didn't want to be anyone's weakness or hold anyone back.

"What were you doing in Delos?" Ivan's question was innocent enough, but I couldn't answer him honestly. Not here, or ever. The secrets were piling up by the minute.

I threw out the usual excuse, "You know, browsing for anything that might be worth my while. I just got done having breakfast with Gerty and Eve a little while ago."

"I know." I looked over at him, curious. Ivan nodded, tonguing the inside of his cheek. "I saw Tam this morning. He filled me in. Said you were looking for me?"

Right. An apology was still needed for last night's trainwreck. Embers of embarrassment burned across my cheeks. "Yeah. I was a mess last night and you came in and helped me. Then I was a dick to you." I exhaled, squeezing his fingers. "I'm sorry." He'd heard this apology before. I knew he was tired of it.

Ivan didn't respond. I thought I might've seen his throat bob as we walked silently towards the busy intersection that marked the beginning of downtown Arcadia. The exhaust in the air stung my nostrils, distracting me from the increasing ringing in the back of my skull.

We stopped, and Ivan looked over at me, his eyes full of things that made my chest ache. His fingers were still warm between mine. I was already mourning the void in my pocket once he walked away. Ivan said, "I don't want you to be sorry. I want you to get better. Be done with this. All of it." It was like the universe decided it was time to fuck with me again. First Cirillo, now Ivan? Frustration threatened to overtake me, but I wasn't about to ruin the nicest thing I'd said all day. Not yet at least.

I pressed the button at the stop-walk and we waited for the lights to signal our crossing. I sighed through my nose before I said, "You know your uncle only keeps me around because of what I am with Ambrosia. What do you want me to do, Ivan?" He glanced my way, swallowing. I continued, "I don't want to burn out. I don't want to be a junkie. But what good am I to Cronus otherwise?" My voice took on a disgusting whine, betraying my fears. At least it was Ivan. He knew who I was beneath my Killer Bee exterior, even if I wasn't sure I did.

Ivan's eyes were warm and full of desperation that made my heart race in my chest. He shook his head, tiny muscles feathering in his jaw. It was a dangerous kind of hope he held. All the same, I wanted it for myself.

I willed his optimism to flood my veins, thirsting for just a bit of it to hit my system. I was left wanting, and Ivan interrupted my thoughts with his own. "I'm going to figure it out. Your days as Cronus' first enforcer are numbered."

My spine went rigid as prophetic warnings rang out in my skull. Either the stars were aligning in my favor, or I was headed for the biggest tragedy of my life.

CHAPTER 9

When I got home, my sister was loudly rummaging through her drawers and closet, talking to herself. I knocked on her bedroom door, and she startled, whipping around with an armful of sparkly things.

Her blue eyes were aloof, but alert. "Ready for the ball?" I smirked. When we were little girls, we liked to play dress up. We'd pretend to be sister princesses, beautiful and strong. Lil always wanted to marry the prince, and I just wanted to be queen. She turned away, tossing the assortment of dresses on her bed. "I was told to dress you up for tonight's *festivities*. So you blend in, or something."

I sighed. "Oh goody." Lil had actually bothered to redecorate her room. All of the kitschy stuff had been jammed in a hall closet. In its place, she'd hung colorful tapestries from home and landscape paintings she'd made herself. It was a snapshot of the real Lilith. The one who created and dreamed. I started thumbing through her picks, but she stopped me. "You need to shower. You look…Just go shower. Now." She shooed me away and then resumed her outfit hunt.

Lil had given me a black, skintight cocktail dress with a plunging neckline that dipped to nearly my navel. My back was similarly exposed. I wondered vaguely how this little dress was going to fare after I'd had a taste of Ambrosia, but the reality was, it didn't matter. If I had a job to do, I'd do it. Even if I had to do it naked. My fear of Cronus paired with that little demon voice inside me all but guaranteed it.

She was slightly more forgiving with her choice of shoes, providing me with a pair of platforms. As I was trying them on she said, "I remembered how stupid you looked when you tried to walk in stilettos." I stuck my tongue out at her. Heels and parties were definitely more up my sister's alley than mine.

My hair was too short to do anything with aside from pinning the front down on either side of my face with sparkly clips. Lil worked her magic while I stood in front of the bathroom mirror. A flustered laugh squawked out of me. I looked more like a pixie than a murdering thug. The partygoers would be surprised, that was for sure. Lil frowned. "What? You look cute." There was a flash of the sweet little sister I once knew laced between those syllables and something broke in me.

In a flood of emotions too powerful to hold back I blurted, "I found a way to get you out of here."

She shook her head, not understanding. "What?"

I couldn't stop. It was coming out. "I got you a forged passport. You can leave Arcadia. Never have to deal with the Othonos family again."

Her frown deepened, eyebrows pinching together. She said, "You want me to run away?"

My stomach bottomed out. She was taking this wrong. "No, I want you to be free. I want you to have a life."

She choked out, "And what about you? You're just going to stay here paying for *my* mistakes?"

I cringed. It didn't sound so good when she said it like that. "I can't leave. There's too much at risk."

Lil blinked in quick succession, holding back tears of anger. "You don't get to decide what I do, Calliope. Not everything is about you!" She pinched the bridge of her nose and continued, "I'm trying to pay for what I did. Don't you think I care? Don't you dare try to play the hero like this. You always want to rescue me, and look where it's got you!"

She might as well have slapped me. I held my hand up to my mouth, shocked at her words. I opened my mouth to say something, but my phone started vibrating. Like the coward I was, I turned and ran for the door.

Nick pulled up and before I could make it to the car, Ivan was getting out of the passenger seat and opening my door for me.

What the hell? Terror and anxiety roared to life inside me, pricking tears from my eyes. Ivan had only heard stories about me—had only been there after to help pick up the pieces. He'd never seen me…in *action*.
Nausea burned in my gut. "Nope. No. You can't come with us. It's not—it's not safe. It's a terrible idea."

My mind was too upset to come up with a viable reason for Ivan to stay back, and clearly, he had come prepared. "I'm supervising. As the new Second-In-Command, I need to make it known that I'm not a pushover." He stared me down, but it was a different Ivan that stood before me. One that was steely and distant.

A pretender.

For a second it was a little too much like staring into a mirror. My anxiety pitched again, sending a flurry of dizziness through me, but I nodded. Even as my mind kept screaming, *all wrong, this is all wrong!* Ivan, like Cronus, never got his hands dirty like this. He handled personnel, worked the bars, but this? Cronus was up to something. Maybe he'd caught wind of our rendezvous; maybe he wanted to show Ivan who I really was. I placed my hand over my stomach, trying to keep my guts from falling out.

Before I got into the car, Ivan gripped my elbow, leaning close enough to whisper, "I'm not afraid of you, so don't you be afraid of me. Got it?" A trickle of calm made its way down my body, not near enough to completely ease my fears, but it was something. I nodded once more and slid into the backseat.

"*So many pretty faces. Who dies first?*"

I rolled my eyes at the voice inside my head, excited and enraged all at once over its insistence for violence.

We have orders.

Oh gods, *we*? I was losing it. Ambrosia lit me up from the inside out like a voracious wildfire, hungry and powerful and endless. I was a battery eager to expend some of this energy in any way that I could, but Cronus wanted a full infiltration. He wanted intel on exactly how he was being double crossed, and then when we had the information he wanted, *then* I could release the madness that so longed to be free.

"*Damn the orders. Who dies first?*"

I'll let you know when I see him.

Rage simmered inside me, the manufactured blending with my own righteous anger into a delicious amalgamation of violence. Tonight was going to be one for the books. In the car, Nick had given me enough Ambrosia to last me an entire twenty-four hours. Clearly Cronus wanted it to be a bloodbath. It had taken every ounce of my control not to lick the entire supply from my palm. Instead, I saved a portion, storing the baggy in my dress as

I mentally patted myself on the back for managing to not
be a *complete* junkie.

Ivan side-eyed me as we made our way through
the gauntlet of people in scandalous party attire around
the mansion's double doors that had been propped wide
open. In this neighborhood, all the houses were mansions.
If it didn't have a pool, two kitchens, and an indoor gym,
then it didn't belong in the Corinthian Heights Community.
Arcadia's rich and famous lived in this gated paradise, and
this home was famous for its endless ragers, and the prince
who lived there.

He wasn't actually a prince—he was the son and
heir of one of Arcadia's most prominent families. And
though he held no formal title, everyone knew the Prince
of Arcadia was Adrian Kordos. The moment we walked
through the doors, my senses went on high alert. I couldn't
help but prowl forward, sizing up each and every party
goer. Who would fight? Who would run and hide? It was a
sickening kind of fun trying to guess. The voice in my head
gleefully played along with me.

"Fight. Then die."

Fight, then run, then die.

*"No contest, they'll just curl up and wait for their glorious
death—"*

I was beginning to enjoy the game too much, losing
myself in the delirious nature of Ambrosia. Nick bumped
into me, snapping me further out of my murderous
musings. The three of us split up. We needed to blend in,
until it was time. I had my phone ready for Ivan's signal.

It wasn't my job to do any snooping, I just needed
to be around for the bloodletting, as usual. I had time to
kill, and a desperate itch to scratch. I needed a non-violent
outlet and soon, or the voice in my head was going to
start screaming. It happened before and trying to think
coherently while the demon side of you wails and moans
about demanding blood sacrifices…Well, it's not exactly

easy.

There was a group of people crowding around together, shouting and arguing. The discord drew me in like a moth to the flame. When I got close enough to see what was happening, the voice inside purred with delight. Arm wrestling. I needed a safe outlet for this growing desire to dominate, so what if I broke a wrist or two while waiting for orders? That happened all the time, didn't it?

"Yes, crush their bones along with their weak spirits."

I licked my lips and pushed my way through to the center of the crowd. Several people cried out in shock at my power, as I easily moved men twice my size out of my way. The two guys who were locked in battle didn't stop to acknowledge me, so engrossed in their struggle.

"Let's take them both."

"I'll take the winner." I didn't yell or raise my voice at all, but my presence had hushed the crowd enough for them all to hear. A ripple of nervous laughter peeled out around us.

"They won't be laughing much longer."

There was a roar of anger from one of the competitors as his arm slammed flat against the table. The hairs on my arms rose in anticipation for battle. I exhaled, trying to soothe the beast inside me. The beast that wanted more than a gods-damned arm-wrestling match, but blood and death and glory. The man who lost swore and spit, turning away abruptly. He didn't even bother to look at me.

"Swine. He'll soon learn who he's dealing with."

I straddled the seat in front of my challenger, not giving a single shit that my panties were most likely on display. Snickers at my position died quickly enough when my eyes found the culprits in the crowd. I positioned my elbow on the table and held out my hand to my opponent, eyebrow raised in a silent challenge. The man was sweaty and obviously drunk. He laughed in my face, hand flexing off to the side.

"Serious? I'll break your arm like a twig."

"This is going to be a delicious victory. Tear his arm from the socket."

"What, are you afraid to get your ass kicked by a woman?" I waggled my fingers, sparkly nail polish glittering in the dim light. He sized me up, and then clasped my waiting hand. The cheers began the moment we touched, now locked in battle. I snapped my jaw tight, lips curling into a silent snarl.

"Make him think he has the upper hand. Make him believe victory will be his. Then steal it away."

I got this. Just shut up.

I did as the voice commanded, allowed my opponent to push my arm at an angle that would spell victory for anyone that wasn't me. I waited, a wild predator playing with her unassuming prey. I held back until I could see the hope in his eyes, the sneer forming on his lips.

Then I destroyed him. My fingers became iron vices, and every muscle along my forearm activated, forcing the man's arm out at an angle. His face took on an amusing expression of horrified shock, eyes darting between his slight opponent and where his limb was headed at an alarming pace.

I didn't make it quick. No, I took my sweet time, slowly but surely extinguishing any chance that this guy would come out a winner. He whined, the strange angle of his joints meeting their limit. I smiled. Sickly sweet, innocent. I bared my teeth when I heard a snap as I sent his arm careening down onto the table. Veins in his neck sprouted like tiny roots, and his scream bled out, mingling with the other shouts in the crowd of my new fans.

"Now take his arm as a reminder of this loss."

That's too far. No tearing limbs. Only breaking. I don't want to ruin this dress so early.

The loser flailed, falling backwards out of his chair while trying to hold his broken arm with his good hand. I continued to sit, enjoying my new position as *Queen of Arm Wrestling*. "Who's next?" I gazed around the mob of would-be contenders who glanced nervously around at each other. Clearly, I was undefeatable.

"This is child's play. Find someone to duel. Find someone worthy of a challenge."

How quickly that voice inside grew bored with limitations. I wouldn't be able to hold back much longer. Ivan and Nick needed to hurry their asses up. The allure of bloody violence was all too delicious in my mind, and each moment I denied my impulse was another closer to absolute chaos. I shrugged off the fears of those around me and rose, pulling my dress down my thighs before making my way out the back doors.

Ambrosia hummed through my body like a race car on a track, roaring mercilessly around every corner just for the hell of it. I stepped through two glass doors, where the indoor pool was, and my platforms splashed through an inch of water that sloshed across the deck. Water cascaded down from every surface surrounding the pool. Pale ivory lounge chairs arranged around the room were sopping. Every curtain, every towel was drenched. A singular tidal wave slammed down, then again while drunken swimmers were helpless to do anything more than cling to their floaties and shriek hysterically as hundreds of pounds of pool water thrashed them.

There was one person at the end of the pool. A very tan, lean woman who looked vaguely familiar. I thought maybe I'd seen her on TV at one point. She was pushing and pulling the air around her like she was a magician. The water mimicked her movements to catastrophic effect. Ambrosia must have imparted this woman with Poseidon's gifts. Lucky her.

Even while high, I was with it enough to know that drunk people and water don't mix. The woman threw her head back and cackled as she sent another wave careening over the others in the pool. More than a few swimmers resurfaced, sputtering and coughing up chlorine as she prepared to smash them all again with another enormous swell. This lady thought she was controlling the water, but really—Ambrosia was controlling her. And if she didn't stop soon, she wasn't going to be the only one hurting.

"Kill her then, end it. Justice out of bloodshed is an honorable thing."

Oh please. I don't need to kill her to stop her.

I stilled the violence that wanted so badly to get out of me, and instead went to the edge of the pool where the woman was standing totally unaware of anyone's existence outside of her own. Without a word, I leaned over, hooked my arms under her armpits and dragged her backwards out of the pool. Her hands went to my arms, grappling for purchase to fight against me, but she was no match for my steel.

Before she could go for my face with her acrylic nails, I put an elbow in hers. A *gentle* elbow tap to put her to sleep. Her eyes rolled into the back of her head and I stood, pissed off that I was now wet. As I tried to shake the excess water off my arms and legs, I watched the people who'd been trapped in the pool pull themselves out of it, clearly exhausted and more than a little shocked at the experience.

"More. More. Kill her. Take her throat in your hands and crush the vile air from her lungs. Kill her!"

I stood over the woman, assessing her with a predator's stillness. Fingers flexed at my sides as I imagined the feel of her soft windpipe beneath thin layers of flesh. So easy to break. So *fun.* I shook my head.

No. I'm in control here. Besides, killing an unconscious woman? That's gross.

"Even villains must have their limits, I see."

I wished so badly that I could reach inside myself and slap the version of me that was so disgustingly obsessed with this violent urge to kill and maim. I wanted to cut it out, to admire it and then cast it away. At least I told myself that's what I wanted. The darkness that hid in the secret corners of my mind was such a part of me now that I didn't know what I would do without it.

My phone buzzed from inside my dress, jolting me. It was Nick.

It read, *Get up here. The party's about to begin.*

"*Finally.*"

I couldn't agree more. Keeping myself in check was clearly getting to a point of futility. I needed action, and I needed it *now*. I forced my steps to remain casual as I made my way inside, towards the solid marble staircase. The room had gone dark, with only fractals of light making their way down to the ground floor. I peered upwards to see what had blocked it, and my jaw went slack. Halfway up the stairs was a mature oak tree. I could have sworn to every single god it wasn't there when we arrived.

I stared in awe at the perfectly geometric leaves, emerald and glossy as they made a canopy over the main floor. Several steps up and I rounded the trunk, examining its bark until I noticed a strange, gnarled collection of knots and indentations at its center. It looked like—

A face.

I'd heard stories about people taking Ambrosia and displaying the gifts of the nymphs—but this? Would this poor man turn back into a human after Ambrosia had run its course through his system? Or was he going to be stuck this way until he could figure out how to turn himself back? The hairs on my arms stood on end. Even the voice inside me was silent. The expression on the tree's trunk was that of surprise, of horror. I hoped it wouldn't be the end for him. I left the tree behind and continued up the stairs.

Ivan's friendly tone drifted out into the corridor. It only mildly confused me. He was probably trying his best to seem agreeable until it was time to pull the rug from under Adrian. I batted away thoughts of fleeing the house so that Ivan wouldn't have to see this version of me. There was too much at risk, and Ivan should be afraid of me. It was for the best.

I rounded the corner into the spacious entertaining area and found Ivan standing beside Adrian, who was every bit the prince you'd imagine him to be. Glistening smile, rings, necklaces, a touch of eyeliner, and beautiful. Absolutely gorgeous. Not even a smile line marred his loveliness. He sat on a pile of velvet cushions surrounded by dozens of pretty people, all vying for his attention. Before him was a tower of sparkling champagne flutes stacked like a glittering pyramid. As I walked towards them, Ivan caught my eye, shook his head a fraction. He wanted me to stay back a little longer.

The time is now. Kill the bejeweled one.

What? Hang on. There will be blood to spill soon. Hold.

My body was alive with the desire to unleash hell. To destroy the perfection in this room, to destroy all those who thought me incapable of such chaos. I would wait. A little longer.

Someone called out, "Rosé!" and Adrian laughed, eyes twinkling as he held a hand out and pointed to the champagne glass that stood at the very top of the tower. The empty glass filled itself with a shimmering pink liquid. Everyone around began applauding and Adrian giggled with self-satisfaction as someone near him pawed at his shoulder. The person who'd called out the drink came forward and took their glass from the tower. They sipped it once, testing, and then gave a smile of approval.

The crowd cheered again, and then people from all over the room started shouting out drink orders. People continued to clamber forward to collect their drinks after Adrian had conjured them into existence, clearly under the thralls of Ambrosia.

The voice in my head whined. *"I want a drink too."*

I think I'm…we're…plenty intoxicated for the moment…A glance around the room told me I wasn't the only one either.

I was going to explode if Ivan didn't make his move. There was so much rage and bloodlust inside me it was threatening to ooze out my ears. I tapped my toe impatiently from my position against a marble column in the corner of the room. Nick was closer to Ivan, working double duty as hired muscle to protect our own prince. Things had better get interesting, and soon.

CHAPTER 10

Ivan called out, "Champagne! Make it two—for you and I." A flash of apprehension breezed over Adrian's expression before he replaced it with calm satisfaction. He pointed to two glasses and they immediately filled, fizzy bubbles dancing at the rims. Ivan took both glasses down and handed one over to Adrian who nodded his appreciation. "A toast! To The Prince of Arcadia. The host with the most."

"Terrible. This pretense of friendship is wretched. Let enemies be enemies."

It's not that easy. Hush.

Adrian and Ivan held up their glasses, and everyone else in the room with even an ounce of liquor in their cup held it aloft to join in on the toast. Ivan drank first and then all followed suit, lowering their glasses and resuming whatever inebriated conversations they were involved in.

Until Ivan kept talking.

"You know, Adrian. I've been collecting your dues for some time now, and recently, well—things aren't adding up and"—he plopped down next to Adrian, like they were two bosom mates, ready for a hang session—"that bothers me quite a bit. I'm concerned that someone is stealing from you. Do you happen to know anything about that? Because if you do, you know when someone steals from you, they're stealing from me. From Cronus. And that's not good." Adrian did *not* share Ivan's expression of ease. He sat upright, his dark eyes fixed upon our second-in-command.

Then Adrian cleared his throat, shaking his head as he said, "No one's stealing from me. Why should they? I have plenty to share, and I always do. You know that." The room became uncomfortably quiet, all eyes glued to the pair on the mountain of cushions. Ivan finished the champagne in his glass, and I thought for a moment that he looked nervous, but it was gone before I could be sure.

Ivan's eyebrows scrunched while he placed his glass on a passing server's tray top. "See, that doesn't make sense. If no one is stealing from *you* then that means that *you* are stealing from *me*." Ivan sat forward, his fingers laced in front of him, the disappointed parent ready to dole out punishment. "Do you know what we do to people who skim? People who think it's alright to share product without paying up? Do you know, Adrian?" Silence stretched outward, tangled in the air like a toxic vapor ready to poison everyone in the place. Adrian's throat bobbed up and down.

Oh, he knows. He knows very well.

Anticipation became intoxicating as it traveled up and down my limbs.

It was time.

I began to stalk forward, hands ready and reaching for flesh to destroy. Ivan held a hand up to me, stalling me yet again. I almost screamed with pent up fury, but I kept it together. Instead, I let it pour out of me like an aura of death. The people nearby seemed to notice, giving me a wide berth as I slowed my pace.

Ivan's voice took on a sharp edge that both excited

and disturbed me. "We don't suffer thieves, Adrian. We kill them." He smiled at me, but it was a smile that was all edges. It wasn't *my* Ivan looking at me then. "Well, *we* don't. Styx does. Styx? Get up here. I've got someone I want you to meet."

"How dare he think to command us in such a way? Is he your superior or equal?"

I didn't respond to the voice in my head. I was too bitter and too surprised to do anything but move towards Ivan. Only a beast to be ordered around, a weapon. My legs carried me toward Ivan while the voice inside cursed him in a million different ways. For once, the demonic voice inside and I were on exactly the same page. It made me want to puke.

"We do not suffer fools; we are a different breed."

Indignance lit a new fire inside me as I responded to the voice. *You got that right.*

I felt it then—It was like shoving the last piece of a puzzle into its place. The flames that had been growing inside me suddenly flared, larger than life in my mind's eye, obscuring everything else except for this feeling of…*joining*. A bridge had been built, and I was afraid I already knew where it led.

I blinked in rapid succession, trying to pull myself back to the present, my heart beating like a bass drum in my chest. Ivan held out his hand to me when I'd gotten close enough to touch. I wished I could hate him with everything I had, but still I placed my hand in his. His eyes were steely and impossible to read. "Styx is one of the hardest working members of our association. I'm guessing you've heard of her?"

Adrian's eyes were wide as saucers as they tracked my movements, his mouth hung open enough to expose his tongue. That was a definite *yes*. Two figures moved in closer to Adrian, no doubt his bodyguards. One was tall, broad shouldered, and lean like a cage fighter. The other was more like a brick wall, squat and made of meaty muscle. Both were in matching blue athletic suits. All that was missing from their cliche uniforms was gelled hair and gold chains.

The voice inside practically vibrated with excitement. *"Too easy. This can't be all."*

I grinned, wishing that my canines were actually fangs so I could look as terrifying as I felt. I glared at Ivan, allowing the monstrosity inside me to shine through my brown eyes. Let them be empty and yet filled with all the things that made Ivan afraid. Of course, I would never *hurt* Ivan. Scare him? Yes. But hurt, *never*.

The part of me that was still human, that still wanted to be loved by the man at my side shattered when his eyes gave no hint of emotion. Wherever he was, I couldn't get to him. Instead of fear, he looked formidable and it was frightening. I swallowed, letting myself simmer in the rage that had almost been lost to me.

Ivan murmured, "We would never want to harm our friend, Adrian. But we do want to send a message. So, we'll hurt Adrian's friends. Styx, you know what to do." Ivan stared Adrian down with such a frigid expression it seemed almost alien.

That look sent me into the full-boil fury that had been stewing in my soul the moment I devoured my first taste of Ambrosia. Cronus had finally turned us both into monsters. I reached out with my free hand and rammed it through the center of the champagne tower. Glass cascaded outward, shattering out into the crowd like confetti.

After every shard finished skittering across the marbled floor, I held my hand out, bloodied but triumphantly gripping a single cracked champagne flute. It had a raw jagged edge, just waiting to taste flesh. I whirled around the room, savoring the looks of pure terror on each and every person's face.

"Weaklings. Kill them all!"

A surge of heat licked at my limbs, and I grinned so hard I thought maybe the corners of my lips might bleed. I jerked around, hard and fast towards the cage-fighting muscle. He was fast, already ducking away as I frantically stabbed outwards.

But I was relentless.

I was a machine meant only for destruction, and it felt so *good*. I thrust my leg out behind him, sweeping him off balance. As he sailed to the floor, arms flailing out in a desperate attempt to regain his hold on gravity, I slid to the ground. I raised my fist, positioning the champagne flute just beneath his landing place. When he hit the floor, his skull made full contact with that beautiful, jagged bit of glass. It did plenty of damage with the force of his body as it slammed down on top of my slight, yet perfect weapon. Screams erupted all around as his brains started trickling out beneath him. I pulled my hand out, felt the warmth of his blood on my fingertips.

A part of me died in that moment of beautiful killing. Not because I enjoyed it. Not because of the horror. But because Ivan was there to witness what I had done. There was no hiding what I was actually like from him any longer. A small slice of my soul was carved away and sent out of my body, leaving behind something aching and desperate. If this had been Cronus' intent, he nailed it.

The voice inside me hissed, *"Let's kill him too, then. He's unworthy."*

It's me that's unworthy.

"You are a warrior, perfect in every way that counts. Do not forget this."

I tossed aside the confusion that came with getting a pep-talk from my subconscious. Blood coated my vision and lay heavy on my tongue. Urged by the power bestowed upon me, I launched myself at Bodyguard Number Two. I no longer held my champagne flute since it was lodged in that other guy's head, but it didn't matter. *I* was a weapon.

This body was a vessel for pure violence, and I would only be sated when I had shed enough blood.

My hands gripped his shoulders as we started falling backwards through the air. I let my entire weight force his trajectory towards a very unfortunate landing. He had no chance of regaining his balance or fighting me off.

There was a disgusting *crack* as his neck made contact with the seat of a velvet armchair. It wasn't as much of a show as I'd been prepared to give, but it did the job. I climbed off his corpse, readjusting my dress so that I was presentable. I tried not to let the rest of my soul break into pieces when Ivan did nothing more than straighten the lapels on his jacket while he rose from his seat next to the stunned Adrian.

Still, I was not satisfied. I'd taken more Ambrosia than I'd thought.

"Who's next? Who will die? The traitorous one who thinks to control you?"

No. Not him. Never him.

"You'll tire of him eventually…"

I didn't respond to the demon in the back of my brain. I pulled a knife that I'd strapped on my thigh and threw it indiscriminately into the crowd as hard as I could. Someone crumpled as the knife found its new home in their stomach. As people screamed, I raised an eyebrow at Ivan, continuing on with my role as the rabid dog chomping at her master's bit. I held out my hands as if to say, "Well?" yet I remained silent. There were no words I wanted to speak to Ivan. I wasn't sure I'd ever be able to talk to him again. He nodded a single time and began making his way through the mute patrons and towards the exit. He made no attempt at eye contact as he breezed past me. He was probably disgusted. Or afraid.

Nick, who had his gun out in front of him, let out three random shots at no one in particular. The crowd scattered to any nook or cranny or window they could find in order to escape us. We raised a sufficient amount of hell in a very short amount of time. I loathed to think it, but I knew Cronus would be pleased. There was nothing he loved more than his brutal reputation.

I'd held out as long as I could, refusing to completely give myself over to the powerful persuasions of Ambrosia, and now its sinful power was leaching away from me. Nick ushered me out of the house, prodding me like I was a cow headed for slaughter. Our phones buzzed in unison, and we both swore.

We need backup at the docks as per Styx's intel. ASAP

Nick glared at me. "It's always your fault when I gotta work overtime. Why is that?"

Cronus knew that every time he pinned something on me, it made my life all the shittier. I rolled my eyes and opened the car door. He loved control any way he could find it. No matter how petty—he could be a real dick. Ivan was already in the front seat. He didn't flinch or even acknowledge us as we settled in. Instead, he turned the music up until the speakers were vibrating as Nick drove us back towards Olympus.

My body was beginning to ache that terrible, hollowed out feeling that ate and ate at me once Ambrosia had faded from my blood. I reached into my dress and pulled the now very sweaty packet of Ambrosia out from between my boobs. I carefully unzipped the tiny baggie and opted to dump the contents directly into my mouth like I was finishing off the last of the potato chips. I tapped the corner of the plastic bag, making sure to shake loose any stubborn remnants. When I brought my head forward, I caught Ivan's stare in the passenger side mirror. The mask from before was gone, and in its place was the perfectly honest expression of a young man who didn't know what the fuck he was doing. I stared back, daring him to say something, do something. He just kept staring, and I hated how I knew exactly what he was thinking. What he wanted to say. And that I *wanted* to hear every single word.

I almost opened my mouth to start an argument. Those pretty eyes couldn't always get him out of everything. It was bullshit. All of it was, but I was overcome with a surge of magical fury as Ambrosia danced through my nervous system, burning into my legs and arms, making me into a warrior.

"You are my warrior. My champion."

The words from inside my head sent me plummeting down from the cresting waves of drug induced euphoria. I was awash with confusion, muddling my sense of reality even further. I knew it was a bit nuts to have a voice pop into your head every time you took a drug, but usually "we" were one, or at least a team…The flames of Ambrosia's power started to eat at my sense of reason, and all deep thinking ceased. Left behind was only the renewed desire to subjugate and destroy. Streetlights strobed through the car windows, casting us in black and white stripes as the car sped towards our destination.

Who are you?

The voice inside asked a question in answer of my own. *"Where do you go when you leave me?"*

When *I* leave? The query dropped down into my gut, each word rotten and heavy. Then I remembered that feeling from before in the Kordos mansion. That snapping sensation, like two powerful magnets clicking together. Was I losing it? Had I overdone it? I'd tried for so long to keep my balance, keep my sanity. My heart ricocheted in my ribcage while I breathed in order to slow its racing.

"Are you a dream?"

My voice was asking *me* questions. Asking me questions like it wasn't me. But wasn't it? How could it be anything other than a new branch of my psyche that was created by my nervous system to help cope with taking Ambrosia. Me, a dream? This was all a dream. It had to be.

I went on autopilot as Nick put the car in park and

we each drifted towards dock twelve. I was too stunned and too high to voice what I was experiencing. Was this what it was like to burn out? In the last three years there had never been a conversation like this. I cursed myself for being so arrogant. So cavalier about taking a drug that killed those who ingested it like they were nothing more than living matches to be ignited and then burnt to a charred stalk.

"Will there be more blood to shed? Is it time to unleash hell?"

That was a little more normal, but even so, the voice had an unfamiliar lilt to it…Ancient. It was as if a wall had been broken down, and I was no longer comfortable in my own skull. I didn't feel *alone*, and that was really fucked up.

The smell of low tide was thick in the air, and there was a deep pulsating warble of machinery as cranes moved slowly above us, rearranging the massive cargo containers that had been recently emptied. The dock we were heading to had a big shipment unloaded this morning. If Sylvia's information was credible and this stake-out led to a real bust, it would help my case with Cronus. He liked to reward his lackeys when they did tricks just to please him.

If it was a false tip, well Nick would be grumpy, but he was always grumpy. Cronus preferred to play things safe, especially when it came to Ambrosia. He was the only one in the world as far as I knew who manufactured it. That's why it was such a hot commodity. You could only find it in Arcadia, and if you wanted it, you had to pay Cronus or one of his dealers handsomely. It was not a cheap party drug by any means.

If I hadn't already been high, the temperature outside would have turned me into a popsicle in a party dress but as it was, I had the heat of Ambrosia flowing through my veins. For all I cared, it could have been July. Ivan and Nick clearly felt differently, both had their arms crossed over their chests, bodies tightened in order to ward off the frigid air. The sky above us was dark and hazy with thin clouds obscuring any glimpse of stars or the moon. As we got closer to dock twelve, we could hear voices and see the shadowed silhouettes of the goons who were usually running this side of the show. They were a rough crew. Any person walking by them in a dark alley would definitely hightail it as fast as they could to get away from the burly, scruffy, nightmarish looking fellas that Cronus trusted to oversee his precious goods while they were transported to and fro.

Ivan went first to chat with whoever was the point person while Nick and I stayed back, neither one of us interested in any kind of interaction with the other. We would just end up trying to kill each other and that wasn't a great look, especially for Nick—because he would inevitably lose, and he knew it.

I let my senses fan out. My eyes tracked over each piece of equipment and crate, searching for any signs that something was off, or something I could use to bait Cirillo, but besides Ivan's muffled conversation, it seemed like everything was as it should be.

I stretched my fingers wide in front of me, remembering they were still covered with that bodyguard's blood. It had dried to a brown crust that begrimed my manicured nails and coated each and every wrinkle.

"A true acolyte. A lust for blood that never diminishes."

My brow wrinkled in discomfort. *Acolyte? What is this? Stop talking to me.*

The voice would not be silenced. *"Disdainful and rebellious. A masterpiece of malice."*

Stop. Now.

My temper flared, and suddenly I was storming over to Ivan, all impulse and no control. It was like I was in the back row of a theater as I watched myself move.

"What's the situation?" *That could have been worse…*

Ivan looked shocked at my sudden nearness for

a moment before his boss mask slid into place. His jaw clenched in displeasure. "When I know, you'll know. For now, we wait. *You* were the one with the warning. Why don't you tell us what was said, exactly."

I twisted my head until my neck cracked, loud enough to make Ivan flinch. "Some guy is supposed to be stealing from this shipment at two." The burly man who stood beside Ivan with his tattooed arms crossed high on his rotund chest slid his gaze to Ivan, then back to me.

"Got something on your mind, lil' guy?" I looked up at him while sucking on my front tooth. I'd already broken one arm tonight and killed at least two other people. Why not cap the evening off with some classic bullying?

The man gave me a sour look then replied, "I've got a new delivery guy. I just hired him yesterday. His resumé was clean enough."

"Get on with it. This is not entertaining."

I shook my head, laughing up into his face. "Well clean resumé or not, he's apparently been blabbing at Delos about how he's going to rob Cronus blind. Tonight. So, where is the little rat?"

"Yes. Where is he so we can exterminate him…"

I didn't want to feel excited, didn't want to like the anticipation of murder, but damn it all, that's where I was. Ivan immediately started cutting into the man with his tongue, giving him a talking-to that impressed even me, but there was no time.

I huffed, "Yeah, we get it, *Boss,* but *where* is this guy?" Ivan scowled at me, knowing full well that later there would be a reckoning for both of us. But not now. No more words were exchanged, instead we all started running towards the sound of a van's ignition as it roared to life.

"There he is."

I shouted to Nick, "Head him off at the gates! We'll catch up!" Ivan and the dock worker were no match for my legs on Ambrosia. I whipped past them, a gazelle in platform heels, racing between crates and over piles of netting and old tires. Headlights flashed across my face.

The van was heading straight for me.

I grinned as I stared into the lights. I couldn't see the driver, but I knew he could see me. Could see the blood lust gleaming in my eyes. I paused where I was only a moment before sprinting directly towards the van.

Ivan started yelling orders to every person who was still on the scene, but I didn't really hear him. I leapt onto the hood of the van and landed hard on my knees. The metal was freezing as my skin pressed against it. I placed both hands on the windshield, and finally I got to look into my target's face.

"After a while, they all look the same, don't they?"

I wasn't sure who said those words, or where they had come from, but it was true. This idiot was a dead man walking, just like all those before him. I raised my fist to punch through the windshield when he slammed on the gas, sending the van and myself careening sideways through nearby stacks of crates and rope. Without any way of holding on, this was going to hurt.

I tried to brace myself for whatever impact was coming for me. I squeezed my eyes shut, as if not seeing would make the impact hurt less. The van slammed into a huge crate and sent me airborne for what felt like an eternity. A flash of bright, beautiful red coated my vision, and then everything went black. Everything except for that voice.

"Where are you going now? Leaving just when things get exciting."

CHAPTER 11

When I came to, Nick was prodding me with his boot while everyone else was rushing all around us, hustling to get the van unloaded. I was mentally drowning in post knockout confusion, but my body still hummed with Ambrosia. I propped myself up on my elbows and from my new vantage point I could see the idiot would-be thief in a pair of very official handcuffs staring at the ground while Ivan spoke to him in a low indecipherable tone. He glanced my way, nodding only once before taking the thief away.

"Prisoner? No prisoners. Kill him. He tried to kill you. Fair is fair."

What is this? Keep quiet, I have to follow orders.

"Pity."

Nick stopped poking me with his boot, now that he was certain I was alive. "Too bad," he muttered before turning towards the van to start helping with the unloading process. I'm sure he was ready to get home and be done with all this bullshit.

I wanted to feel that way, but I never did. I just

wanted to fight. To destroy. To burn the world down and laugh while it turned to cinders.

I was partly terrified that my body was damaged in the crash, but as far as I could tell, I only felt stiff and bruised. There was no obvious throbbing that came with a broken bone, no limbs that refused to respond to my brain. It could have been much worse.

Ambrosia made me strong, fearless. It made me fast, too. But it did not make me immortal. When I stood, there was a funny rushing sound and a warm sensation of something trickling down my face. I pressed a hand to my left cheek; it came away with a fresh coating of crimson, this time it was *my* blood. I tried to care about my flesh wound but came up wanting. I would tend to myself later when I was alone and less high. For now, I let it add to my already terrifying visage.

I sauntered over towards the back of the van where men had formed an assembly line and were passing things down and into another van. This one had obviously been rendered useless in the wreck. Its front end was all smashed up, no doubt the axel was fucked.

Every person I passed glued their eyes on me. The predator. The bloody killer in a pretty dress. The woman who was afraid of nothing and ready for anything. I smirked before finding a spot in the line. It took a moment for the guy next to me to realize I was there to help and not to murder him, but then he passed along the next several bricks of what was clearly Ambrosia.

I had to keep myself from drooling over each package that went through my hands, eternally thankful to be able to pass it off immediately to the person beside me. Only the fear of discovery kept me from stuffing a brick under my dress. Shame rose up into my throat with a healthy coating of bile. I wasn't a total lost cause. Not yet.

As the Ambrosia began to fade from my body, so did my capacity for executive functioning. I'd rarely ever gotten high twice in one night. I knew the come down for this was going to hurt and there would be no way to avoid it. No way that didn't turn me into a full-blown junkie.

My arms grew heavier by the minute and soon I was the only one working the assembly line with just one more brick left to switch over. Apparently, I wasn't the only goon who no longer gave two shits about orders. I scanned the area; Ivan was nowhere to be found and Nick had already left. No keeper, no job. I was done. The voice inside was only a whisper but I could feel it lingering silently inside my mind. I couldn't remember a time when I'd had its company for so long. Usually when I started aching, I was left with a head full of nothing but misery.

The voice murmured, "*And what is the reward for our deeds? What is our prize?*"

I shrugged. *We get to live another day. Fight another fight. That's it.*

There was a stretch of silence, but then one of Cronus' delivery drivers circled around. "Is that the last of it?" He eyed me up and down, waiting for confirmation. I swallowed, jaw clamping down tight as I tried not to look at the one remaining package still sitting in the squashed van. My arms hung heavy at my sides like useless weights. The chill of the night began to eat at my skin, taking little bites of my warmth with each minute.

"*This misery, for only a trifle moment of glory? Shameful.*"
Better to be miserable than dead, don't you think?
"*I suppose.*"

I ignored the voice, hoping it would grow quiet, hoping it would leave me be. I was done communicating for the night, with myself or otherwise. I was free falling from the high of Ambrosia, and soon I would hit the bottom, and oh how it would hurt. The driver scowled at my silence. "Well?"

"Take it all. It is the least you deserve. Warrior."

The desire for Ambrosia wrapped its hands around my vocal cords summoning the words, "Yep. That's it." Before I could stop myself, I was slamming the loaded van doors shut, signaling the driver to head out. I stood there, every inch of my being aching with want as the van's red taillights faded to nothing as it drove away from the docks.

All reason, all sanity fled as I lunged into the back of the smashed van and scooped the brick into my arms. Like a maniac I hauled ass through the gate towards home, praying to every god in the Pantheon the cameras hadn't caught what I'd just done.

When I came through the door, Lil was passed out on the couch. She was in pajamas this time around. I closed the door with a soft hand, unstrapped my feet from their platform prisons, and hobbled as quietly as I could to my bedroom. Every cell in my body screamed at me for relief, but I needed to figure this shit out.

What the hell was I doing? I put the brick on my bed and stared at it for a solid minute before pacing back and forth in front of it, never taking my eyes off it. It was enough to kill an elephant three times over. It was also enough to buy at least half of Lil's debt. But selling it would be impossible to get away with, at least not for long anyway. If I gave this to Cirillo, would it help my case? Would it be enough to persuade her to keep her word and buy our way out from under Cronus' boot?

It was a stupid idea. She could have bought Ambrosia if that's what she wanted. Gods, I was so fucked. What was I going to do with this thing? It was going to kill me if I left it here. I could only hold out for so long. And it hurt, it hurt every single part of me to stand here suffering while the key to my comfort was sitting on my bed. I reached out for it, the desire so terrible it drowned out everything else.

My fingers shook as I reached towards the white

crystalline drug. I'd never really considered I was lucky when it came to Ambrosia, but after seeing that person-turned-oak in the Kordos mansion, I realized it could have been much worse. *At least I'm not a tree.*

My hand hovered over the package and then I snapped out of my drug haze.

Blood.

Oodles of it still covered my skin. I recoiled and with as much haste as I could muster, I shoved the brick into a random bag and stuffed it under my bed. I would find a better hiding spot for it later.

I left for the bathroom to try and rinse away the night's gore. I knew that no matter how much I scrubbed, it would leave a stain. Not just on my skin, but on my soul. There wasn't much clean space left anymore. Soon I would be completely altered from my original state. The old Calliope was almost dead. I didn't want to think about that. I just wanted to find some sliver of peace that would get me through the night.

I gasped when I saw my reflection in our grimy mirror and every sensation before that fluttered away. A jagged cut that began at the center of my left eyebrow and ended at my jaw had bled a considerable amount.

"Like Enyo, goddess of battle."

The voice faded into the background as I examined my cut. Blood had spread across my face and crusted in patterns that reminded me of a dried-out riverbed. I was disgusting, and maybe needed stitches. My left eye was swollen shut, eyelashes gunked up with blood. My arms and legs were covered in bruises and cuts. I was a tapestry of brutality. It was hard not to admire the bluish splotches staining my skin. I poked and prodded, testing for pain, but besides a general achiness reverberating throughout my being, I wasn't in terrible shape.

After the world's hottest shower complete with insane amounts of soap and scrubbing, I found myself still restless and unwilling to stay in my room, or even my house until I had a plan for…I didn't even want to think about the *word*—until I had a plan. I found myself tugging on my bathing suit then pulling sweatpants and a hoodie over it. I tossed my still damp towel over my hair to ward off the chill for the brief walk and snuck out while Lil continued to snore.

The indoor pool was only occasionally locked, and when it was, finding an alternate entrance was never difficult. It was kind of an unwritten understanding at Olympus. Arcadians loved swimming, and nobody held dominion over any time slot. Well, nobody but me. It was my pool when it was this late, or early, depending on your perspective. I tried the front door. The handles were bitingly cold as I tugged at them and when they gave, I threw the right door out wide, allowing myself entrance. I locked it behind me.

Only the sound of electricity running through the walls and a slow dripping faucet kept me company as I walked through the changing room. The walls were tiled with white hexagons, all polished and ready for tomorrow's Olympian swimmers. This was the one place on the compound that I didn't completely despise.

The natatorium was almost completely dark. A streetlight from outside illuminated the surface of the water, casting peachy light across the lanes in wavering beams. I flipped the switch and the underwater lights turned on, washing the room in the water's mirage. Turquoise ribbons danced on every wall as I tossed my towel and clothing on the nearest deck chair. Without waiting another second, I stepped to the pool's edge and dove in headfirst. The chlorine stung my face for a moment, but the shock of the cool water wrapping around my body helped me forget the pain.

One of my favorite things about swimming was testing my lungs in a battle of wills. My brain knew there was more oxygen inside me, more time to swim beneath the water, but my heart, my lungs, my cheeks, they didn't know. They didn't believe there was time to spare. It was a war between logic and fear. One that no matter how many times I fought, I always lost. Logic *or* fear, it didn't matter, because in the end I was still mortal. I would always need to surface. To start again.

I moved slowly, allowing the water to carry my weight for me. I wanted to feel nothing, to forget I had bones that ached and a face that was cut to shit. I allowed my limbs to still as I rolled onto my back, rising from under the water. My arms and legs drifted apart, and my body formed the shape of a star.

If Cirillo found her own way to sell Ambrosia she could totally compete with Cronus. One little stash of it wasn't enough to set her up for success. And it would ultimately get me in trouble—I knew that without a doubt. I only had one chance to find what Cirillo deemed helpful, and if I fucked up, I knew she would make good on her promise to send me to prison. That made my stomach go all watery inside. I wouldn't survive prison.

I flexed my ankles in the water as I racked my brain for ideas. Connections. People who could help without getting too involved. Maybe I could get someone to figure out what Ambrosia was made of…I didn't know the first thing about science, or manufacturing, and had no idea who would. Even though Cronus used my "services" constantly, he kept all of his machinations close to his chest. I doubted even his idiot brothers knew much more than I did.

It's not like I could just walk around asking people if they knew how to make drugs, obviously. I smacked myself in the head and hissed when I made contact with the edge of my cut. I was going to have a terrible scar. My stomach lurched again when I realized I would have to lie to my mom and dad about what happened to my face. *Oh gods.* Bike accident? That would have to do. Mom would buy it, but Dad?

The pool filter kicked on, sending a whirring sound through the water and into my submerged ears. Above the surface, an annoyingly familiar figure appeared through the men's changing room entrance. I refused to move or even acknowledge Ivan's presence. Instead, I closed my eyes. His voice came out garbled. Clearly, he wanted to talk to me. *Fuck that.*

I took in a lungful of air and dove under the water, kicking off the bottom towards the other end of the pool. I wasn't sticking around to hear whatever it was he wanted to say. I needed more time to process the stranger that had so abruptly arrived and taken Ivan's place tonight. The frozen prince who didn't even stick around to make sure I'd be able to walk away from the crash. Cronus was determined to take everything from me. Every single inch of my life that I tried to keep for myself was slowly slipping through my fingers. The Ivan I knew had been replaced by some other cold, cruel version that I wanted no part of.

I stayed submerged for as long as my lungs could stand. I breached near the step ladder and grabbed hold of the railing before I was above water. When I hauled myself up, Ivan was an inch from my face, leaning towards me over the pool's edge. His eyes were pleading, begging me to hear him.

I growled in frustration, letting go of the handlebars, falling backwards into the pool where I promptly began back-stroking away from him as quickly as I could. All the feelings of being turned into an object of death by one of the very few people I trusted was revived. I never wanted this. Any of it. And now I was determined to break free of my chains. It didn't matter who held the leash, I was done being a tool.

Again, he tried to speak, but the roar of my arms impacting the water distorted the sound for which I was eternally grateful. I knew if I listened, I would forgive him.

I knew I would melt into a puddle of mush and accept everything he wanted to tell me, but I wasn't ready for that. Not yet.

CHAPTER 12

When I reached the other side of the pool, I hauled myself up onto my elbows first before kicking my leg up and onto the deck. Each limb weighed even more than before, exhaustion dragging me down. It was going to take me forever to get out of here.

Ivan's voice echoed across the room. "Are you kidding me? The woman I watched kill two people tonight is running away from a *conversation*. Am I getting that right?" I wished I wasn't the type of person to take easy bait, but I was. He knew it too. There was something insatiable about our arguments. I couldn't seem to get enough of them, and neither could he.

I twisted towards the sound, not entirely sure where he was. "That should tell you something about how I'm feeling. But clearly you can't take a hint. You're the idiot who thought now was a good time." I stood up, albeit incredibly slowly, each joint locking into place as my bones stacked one on top of the other.

Ivan came into view close enough now for the pool lights to illuminate the contours of his face. The water lapped at his chest. His hair was wet, dark strands curling around his cheeks. His usually warm eyes were veiled, keeping me from reading him clearly. There was a harsh line to his jaw, and I wanted to run my fingers over the curved angle. So many nights we'd spent circling each other in this water, playing, happy. Now those memories felt tainted with my sorrow.

My heart ached as I looked at him. So many times we'd hurt each other in the last three years. This was just one more occurrence. I'd tried to keep him at arm's length. Tried to cut myself off from him, but here he was, looking handsome and earnest and daring me to forget everything. If looking was all I could do, then I would take my fill.

"Just say what you want to say, Ivan." I put a hand on my hip, hoping I looked more pissed than upset. Ivan swam up to the edge of the pool at my feet and rested his forearms on the deck as he looked up at me. There was a shine in his eyes, one I'd seen often in the faces of my victims. I threw my head back, exhausted from all of these gods-damned feelings. "Spit it out already."

Ivan sighed and said, "I'm sorry about everything. Tonight was awful in every way." He stared up at me a moment longer, until my gaze was too much for him to handle. He ran a hand through his curls as he looked away. "I hated that version of myself. What I said, what I told you to do, the *way* I told you to do it." He brought his hand to rest at the base of his throat as though he might be sick.

I sucked on my cheek before I relented and sat in front of him, dangling a foot into the pool. His hand found my ankle beneath the surface, his fingers circling my joint while he waited for me to say or do anything. I wasn't sure myself what was going to happen yet.

I swallowed, knowing that behind his words there was pure sorrow, a kind that I didn't have access to anymore. Thanks to Cronus, and now by proxy, Ivan. "I don't have a choice. The things I do, the people I…But you do." Ivan's neck tensed, and his brow came down over his eyes, but he didn't interject. "Just because you're Cronus' nephew doesn't mean you have to be *him*. And if it did, is that really what you want?"

Ivan released his grip on my ankle and swam a meter or so away from me. I couldn't help myself, the words kept tumbling out. "Because the man I saw tonight, that wasn't you. It was Cronus," I exhaled hard, knowing I needed to say everything in my head, "and I hated it, too." I could blame Ivan all I wanted for the monstrous things I'd done tonight, but in the end, it was all me.

I pushed off the deck and slid into the pool towards Ivan. He was treading water, arms and legs moving in slow, practiced circles. I started mirroring his movements, silently challenging him to a contest of stamina. He raised an eyebrow acknowledging the game. We bobbed there for what could have been mere moments or hours. The time we had together was fleeting. Fragile. This was a fairytale that would be over soon. Real life wasn't easy like this. Life was a tragedy; we were merely delaying the ending.

He spoke first, pulling me from my thoughts, "I should have stayed and made sure you were going to be alright. I hated not being able to check on you. Knowing you might be hurt and that I had to act like—like I didn't give a shit." His eyes traced the cut on my face, and I did hate him for a moment, for leaving me when he could have chosen to stay. My sins in comparison were unforgivable. The Killer Bee, ready to destroy at my master's request. And now I was a thief, too. Ivan still had a chance to be good, to live without blood tainting his soul.

Ivan swam closer to me, until his legs brushed against mine. And then his nose grazed my cheekbone. I refused to back away, challenging him yet again. His hands found my waist, pulling me closer before his lips, wet with pool water, glanced across mine. They were so familiar and so new. Soft, decadent. He kissed me again, and it was like a secret. One that no one would ever repeat, even though I desperately wanted to hear it again. And so, I kissed him back. My lips met his while I pressed my body against him, needing him so much more than I wanted to admit.

When I pulled back, our chests were both rising and falling in quick succession. I pressed my hand against his collarbone, gently pushing him away. He stared into my eyes, confusion and a faint flicker of hurt danced across his gaze. I was always hurting him. I cleared my throat and said, "This is a bad idea. We both know how bad of an idea this is, right?"

Ivan swallowed, his hazel eyes drifting towards my lips. "I've never agreed with you on that front. You know that."

Ivan was convinced we could have a normal relationship and no one would think twice. He wanted to believe we could be like everyone else. It was sweet, but stupid. He leaned in for another kiss, but my hand stayed firm against him. "I am, like, the easiest bargaining chip for your uncle to use against you, or you against me. Or any other number of painful combinations. It's just dumb. And I don't want to hurt you."

Ivan's hands slid to my back. "I don't want to hurt you either." He found a way to get close enough to nuzzle my neck before placing a delicate kiss where his nose had just been. "But this day in and day out of seeing you, talking to you, and nothing else? That hurts. It really hurts. Just let me keep you."

There was no coming back from that. I melted like I knew I would. I leaned into him, giving him full access to my neck, my mouth, my heart. All of it. Just like the idiot I was.

Ivan's lips trailed along the column of my throat, then back up to find my lips. His kiss was insistent, and his tongue slid easily into my mouth. I found myself losing all sense of right and wrong. I kissed him back, bringing my arms around his neck to pull him closer to me.

I was tired of fighting off my feelings, but I still had to maintain some sort of agency against Ivan's charm. It would be all too easy to get mushy and lose myself in the mythology of the romance we could have. The life we could forge for ourselves. We couldn't afford those kinds of dreams. Cronus would see to that.

I swam away from Ivan, towards the ladder nearest the changing rooms. "This has to stay between you and I. Promise? Your uncle would eat me for breakfast." And if anyone caught wind of our…whatever we were…Well, I had plenty of enemies inside and outside of Olympus who would jump at the chance to see me bleed. The problem with delimbing people is, they remember you. And while they might not be brave enough to fuck with me or Cronus out right, they would jump at the chance to hurt the person I loved most.

Ivan stayed put, but I felt his eyes watching me through the dim lighting. "You really think my uncle would use either one of us like that?"

I spluttered, trying to hold back a shocked guffaw. "Was tonight not a big enough sign to you, that yes? He will and does use anyone he wants." I didn't turn to look at him, I didn't want him to see my face. "You think he cares that I've got so much blood on my hands I could paint the town in it? No. All he thinks about is power, and how to hang on to it." I stopped moving, waiting for his answer. "You can't honestly tell me you believe that he wants to give you the reins?" He couldn't be that ignorant, could he? Usually, we kept shop talk out of our conversations, but if he was going to make attending my jobs a routine, we needed to have it out, now. Finally I broke, facing him so he knew I wasn't going anywhere until this was done.

Ivan's voice was soft as he said, "I'd always been adjacent to whatever you had to do for Cronus. I didn't know it would be the way it was. I mean I *knew*, but—I didn't really." His next words were so quiet as they floated across the water, I could have missed them. "I don't want to be like him. I don't want you to have to be like that. Not for *him* or *me*."

My heart, already weakened from his kisses, twisted inside me. I wanted to tell him there was a way, there was a splinter of hope. I could be free. *We* could be free. But was he ready to hear it? Did he really want to stop this runaway train before it went off the rails? "Just because you don't like it doesn't mean it isn't going to be that way. You're Cronus' nephew, not his right hand, no matter what he tells you. Don't kid yourself into thinking he won't break you just to prove a point."

Ivan groaned, kicking his way closer to me. "Gods, Styx, why do you always have to say things like that? Like I'm just some puppy-eyed idiot who doesn't get anything? I know who my uncle is. I know. Trust me. I've been around him longer than you have. There's a reason my dad hates that I have anything to do with him. Well, plenty of reasons actually."

I sighed, bobbing on my back. "You *are* a puppy-eyed idiot. And I say it because I care about you, and I don't want you to dupe yourself into thinking you're safe from his bullshit."

My mind shifted unwillingly to the bag hidden beneath my bed, to the contents inside waiting for me…I swallowed, forcing the image away. I couldn't stop the words that barreled out of my mouth. "Where did Ambrosia come from? Cronus doesn't seem like the type to dabble in drug manufacturing…" *Oh gods.* I sounded like a junkie. We *never* talked about it unless Ivan was trying to convince me to go easy on the stuff. I'm sure he felt even more strongly about that after seeing me in action tonight— Last night? It was hard to tell what day it was.

Ivan drifted close enough that I could almost feel the suspicion oozing from him. "I don't know. Why do you care?" I wanted to submerge myself, hide away until my breath gave out to avoid the feeling of foot-in-mouth shame.

But I stood my ground. I could take it. "It seems like it's the only wildcard he's got. Just like Cirillo and the other fools in town, he launders like there's no tomorrow but Ambrosia's the one thing that's uniquely his…What if—never mind. Forget it." What was I doing? I twisted and started to make my way up the ladder, my toes curling around the cold metal steps.

Ivan's voice took on a strange weighted quality. "What are you thinking? Tell me, Calliope." My stomach clenched when he dropped my real name. When we'd first met, he'd refused to call me anything but that, until Cronus threatened to give me an even worse moniker. Since then I'd forgotten how much I loved the sound of my real name on his lips. He had to have some inkling of what I was doing. I was about to be in deep shit if Ivan turned on me.

Lying had never been my strength, so I figured, fuck it. Maybe it was the high of being close with Ivan again, but I felt a sense of rightness, of peace. I decided to lean into that feeling. "Cirillo propositioned me yesterday." My knees threatened to buckle but I kept climbing the last steps out of the pool. This was the moment of truth for me. I felt myself standing on the edge of a precipice. Waiting for Ivan to decide whether or not to push me.

"I know."

I whirled around, my one good eye snapped wide open. "How?"

Ivan smiled and his perfect teeth glowed in the dark. "I have my ways."

Son of a bitch. "Cap? He ratted me out?" My pulse couldn't decide whether or not to race or simply stall out on me.

Ivan shot a solitary finger gun at me while he clicked his tongue between his teeth. "Bingo. I've been keeping an eye on you. I kind of like you, you know." Heat bloomed across my face as Ivan continued. "So, what did she say?" He followed me up the ladder, gripping the rails with both hands as he lifted his body out of the water. The muscles in his chest flexed with the effort, momentarily distracting me from my storm of emotions.

I turned from him, putting more space between us as I went for my towel. "She offered to free Lil and I from our debts. She also offered to send me to prison if I didn't deliver."

Ivan shook his hair like a dog, confirming my earlier opinion. "What does she want?"

I scooted back on the chair, stretching my legs out on the chaise. I began toweling off my legs, and after a deep exhale I spilled. "She wants intel on Cronus. She wants to take him down." My voice was an echo, slowly and quietly reverberating off the surfaces in the room. The one person I'd hoped to spare from this chaos was now steeped in it, and I wasn't sure I wanted to take it back anymore.

There was nothing but silence paired with the *drip drip drip* of water as it fell from Ivan's swim trunks. Ivan's face twisted and my stomach bottomed out. "I didn't just hear that. Right? Tell me I'm dreaming."

I knew this was a bad idea. I knew, and yet here I was, ruining every single good thing that came my way. "I'm not asking you to help me. I'm just telling you because I didn't want you to feel…"

"Betrayed? Lied to?"

My guts kept tumbling inside me in an endless spiral. This wasn't about Ivan. It never was, but it could be, if he wanted to get involved. I held my ground. "It's got nothing to do with you. What would you do if you were in my shoes? Would you really walk away and go to jail for a man like Cronus?"

There was a heaviness between us as Ivan finally realized the full weight of my servitude. My "role" had always been a problem for Ivan. He wanted to believe that I had as much choice in my affiliation with Cronus as he did, but the blood that bound Ivan to his uncle was different from the blood that ran between Cronus and I.

Ivan had to know to deny me this opportunity, no matter how suicidal it may seem, would be to acknowledge my enslavement to his uncle. I didn't want to live in a world where I was beholden to anyone, and now, sitting in this empty pool room, I knew I would do whatever it took to reclaim my freedom. Three years was long enough. I'd take Cronus down, then get the hell out of here with Lil.

Ivan sat beside me, still soaked. He took my hand in his and held it without saying a word. We continued to stew in silence until he said, "It doesn't matter what I would do. What does matter is that *you* are going to fight tooth and nail to get what you need. Because that's who you are. And I won't stand in your way, because I'm a big pushover."

I swallowed, wanting him to get it, to really understand what this meant for him. For us. "Even if it means giving up your family? Even if it means destroying all that Cronus holds dear?" If I found a way, I would hold the match and look on as everything in Cronus' world burned to a fine crisp, and I'd do it all with a smile.

Ivan's knees collided with my legs when he twisted my direction. He squeezed my fingers so tightly they began to tingle. "Last night I saw what it meant to be in his good graces. And I never want to be there again. I'm the son of a mechanic. Not whatever it is Cronus wants me to be. If there was a way we could both be free…I'd consider it."

The muscles in his jaw feathered lightly, and I wanted to pull my hand free of his just so I could touch them, feel them under my fingers. "I…I don't even know where to start." I bit my tongue and looked the other way, fighting tears. "You're unhinged. You know that right?" I blinked in quick succession, still trying to chase those stupid tears away.

To have trust like this was like having a luxury good. It felt sumptuous and delicate. I wanted to savor this feeling, to believe that it could be as easy as this to have someone to count on. Someone who might be able to count on me. Maybe it was too good to be true, but I savored the moment while it lasted.

Ivan continued holding my hand. He was still looking at me like this wasn't some terrible plot meant to destroy us all. I wanted to look back at him with that same feeling, but I was too afraid to give in to hope. Instead, I squeezed his fingers between my own and kept staring into the dark.

"Want to get out of here?" His voice was low, like he was afraid of my response but too desperate not to ask. I swallowed. Instead of answering I stood, tugged on my sweats and hoodie and held my hand out to him.

CHAPTER 13

We kept to the shadows, Ivan trailing behind me as we sped back to my bungalow. It was closer than Ivan's place which was nearer to the front entrance of Olympus. I knew if he was with me, I wouldn't dare to drag that bag out from under my bed. The shame would be far too immense. Too afraid to wake Lil, I jimmied open my bedroom window, and climbed inside. A few moments after, Ivan's damp curls made an appearance before the rest of him stumbled into my room.

Neither one of us spoke as I turned away then started to peel off my wet clothing, letting them fall in a pile. I heard the smack of Ivan's trunks as they hit the floor. Ivan cleared his throat, but I refused to turn. I knew if I did, I wouldn't be able to stop myself from taking all that I wanted from him. We needed to go slow. I focused my attention on my dresser, digging through the last dregs of clothing I had that were clean. I tossed Ivan a pair of basketball shorts over my shoulder and threw on some underwear and an old T-shirt.

He cleared his throat again and said, "Thanks. I

think these are mine?"

I turned to see him still fully naked, considering the shorts in his hand. "Gods, Ivan! Get dressed. And yes. Those are yours. Well, they *were* yours." There was no shame on his face as his lips curved into a small knowing smile. He was so familiar, and yet here I was drooling over him like it was our first date or something. I stalked towards my messy bed, fumbling with the sheets and blankets, anything to keep me occupied as he bent down and pulled his shorts on way too slowly to be reasonable.

I flopped on the bed, staring at the ceiling. "We can't get carried away. Okay?" I felt the mattress shift as Ivan settled in beside me.

His bare skin caressed my legs, cool yet welcoming as he curled against me. He whispered, "Can we cuddle?"

Heat rose to my face, my heart beating two times faster. "We can cuddle."

"Can we kiss?"

I licked my lips and breathed. "Yes." Ivan's fingers grazed the swollen edges of my face, whisper-gentle. His hand moved to wrap around my waist, tugging me closer against him. His lips found the shell of my ear, then the nape of my neck and a riot of goosebumps broke out all over my body. I felt him smile against my skin.

"Calliope?"

"Mhmm?"

"Why is there a book under your pillow?" I blushed, twisting around to see Ivan thumbing through a Spanish language guide. In the darkness I could still make out his smile, one eyebrow cocked upwards as he skimmed the page he'd landed on. I fought the urge to snatch it from him. I don't know how many times we'd argued about which was better, fiction or nonfiction. I preferred to keep my mind grounded in reality while Ivan couldn't get enough of the escapism found in his favorite fantasy novels. He handed it to me, whispering, "You know you can't just sleep on it, you actually have to read the words to learn."

I grinned, lightly shoving Ivan before turning over to set the book atop the tower of other books on the side of my bed. "I was hoping if I fell asleep reading it I might get some practice in my dreams."

Ivan chuckled, wrapping himself around me once more. "Get some sleep." My heart squeezed inside me. Stupid, good, honest Ivan. But before I could argue or give into my feelings of lust, sleep overtook me.

The sun decided to stay away from Arcadia, instead, massive billowing clouds hung over us threatening a downpour at any moment. When Ivan left, I had been too afraid to stay and face what was hidden beneath my mattress. I should have told him about it but that part of me that I hated wanted to keep it hoarded away like treasure. That was why I was wandering around Olympus looking like a ragamuffin in my mixed-match ensemble of "whatever's clean."

No one would dare give me shit about my outfit choice, no one besides those who knew I loved them enough not to kill them. For the most part, the goons who shared the compound with me were asleep. Some of them were probably still out working their shifts at the many establishments the Othonos family "helped" maintain. There were still a few early risers getting their runs in, pretending not to see me as they trotted past.

My thoughts spiraled around in my head, almost coherent before evaporating in a maddening cycle. I couldn't understand why after so many times, so many highs and lows with Ambrosia, this morning was *different*. I kept going back to that moment, that bizarre feeling of connection between the voice inside and myself. The sensation that there were *two* of us in there was unsettling to say the least. And this morning? I was on my feet—not a burning pile of ash and pain from the comedown. The usual lingering aches, the migraine, completely absent. I felt awake and ready. I didn't understand.

Tam's bouncy gait caught my attention. He'd just locked his car and was making his way up the road towards the guard station, tucking his keys into his coat pocket. And then a terrible, disgusting idea crept into my skull.

"Hey Tam! Wait up." Tam whirled around, already grinning from ear to ear at the sound of my voice. Not many people in Arcadia felt happy when they saw me coming, it made me squirm knowing what I was about to do. *Sweet innocent Tam, why did you ever want to work here?*

"Hey there, Styx! Did Ivan catch up with you? How did your coffee go yesterday? Did you have the whole day off? Where are you headed now?"

I patiently waited as Tam continued to rattle off the next chain of innocuous questions, trying to decide which one I was willing to answer, which one would lead our conversation the way I needed it to go. "Things got pretty wild after I saw you yesterday. Actually, I'm glad I ran into you. I've been asked to do some research." *Okay, so far not lying.* Tam's eyes twinkled and I knew he was excited to be privy to whatever it was I was going to say next. I was a terrible human being. "Your mom works in a lab, right? Am I remembering that correctly?" I had caught up with Tam, now our paces slowed as we grew closer to the guard booth.

Tam's head cocked to the side, curiosity running rampant. "Yeah, she's a lab tech at Asklepios." He shrugged. "She's been working there since I was a little kid. She's not like a chemist or anything, though. She mostly manages ordering equipment and chemicals." Asklepios Corporation was one of Arcadia's leading employers specializing in all things medical, as far as I knew.

I pursed my lips. It wouldn't help much to have access to a lab with zero chemistry knowledge. "Oh, well damn. I need a favor, but it's…definitely got to be under the table. I'd hate to get you in trouble. Don't worry about it." *Take the bait, take the bait, take the bait…* I started walking away, like I was headed back to my apartment. Like Tam was the only reason I'd bothered to be awake this early in the day.

I'd only walked a few steps when Tam called out, "Wait! I took three years of advanced chem in high school, do you think I could help? My mom lets me go to the lab with her all the time. She says it's a good way to get recruited once I have my degree." *Bingo.*

I smiled, but on the inside, I was dying. I recalled the words that mysterious voice had spoken the night before. *Even villains have their limits.* Apparently, my line was a bit blurry. "Hmmm, do you think you could look at something and figure out what types of chemicals it's made of?"

Tam's eyebrows went down as he thought it over. "That's basically what chemistry is, Styx. I'm pretty sure I could figure it out. Why not let me try?" Ivan was going to murder me.

I nodded, then continued with the execution. "What time do you get off today? I have a sample at my apartment that I can bring to you."

A brilliant smile lit up Tam's face at the idea of being useful to the Othonos organization. My guts went watery, all feelings of goodness immediately replaced with self-loathing. It coated my insides like sticky tar. "I'm here until one. What's the sample? What's the goal so I know what I'm looking for?" I moved closer to Tam, close enough to put a heavy hand on his shoulder.

I looked into his eyes, pouring every ounce of fire into my stare. "This is top secret, Tam. What you are doing will be illegal. Your life will be ruined if anyone finds out about this." I paused for emphasis. "Do you understand? By agreeing to do this, you are officially dipping your toes into the dark side of Arcadia."

I applied pressure to his shoulder through my fingers, unrelenting with my glare. He needed to be afraid if this was going to work. He needed to be *very* afraid. "If you get caught, you could get arrested, or even killed. Are you up for this?" I watched as my words sank in, as the blind ambition inside him flickered and a new wariness bloomed across his face.

Tam swallowed, commendably holding my gaze. "So, this is the big leagues."

"Sure is. One more thing."

Tam sighed, the fear in him palpable. "What is it?"

"Don't tell Ivan. Don't tell anyone." Tam nodded, and I wanted so badly to trust him. "I'll bring the sample in a bit. It's got to stay totally hidden. Can you do that? I'll put it in a backpack for you."

"Yes. Got it." I couldn't help the relief that washed over me. The brick of Ambrosia would be out of my grasping, addicted hands as soon as a few minutes from now. And even better, I'd be one step closer to solving my Cirillo problem. My freedom problem. I had to keep myself from sprinting back to my apartment so I could rid myself of the drug; I wasn't done quite yet.

"Your job is to find out everything that makes the substance. Every chemical, every atom, whatever. Find out what it is. And don't get caught. I need results as soon as possible. When can you get to your mom's lab?"

Tam sighed again, his boyish smile inching his cheeks up under his eyes. "I told you it's not her lab, it's Asklepios, and she's a tech there. But I get it. I have a day off coming up, so I'll go up to the lab with my mom then."

"The sooner the better, got it? I almost forgot; I'll pay you for the extra work." Tam looked relieved to hear his efforts would be rewarded. I returned his smile with my own, a small wretched thing stretched across my traitorous face. "See you soon." I turned and fled back to my apartment.

I ignored my conscience as it railed at me for involving a minor in my trainwreck of a life while I frantically dressed in some clean clothes, dug out some cash, and crammed the brick of Ambrosia into an old backpack.

I blamed a torn corner in the package for the granules of Ambrosia that somehow gathered into the palm of my hand. Just a small lump, inconsequential really. No one would ever know I'd done it, no one needed to know either. I held my hand to my mouth, and my tongue darted out, scraping up every tiny grain. That familiar, scintillating surge of power was smaller this time after such a miniscule serving. It felt different, more like the hand of a friend pressing their warmth and love into my very bloodstream. I needed more. Wanted more. And here it was. In front of me.

With shaking fingers I tore open the package even more, wide enough to get a fist inside and then without a single thought of the consequences, I filled my mouth. A manic laugh peeled out from me as the delicious heat of Ambrosia coursed through every vein in my body. Blinding ecstasy surged in me, as I continued to gorge on the sweet manna before me. Mouthful after burning mouthful. Like an empty vessel being filled, I began to overflow with the power of the drug. The flames of rage and blood and battle welled up inside me, threatening to consume me entirely. There was no fear, only strength. And I wanted more.

"Acolyte, we meet again."

That's when I froze. For in my mind wasn't just a voice, but now I knew without a doubt there was *someone else*. An image, brief and terrifying, flashed across my brain. It was a being carved from iron, forged from the fires of the gods. One we'd all learned about as children studying our nation's history and lore. One we all believed was slumbering for eternity.

Ares.

Ares, god of war, was in my head. Talking to me. I closed my eyes wishing to shut the image out, but there, behind my eyelids was his face, another flash of brilliance. His own eyes glowing like embers, hungry. He was so very hungry. That's when I became frightened.

Why is this happening? I didn't know if I was speaking to him or to myself, but I was definitely trying to get a grip on reality.

"Does it matter why? Can it be enough that I am here because I am called by your spirit?"

I don't understand. Called by my spirit? Why would a deity respond to *me*?

"Understanding is for philosophers. Action is all we need."

I remained mute as I shoved the deflated half-empty package of Ambrosia into my backpack. I wanted to revel in Ambrosia's effects, but instead I was toeing the line of frightened sobriety, jittery and afraid that I might be burning out. Panic flared when I realized what I'd done.

No one really knew what happened to a person mentally while they were being consumed by the drug. What if this was part of it? Was I dying?

Ares purred, completely nonplussed by my rising anxiety. *"Is it time to unleash chaos? Have we been called to war?"*

No. No fighting today. Are you…going to kill me?

There was a startled silence that followed, a blankness. I took advantage of the quiet and hurried out of the apartment after securing my boots to my feet, as if I could run from the being inside me. The backpack felt red hot against my spine, like the Ambrosia inside was fighting its way through the fabric to get to me. The desire to finish off the brick was rising, battling with my horrified disgust. I cracked my neck with one hand while gripping the left strap with my other hand. I had to get rid of it. Now.

"Killing you would end my fun. If we will not have blood, then what shall we have? Chaos? Rebellion?"

I was going insane. This was it for me. This was burnout.

Fuck it. I swallowed, responding to the god in my head. *How about lying, stealing, and then maybe some drinking?*

"I am satisfied."

I couldn't help the small smile that appeared on my face. Was it wrong to be this okay with a god sharing space in my mind? I would rather have a god in my head than go nuts. My Ambrosia high had doused the fear of insanity, and instead it was replaced with a chaotic kind of giddiness that would have terrified me otherwise.

The walk from my apartment to the gates of Olympus was a blur of adrenaline and bliss. A flock of swans trumpeted as they flew in a white *V* across the dark clouds. My boots hit the pavement one heavy step at a time, fast, but disjointed and strange. The minutes didn't matter, the steps, none of it. All that mattered was getting rid of the stash attached to my body and finding a way to survive whatever was happening to me.

Tam was doing his best impression of someone playing it cool, no more smiles or excitement, just a single head nod as he recited what his task was: "No one can know. Figure out what's in it. As soon as possible."

"Good, that's right." I tugged the money from my pocket and held it out to Tam. I didn't know how much it was, but it didn't matter. I'd give Tam my life savings if it would take away the sick feeling of shame that ate through my high, threatening to kill me. "Please, please be careful, Tam. Swear to me. You'll be safe."

Tam's eyes were somber as he nodded. His expression eased the misery welling up inside me just enough. "I swear."

"Swear on your family's seal." I needed Tam to know how serious this was. To understand that his life would be in danger if he so much as put a toe out of line. I'd been killing people for so much less these last three years.

He swallowed but nodded, his expression becoming stoic with the weight of his words. "I swear on the Pappas seal."

I tried to keep the grimace off my face. It was always uncouth to ask someone to swear on their seal. It was a threat in itself, daring someone to put their entire reputation on the line. If I was sober, I probably wouldn't have crossed that line. "Now keep me in the loop. If you text me, don't say *anything* about this mission. Only text if you want to meet to discuss in person. Give me your phone." Tam reached into his back pocket and handed over his cell. I typed in my number and saved it for him before giving it back. "I've got my eye on you, Tam. Don't fuck this up."

He ate that up. I watched him grow two inches taller. "I won't. I've got this." Great. I was trusting my future, my life, and my sister's life to a high school graduate with a couple of semesters of science under his belt. This was genius.

I gave him a solitary wave before walking through the gate. The massive amount of Ambrosia coursing through my blood should have been enough to keep me awake for an eternity, but I was growing achy and weak by the second. I would have been afraid, but the drug had stolen my fear. Instead I was only angry. At myself. At the world.

Ares murmured, "*Interesting. This place has much to hold my attention.*"

I laughed, a cold grin slashed its way across my face. *Glad I can amuse you with my miserable existence.* I turned back for home. I needed a safe place to come down and hopefully not die.

CHAPTER 14

The heater rattled to life, pulling me from a bottomless pit of sleep. I kicked, trying to untangle myself from the sheets. It had been so long since I'd slept that soundly. I felt fresh. I might've even dared to call it, *optimistic. What's happening to me?* A cold sensation curled up my spine. I could have died. I could have burned out. I *should* have burned out. Why didn't I?

I rolled to the edge of the bed, reaching for my phone on autopilot. Three unread messages. Eve had texted twice with vague check-ins. And then there was Ivan's message, which was very business-like and had no personality, whatsoever. Thank the gods.

He said I was needed to go over the plans for the Expo. Which meant Cronus was going to have us check every tiny detail ten times over if he felt it was necessary. Or if he felt like picking on me, which wouldn't be that far of a stretch. It wasn't like I was head of security or anything, but I was the muscle with the most—shall we say, panache? Cronus probably wanted to put me on display for the rest of his goons. Show them all his fighting dog was ready for action. That's what Cronus loved best of all. The knowledge that he controlled the one with the gift of Ares.

"This man knows of me? Are you his personal guard?"

Ares was apparently making himself at home in my thoughts. *Will you please stop talking? Please. It's incredibly distracting.*

"I understand now. You are his, not by choice, but by the chains of fate."

Seriously, stop talking.

I thrashed out of bed, panic filling my body with an urgency to do anything other than sit still. Why was *he* still here? I thought the Ambrosia faded from me hours ago. So why was I still host to Ares? My heart ricocheted inside my chest as I held the back of my hand against my forehead checking for a fever. It felt cool, not even a drop of perspiration. I took a deep breath, at least I wasn't burning out. I was just losing my fucking mind.

Why are you still here? I couldn't see Ares, but I could *feel* his presence, like the gentle pressure of someone's finger as they poked around in my skull.

"It seems your summons has not expired."

I wondered if he could see me when I rolled my eyes. *It definitely has. I have zero Ambrosia, and so ipso facto I should have zero you. Be gone? I release you? What do you need to hear in order to leave me alone?*

"You said there would be debauchery. We have not even begun. I will stay until I deem it wise to leave."

I was too stunned to respond. My brain was a very loud place at the moment, but otherwise, the heater was the only sound in the apartment. Even though I knew I wasn't, I felt very *very* alone. Did everyone who took Ambrosia end up insane or dead? I wasn't ready to even think about a possible third option. Which was worse? The clock hanging above my closet, with its palm tree design obscuring the numbers just enough to be annoying, was *tick-tick-ticking* around in slow circles. I could handle crazy. I could deal with this. Whatever *this* was.

Sorry Ares, no debauchery yet. Just boring strategizing. You might as well check back later when the action is hot.

There was a strange burst of heat from inside me, like the surge of a fever—Ares was unhappy. What a surprise.

His voice was steely as he said, "*I shall decide when I leave. Never before have I been given free reign over my time spent alongside you, acolyte. I will maintain a watch on any possible opportunity for fun.*"

His demeanor didn't frighten me like I thought it would. *Oh goody.*

Unable to deal, I tried my hand at some simple routine. I shot a reply to Ivan then Eve, who responded almost instantly. She said she was going to watch the fights tonight, since Gerty *of course* took another bouncing shift. There was always a seat open for me at the arena. It was one of my favorite places in the city. I texted her back letting her know to expect me. Hopefully Cronus' briefing wouldn't last all damned day. I needed to talk to someone.

The apartment was dark. Rain sounded like gunfire as it assaulted our shitty roof. I shuffled to the bathroom, very much aware of how once again there was no ringing in between my ears, no pain zinging through my nervous system. I flipped on the lights hanging over the mirror and almost lost my balance. I'd expected to see black and green bruising with a nasty looking cut down my cheek but— there was nothing. I sucked in air and leaned closer, probing my skin for any sign of damage. There was hardly a scar, just a tiny white line—like it had been there for years.

Option three was quickly becoming the only option. There was *actually* a god inside me. *What are you doing to me?* I peered into my own eyes, searching for any hint of Ares hiding out in there. He remained quiet, but his presence was still needling me from the very back of my subconscious.

He probably didn't know either. From what I remembered, Ares was never known to be the smartest, or wisest of the gods. In fact, he was usually the most disliked among The Big Twelve. It figures I would get saddled with a—

"A god? A deity of endless power? Choose your next thoughts wisely, acolyte. Or should I say… Calliope?"

I swallowed, feeling the heat of Ares' words inside my blood. *Point taken. So, do you know? Why am I suddenly fit and ready for battle?*

"A soldier must always be prepared for war."

Is that another way of saying I don't know?

After that he was quiet, which meant I was right. I brushed my teeth and got myself ready for the night. I tried to tame my hair. Letting it air dry with pool water in it had been a mistake. I winced when my comb snagged in my chlorinated hair. Once again I found myself feeling grateful I'd cut it all off, otherwise I would have combed for an eternity trying to free my hair of snarls. Short was much more practical.

I stood in front of a mostly empty closet. Doing laundry was becoming an unavoidable necessity. If I didn't make time for it soon, I'd be running around town in nothing but my birthday suit. After searching for literally anything else, I settled for the last pair of jeans I had. They were baggy, comfortable. I rolled the cuffs and belted my waist. I had to ransack Lil's bedroom for a shirt, which was only slightly less disastrous than mine. I found a dark blue long-sleeved T-shirt that I'm pretty sure was mine anyway.

I shoved one of the last brown bananas into my face while looking for my raincoat. It was crumpled in the corner behind the front door. Gods, if Mom knew we were living like this, she would have many things to say, and maybe throw, while she berated us for our terrible upkeep. She definitely taught us better than this. But, in my defense, I've been pretty busy lately. Too busy. Thoughts of an angry mother kept me from tossing the banana peel on the counter. Instead, I made sure it found its way into the overflowing garbage bin under the sink. Someday we would have the kind of life where cleaning the apartment was the biggest annoyance of the week. I hoped.

I pulled my hood down low, keeping the rain from slithering into my face. I usually didn't mind being carless, but nights like this, or when the snow decided to pile up, I really hated it.

"A warrior can handle any climate, any terrain. It is only a bit of water."

A warrior can be grumpy when she wants. I'm not a machine.

Then Ares laughed. It was the sound of swords and shields clashing, brutal and a little terrifying.

I wasn't going to be pushed around while he maintained his unwanted guest status in my head. *Laugh all you want, You are safe and dry, while I deal with the weather. You don't have to worry about getting your boots wet.*

There was a feeling of piqued curiosity from his end of our connection. *"But I can feel the rain, at least in some fashion. You are my vessel. I am your guide."*

I wasn't ready for this kind of mind fuckery. It was all too surreal and icky feeling. I pushed back mentally. *Just because you're somehow in my thoughts, doesn't mean you're in control. I am my own person.*

There was a chuckle, cruel like the sheathing of a sword. *"Spoken like a true acolyte. I wouldn't have it any other way. Life holds no joy without a fight."*

Acolyte? You know what? How about you keep that watch of yours silently.

Ares huffed but remained mute.

By the time I got to Cronus' mansion, I felt like a drowned rat. Even my coat hadn't been able to withstand the rain. The butler sniveled at me as I stomped through the double doors and handed over my sopping wet coat. I grinned at him, enjoying the distasteful look he gave me. "If you've got a towel somewhere, you might want to bring it to me. Otherwise, I'll be tracking dirty water all over Cronus' palace. I'm sure you'd hate that."

He turned on his heel and left me standing alone, still grinning as rainwater continued to drip off of my clothing. I peered around the corner of the vestibule, leaning towards the sound of echoey voices floating down the hall. Sounded like everyone was present. I rolled my shoulders, once again savoring the forgotten feeling of balance in my own body. Maybe Ares wasn't all bad.

Nick appeared from a room off the hallway. "Look what the cat dragged in. When are you gonna get wise and buy your own set of wheels?"

I steeled my nerves and turned the other way. "Why should I, when I have you to chauffeur me around town?" I flashed Nick a sour smile, wrinkling my nose in mock playfulness. He stalked towards me scowling like usual. He moved in close, too close. I stood my ground, glaring at him. He stared back and my skin started to crawl.

Ares sneered. *"Fool. Why is he still alive?"*

I was about to open my mouth and talk a little more trash, but Nick surprised me. He knocked my chin with his fist, in a move that was anything but friendly. "You're not as intimidating as you think you are." Without another word he continued on his way towards the dining room.

A burst of fury burned my skin, turned my face beet red. I clenched my fists in silence, trying to get a hold on my emotions before I followed after him.

"Why hold back? You would normally break every finger in his hand to prove a point."

Now's not the time.

"Afraid, are you?"

Shut up.

The butler arrived, tossing a towel into my hands before motioning me towards the meeting. "You are the last to arrive." I toweled off my face, taking the opportunity to hide my crimson cheeks. I stalked in behind the butler, eyeing my options for seating. There were goons leaning against every inch of wall space and around the massive table where Cronus sat at the head. He was wearing black from head to toe, with a matte tie in a double Windsor at his neck. His blue eyes latched on to me, assessing like I was a prized horse he'd spent oodles of cash to own.

Ivan was to his right, a symbolic move that was so painfully obvious you would have to be an idiot to ignore. I couldn't afford to glance long in Ivan's direction. He knew better than to look at me.

I tucked myself into the last open seat that was a few down from Cronus. As I looked around the room, I noticed a few more familiar faces. I usually worked only with Nick, the rest had seen me in action by happenstance or merely heard rumors. I could feel their eyes on me. These people didn't have to get their hands dirty like I did. They thought they wanted it, the power. The reputation. They had no idea what it was really like.

Cronus spoke first and the room became silent as everyone straightened to attention. "The Exposition is coming up quickly. I need every one of you to be prepared to protect this compound, and my relations. This is the next step for the Othonos family. If all goes well, I'll have a whole line of new clientele, and some of you may be traveling overseas to make it happen." Several men grunted in approval. "My home will be open to everyone, even those we do not often…get along with. This is a show of strength. You know what they say. Keep your friends close, and your enemies closer." I snorted. If he actually invited Cirillo that would make things even more…hairy.

The excitement was growing, and with it so was my unease. Too many opportunities for shit to go sideways. Cronus continued, ignoring the quiet outburst. "Soto and his associates will also be arriving two days before the

Expo. I need you all to be sharp, cutthroat if you have to. Show them our teeth, but also show them we know how to treat those we work with. Got it?"

There was a collective murmur of "Yes boss" before Cronus said, "Good. Ivan's already been given the details for security. Who to watch, who to follow, and who to schmooze. Ivan?" Cronus' silvery eyes slid towards his nephew, and everyone else's gaze followed. Having permission to look at Ivan was a blessing and a curse. I clenched my jaw as I tried to convince myself he wasn't sitting there looking gorgeous in his white button up with his hair tousled, still damp from the rain.

Ares snickered in the back of my brain, distracting me from my yearning. Until Ivan cleared his throat, and his bobbing Adam's apple took my attention hostage again. There were definitely words being shared, important plans, points, and details that I would need to know, but they whirred around me in a jumble of incoherent sentences.

Ivan's charismatic nature filled the room with a kind of warmth that put all of us under his spell, until I realized Nick was staring at me. Like I was something to dissect, or maybe eat. I didn't need Ares to goad me on. Who was Nick to think he could ogle me in a room full of the most formidable people in Arcadia, including yours truly? I sent back a glare of my own, full of hellfire and the promise of a slow death. Nick didn't seem to clue in until I mouthed the words—

Fuck. Off.

He sneered, then zeroed in on Ivan who was still talking, completely unaware of the mental fist fight between us. What the hell was wrong with Nick? Icy suspicion curled up my spine, freezing all the fury from our staring contest. Did he know what I'd taken? Had Tam spilled his guts? I tapped my toe, disguising my fear for impatience.

Another glance around the room and I realized

Cronus had been watching the whole time. His eyes sent more glacial anxiety up and down my being. I fought the urge to swallow. Cronus would sniff out any hint of weakness and devour it for his own gain. Instead, I held a neutral yet dispassionate expression, complete with the lazy sniffle of someone who was still getting warmed up from her rainy walk.

"Styx'll see to that, won't you?" Ivan wrapped his knuckles against the table. *Shit.*

I had to dig deep for the sardonic smile they'd come to expect from me. "You got it, boss." I looked out among the faces in the room, not a one of them appeared pleased to hear from me. I'd no doubt just promised to kill them all if they messed up next week. That's what I got for not paying attention. It didn't matter. In the end, Cronus could tell me to kill every one of them and I wouldn't hesitate. It was us or them, and I would always choose us. Always.

CHAPTER 15

After Ivan and Cronus finished their briefings, we were released for the evening. I hoped the rain had stopped, knowing my coat was still too wet to wear. I stood and meandered to the front doors, but Cronus called out to me, stalling me in my tracks. "Styx, I need you." I released a shaky exhale as I turned to face him, trying to keep my spirit from leaving my body. This was it. The cameras had spotted me. He'd seen what I'd stolen last night. He knew Cirillo had propositioned me.

"Breathe. The swine knows nothing. Stop letting fear dampen your prowess."

Feeling oddly comforted by Ares' words, I steeled my panic and followed Cronus as he steered us towards his study. When we entered the room, the air was thick with cigar smoke. Crius and Hyperion, Cronus' brothers, were sitting together in a pair of matching leather wingback chairs. The smoke almost obscured the towering bookshelves that lined three walls of the study. They were packed with titles I was certain Cronus hadn't bothered to read. He'd probably hired an interior decorator to pick them out and never thought twice about them. He wasn't the type to sit around and thumb through the pages of books.

Ivan had his back turned, looking through the wall of windows that faced Cronus' front lawn. The world beyond his silhouette was dark. Rain made snaking trails down the panes of glass. Arcadia was a blurry blob of glowing oranges and neon reds. There was a whole city out there, hidden by the night. Cronus found his way to his chair, and I glanced backwards, longing to bolt through that door. To freedom.

"These men are below us. You are a god's chosen. What are they?"

They own me, so do with that what you will. Wait, what?

Shocked silence rang out between my ears as I mentally stumbled through the standing arrangements, willfully blocking out what Ares had just called me. Too close to Crius and he was likely to try and fondle me. Which would lead to a very unfortunate, violent turn of events I really needed to avoid.

Hyperion was less troublesome in the pervert arena, but he was twice as arrogant, and standing near him would inflate his ego too much. Ivan was obviously a no-go, so I resigned myself to stand behind Cronus. I knew he would eat it up; his favorite killer standing guard at his side. It was the best option, even though I hated it.

A billowing cloud of smoke exited Crius' nostrils. "Ah, the angry sister joins us. Where's the pretty one who makes the cocktails? I could really use something sweet about now."

Ten seconds in and he's already pissing me off.

"Should we kill him?"

Kill him and we'd be dead in an instant. They all have guns.

Cronus responded as he lit a cigar of his own, "She's running *The Siren's Lair* tonight. You'll have to settle for your cigar. I doubt Styx will submit to stirring your martini for you." Hyperion and Crius both chuckled, and I willed my body to stay still, my arms crossed over my chest, staring ahead. No emotions. They would like that too much.

Ivan joined the group, sitting in the empty chair nearest Cronus' desk. He leaned forward, elbows on his thighs then clasped his hands between his knees. "Uncles. Why are we here?" Hyperion just shrugged, looking towards his older brother.

Crius raised a brow, still casting pervy glances my way. "Yeah, Cronus, please don't keep me waiting. I have a date at *The Siren's Lair* with my favorite cocktail waitress." I didn't need Ares in my head to rile me up, this piece of shit was doing fine on his own. I only wished there was more power behind my anger. I was totally useless without Ambrosia.

Cronus didn't laugh, or smile. Instead, he puffed his cigar, sending acrid smoke up into my eyes. "It appears the thief wasn't alone. Whoever was working with him was able to get away with enough Ambrosia to buy a new yacht."

Oh gods. My stomach clenched. I started screaming on the inside, panicked while I forced my face to remain stoic.

Ivan spoke up first, "They must have split up before we'd caught up to them. By the time we'd figured out he'd weaseled his way on staff, the guy was already gunning for the exit. Styx, did you see anything? You stuck around after I left, right?" All eyes landed on me.

I shrugged, making a show of trying to recall the events of last night's bust. "When I came to, everyone was busy unloading the pulverized van, so I joined in. Whoever it was, they were long gone." Cronus turned his head so he could see me as I talked.

There was a cold assessment in his eyes as they raked over every inch of my person. He said, "That's right,

I heard you tried to take on the van itself. You don't look much worse for wear, though." I wanted to swallow, but my mouth had gone dry.

Reassuring warmth curled up the back of my neck. *"Steady. Hold your ground."*

I shrugged again, wanting very much for Cronus to stop staring at me like I was for dinner. "So, did the creep say anything specific about this accomplice?"

Cronus continued to look my way, like he was imagining peeling my skin back to see what was underneath. I was just an insect to him. "He unfortunately…expired…before he was able to tell us anything. So, I'm asking all of you—Crius, Hyperion, Ivan, Styx. This brick needs to be found and it needs to be found now. You will find the missing Ambrosia or find the one who took it. Then you'll make them pay up, just like always. The Soto Group needs to see we are infallible. We are invincible. They will not partner with us for anything less formidable. There will be no leaks in our ship. Got it?"

The joy I saw in Hyperion's face was terrifying. Cronus hardly ever asked his brothers to get their hands dirty like this. They had their own rank and file criminals to do their bidding, and rarely were they involved in the business of Ambrosia. Cronus kept his own dealings close, untrusting of even those who were supposedly his near and dear ones. Clearly he wanted the foreign gang to recognize his power and was willing to bring his brothers closer into the fold in order to make it so.

I sent a prayer out into the void, *please keep stupid Tam safe.* It was unlikely they would think to look at Asklepios for an illegal drug, but the Othonos family had people everywhere. I found myself itching to send him a text, just to check in, make sure he was still breathing. Later.

Cronus continued, scaring me back into the present. "Look into any rumors of people suddenly coming into good money. Send your people out to shop, to snoop, find the thief. Then when we've found them, send them to Styx." He eyed me once more and I thought I might die. "She knows what to do in order to make my point." I could see the unspeakable things he was envisioning, the orders he would give, and the cruelty I would be enacting…

It would *not* be Tam. I swore that to myself then and there. I would throw myself on the sword for his sake.

"Noble, very unlike you."

I have my moments.

I raised an eyebrow, digging into my role as enforcer. *Fear me.* Hyperion leaned back against his chair, and that was enough for me. He could act the part of Titan and he played it well, but he was still only a man, a man with nothing on me. I had a warrior god fueling me. Oh shit, I *had* a warrior god fueling me?

Cronus rose and everyone in chairs followed suit. "Our guests will be here soon. I expect this to be taken care of well before they arrive."

Ivan glanced my way. His eye contact brought on a panic that could've dropped me flat on my ass. I looked anywhere but back at him. He was such a gods-damned fool, I wanted to smack him for daring to look at me like that right in front of his uncle. Ivan reached out his hand and Cronus took it in his own. "I'm counting on you, Ivan. Find the scum. And feed them to the hound."

There was fire inside me. Hatred for the man in front of me, who'd turned me into a murdering ghoul. But the fear that overpowered it every time was that much stronger. It was fear that kept me from using my hands to hurt Cronus, very badly, in that moment. Shame forced my eyes downward, shielding me from seeing Ivan's reaction to his uncle's cruelty. If he was smart, he'd keep his face stone cold. I was nothing more than a beast, let Cronus believe that lie.

"You are so much more than a cold-blooded servant."

I mentally balked. *Thanks?*

A compliment from Ares? Things were getting stranger every second. Crius flicked the end of his cigar then stubbed it out in the ashtray on the table beside him. "If that's all, I'm off to find a siren." The men took turns shaking hands while I stood by. Curtsying was definitely not on my agenda nor was doing any more ass kissing than I had to. I was more concerned about making sure Lil wasn't about to be ambushed.

Ivan and his uncles drifted out of the office, and I started to follow suit, but Cronus stopped me, one of his hands landing on my shoulder possessively. "Styx, one moment." He watched his brothers and nephew leave the room, waiting until Hyperion closed the door behind him. My blood started thrumming in my body. I hated being alone with Cronus. The feeling of vulnerability was repulsive. His icy eyes shined, lips pursed a second before he said, "You've done me proud with the intel you uncovered. If I didn't know better, I'd say you were warming up to the idea of being my best enforcer." He put his hands in his pockets, leaning against the top of his desk.

Anxiety wormed around inside me. You'd think after three years I'd be able to handle a simple one-on-one with my boss, but no. I was afraid, always afraid. This time though, I was afraid of getting caught in the web I was tangled in. I had to be clever. Think of something to say that would make sense. "I thought maybe you'd consider knocking off some of Lil's debt if I did something extra. Any chance of that?" I shrugged, not really caring about his answer.

Cronus frowned. I knew he'd never do anything more than what he'd promised me. Do the blood work to pay Lil's debt, with interest. Do the dirty work, and he'd keep my family's name clean. "I'm not above rewarding those who go above and beyond. Take this." He opened a drawer and pulled out a neatly banded stack of bills. Cronus thumbed through the money, fanning it out so that I might see all the ones and zeros. "I'll consider your proposition if you find the thief before the others." I smirked, letting the sight of money overwhelm the fear in my belly. It was peanuts compared to the mountain Lil had racked up during her insane gambling binge. I held out my palm and Cronus smacked the money into it.

"Thanks."

He grinned, and my stomach churned. "No, thank you. Don't go spending it all in one place." It would be a lie to think all this money wasn't just going to circulate through the city once before ending up back in Cronus' drawer.

I stood there, feeling unable to leave without his permission no matter how badly I wanted to bolt, and he knew it. He watched me the way a scientist watches cells dividing beneath a microscope's lens until I couldn't stand it any longer. "So…can I go now?"

He nodded, just once, before moving back to his cushy armchair. No more words were exchanged. I turned on my heel and walked as surely through his palace as I could. It wasn't until I made it out of the main doors and into the black rain that I remembered to breathe. Something had been rattling around in my mind, something Ares said earlier.

Did Cronus know there was a god inside me?

CHAPTER 16

There were few things I loved more in the world than a good fight. Ever since I was just a little girl, the idea of hand-to-hand combat held me captivated. In the ring, there was a winner and a loser. It didn't matter who was bigger, who looked stronger, because in the end it always came down to one brilliant move. One flash of lightning in order to turn the tide.

Lil hadn't replied to my texted warning about Crius, but I wasn't too worried. She was probably still pissed at me for trying to save her from this awful life. Anyway, she was used to his bullshit at this point. There was little else I could do short of kicking him in his favorite parts, and that would get Lil and I both in more trouble than his stupid harassment was worth. The bar would be busy tonight, with people seeking refuge from the frigid downpour in a fake tropical oasis. I hoped it was—it would be easier to keep out of Crius' nasty reach.

The rain slapped at my coat. The noise of it deadened my senses while I waited in the darkness outside of the gates of Olympus for my cab. Ares let out a warning hiss, and I glanced to my right, feeling the weight of another's shadow.

"Madame Cirillo is concerned you aren't taking her seriously. She wanted me to remind you of your deal."

My stomach clenched, but I feigned nonchalance as I slowly looked Mr. Meathead up and down. He was holding a massive black umbrella overhead that completely obscured his face. "Trust me, I haven't forgotten. Are you nuts or something? Don't you realize where you are right now?" I gestured towards the iron gates behind us. This was a bad idea for the both of us.

There was laughter in his voice now. "Right, Madame also said I needed to make it look legit." Every sense in me flared to life as I prepared too late for the impact of his giant fist. He sent it careening right into my gut. I doubled over, catching myself only barely before landing in a puddle.

"Fuck…you…" I gasped the words, the wind thoroughly knocked out of me, but not my shitty attitude. When I finally had enough air in my lungs to fight back, he was already halfway up the block. "I won't forget that!" I yelled, but it was too dark to tell if he heard me, or even cared. I glanced back at the gates, wondering if anyone had witnessed our meeting through the security cameras. I was in some serious shit. When my cab pulled up, I was relieved to be out of the rain, but my mind continued to race past all the terrible possible futures that might be mine if I didn't figure something out soon.

My cab dropped me right at the front doors of the arena. Gerty was working the ropes at the entrance. Her blond hair was in two tight rows of braids that trailed down her back. She was in all black athletic gear that showed off her toned musculature. "Styx, hi! Eve's already inside. She's got a seat saved for you. Same spots as usual." Gerty dropped the rope and wrapped me in a hug that lifted me off the ground.

I laughed, feeling ridiculous and giddy as she put me down. "Thanks babe. See you inside?"

"Not for a while, I've got a few more hours working the door. Stick around, okay?"

I said, "I'll try, but you know me. No promises." Gerty smiled and put the rope up after I stepped through. People were lined up at the bar, crowding together elbow to elbow as they waited on drinks. Spotlights trailed around the arena, shining intermittently on random strangers as they made their way to their seats. Music was playing, but the bass was turned up so loud it was all I could hear. As I got closer to the ring, the smell of sweat and blood became more pronounced, setting my senses on high alert. It was instinctive at this point in my life.

"It is a gift to come alive at the scent of battle and not cower from it. Be grateful you were born to fight."

I am. Trust me, I am.

There was never a time in my life when I wasn't fighting. It didn't matter who or when, all that ever mattered was keeping those I called mine, safe and sound. Eve's voice managed to rise above the strobing bass, "Over here, Styx!" She was parked on the far end of the third row, her arms were both in the air, flagging me down.

She was wearing a burgundy top with a sweetheart neckline that accentuated her decolletage. Her dark curls swept over one shoulder, like being that gorgeous was easy. She made me wish I'd bothered to fix my eyeliner or something before showing up. As I got closer, I noticed her eyes. I could only guess she was still worrying about me; about the pile of shit I'd gotten myself into. I took off my satchel and sat beside her before giving her an awkward yet heartfelt one-armed hug.

Eve and I went way back, but we'd lost touch after high school. Until she'd been walking home from a night of bar-hopping while I was on my way to do the standard delimbing. We met in a grimy alley where idiot men thought they could do whatever they wanted to sweet innocent Eve. I did some additional delimbing and just like that, our friendship was rekindled.

When I let go, she kept hanging on. Her hand clung to the back of my jacket like she was afraid I would jump out of my seat. "I'm so glad you were able to make it out." She glanced around us at the sparsely filled seats. Most people preferred to loiter around the bar, and when the fight started, they would all crowd in as close to the ring as possible. Seats were for the well-to-do, the people who came for business, to have a chat while getting some entertainment on the side. Me? I just liked watching people kick each other's asses. Eve said, "We need to talk."

I leaned back into my chair, forcing Eve to relinquish her grip on me. "I know, I know. Is this really the best place?" I had things to tell her too, but I was scared of what she might think. There weren't many people in my corner these days, and I couldn't afford to lose anyone.

Eve said, "It doesn't matter where we are, trust me, you want to know this, *now*." Her words unsettled me. Eve was dramatic, sure, but serious? The tone of her voice held too much weight.

"What's going on?"

Eve glanced around again and then leaned in close to me. She opened her mouth to dish whatever it was she wanted to share, but the lights cut out and the announcer's voice blared over the speaker system, rolling like thunder as they announced both fighters. Two women made their way into the ring, bouncing on their feet with hands wrapped and ready to go. For a moment I was a child again, sitting with my dad, little legs swinging as we cheered for our favorite fighter when they entered the arena. All that was missing was some popcorn.

We watched as the match commenced, each fighter throwing jabs and kicks at the other, powerful gladiators sparring.

"I like this very much."

Of course you do. What's not to love? Two badass women going toe to toe for the hell of it? That's right up your alley.

"Fighting for the glory, for the joy of the carnage is an ancient endeavor that should always be celebrated."

I think we're beginning to really bond here. Sweet.

"Hello? Earth to Styx? You in there?" I blinked in rapid succession. I must have looked like I'd gone to space while I conversed with the god squatting in my brain. Eve's eyebrows were raised as she waved a hand in front of my face. "Where did you go? Forget it. I started doing some looking into that certain thing we talked about? That certain substance, you know, that's like the thing we need more information on?" I rolled my eyes and twirled my finger in a motion for Eve to get on with it. "Okay, so I did some research. Do you know how many people have OD'd in the last three years?"

My first encounter with someone burning out was the very same day I'd sealed my fate with Cronus. I'd been blamed for that man's death as well as the guy I actually stabbed, but clearly, he'd died from Ambrosia. "How many?"

"Hundreds, at least in the first year. Every year it continues to circulate, and more people die. Lots more." I didn't mean to, but I shrugged her off.

"Yeah? So what? We all know what drugs do to you when you go overboard. Even the more benign drugs out there will get you killed if you take too much or if you get a bad batch."

Eve smacked my leg. "Be serious for one second. Here's the thing—" She looked into my face, like she was bracing me for something awful. "Almost all users who've burned out, did so only a few weeks after taking the drug. The way it interacts with the brain short wires a person's ability to have any impulse control whatsoever. They binged on Ambrosia until it destroyed them from the inside out, and they didn't take long to do it."

I frowned, waiting for it to make sense. "I don't get where you're going with this. Again, I know how drug addiction works." A bell rang out in the arena, signaling the first round had ended. The crowd roared, and I joined in out of instinct, wanting to be able to enjoy the match and forget about this terrible conversation.

After the cheering died down Eve went on, "What I'm about to say will come out harsh, but believe me it's not what I want, I just don't know how else to say it."

"Oh my gods, Eve, just spit it out. You know I'm tough enough to handle whatever it is you want to say."

She sighed, chest heaving. "Okay, so if people who routinely take this drug are dying left and right, why aren't *you* dead? Because, based on the science that's come out, you should be. A couple times over."

My jaw fell slack. There was nothing I could say, nothing that would make any sense. I glued my eyes to the fighters in the ring. Their movements were fluid and powerful, arms and legs swinging out like scorpion tails full of venom. "I guess I'm tougher than the average junkie."

I didn't know if Eve heard me or not, but she took my hand in hers and squeezed. "You are. Or your brain is at least. Maybe it's because you only take it when you're supposed to work, and you don't take as much as you want. I don't know." I flushed. If she knew about my binging on Ambrosia she would be so ashamed. I was. I squeezed her hand back and kept watching the fight. We both sat in silence while the rest of the club screamed their heads off as the women in the ring danced around each other in a vicious waltz.

"You are a god's chosen. You will not fall so easily."

I don't like cryptic bullshit. Say what you mean or don't say anything at all.

"Where do you keep drifting off to? I know you've got a lot going on right now, but you keep getting this weird look on your face. Your eyes go all out of focus and your eyebrows come down like you're trying to hear a quiet song playing on the radio or something. It's pretty off-putting if I'm honest."

Eve's head was cocked to the side as she looked me over. Her gaze wasn't accusatory or dissecting like Nick's or Cronus'—no it was full of concern and love. Her long lashes fluttered around those big doll eyes. It was impossible not to love her back. I wanted to tell her what was happening to me, *who* I was listening to, so badly it started to hurt. Was it wise? No, but then neither was I.

I cleared my throat, letting my eyes drift back to the match. "Did you happen to see anything in your research about users…hearing voices? Well, more like one voice." I allowed myself to glance briefly back at her, just to gauge her reaction.

Eve's eyebrows were down low, eyes squinting as she fought to recall the information she'd found. "Actually…yeah. Some users claimed to hear a voice giving them orders they had to obey. The most frequent order given was *Take more*. And they did and died." One of the fighters landed a ferocious left hook into her opponent's jaw, sending her sprawling backwards on the mat. The one who threw the punch descended upon her, sending a flurry of blows down until the ref pulled her back. The bell rang again, and the ref grabbed the standing fighter's hand, holding it high as the announcer bellowed the champion's name to the roaring crowd.

I didn't know whether to feel frightened or comforted by the fact that other Ambrosia users also experienced this same phenomenon of being invaded by a god. At least I wasn't crazy. There was that. Eve and I both stood, clapping wildly for the victor of the match. The fighters left the ring, and the cleanup process began in order for the next two fighters to take the stage.

We sat and I grabbed Eve's hand again, this time

giving her full-on eye contact. "Eve, I'm hearing a voice too." Her eyes widened, but she looked intent, ready to hear more. "I've heard it since the very first time I tasted…you know. I've heard him—Ares." Shock cascaded over Eve's features, and my heart raced in my chest at the honesty I'd just spilled.

"Ares?"

"The very one."

"But, how? It's not possible. The gods are sleeping. Why would they get involved with lowly mortals who do drugs?" *Ouch.* She wasn't wrong. I was just as confused as she was over Ares' choice for companionship, but she didn't need to call me a lowly mortal like that. The average Mycenaean like Eve believed the gods had finished dallying with humans long ago. The present was ruled by man and man alone.

"I don't know, Eve. I'm just a fighting dog, remember? He's only just recently revealed himself for what he is, so trust me—we are *not* that well acquainted yet."

"Gods do not get well acquainted with mortals. It is not necessary."

Well, it sure wouldn't kill you to introduce yourself before three years had passed, don't you think?

"Are you talking to him now? Are you high?"

I shook my head. "No I'm not high, that's what's so weird. He used to only show up when I was, but now—he's just in there. He won't leave."

Eve's head jerked back in disgust. "What's he saying? What's he like?"

I scratched at my forehead, feeling a tangy mixture of relief and regret over telling Eve about Ares. "He's glad to be watching the fights. He likes violence just like you'd expect, and we have somewhat of an understanding."

Eve leaned back in her seat, mind completely blown. "Whoa. It's like you have an immortal, magical parasite in your brain."

It was my turn to be disgusted. "No, it is not like that at all. Don't ever say I have a parasite again. Sicko. It's more like having an extra conscience that likes to get me to make the bad choice, or at least the choice that's going to cause the most chaos. Not really that different from what already goes on in my thoughts." I shrugged.

"The world is a chaotic place, to go against the nature of things would be futile."

My point exactly.

Eve nodded, "Okay but the question still remains… why you?"

"He says I'm *a god's chosen*, whatever the fuck that means."

I was about to go on, but the announcer started calling out the next two fighters' names, and one caught both of our attention.

"Gerty Galantis, *The Amazon of Arcadia*!"

Both Ares and I were completely in sync as we thought, *This is going to be good.*

CHAPTER 17

"No, she didn't. She said she was working the door all night! That little liar." Eve was on the edge of her seat, eyes pinned to her girlfriend, who was busy dancing on her toes in the ring in front of us. Gerty had only glanced our way briefly, flashing that devilish smile of hers before she honed in on the fight ahead of her. Eve's expression was a mixture of anticipation and anger. She always worried when Gerty got into the ring, but her worry was usually unnecessary. She was almost always the one left standing at the end of the match.

"This friend of yours is also a warrior?"
Yeah, but she's the real deal. Not like me.
"You seem real enough to me…"

Eve was busy white knuckling the armrest of her chair, probably imagining all the knicks and cuts she'd be helping Gerty clean up later tonight. And all the words she'd have for her. I too was alive with focus, but it was different for me. Getting to watch Gerty kick major ass was one of the few joys in my life. Her opponent had a shaved head and eyes that glared at Gerty with defiant energy. She was about six inches shorter than Gerty, but in a fight, skill was king—not size.

"I'm glad Lil is working, or she'd be chomping at the bit to put down serious money on our girl. It's going to be okay, Eve." I patted her leg.

Eve rolled her eyes. "She's been hurt before. It's not fun, trust me. She acts tough as nails out in the ring, but the minute we get home, the baby starts whining and demanding to be coddled. The injuries are *so* not the worst part, it's her attitude."

I smiled back at her. "You know you love it. Otherwise, you'd be throwing way more of a fit right now."

Eve's cheeks darkened with embarrassment. "Maybe. Shut up." We screamed as loudly as we could for Gerty. When the bell rang, neither of us took a breath. We couldn't. Immediately both fighters charged, fists rolling out between them so fast, so hard, we couldn't do anything else but watch. Gerty's opponent landed a hard right into Gerty's center, a move that surely knocked the wind out of her. She stumbled, and Eve grabbed my wrist, squeezing so tightly it hurt. But then Gerty looked up, right into her opponent's eyes and the crowd gasped. We all knew it was over for her.

Gerty swung her leg up like a hammer, and her heel landed square with the fighter's nose. She remained standing, arms flopping down in momentary shock. Gerty took the opening in stride. She came down hard, sending a flurry of lefts and rights into her face. Again and again, until the ref intervened, shielding the stunned woman with his body.

The ref signaled the fight to resume after giving her a minute to breathe, but Gerty was relentless. She was all fists, elbows, knees, heels, everything with undeniable raw power. She was untouchable and the arena roared with bloodthirsty glee. The bell rang, and we jumped out of our seats, cheering like complete maniacs.

"Most impressive."

The second round began with Gerty's opponent instantly pinned after Gerty had taken her by the leg and threw her to the ground. I smirked, jabbing Eve with my elbow. "See? Told you. She's hardly got a scratch on her. I bet she's going to be in a *really* good mood tonight."

I waggled my eyebrows at her, and she giggled. "Just watch the match! Sheesh." I swear to all the gods that every single person in the arena had their jaws hanging slack. Gerty was an Amazon, that was for damn sure. She landed an elbow into her opponent's back when she went to take Gerty to the ground. Her opponent stumbled from the impact and Gerty pulled her knee up hard, smashing it into the fighter's chest. She went down and didn't come up.

Gerty turned our way and grinned with her purple mouthguard on full display as the ref took her hand and hoisted it aloft, declaring our girl the winner. The club exploded in applause and we joined in, giddy over the victory.

For a moment, I was just a person enjoying a night with her friends. Doing something I loved. But the moment evaporated quickly enough. All it took was one word from Ares to remind me that I was anything but an average woman.

"But why not kill the loser? There is no honor in surviving such a shameful defeat."

This kind of fighting is just for entertainment, not for murder.

"It's not murder if it's done out of mercy."

That's where the law would strongly disagree with you.

"Gods are above man's law."

Oh right. How could I forget?

Eve and I sat back down, gathering everything we'd dropped in our excitement. Gerty ducked under the ring's ropes and trotted over to us, squirting water into her mouth from a massive bottle. "Did you enjoy the show? Thought I would surprise you ladies with a little demonstration of my amazing abilities."

Eve crossed her arms harrumphing, while Gerty and I bumped fists. "You kicked serious ass! When you put that elbow down, I felt it in my own back. Brutal move!"

Gerty grinned even wider as she scooched by me and sat in the open seat on the other side of Eve. "Thanks bud. Eve? What did you think? Did you like my moves too?"

Eve tried to fight a smile, but it came out anyway, lifting her adorable round cheeks. "I always like your moves, even when you are a big fat liar about them!" She playfully smacked Gerty's bicep and leaned over to plant a kiss on her girlfriend's still sweaty brow. "Good fight. Now relax and watch someone else kick ass for a minute." We all leaned back in our seats and waited for the next fight to start.

The rain had become a chilled mist, pools of water collected intermittently along sidewalks and potholes in the streets, reflecting the neon lights of Arcadia's bars and clubs. This section of town was more modernized, stucco walls painted bright shades of peach and turquoise brightened up the night, the upper levels were living spaces, condos and apartments mostly. Empty laundry lines swung limply on the breeze.

Gerty and Eve were bickering on the corner about the next spot they were going to hit up while I checked my phone. Lil had responded eventually with an *Okay* and nothing else. As I tucked my cell into my pocket it started vibrating.

"Hello?"

"This is Jason. Come get your sister. She's getting sloppier by the second." He hung up before I could respond. Before I could really wrap my head around who *Jason* was…But then it clicked. Lil's favorite spot to end a wild night. Her shift must have been a real doozy for her to be so faded this quickly. It was barely past midnight.

"Hey you two, I'm heading to Jason's. Lil's already there." Eve and Gerty exchanged a look. They both knew exactly what that entailed, and both of them loved witnessing my younger sister's debauchery.

Eve pulled a set of keys from her purse. "Let's take my car." We followed her as she navigated in and out of groups of people exiting the club. The smell of rain on concrete permeated the air, masking every other stench. The lingering odors of blood and sweat from the fights slowly faded into memory.

A few stoplights later and we were clamoring out of Eve's tiny two-door right outside Jason's Bar. The front facade was covered in a faded mural of dolphins jumping above geometric waves. An homage to his past life, I supposed.

When we entered, Jason just scowled at me and pointed with the glass he was drying. My eyes followed his gesture which led to Lil, browsing through songs on the jukebox in the back corner. *Oh gods.* I glanced backwards at the girls who were grinning ear to ear when they saw what Lil was doing. We all knew what it meant when she started obsessing over music. Dancing on tables was not far behind unless I stopped her, which wasn't the easiest of feats.

I sauntered over to my sister, hand on the strap of my satchel. "Hey babe. Whatchya looking for?" Lil looked up at me, her eyes glossy and red rimmed like she'd been crying. That could mean all sorts of things since Lil cried at the drop of a hat.

Her words were only slightly slurred when she spoke, "What does it look like? A song. Duh."

I sighed, leaning into her close. "Why don't you let me pick? I'll surprise you."

Lil sneered, "You only like boring music. I want something I can dance to!"

I could hear the murmurs of Eve and Gerty ordering a round of drinks and wished that I could enjoy the impending show as much as they would. "Jason hates when you dance, Lil. Come on, act like an adult for once."

Lil scoffed and threw her hands up in the air, shouting, "Why are you such a fun sucker?" The three other bar patrons glanced our way, their snickers peeling out into the room.

I shook my head, bumping my hip against hers, trying to get her to lighten up. "Oh stop. I'm not always a fun sucker. Just when you do stuff that gets us kicked out of public places. I would love to let you crawl up onto Jason's bar, flashing everyone around your underwear—if you're wearing any—and enjoy the show as you drool into your hand while you scream into it like it's a microphone."

Lil's nails tapped on the glass. "Whatever, get me a beer then. I'll go sit down with your friends." I stood by a moment longer, waiting for her to prove it. She sighed and tramped over to the booth where Gerty and Eve had stationed themselves. I made my way to the faded oak counter where Jason was still sour faced, but at least his shoulders had dropped from around his ears. Progress.

I leaned against the bar top. "Sorry again, Jay."

He huffed. "Sure you are. What do you want?" I eyed the tap list before choosing the lightest beer available for Lil and I. Jason filled up two glasses and slid them over the counter to me.

"Can we get the fried sampler plate too? I'll pay my tab tonight. Promise."

I threw the *promise* in after seeing irritation bubbling out of him. "Yeah, sure. I've heard that line before." Jason threw his towel over his shoulder, turning his back to me and I returned to our table.

Lil continued pouting even after I'd handed her

beer over. She slurped the foam from the top, hiccupping into the rim of her glass. Eve and Gerty had both decided on margaritas. I sipped on my beer, silently enjoying the feeling of being surrounded by my loved ones.

Eve looked over at Lil and asked, "How was your night?"

Lil took a deep swig from her beer. "It was going great. It was busy, the tips were flowing, people were happy. And then *he* showed up." Even when tossed, she had enough sense not to utter Crius' name aloud in a public space. Everyone leaned in over our drinks, cueing her to go on. Lil stared into her cup and kept talking. "With a bunch of his gang. They all ordered super hard to make cocktails." She gulped down more beer and sighed, "They crowded the bar so no one else could get in to order drinks, and I could hardly get around them without their slimy paws groping at me."

My blood started boiling, my grip around my glass tightening with every new piece of awful information.

Ares purred in between my ears, *"This Crius surely deserves to suffer. Let's go find him."* Something in me surged, and then my fist tensed, and beer cascaded over the table. I'd cracked my glass into three massive chunks.

"Hey! What the fuck, are you high right now?" Lil drunkenly tried to brush the spilled beer off the table, sending it into her lap instead.

I stared at my hand, at the glass, the beer, all of it. The table was silent, everyone stared at me, the same question in their eyes. "I'm not. Swear to gods. I haven't been high since…" My words dropped off, confusion pooling inside me. Eve shook out of her stupor faster than Gerty, giving me a knowing nod before getting up to ask Jason for a towel. I shouted after her, "Can you get me another beer too?"

Jason called out from behind the counter, "I'm still charging you for the last one. And the glass." I waved him off. He was in a surprisingly good mood tonight.

Lil cleared her throat as Eve helped sop up the spilled drink and said, "*Anyway,* they ruined any chance of getting extra tips, and they were just plain gross. It sucked."

Jason came over with a massive plate of fried goodness, placing it in the middle of the table. Gerty's hand launched out for it first and she stuffed a fried macaroni and cheese wedge into her mouth. A microsecond later, she was red in the face, spitting the half-chewed ball into her hand. "Ith hoth! Hoth!" She fanned her mouth while Eve held her margarita up for her. I started laughing, then Eve and Lil joined in on my cackling. Pretty soon we were all doubled over. My sides started aching as laughter continued to bubble out of me.

Lil dabbed at the corners of her eyes with the knuckles of her pointer fingers, catching the tiny tears that gathered from her fit of giggles. She looked my way, raising her eyebrow. "I thought you were going to put a song on the jukebox?"

I grinned at her and sipped my drink. "I think we're having plenty of fun without the singing and dancing on tables part of the night. Just eat some food and relax." Lil only harrumphed a little bit before taking a plate from the stack and delicately piling it with each item on the sampler tray.

Ares piped up, reinserting himself into my psyche. "*Strange are these spoils of battle, and yet so very familiar. Aren't you going to partake? Eat, champion. Sate yourself with food.*"

And so I did.

CHAPTER 18

We hugged and kissed the girls goodnight outside while Jason hastily locked his door behind us. Eve ruffled my hair and said, "Don't leave me hanging. I want updates."

Lil eyed the both of us, questions dancing in her glassy eyes, but I ignored her silent prodding. I said, "I'll do my best."

Gerty tugged the keys out of Eve's back pocket and twirled them around her finger. "Let's get out of here, baby!" Eve linked her arm in Gerty's and the two sauntered towards her car, leaving us to walk home. Nights like this were rare. When there was nothing but time to kill. Come to think of it, I didn't know the last time I'd gone so long without receiving a text from my overlord.

Lil's voice broke into my revelry. "You're different tonight."

I shrugged, stuffing my hands in my coat pockets. "I don't know what you want me to say to that."

She sighed. "You seem, I don't know—Just tell me what's going on. You've never been good at keeping secrets, you know that."

I rolled my eyes at Lil, but she was right. "Want to have a sleepover with me?"

She crinkled up her face. "We live together. Every night is a sleepover."

"Yeah, I know, but we could watch a movie and eat some junk food or something. Like when we were little."

"If I put one more bite in my stomach I'm going to explode. But yeah, let's have a good old-fashioned sleepover. Don't be mad if I pass out right away." Right on cue, her heel caught a dip in the sidewalk, sending her stumbling forward in a way that screamed, *I'm drunk but I'm okay!*

She scowled and I snickered. "Oh goody. Let's watch something scary."

"You know I hate scary shit. I want to watch a musical."

"You always want to watch a musical."

Our sisterly bickering continued down street after street. The city lights blinked on and off, neon strobes cascading colors onto the wet sidewalks and brick buildings. The bars and clubs were closing one by one, bouncers shooed the stragglers who refused to take a hint, and cabs lined the busier intersections hoping to get one last fare before they ended their shifts.

It was *this* Arcadia that enthralled me as a kid. This wild raucous wonderland where people stretched themselves as far as they wanted. Dared to do things a country bumpkin might never have dreamed up in all her life. But there was a hunger in this city, and it was fierce and bottomless. No matter how many people it devoured, it wanted more. Always more. It was easy to forget that on nights like this one.

Lil had settled for a scary movie we'd both seen at least twenty times. As she shimmied out of her party clothes and into her pajamas, I was scrounging the cabinets for anything remotely snack worthy. I found a package of microwave popcorn that had its plastic wrapping removed. *This'll work.* I stood watch, eyes glued to the little window to make sure the popcorn wouldn't burn. The bag was mostly inflated, with enough fully popped kernels in there to satisfy me. I couldn't believe how hungry I was. Usually, Ambrosia zapped all other cravings except for more Ambrosia.

Lil shouted, "Hurry up already, I can hardly keep my eyelids open!" When I popped back into the living room Lil was spread out on the couch, her head on the armrest closest to the door. Her blond hair was in a messy topknot, reminding me of the teen who used to run track with the best of them. Before she discovered the party life. The life that had led us both to this place.

I shoved her legs aside so I could squeeze in and pulled a blanket up over my lap. Lil promptly piled her legs on top of me, giggling as I groaned. "Sleepover time, right? Don't forget I'm the annoying younger sister."

"How could I ever forget that? You remind me constantly." I snorted at my own joke while the movie started. A thought occurred, one I knew that would make both of us feel a little better. "Let's send a photo to Mom, so she has something to tide her over for the time being." Lil swiped her phone from its spot on the cushion, and leaned over so we were scrunched up close enough to have both our faces on the screen. Without a beat, the two of us plastered on our best cheesy grins. Lil snapped the photo and sent it with the caption "Sleepover time! Love you Mom." Let her believe the fantasy. It was too painful to even think about our parents' reactions if they knew the truth. I prayed they would never need to know.

We moved back to our spots, settling in for the

movie. The smell of buttery goodness filled the air as I tore into my half-inflated bag of popcorn. Lil hardly waited for the opening credits to finish before she started probing. "So, what's with you? Did Cronus make you do something really bad?"

My stomach bottomed out, but I kept chewing my popcorn, trying to come up with an answer that wouldn't lead to chaos. "I know you don't want to run away, I get it, but do you really think Cronus will just let us go?" Lil's eyes stayed glued to the TV but her head moved in a single nod. I swallowed, the salty popcorn gummed up my throat but I continued. "Having a backup plan isn't so bad, right?"

"I guess. I'm just tired of you throwing yourself on the sword for me. I'm my own person. I can deal with my choices, I have to." *Gods.* There it was. The stark, brutal reality. She was right of course. I tried to say something, but the air was too thin.

A massive funeral pyre burned bright against a midnight sky on the TV screen as people wailed in the background. Lil wasn't going to let me off the hook though, she angled her body so that she was somewhat upright enough to glare at me. "Say what you want to say, Cal." The use of my childhood nickname made me want to cry.

I rubbed at my temple. "I got you that passport so you *could* leave, and if you *want* to leave, you can." I pushed Lil's legs down and raced back to my bedroom.

I heard a muffled "What the hell?" as I knelt down in my closet and pried the floorboard loose. The bag I'd gotten from Chester was still tucked safely inside. I reached in and pulled out what I'd come to get. When I returned to the couch Lil was waiting, a look of pained confusion stamped on her face. I smacked the item against my hand once as I exhaled, then tossed it at her face.

"Hey!" She failed to catch the small envelope and it slapped her right in the mouth. She pulled out a slim red booklet. Gilded in gold letters with, *Official Passport of Mycenae* stamped on the cover.

"If the time comes, you'll be able to *walk* away, completely free. You can go anywhere you want. For as long as you want, without having to look over your shoulder."

She read the fake name inscribed on the inside of the passport as she said, "Calliope, that's impossible. Cronus, the Titans—you know how they work. Explain this to me so it makes sense." Oh, how I wanted to, but giving Lil too much of a good thing was always a bad move.

Much as I loved her, I knew not to trust her with something so big. "I can't. It's too dangerous for you to know. Put that somewhere no one but you can find." Lil's frown had deepened, casting shadows on her face, but she nodded, still looking at her photograph. "Like, now Lilith. Hide it right now."

"Oh shit, okay." She jumped up from her seat and twirled around to face me, "Close your eyes."

"Really? In the living room?"

"I don't want you to know which room! Duh." I shook my head but obeyed. A few moments and some rustling sounds later Lil was back in her seat, "You can open your eyes now." She tuned into the movie for a few minutes and everything felt so mundane I almost thought that conversation hadn't really occurred. But then Lil reached over and silently squeezed my hand, long and hard. "Don't you dare get yourself killed."

"I'll try."

The movie rolled on, and neither one of us said anything more. I munched all the way through the bag of popcorn, which tasted pretty good, all things considered. I could feel Ares watching the TV from within my psyche. A spur of fear stabbed me—what if he *couldn't* leave? I knew the feeling of imprisonment and I didn't want to be the reason anyone was trapped, god or otherwise.

I asked, *Why are you still here?*

"*I am observing. There is much to engage me.*"

I would have thought the gods had better things to do. I expected to be rebuked but was met with internal quiet for a long while.

A woman on the screen was about to plunge her ceremonial dagger into her unwitting target when he replied. "*The gods love nothing more than to be noticed, and here you are. Noticing me. It is too good to forfeit.*"

Whatever. I think you're a liar. I think you're stuck in there, and you can't figure out how to escape.

Ares laughed, a sharp cut into my smug thoughts. "*Do not be so foolish.*" Either he was bluffing, or I was an even bigger idiot than I'd ever thought, because I had no fucking idea what was happening to me—to us.

Lil jabbed at me with her toe, and I jerked to attention. "What are you thinking about? I can tell right now you are *not* thinking about the onscreen carnage. Why won't you let me in?" She gave me her famous puppy dog eyes, and I was almost helpless against the guilt that threatened to overtake me.

But I had one ace up my sleeve. "Oh, well—Ivan and I, we're…maybe—"

"I already know about *that*."

I gasped, instantly mortified that Ivan had been running his mouth when he swore up and down not to say a word. "*How the fuck do you know?*" I couldn't help but scream the words, well, shriek is more like it.

Lil rolled her eyes. "I saw him leave the other night. It wasn't hard to guess you two were back on again." *Oh shit.* I didn't have time to wonder about who else might have spied Ivan's departure because Lil continued, "There's something else. Are you okay? Like, mentally? Are you having a psychotic break or something?"

I stood up, dragging the blanket I had with me. "Shut up. I'm just tired. Let's go to bed already. The sun's going to be up soon."

Lil followed after me, murmuring, "Killing people and doing crazy drugs and shit, that would make anyone lose their mind…"

"*Goodnight*, Lilith."

As I curled myself up into bed, adjusting my crumpled pillows until they felt just right, I felt the smallest sense of release, some pent-up tension from deep within me eased. Lil had a way out. That passport was as good as gold, and even if everything went to hell, she could use it to escape. At least one of us could get out of this dump.

Lil's drunken snores started bleeding through the thin wall between our rooms, settling me further into my state of calm. There was always hope, even if I hated to admit it. Even if it scared me to death. My eyelids drifted closed, weighed with the heaviness of exhaustion. In the darkness of my mind, I was not alone.

Will you ever *leave?*

"I shall depart when you sleep."

I was too tired to doubt him, too tired to care. *Whatever.*

I didn't know how long I slept, but it felt like mere seconds when my phone began vibrating like a seizing animal on my nightstand. I wanted to ignore it, to chuck the damn thing out the window, but that would be stupid. I forced my eyes open enough to read the screen.

Oh gods.

Tam. He'd already called me three times. Without hesitating I slammed the accept call button, smashing the phone against my face. Half a ring later and Tam's voice echoed through my skull.

"Styx, we need to meet. I think I've figured out what—"

"Shut up about it right now. Where are you?"

"I'm at Asklepios. My mom is on shift for another two hours."

"I'll be there in twenty." I'd never been close enough to the massive medical complex to even begin to know where to find Tam, but a cab could at least get me to the parking lot.

I could hear Tam's excitement and the terror it triggered every one of my senses to come screaming to life. "Okay. Call me when you're here." I hung up then hauled ass out of bed. One glance at the clock told me I was going to be tired all day without some serious caffeine. I threw a beanie over my greasy hair and pulled on the same clothes I'd worn the night before.

There was no rest for the wicked.

CHAPTER 19

Asklepios Corp was a collection of chromed out buildings with curving architecture and green roof spaces. Vines cascaded down the shiny windows on each of the seven structures of varying sizes that were spread out on a sprawling campus fifteen minutes south of downtown Arcadia. When the sun hit it just right, the effect was almost blinding, but not this early in the morning. Instead, the metallic surfaces gleamed only faintly in the murk of predawn.

The cab driver was playing retro music through his busted speakers, so only half of the vocals came through on the driver's side of the car. The dissonance paired with my mounting anxiety was enough to set my teeth on edge. I strummed my fingers against my thigh while I scanned the cluster of labs and offices when the cabbie piped in, "Where do you want me to drop you off?"

"The parking lot is good."

He turned around to look at me, clearly confused. "Yeah…Which one?"

I glared, refusing to display an inch of humility.

"You pick." He looked back at the windshield, shaking his head at my asshole-ishness. A figure dashed out of one of the taller buildings towards the back of the complex—Tam. I tapped the driver's shoulder, pointing to him. "Take me to him." A few moments later, I was sliding out of the cab as Tam hustled my way.

I wasted no time with pleasantries, mostly because there wasn't a single ounce of pleasantness in me at the moment. It was too early to be nice. "What'd you find?"

Tam nodded enthusiastically, completely dodging my sour attitude. "I made a list of the chemicals found in the…substance…and compiled all the possible ingredients where you might find these chemicals. It's surprisingly— organic? I was expecting a lot of hard-hitting stuff, but for the most part it's very medicinal." Tam dug into his pocket and pulled out a yellow legal sheet that had been folded several times over into a thick little square. The grin on his face was endearing and dumbfounding all at once. Why did it feel like this was too easy? I snatched the paper and unfolded it, tearing a corner in my haste.

Nepenthaceae
Claviceps purpurea
Mandragora officinarum
Datura stramonium
Hyoscyamus Niger

I looked back up at Tam who was still grinning like a schoolboy, waiting for more information. He glanced from the paper to my face, and back to the paper twice before realizing I wanted more.

"Well? That's what it's made of."

I tsked, feeling underwhelmed by the results. This didn't feel like the winning ticket that would get Cirillo on my side. "I guess that's what I asked you for. Thanks Tam." I reached into my coat pocket, searching for the money I'd promised him.

Tam said, "Sure thing, Styx. I honestly didn't

expect it to be so easy. Are you sure you want to give me this much? Really, it wasn't such a big deal at all. The labs are almost always empty this early in the morning, and my mom had no clue what I was up to."

I was only half-listening to him go on and on about the slice of cake job. In my mind I was remembering something Sylvia said the last time I saw her at Delos Park. What was it? That I needed guidance or some shit?

"No wonder this stuff is so dangerous, right?"

I raised an eyebrow. "What do you mean? Drugs are usually bad news, Tam—that's one of the many downsides to using them."

Tam's smile curled. "I was saying that all of these ingredients are poisonous."

My stomach clenched, a mixture of fear and fury fermenting inside me. "What?"

Tam nodded, thumping the wad of cash against his palm. "Very classic poisons. Most of these things have been around for thousands of years. That's what I was saying earlier. It's old school—like *really* old school."

Cronus was selling a drug that was a blatant mixture of poison.

Cronus had forced poison down *my* throat. Forced me to take it again and again and then rage at me when it began noticeably killing me.

Tam must have had enough sense in him to realize I was upset. He pulled his phone from his jeans. "I'll call you a cab."

I shook my head, looking down the hill towards Olympus in the distance. The False Sea was a dark green to the west, nearly still without a breath of wind. My mind was bursting at the seams with all of the terrible things I wanted to do to that vile excuse for a man. "Don't bother. I feel like taking a walk." I spun on my heels, leaving Tam behind me.

Silver sunlight peeked out from behind gray clouds

that threatened to kiss the tallest skyscrapers in Arcadia. There was only a hint of dampness in the air, mingling with the bitter tang of coffee beans as professionals zoomed into their favorite cafes for a shot of energy before starting their days. Meanwhile, I wandered like a lost cat, slinking up and down alleys searching for some kind of solace.

My head felt heavy, but strangely empty—Ares had done as he'd said. There hadn't been a single hint of his presence since I'd awoken. I raged internally and almost, *almost* wished he would pipe up with his own fury, but I was alone. More alone than I'd been in a long time, and I began to hate it. My steps became more planned as I turned around corners cutting the fastest path to *Old World Diesel Service*.

When Cronus sunk his teeth into my life, I'd lost the one person I could always talk to about anything, my dad. Right after moving to Olympus I was so lost. Angry at my sister for ruining everything and mad at myself for being the one actively doing all of the ruining. At some point Ivan's babysitting had turned into companionship, and he'd taken me under his wing. One night he'd brought me here, to his dad's shop.

Tobias had married Cronus' only sister, who passed away before Ivan could even remember her. Since Ivan was the only male heir in the Othonos line, Cronus glommed onto him from an early age, but not without Tobi fighting his grip every step of the way. He'd known the kind of life Ivan would lead if Cronus had his way and he railed against that possibility.

Spending time around the two of them made me ache for the company of my own father, who always knew just what I needed to hear. Or not hear. From then on, Tobias' shop, *Old World*, was a sacred place. He seemed to understand that I was a refugee, even though I don't think he knew much about why I was stuck answering his brother in law's every beck and call.

And he listened to me. Or at least he let me ramble on while he fiddled with tools and engines from within the pit. Even when Ivan and I were on the rocks, this place was neutral territory for us. Gods bless Ivan and his sincerity.

When I showed up this morning, Tobi was already underneath a hulking machine, his legs barely visible from beneath the massive equipment. There was a fumbling sound as something metallic clanked hard onto the concrete surface of the garage, then a groan followed as I assumed Tobi had to stretch some kind of way to reach the item he'd just dropped. The air was coated with grease and oil, and above it all the scent of burnt coffee beans. I helped myself to the bubbling coffee maker, pouring myself a cup into a random mug on Tobi's messy ass desk. I let my fingers thaw against the warm ceramic as I slipped into the swivel chair stationed at the cashier's desk in front of Tobi's workbench.

"Thanks for the coffee." I slurped up some of the acidic brew, noting how Tobias' legs went rigid at the sound of my voice. Maybe I'd scared him. "Sorry! Didn't mean to catch you off guard. It's just been…a *crazy* morning. I know it's not even eight o'clock yet, but holy hell. Crazy doesn't even begin to describe it." Tobi didn't say anything, but his limbs seemed to ease up and the clanking of tools resumed. I went on, "Have you ever had that realization that you're an even bigger idiot than you ever could have imagined? Like—The gods hate me. And I just—poison! Poison, can you believe it? And even still after all of that, I still want another taste. *So* badly." I sighed, embarrassment burning my cheeks at the admission.

Tobi continued to work silently which was somewhat of a comfort considering I probably sounded like an absolute mess right now. The sun rose, illuminating the dust motes in the rafters. The traffic outside grew heavier with every moment.

A strong arm curled around my shoulders, shocking me so much my coffee mug nearly tumbled out of my hands. "I haven't seen you in a little while! How are you, darlin'?" I twisted around to see...*Tobi*? Then who the fuck was under...

I looked back and saw Ivan sliding out from beneath the machine, already red faced from being caught in his ruse. He flashed me a painfully bashful smile as he muttered, "Morning, Styx."

I didn't know whether or not to feel relief or even deeper mortification. Deep inside, was a tiny bit of me that was glad it had been him under that engine, because there had been no need to gloss over the terror I felt. There had only been raw truth. A truth Ivan needed to hear.

I searched Ivan's eyes as I responded to Tobi. "I'm alright. I've been better that's for sure. Thought I would come have a cup of your delicious coffee before I started my day." I reached out with my free hand to slap him on the back as I cheersed him with my cup. "It's nice to see you two working together."

Ivan snorted. "Does this look like working *together*? The old man is using me for free labor. It's extortion!"

Tobi assessed his son, pride oozing out of every single pore. "Yeah, yeah, and yet here you are, doing the work anyway. You just can't admit that you'd rather be here working with your *old man* than anyplace else." The love in this garage was a balm. It smoothed over the blistering pain of my own naivete, my weakness. I wanted to soak it up and save it for later, for I was sure there was going to be more pain. More hell.

Ivan swiped a dingy red towel from the floor where he was stationed and wiped at his hands, trying to clean the oil stains from them. "Styx was just telling me how much the gods hate her, weren't you Styx? She says they've been picking on her, making her feel like an idiot. What do you think about that, Pops?" I chose to enjoy this moment, to let the teasing just be that. Friends enjoying a moment together. No challenges, no posturing.

Tobi smiled down at me, the resemblance between the two men was charming. He said, "I think the only person who should make you feel like an idiot is yourself. Don't let anyone, god or man alike, let you think for one second you aren't a fantastic person." Tobi squeezed me again, his burly arm radiating warmth into my bones.

Grinning, I said, "Thanks, Tobs. See? I knew I came here for a reason. Go on, keep saying nice things about me. This is exactly what I needed." I nudged Tobi with my shoulder as Ivan walked over to us. He leaned against the cashier's counter, resting his forearms against the surface as he leaned towards me.

Tobi laughed and glanced at the coffee pot. "Looks like we need a refill. I'll be right back." He shuffled towards his office, leaving the two of us, if only for a moment.

Ivan's mouth curved into a smile, his hazel eyes twinkling with mischief. "I don't know Styx, if we talk you up too much, you'll start thinking you're too good for our company." He quirked his head to the side. "Hey… did you finally realize what a terrible mistake you made?" I scrunched up my face, trying to figure out what Ivan was trying to say when he pulled my hat from my head and wiggled it in front of my face.

I tried to snatch my hat back from him, lunging forward, well aware that I was making myself easy prey. "Oh please, you know you like my new hair." Ivan caught my wrist as I reached, pulling me even closer to him.

He dropped my hat on the counter and smoothed my hair back, his fingers resting at the nape of my neck. "It's growing on me." He leaned in, pressing his lips to mine. He tasted like toothpaste and coffee, like morning and real life. I stood on my toes, stretching myself across the counter to taste him more deeply. Tobi returned coughing and sputtering in embarrassment. Ivan smiled against my mouth before leaning away from me. "Sorry, Pops. Styx has no self-control. She just sprung herself on me the minute you left the room. You should kick her out."

I rolled my eyes and smiled, basking in this rare feeling of contentment. It was fleeting and fragile, but I craved it all the same. "I'll kick myself out after another cup of coffee. Otherwise, Ivan will just sit here drooling over me all day, and then how will you get your free labor?"

Tobi nodded, still blushing as he poured more hot coffee into my mug. "Maybe stay for three?"

There was something in me that couldn't spill the entirety of what I'd learned from Tam in front of Tobi. I knew the truth of Ambrosia would be the final nail in the coffin for Cronus and Ivan as far as Tobi was concerned. To know that his own kin was poisoning people for money would cause a rupture so deep there would be no chance of repair. I didn't want to be the one to start that chaos. I would tell Ivan, I would. Just not in front of his father. Not like that.

We shot the shit for another hour or so, but then customers started trickling through the bay door and I felt like too much of a nuisance to stick around any longer. Ivan walked me around the corner, careful to keep his distance as we said our goodbyes.

He said, "Tell me you're okay. I don't need to hear anything else right now." I wanted to reach out and brush his dark curls away from his eyes, but instead I clenched my fist around the strap of my bag, afraid my hand might betray me if I let go.

I licked my lips, deciding on the truth. "I can't tell you that because I don't want to lie. I'm done with Ambrosia. Done. Don't let me take it ever again." Ivan clenched his jaw and I knew there were too many words to be said, too many emotions that would give us away. He shoved his hands into his pockets and nodded, those hazel eyes trying to read me like one of his novels.

"Deal." Our gaze held for a long while, until I couldn't stand the tension anymore and turned the other way. I didn't look back. I needed help.

CHAPTER 20

    I kept my head down as I navigated the narrow corridors that made up Delos Park. I passed an airy little booth that was all white gauze and shells and stones. I'd always thought stuff like charging crystals beneath full moons and patron gods were just fluff, but so many people in Mycenae clung to the old ways. To the Pantheon and all its gods and monsters. They bathed naked in mountain pools and sacrificed animals on altars that had long been deemed more decorative than anything else.

    To the *Epoptai* or "beholders", our gods were still alive and well—awaiting the day when man would collectively remember enough of them to bring them back to their full glory. The *Epoptai* stood on street corners, peddling the message of the gods, hoping to get some people interested. Those who were curious flocked to spiritual temples and odd shops like this one. They dabbled in the ancient arts, doing all sorts of strange and nasty things to entice the gods out of their slumber.

    I was just beginning to understand that at least some version of them lived, and one of them had decided to hang out in my mind. I must have expelled all of the Ambrosia from my system and that's why Ares had finally gone silent. Maybe that was all it took to get rid of him. I just needed to stay away from that shit. Stay clean. I swallowed, hating how my jaw tightened in reminiscence of the drug's tart flavor. *It's poison, you idiot.*

Sylvia's stand came into view as a torrent of unsettling realizations flooded my head. How does poison make a person have superpowers? How does poison *invite a god* into our brains? That hideous human-tree from Adrian's mansion flashed across the backs of my eyes. Mere plants couldn't do that. So, what in the gods-damned hell was going on?

I tugged at my satchel strap, trying to readjust my coat without my hands. A splash of surprise crossed Sylvia's face when our eyes met, but then something else took its place. "Hey honey, I wasn't expecting you back so soon. Everything alright?" Her brows crinkled as she looked me over, and I knew I was doing a shit job of concealing my growing horror.

Sylvia held her bony hand out to me, beckoning me closer. "Come, let's get some privacy." She went to her register and locked the drawer, flipped her welcome sign, and waved for me to follow her behind her stall, where her yellow camper was parked.

For a moment I was frozen. Unwilling to expose myself to the lunacy that was sure to come out of Sylvia's mouth. What was worse, was that I was terrified it would all make sense. I exhaled and forced myself to follow her. I squeezed my hands into fists, willing my fears to dissipate enough so that I could lift my feet from the ground.

In front of the camper was a bistro table with two chairs beneath an awning. Sylvia took a chair and patted the other seat for me to join her. I balked, the watchful survivor in me wanting to remain standing in case I needed to flee.

She smiled, and it was the same kind of smile my

mom would give before sharing hard news. I sat down in resignation. She waited until I was settled. Sylvia's voice was even when she asked, "What is it, love?"

Apprehension frittered around inside me. Why should I tell this woman anything? *Screw it.* I exhaled the word, afraid of what she was going to say next. "I think…I think Ares is in my head."

Shock flashed in Sylvia's eyes. "God of discord? Are you sure? I thought I saw some fire there, but really?"

I guffawed, "Oh yeah." I stared her hard in the face, hoping she would understand without further elaboration. She knew enough about what I did.

Sylvia leaned forward. "And how did you become his chosen?" My stomach coiled into a million tight knots. Just the thought of Ambrosia made me feel weak with desire.

I curled my toes in my boots, a mixture of shame and want curdling in my gut. "Ambrosia I think. When I started using, he started talking."

Sylvia lifted her chin. "*Ambrosia.* I've heard people say it's another way to make communion with the gods. I assumed it was just a gimmick to sell more…" There was a long pause as she continued studying me. I felt more like one of the items on display in her stall with each passing second until I couldn't stand it anymore.

I thumped my fist against my thigh. "*Apparently,* it's not just a gimmick. Because he's in there, well. Not right now he isn't…I think it has something to do with how much I take. Or how long I use…Here." Before I really understood why, I tossed her the wadded-up list Tam had given me. She snatched it out of the air, tilting her face downward as she unfolded the paper like she was opening a gift. Sylvia's eyes tracked across the crinkled yellow page again and again until she dropped her hand into her lap.

She glanced up at me with that same bad-news look and I found myself feeling petulant about how much power this stranger held over me. I sighed. "That list of poisons in your hand is what makes Ambrosia. Pretty fucked up, right?"

Sylvia shook her head, still staring into my soul. "It isn't that simple, and I think you know it. These aren't just random toxins."

My jaw tightened, frustration and fear warring inside me. "Tell me what I know then. Go on, spit it out. What am I thinking right now?" I rose from the chair and turned away from Sylvia. I couldn't handle the kindness in her eyes. The pity. I would have walked away if I'd had a few less brain cells. I prayed to the Pantheon that she might have even a tiny kernel of knowledge that would help me. I wasn't going anywhere until I got every ounce of it from her.

Her voice was quiet, calculated. She knew how lethal I could be, how precarious this moment was for my sanity. "The plants on this list are some of Mycenae's most sacred. Many of them are only grown in heavily sanctioned spaces, protected by the Epoptai. They are the ancient ingredients that have linked man with the gods for millennia."

"And? What exactly does that mean for me?" I hated how my voice wobbled out of me. I took in a few measured breaths that felt more like seething than anything remotely therapeutic.

Sylvia said, "Oracles would ingest doses of these herbs to commune with the gods. To invite the gods into their bodies to be used as vessels. The gods would share messages—tidings, warnings. To ingest these drugs again and again, risking death each time…" Her voice faded, the terror I felt had become thickly intertwined with rabid curiosity.

I spun on my heels to glare at her. "*Just say it!* For the love of the gods, *please.*" A wave of nausea crested inside me, and I doubled over, hands on my knees, waiting for Sylvia to knock me clear off my feet.

She reached out, squeezing my wrist. "There are few who could survive what you have survived. Most people don't have the strength to house a god inside them. Most people would be destroyed from within as the god tried to commune with them." I looked up, stared into her wrinkled face, needing her to spell it out for me. She nodded as she continued, "You, my sweet, are an Oracle of Ares. *Makarios.*"

My mouth ran dry. Eve said that most people hooked on Ambrosia died within weeks. My knees started to wobble. "I think I'm going to be—" Sylvia rose, swiftly pulling a trash can from behind her, moving it under my face just in time for me to vomit up all the coffee I'd consumed with Tobias and Ivan. I continued puking while Sylvia went into her camper. She returned when I'd finished, holding out a glass of water and a box of tissues.

I plucked out two tissues, wiping away the tears that had streamed from my eyes and the mess that dribbled down my chin while muttering my thanks. She placed a tentative hand on my shoulder as I sipped at the water she'd given me.

Reality started pressing in and panic right along with it. There were so many sharp edges to this, and all of them lethal. I looked up at her. "You can't say a word of this to anyone. The Titans will kill you. Or more specifically, they'll make *me* kill you."

Her eyes flashed. "I swear, I won't tell a soul. You have my word, on my family's honor." She put her hand over her heart as she spoke, and I knew she meant it.

"Good." Ambrosia was a literal gateway drug, and it was killing its users. No—Cronus was killing them. Cronus was feeding it to the masses, not giving a single shit what it really was. He *had* to know. I would never consider myself a religious person, but this was wrong on so many levels.

The water cooled my scorched throat as I downed the last of it. I took my beanie off and ran a hand through my hair. "Is there anything else I should know about being an Oracle, or whatever?"

Sylvia found her seat again and sighed. "I'm sure you've learned at least a little of our history from school, right?"

I nodded. "Yeah, but we covered Ancient Mycenae in, like, eighth grade. Oh, and back then I was pretty sure it was all bogus, so I didn't really take it to heart. *My bad.*" I wielded my sarcasm like a shield from the impending avalanche of existential dread that was sure to bury me any moment. It was flimsy and pathetic, but I didn't care.

She didn't seem to notice either. "Oracles were *Makarios,* or blessed, and each god chose their Oracle based on many things, including common traits. Once a god had chosen their Oracle, they would imbue them with gifts. They would protect them. And do their bidding through the Oracle."

"But I thought the gods used to be able to walk around like people? Why use us like pawns?" I swallowed another swell of bile. Was I stuck being somebody's fighting dog for the rest of my life?

Sylvia shook her head. "The gods haven't been able to walk among us for centuries. When people started to view the Pantheon as more of a cultural pillar than a religion, the gods lost the ability to leave their heavenly confines. An Oracle is the next best thing."

There was one question I had to ask. "Is there any way to get out of being an Oracle?"

Sylvia leaned against her chair, the sad-mom look back on display. "The only way is through death."

I exploded. "Fuck! This is *so* not how I envisioned my life going. Are you sure? What if I just stop taking Ambrosia? Maybe he'll go away?" I paced, feeling like an animal in a cage. Any hope of freedom turning to ash with each step.

She shrugged. "Perhaps…Why not try and see what happens? Microdosing poison can't be that great for your health in any case."

I would've laughed if I wasn't on the verge of having a heart attack. I had to get out of there. Reality started closing in on me, another prison to hold me captive. "I have to go." I pulled my hat back over my head and raced away as fast as my wobbly legs would carry me.

CHAPTER 21

I was grateful for the cold air on my clammy skin. I sent a text to Eve who was working on a project at home, telling her I was coming over. My stomach ached from a lack of sustenance, but my appetite was nowhere to be found.

All that existed within me was an endless sea of disgust and rage. I wanted to murder Cronus. I wanted to burn his empire to the ground. Not only had he held me hostage for three years, but he'd also made me a prisoner in my own body. Someone would always have their hands around my neck, no matter how far I ran.

I cut through an alley off to the right, crowded with industrial-sized dumpsters and a few people dozing beneath tattered sleeping bags. The smell was rank, but it was better than losing my shit in public. I tiptoed around the sleepers, watching my boots as they made contact with the pavement. I stopped a block later when I noticed a pair of leather shoes I recognized straight ahead.

I looked up into a face I really didn't want to see. *Nick.* I groaned. "Not now buddy, I've got places to be."

He smirked, but something about that look sent alarm bells ringing in my ears. His arms were crossed, and his eyes glinted like steel as he looked me over. How did he know where to find me?

Something was wrong. My mind started sprinting past all the possibilities, each one worse than the last.

He sucked on a back tooth then said, "You busy hunting down whoever it was that stole from Cronus? Cause that's what you should be doing. However, it doesn't seem like that's your number one priority right now." He stepped closer to me, clucking his tongue like a mother hen. I gripped my satchel's strap as a powerful wave of craving sent shivers of sharp desire through my limbs.

I deflected, "And what about you? Taking a break to go shopping for an even bigger gold chain?" I pointed at the necklace he wore. "That one makes you look puny, by the way."

He cocked his head, taking yet another step in my direction while I fought the urge to bolt back the way I came. Without Ambrosia, I was nothing, and he knew it. I didn't even have a knife on me, but I glared at him like I did. I sent every murderous thought through my stare as I waited for whatever was about to happen. I thought I smelled the faintest hint of blood in the air, but maybe I was merely thirsty for it.

He reached into his pocket. "I came to see if you needed any assistance. You seemed like you might be lost." Then held up his phone. A tiny digital map filled the screen, complete with a blinking red dot that hovered over this alley. *Shit.*

"Are you *tracking me?*" I reached out to snatch his phone, but he was too fast for me. He grabbed my wrist, and I snarled at him, already raging from the hell that had been my morning.

His breath assaulted my face, it was sour and hot. His beady eyes filled my vision and I slipped further into my fury. "You've been acting strange lately, Styx. Taking midnight walks…spending considerable time with people I'm sure Cronus would be eager to hear about. Not to mention the fact that all of a sudden, you're scratch-free after nearly being squashed flat by a van." He stuck his sausage finger right in my face. "You're hiding something."

I ripped my arm free of his grip before shoving him once in the chest, then I stood up on my toes, pushing my face into his. "You mind your own fucking business, Nick. I work for Cronus, *not* inconsequential pricks like you." I spit and the acrid wad landed square on the toe of his shiny shoe. I tried to push my way past him, but he lunged for me, slamming my body into the dumpster beside us.

My shoulder was singing with pain, but it was paltry compared to what I'd already survived. Nick laughed like a maniac. Any minute now he was going to sprout fangs and start shooting venom at me. "You're such a stupid bitch. All talk and no walk. You think you can take me without your superpowers?" He grinned as he slid a pair of brass knuckles over his fingers. He was right. Nick towered over me, and the look in his eyes was downright murderous. I cursed myself for all those times I'd tormented him while high off my ass on Ambrosia. It seemed like a good idea at the time.

This was it. I was going to die in a dirty alley.

In spite of the odds, in spite of my impending doom, I squared up. I held my fists in front of my face, my stance wide and low, just like my dad had taught me. "I think I can take you with just my little finger, but where's the fun in that?" I wiggled my pinkies at him, flashing him an acidic grin of my own. "Let's do this."

Nick wasted no time clearing the space between us. He prowled forward, already swinging wide. His reach went further than I anticipated, and he grazed my cheek so faintly I could just feel the cool of the metal. I ducked out of the way, sneaking in a jab of my own at his ribs. I barely made contact before I was forced to back up, otherwise his fist would have found its mark. I danced on the balls of my feet, praying that somewhere inside was an ounce of fire left from Ares. Anything to keep me alive for at least another day.

Please.

Nick continued to advance, this time he swung at me with both hands, left and right in a continuous arc of violence that I wasn't quick enough to escape. He sent a right hook flying up into my chin.

For a moment, my gaze was forced upward, and I caught a glimpse of a pigeon taking flight from the eaves high above us as my teeth slammed together. There was an audible clack paired with exquisite pain that told me I'd broken at least one tooth. The moment ended and suddenly I was down on my ass.

Nick laughed at me while I jumped back to my feet, wiping a splatter of blood from my lips. I couldn't help myself as I said through my broken teeth, "That all you got? My grandma hits harder than you." I spit out a mouthful of blood and detritus, not daring to look at the bits of enamel that most likely littered the ground.

He shook his head. "I've been waiting to shut you up since the minute you came waltzing into Olympus. Don't worry, I'm just getting warmed up. Only one of us is leaving this alley." His teeth gleamed, brimming with spite and unspent anger over something as stupid as jealousy. There was nothing left to do but fight until I couldn't anymore. So that's what I did.

I lunged at him, but he was too strong. His arms went around my neck and shoulders, twisting me into a headlock. His forearm started crushing my throat, sending stars streaming across my vision. He laughed again as I coughed and sent my legs backwards, trying to kick him in the crotch. He was too tall for me to reach. I scratched at him with my nails and bucked, thrusting my head against him. As the seconds wore on and my lungs emptied of anything useful, I grew weak until I was flailing like a fish caught in someone's net.

My vision was down to a pinpoint when I felt the fire. A burst of flames, vicious and beautiful, surged from a hidden place beneath my skin.

"Take his eyes. DO IT NOW."

The fire inside me leapt up to my arms, to my fingers, and in that fire was power. Raw and hungry for blood. I could hardly see, but my hands knew the way. They gripped Nick's meaty forearm as I summoned newfound strength to haul him over my head to the asphalt below. My legs burned from the effort, but I stood before him only a moment before kneeling hard on his chest.

"A spy is no good without their eyes. Take them."

The act was pure instinct. My fingers launched into his socket, pinching the soft organ between my thumb and index before snatching it out. Nick's scream rattled my bones as it ricocheted off the dumpsters and into the streets of Arcadia. His hands went to his face, shaking as they tried to cup the empty, bloody socket.

I remained kneeling on his chest, still clutching his eyeball until his wails were little more than moans. I took his hand and placed the detached orb in his palm. "You might have a tougher time finding that missing supply now. Better keep your eye on the prize."

His fingers curled around his eye, and he growled rather pathetically, "You fucking bitch."

"You are too benevolent. Take both eyes. He tried to take my champion. There must be more pain."

I considered Ares' words for only a moment. "If I catch you spying on me, or telling anyone how you got that injury, I'll take your other eye. Maybe your tongue too. Keep that in mind." I rose from my position, making sure to dig my knee into Nick's sternum for added emphasis. As

I headed towards the end of the alley, I stopped to wipe my bloodied hand on an old newspaper that was flapping in an errant breeze. It was yellowed with age, but it did the job well enough. I glanced at the headline, *Police Mystified Over New Drug Surge,* back when Arcadia actually gave a shit about what was going on in the underbelly. Before Cronus controlled everyone at city hall. My mouth ached, but not as terribly as I'd imagined. Maybe the damage was less than I thought.

It dawned on me then that Ares had saved me. *Sans Ambrosia.*

How did you get back in there?

Ares chuckled, a chain sliding across stone. "*You needed aid. There are few loyal to me, and I them. Count yourself blessed.*

Yeah, I heard about that. I guess I should be thanking you.

"*I would also accept a human sacrifice.*"

I snorted, *How about you take the fact that I actually took your advice for once as a gift?*

"*It will suffice…for now.*"

I couldn't help the indignation that flooded my veins. *I suppose squatting in my mind and body isn't enough of a tradeoff for you?*

I could feel Ares' frustration simmering. "*I am a god, not a squatter.*"

Could've fooled me.

"*Why was he trying to kill you?*"

He obviously doesn't like me. I shrugged as I dropped the soiled newspaper and continued back onto the main street, towards the girls' apartment. I didn't want to think about the possible repercussions to this little interaction. Nick was a fool. He was lucky to be alive. But that made him dangerous. Maybe I should've killed him.

Ares grumbled, "*You should have plucked his other eye out and made him eat it.* Then *killed him.*"

Well, you're just delightful, aren't you? I'd be lying if I said I wasn't afraid for our future together.

There was a lull in our mental sparring while I walked as quickly as my legs would carry me. The people I passed on the streets only glimpsed my way before hurrying away or even crossing the street to avoid me. I must have looked completely unhinged.

"You seem…harried. Is there trouble? Are we headed into another battle?"

I've got a lot on my mind. Including you. I have to know. Why me?

"Why you?"

Yeah, why am I the one who has to share headspace with the god of discord? Why me? There was a heavy silence that followed, and I almost worried I had hurt his feelings. An ancient god couldn't be that sensitive, right?

"It is a solitary existence to be so singular, is it not?"

I thought about that for a moment. *Yeah, I suppose so. What's your point?*

"To have a comrade in battle is a rare gift. One I've not had the honor in a very, very long time."

Comrades? Not slave or servant or messenger?

Ares paused again until I could see my destination up the street.

Then he said so quietly I almost missed it. *"Never."*

I'll believe that when I see it. Or…Hear it. I guess.

When I arrived at Eve and Gerty's stoop, Gerty was out smoking a cigarette. She waved me in, shouting to Eve, "Styx's here, babe." Gerty looked at me, wincing. "What the hell happened to you? You've got scary clown vibes."

My eyes bugged out of my head. *Scary clown vibes?* I made a beeline for their bathroom, walking right by Eve who sat at her computer chair, headphones around her neck as she called out to me, "You gotta pee or something? Thanks for saying hello!"

I leaned against the bathroom counter as I stared at my face in the mirror. My lips and jaw were disgustingly swollen. I'd smeared the blood from my mouth around my lips instead of wiping it away, and a browned trickle had crusted down the side of my neck. Not to mention the fact that I was still unshowered, wearing yesterday's clothes. I opened my mouth to inspect my teeth. One molar was totally missing, and my bottom left canine was only partially intact. I poked at them gingerly with my tongue, wishing immediately that I hadn't.

I shouted through the bathroom door, realizing I needed a minute, maybe several—to get my shit together. "Hey can I rinse? And maybe borrow some clothes?" I didn't bother to wait for a reply as I turned the faucets on in the shower, peeling off my grimy clothing.

If you're still in there, go away or close your eyes or something. I need privacy. There was no reply from within and my head felt empty except for my own thoughts. Where did he go when he left? I let the question drift away as I focused solely on getting myself cleaned up. The water pressure wasn't spectacular, but it was hot, and as it poured over me, I tried to imagine what it would feel like to have all my transgressions simply wash away down the drain. Each and every wound I'd inflicted, gone. The pain erased. But it wasn't that easy, and I wasn't sure I really wanted to forget.

CHAPTER 22

I might have gone just a bit too long without taking a decent shower. It took a considerable amount of soap and time before the water was no longer murky as it made its way down the drain. My head throbbed, a dull ache that started in my chin and radiated up to the crown of my skull. My tongue felt fat inside my mouth as I tried to avoid touching it to all of the raw parts where my teeth had been broken.

When I finally pried myself out of the shower, Eve had laid a towel and some sweats on the counter for me. They were Eve sized, which meant they were wonderfully roomy in the ass and chest areas, leaving me plenty of extra fabric to be ensconced in. While I toweled off my head a thought occurred.

Ares? I waited, feeling immediately sheepish after being a constant asshole to the immortal in my mind.

"I am here."

You were in there the whole time? Ew!

Ares laughed, and it sounded so nearly human I thought maybe it was coming from somewhere in the apartment. Oh gods, that would be terrible. *"I have no interest in dallying with my champion. Comrades, remember?"*

Somehow that calmed me down. *Right. Comrades.*

"Have you called to prepare for battle?"

I swallowed. *There will probably be fighting soon. I don't know when. But, in the meantime…think you can do anything about my teeth?*

Ares said no more, but a burning sensation surged up my back and filled my mouth. It was so jarring, so painful I stumbled and fell over the toilet seat. My hands went to my mouth as I screamed. A moment later the fire had subsided. I was wedged between the tub and toilet when Eve and Gerty tumbled in through the small doorway.

Eve lurched forward, getting down on a knee to haul me up. "You are scaring the shit out of us. Get your ass out here! You need to start explaining and start right now." Her tone was enough to terrify me, so I did as she said.

Eve wrapped an arm around my waist like she was afraid I might bolt away if she didn't hold on tight to me, and Gerty walked backwards keeping both eyes glued on me like I was some criminal—well. Like I was dangerous. To them. We shuffled awkwardly towards their living room that was festooned with records, some still wrapped in plastic. Gerty must have gone shopping with her extra fight money.

Eve shoved me down onto the doughy surface of her couch and sat close enough to me our thighs were touching. Gerty completed the sandwich, sitting to my immediate left. Without thinking I reached out and took their hands in mine, squeezing them with emotions I had shoved so deep inside me I didn't know they existed until then.

Eve sighed, breaking the heavy silence. "What happened this time?" I let my head fall back against the sofa cushions, my tongue running over each tooth as

I silently thanked Ares for his gift of healing. Where to begin? My body no longer ached, but my soul—or what was left of it—was weary. So damnably weary. Eve squeezed my hand harder. "Styx, you're scaring me."

My eyes stared straight ahead at the painting hanging on the wall. It was an abstract of the city skyline. Blobs of magenta and black stretched across the canvas, dotted with white and yellow splotches of paint, like stars, or lights. It was a fantasy. A mirage of something no one could ever really find. Instead, we all rotted away in those buildings and between the cracks, fading to nothing while Arcadia feasted on our dreams. I squeezed back. "Nick tried to kill me. He's been watching me."

The anger rolling off my friends was palpable as they both went rigid in their seats. I could almost see the steam coming out of Gerty's ears when Eve said, "Did you kill him?"

"No. He almost had me. But I was able to take him down. I…pulled his eye out."

"What the fuck? Styx, that's—"

"Look, he was trying to kill me! I could have just stomped on his windpipe and been done with it, but I went for a more subtle approach."

Gerty snorted. "Yeah that's subtle alright. No one will notice his *missing eyeball*."

"He likes to wear sunglasses. I'm not worried about him."

I shrugged and Eve shoved me with her shoulder. "Did he hurt you? Are you okay?"

"Yeah…My *comrade* helped me out. Nick managed to break a few of my teeth, but they're all good now."

Gerty leaned over to stare into my face. "What do you mean *they're all good now*? Teeth don't just grow back like fingernails, Styx."

I sighed, *might as well get this part over with too.* "They do when you're *Makarios*." I threw my hands up in the air and let them flop down into my lap where Eve proceeded taking one back up in her grasp.

Gerty's eyes went wide. "Who are you?"

I licked my top lip, feeling incredibly foolish. "I am... *The Oracle of Ares.*" There was a pause when all three of us tried to absorb the insanity spilling from my mouth and then Eve and Gerty started laughing. Hard.

While the howling commenced, Ares mumbled, *"They do not believe you? Why not show them? The tall one can fight, yes? Take her down."*

You don't take down your allies. Even when they tease you.

"I loathe this teasing."

I think you'll survive.

Gerty smacked my leg. "Like in that one movie? Where the guy has to get the golden fleece or whatever?"

I smacked her leg right back. "No, not like the fucking movie. Like, for real. He's in my head. Right now. And he fixed my teeth." I grinned at her to further illuminate my point. The air went out of the room as Gerty absorbed the truth of what I said.

"Ares... God of war and all that—is in *your* head? How the hell did he get there?" Gerty's eyes kept darting between me and Eve, plainly checking her girlfriend's take on my statement. Eve stared right back, and I knew she really believed me.

"Today was a day full of exciting truths for me. Basically, Ambrosia is a gateway drug that invites gods into human bodies. It's also a mixture of deadly poison. And I'm one of the lucky few who can host a god. *Yay!*"

"Comrades do not tease."

Yes, they do.

Eve cleared her throat. "What happens to the people who can't?"

I blinked, thinking again of all those who'd taken Ambrosia and burned out. "They die." Her eyes darkened, and I knew she was counting her blessings for having enough sense to stay far *far* away from the stuff.

Gerty asked, "And what happens to you? What does Ares want with you?"

"That's a good question. I thought he might leave if I stopped dosing it, but I haven't had any in a few days now, and he's still sticking around."

Eve surprised me with a hug, pulling me in against her bust. "I'm so proud of you! See, I knew you would get yourself cleaned up."

I couldn't help the rush of heat flooding my face as she showered me with praise. "Don't get so excited. It's an active job right now." Just the thought of Ambrosia made me salivate. *It's poison. It's poison. I'm* not *a junkie.*

Eve refused to let me go as she said, "I will get as excited as I want, this is huge. And I will *not* let you slip up."

"Thanks."

Gerty leaned over and wrapped her long arms around the two of us. For a moment, we were merely friends sharing a bit of tenderness.

Then it ended when Gerty asked, "What about Cirillo?" And my stomach bottomed out.

"I've got what she wants."

"This *has* been a big day for you. What did you find?" Eve pulled back to look into my face.

I swallowed, glancing towards the bathroom where Tam's note was still wadded up inside one of my pockets. "The recipe."

Eve balked. "The recipe for Ambrosia? You're just going to hand it over to her like that?" Her voice pitched, threatening an argument.

"What else am I supposed to do? Go to jail? This is my shot. My *one* shot." A bitter taste began to coat my mouth.

She recoiled from me and that alone was enough to rekindle the self-loathing which had been my constant company since I became Cronus' plaything. Gerty pulled in a breath like she was about to say something, but Eve went on, "You don't care even a little that with *two* Ambrosia dealers there would be *twice* as much death?"

My teeth ground together hard enough to bite through metal. Eve continued, "You know if Cirillo gets this, she's going to make it worse. She's going to sell it cheaper so that she can have more clientele. It won't matter to her one bit who burns out from it as long as they pay up. And you know what else?" I glared at Eve, hating every truthful word out of her mouth, waiting for the *what else*. She was just getting started. "Even if you do this for her, who's to stop her from using you like this again? It's not like she's known for being honest."

I snapped, "That's just great, Eve! Thanks for reminding me that no matter what I do, I'm nothing more than someone's pawn. You think that's not on my mind every single gods-damned second of my life? You think I'm okay with the amount of blood that's soaked my hands? Do you?" I lurched up from the couch, forcing distance between them and me. I rushed into the bathroom to grab my stuff, wrapping it in a bundle in my arms.

Eve spat out, "You can't just keep running like this, Calliope. It's fucking bullshit and you know it." Her dark eyes were burning pits of righteous anger. I saw myself in them, small and afraid.

"Just because it's bullshit doesn't mean it's not my reality." I started for the door, too humiliated to stand another second with the best people in my life, but Gerty was faster than I was. She bolted in front of the door, her long arms out wide to keep me from sneaking around her.

She gave me a sympathetic nod but held her ground all the same. "Let's talk about this. We want to help you, so just get over yourself and let Eve and I actually support you for once."

My shoulders sagged, the weight of my world threatening to bring me to my knees. Instead it was my two closest friends who forced me to remain grounded. "I'm not going to prison, and I'm not going to be anyone's tool ever again." Both women nodded, wearing similar expressions of grim empathy. I took a seat on the floor, too tired to give a shit. "Do you have anything to eat? I'm starving."

Gerty went to the fridge and started pulling out leftover takeout boxes. "Sweet and sour chicken or veggie lo mein?"

"Yes."

She chuckled while delivering the cold meal on a plate. I wasted no time before I began devouring noodles and chicken. Through my stuffed face I asked, "Any genius ideas to get me out of this awful mess?" I looked up at Eve through my lashes, still feeling a tad sheepish about my almost storming out.

Eve pulled her legs up on the couch as she watched me eat. "What if you expose them? Like, sell the information to the papers? Or the news?"

It was my turn to chuckle. I slurped up a bamboo shoot. "What would I say? And why would they even care? I'm sure Cronus has at least some members of the local media force on his payroll."

Gerty chimed in next, "What if you challenge Cronus? With Ares on your side, you could probably take him down."

"Cronus likes guns, Gert. He'd just put a bullet in my brain. He's threatened it before." Gerty went pale.

"Guns?"

A weapon that makes killing far too easy.

"Hmmm."

I went on, "Ares doesn't even know what a gun is, so that would be wildly unfair. Next?" My phone started buzzing in the pile of clothing I'd dumped on the floor beside me. When I uncovered it, Ivan's contact info was flashing on the screen. I held up a finger signaling the girls to hush up before I answered. "This is Styx."

There was a jagged edge to Ivan's voice. An edge that told me he was in the company of our boss. "We've caught the thief."

"What?" A wave of lightheadedness crashed through me, and I forced my lungs to breathe in and out as he replied.

"We've found the stolen brick. Report to Olympus *now*."

The phone slid from my hand as agony tore through me.

Tam.

CHAPTER 23

One look at my face and both Eve and Gerty knew something was horribly wrong. Gerty tossed me her keys and said, "I'm not working the rest of the week, take my bike." I nodded while forcing my baggy sleeves through the arms of my coat.

I pulled the yellow paper out of my pocket and handed it to her. "Keep this safe. Hide it. No—put it on a thumb drive, then burn the paper."

Eve's eyes were round with fear. "Okay." I made my way to the door, forgetting everything but the terrible wrong I'd committed. Eve's voice cut into my mental torture. "Don't forget the helmet!"

"Oh duh, hang on, Styx." Gerty pulled her black helmet off the bookshelf in the hallway then handed it to me, her blue eyes darkened with anxiety. "Be careful. You know how much I love my baby."

I couldn't bear to look either of them in the eye. They had so much love for me, so much concern that it was painful. They didn't know what I'd done. They didn't know what tragedy I was about to bestow upon an innocent kid. I squeezed my eyes shut for a moment, forcing all the sorrow I felt into that box in my mind. For a second I thought it would break apart, spilling out all of the awfulness that I'd stuffed inside, but it held. For now.

I shoved the helmet over my head and bolted.

I'd only ridden Gerty's motorcycle once or twice, just around the neighborhood, or home from the bars if Gerty was too tossed to get it there herself. It was heavier than I remembered. I lost all sense of time and place as I flew towards Olympus. The engine purred beneath me, but everything felt distant, like I was in that place between dreaming and wakefulness. The January chill wasn't on my radar, even though it was probably close to freezing out. My knuckles should be ice cubes, but there was nothing. Until Ares pulled me from my catatonic state, his voice filled with hectic glee.

"This chariot is fit for the gods! You should keep it."

Gerty would kill me if I tried to keep her precious motorcycle.

"Then acquire one for yourself. The Champion of Ares deserves no less."

I'll get right on that.

"How fast can we go?"

Instead of responding, I rolled the throttle grip towards me while clenching my thighs against the bike in order to keep from flying off. Ares cackled inside my head, and for a split second I was there with him, exhilarated. But it didn't last. The exit for Olympus was swiftly approaching and my personal doom along with it. How did they find Tam? What went wrong?

I'd probably lead them right to him. *Nick, that sonofabitch.*

"Are we going to battle?"

I think a friend of mine is in trouble because of me. And I think Cronus is going to make me hurt him.

"You owe no one your allegiance. Except me."

If I don't, he could hurt Lil. Or me. Remember what I said about guns?

"I will guard your back."

I paused, sensing something new, something akin to actual friendship growing between us.

Thank you. I leaned forward, pulling the throttle again as I sped down the off-ramp towards Olympus.

When I pulled up to the gate it was already open, and Ivan was waiting for me. The grinning boyfriend from this morning was nowhere to be seen. Instead, I was greeted with cold steel as he stood with arms crossed and a mouth that was flat with forced apathy. I didn't want to face him. I was too afraid of what he was going to say. Instead of slowing down and dismounting from Gerty's bike, I rushed past him straight for my house. I'd use the excuse of needing to change out of my borrowed clothes so I could come up with some sort of plan. I promised myself Tam would be safe. I was not about to be made a murderer *and* a liar.

It was clearly stupid to think of anything like style in the moment, but that sliver of control, of normalcy was all I had to cling to in the cascade of chaos that was my life. I was powerless, a coward. At least I could look decent while being the scum of the earth. I scanned my closet, then resorted to rummaging through Lil's because mine was basically empty. I settled on a pair of black pants and a gray sweatshirt.

I threw them on over a clean pair of underwear as Ares began to talk me up. *"Do you have weapons?"*

Good thinking. This is probably going to be messy. In the top drawer of my dresser was a stash of knives, brass knuckles, a taser, and even some throwing stars. I left those but grabbed everything else.

As I stuffed them into my pockets, he went on, *"Small tools for such a mighty master of mayhem."*

Thanks? They do the job.

"But no gun?"

I'm not allowed.

"This seems like a strange rule to follow, does it not? You break all other rules quite easily it seems."

I sighed, *Honestly? Guns kind of freak me out. I do enough damage with my own bare hands.*

"There is a weapon for every situation. Perhaps there will come a time when a gun is most advantageous."

I'll think about it.

There was a loud banging as someone slammed the front door open when I slid the last of my knives into a hidden pocket in my jacket. "What the hell is taking you so long?" There was an edge to Ivan's voice, but I couldn't tell if it was because he knew what I'd done, or if he was just stressed in general about the whole situation. I grabbed my satchel from the floor and tossed the strap over my shoulder.

"Say as little as possible. Test his knowledge."

"I'm coming. I needed a fresh pair of clothes, is that a crime?"

Ivan grumbled, "It is when you have an angry Titan breathing down your neck. We've got to go."

I tried to wrangle all of my frantic energy, tried to pilfer it away, pretend that I really was bad ass enough to be the champion of Ares and not just some terrified twenty-three-year-old who didn't know shit. One look in Ivan's hazel eyes and I knew he could tell I was off. He pursed his lips as his gaze tracked up and down my figure. He was trying to read me, to see if there was any physical sign that confirmed his suspicions. I shrugged, giving him my *what are you staring at* look.

"Cronus wanted me to give you this—" He held

out a baggie, filled with so much Ambrosia it was bulging at the seams. Saliva filled my mouth and a longing so powerful, so brutal I almost buckled. Ivan licked his lips then said, "But I'm not going to. Because that's what you want, right? No more drugs?" I hated how every other worry in the world floated away from me, all but one—how to get that baggie into my hands. I hated that I considered snatching it from Ivan and devouring it all like a lunatic. A tidal wave of shivers racked my body. It hurt. I wanted it so much that it hurt.

"Steady. Hold yourself true. Do not let yourself be commanded by anyone, or anything." Ares' words were like a shield. After he'd spoken, the need for Ambrosia began to slowly wither until it faded to nothing.

I swallowed. "Get that shit away from me." He nodded and stuffed the baggie into his pocket.

He eyed me again. "How do you plan on executing Cronus' commands…without it? Are you really capable?"

Executing his plans… I squirmed internally at the words. More like executing Tam. *Oh gods, what was I going to do?*

"Survival is what I do best. Stay alert and listen to me. We will be victorious."

I promised I'd keep Tam safe. He has to make it. No matter what.

"A rescue mission? This is novel."

"Styx? You in there?" Ivan was waving a hand in front of my face, snapping me out of my internal discussion with Ares.

I swatted his hand away as we left the house and made our way to Cronus' palace. "I'm capable. Don't worry about me, I'll do what I need to do."

Ivan's brows were creased, but he didn't look back my way. There were eyes on us now. "I *am* worried. Did you hear something?"

"Nothing." A knot the size of a melon throbbed in

my guts. What would Ivan say when he learned the truth? When he realized that I was the reason for…I didn't want to finish that thought. Somehow it was going to be alright. Even if it wasn't alright for me, at least Tam could make it out— *would* make it out.

The sun was a watery red circle hanging low in the sky. It would be dark as shit soon enough. When we walked up the steps to the double doors of Cronus' palace, they flew open before we had a chance to knock. Lil burst through the other side, wearing a lavender mini dress and silver pumps. Her makeup was flawless as usual, but the look in her eyes was that of a rabbit forced into a corner by taunting children.

She was on the verge of a meltdown. "I gotta get the fuck out of here." She brushed past Ivan and I who exchanged looks of panic. "Good luck. The Othonos brothers are on a rip."

I steeled myself, clinging to my smoldering indignance. Ivan moved swiftly, outpacing me as he prowled towards Cronus' dining room. Before I caught up to him, he was already tearing into someone.

My eyebrows lifted at his tone. "I just saw one of your serving girls. She was so upset at your treatment that she was afraid to come back in. What the fuck is that about?" I nearly died of shock. *Ivan* was yelling at *Cronus?* Dear gods, I'd broken him.

When I entered the room, Crius and Hyperion were staring slack jawed at their nephew who stood toe-to-toe with their oldest brother. I froze in my tracks, wishing I'd had sense enough to stay back and just eavesdrop.

Cronus' blue eyes looked like they might freeze Hades himself as he spoke. "Ivan, though I am pleased to see you've grown some balls, I will remind you of this only once. I do as I please. Especially when it concerns those who've royally fucked me over. That *serving girl* is paying her dues."

Ivan leaned in, and the audacity of it sucked all the air from the room. "She's working off her debt, like you required her to do. She's not your whore." My heart leapt from my chest. I would have tackled him if I had less brains.

"I see why you continue to be fond of this man."
Told you he wasn't so bad.

Ivan and Cronus held each other's glares while the rest of us looked on in complete silence. Waiting to see who would come out the winner. And what would become of the loser.

Cronus raised a silver eyebrow. "You're right, nephew. She's far less than that. She's nothing but a silly Lily, waiting to wilt into rot." My fingers curled to fists, and the big sister's urge to defend Lil, that same urge that had landed me in this position three years ago, nearly overwhelmed me. I'd at least learned that lesson.

Hyperion cleared his throat and Cronus grinned, the loving uncle just teaching his progeny a lesson. "Let's move on, shall we? There's been a development. Come, sit. You too, Styx." My face was hot with anger and I'm sure they could see it, but I did what he said, pulling a heavy chair out from beneath the marble table.

I surveyed the room, realizing that a certain one-eyed bodyguard was nowhere in sight. He must be licking his wounds still. Cronus motioned to Crius, his pinky ring glinting. "Tell everyone what you've learned."

Crius licked his lips and leaned forward, giving each of us way too much eye contact. "Somehow, it's making its way through U of M's campus. Nick tells me some kid's been showing up to parties with it, doling it out for petty cash."

There were not enough swear words to sufficiently illustrate my internal terror. Tam was *dealing*? I kept my face neutral while I died on the inside. This was so much worse than I could have imagined.

Crius went on, "Nick's collecting him now."

"What?" The word flew out of my mouth like a gust of wind. *No, no, no.* Getting Tam out of this would be all but impossible with the entire Othonos family waiting for his arrival.

Cronus sipped from the wine glass in front of him then said, "We need to send a message. A very loud message. Stealing from us is a deadly crime." My blood curdled.

The four men turned their gazes behind me, and a voice—the butler's—announced, "They're here sir."

Cronus set his glass down and rubbed his hands together. "Excellent timing. We can show the Soto Group how the Othonos family deals with problems. Bring them in."

"Yes sir."

Cronus leveled all of us with an icy stare. "These people are our *guests*. Let's make sure to have some class while they're with us." His eyes lingered on me, and I had to clench my teeth together to keep from sneering at him.

The butler returned, and behind him were six people. In front was the man I took to be in charge. He was tall, taller than Cronus, and bronzed to perfection. He wore a white button down tucked into very slim black slacks. The others in his entourage were similarly styled, polished and pretty.

Cronus rose to greet him, and we all followed his lead, standing by our chairs in silence while Cronus spoke. "Welcome to Olympus, Leon. So glad you could finally come." Leon grinned, and I swear to gods, a golden tooth glinted where a canine should have been. They clasped hands, both staring at the other far too long for it to be comfortable or natural. This was a pissing contest, and we all knew it.

Leon gestured behind him, a lazy arm waving at his crew, "These are my associates. They'll be joining us for the Expo." A rather bulky fellow standing to Leon's right crossed his arms and I took him to be the bodyguard. His brown eyes connected with mine, and while he was formidable in stature, I sensed a softness in him that I logged away for later. Soft people could be manipulated. I knew that from personal experience.

Cronus said, "We were just getting ready to host another *guest*. Would you care to join us? The more the merrier."

Leon eyed his men for a second and turned back, a cruel smile splitting his face. "I think I'd like that."

"Hold steady. You could destroy every being in this room. Do not forget that."

I could?

"We *could*."

I let Ares' darkly comforting words sink into the black depths of my soul. I hoped it wouldn't come to that. But if it did, I would be ready.

CHAPTER 24

No matter how stupid Tam had been, he was still only eighteen. But I knew better. Lil was the same age when she first got mixed up with borrowing Cronus' money. He had no issue putting a hit out on her. Why would some unknown thief be any different? I paced out on the Palace's front lawn, gazing distractedly at the dark streets of Arcadia. I wished it would all burn to the ground. Let Arcadia crumble into ash.

"The world shall be made anew from the fires of discontent."

That's kind of pretty, did you just make that up?

"Perhaps."

I nearly choked as I wondered what Cronus was going to force me to do tonight. Where was the line?

"Everyone has a limit, young acolyte. You must find yours. Then hold to it. When your will is unshakable, so is your power."

Someone's feeling quite poetic tonight.

"The promise of bloodshed does things to me."

Delightful.

I didn't want them to arrive. Where this night was

headed, there was no returning. Not for me. Headlights strobed up the driveway, signaling my impending doom.

The Othonos brothers moved like a giant mass as they filtered out of Cronus' palace, followed by Leon and his soft looking guard. I prayed that Tam had pawned the drug off on someone else, that it wasn't actually him doing the dealing.

I moved to stand beside Cronus, Ivan on my right. Our shoulders almost grazed but I leaned away before we could make any kind of contact. Soon I doubted he would ever want to touch me again. My heart twisted. Just when things were maybe going to be okay between us. The gods really hated me.

But not all of them.

"Are we going to massacre your captors at last? Will this be the final battle?"

All I want is to get Tam out of here. I don't know what that means for me—us. I felt a surge of heat course through my body, not unlike the high of taking a hit of Ambrosia. I understood it for what it was— a sign that Ares was preparing me for the fight ahead. My limbs came alive with raw energy, the fire of an angry god poured through me.

As I adjusted to the feeling of unfettered power, I obeyed a new and overpowering urge to check all of my weapons. I felt the impression of my favorite knife where I'd tucked it into my front pants pocket. I didn't know what good it would do. Cronus and his brothers were most definitely packing heat. I didn't know what was going to happen, but I felt the increasing weight of looming consequences pressing me further into my own hell. Nick got out of the driver's seat, and hit the fob twice, popping the trunk. As he rounded the back of his car I exhaled, *Ready for this?*

"With every ounce of my being."

Let's fucking go.

Ares opened the floodgates, and even more fiery

energy filled my body, raging down the ends of my fingers and up through my spine, burning up any hint of fear. Ares consumed all doubts with his power.

Cronus stepped forward, as Nick dragged a hooded figure towards us. His one good eye gleamed when our gazes met. The Titan bellowed, "The Othonos family doesn't take kindly to thieves. Let's see who this little shit is." Nick shoved the person forward, and they stumbled, landing hard on their knees before Cronus. He looked my way and nodded, signaling me to remove the black bag from their face.

I held my breath, my stomach doing somersaults inside me as I gripped the fabric and yanked.

Fuck.

Tam's eyes were so wide they almost swallowed up his whole face. He saw me and the terror in him visibly multiplied. I had no time to prepare him, to even hint that I was trying to help him.

I lunged for him, ripping him up by his bicep. "You *fucking moron.* What did you think was going to happen?" I couldn't help the fury laced in my words, even though it was more for me, not him. I shook him once for good measure as Hyperion and Crius circled around us, blood thirsty smirks ruining their good looks. Hyperion said, "Now kill him, Styx." I froze, trying to think of anything that would help in this situation. Tam started hyperventilating.

"Stall them."

"I thought you wanted to make a big statement." I tried to make myself sound bored, summoning the cruelty I knew lived inside me.

Cronus frowned, "Kill him, then cut his head off. I want a souvenir for the Expo." I squeezed Tam harder, feeling his body vibrate with anxiety.

He's a fucking monster.

"Feel your strength. Be ready."

"Okay then. Outta my way, fellas." I pushed at the wall of Othonos men, making sure to shove them as hard as I could. I needed a clear path. I tried to avoid Ivan's face, having realized who he was about to watch get murdered and decapitated, but there was no escaping it. The depth of sorrow in his eyes was endless. Ivan knew there was nothing he could do. Not in front of Leon, not after his spat with Cronus earlier. I dared him silently to look at me, to see the sorry in me. I knew there would be anger later, when he learned how I'd betrayed them both with my own selfish need. Who knew if I'd be around to defend myself.

Tam was crying now, severing me from my callousness. "Please, it wasn't supposed to go this far. Please. I just thought I could add a little more to my college fund, you know? I didn't mean for it to be like this. I'm so sorry! Please, please just give me another chance." He started pulling against me, but my grip on his bicep was stronger than steel. There was no escape, not for either of us.

His pleas were all too familiar. So many people had cried to me in the same way, so many had been dispatched for the same reason, but not again. I swore to myself then, *never again.*

"The line has been drawn."

There was a growing crowd of goons and palace staff hovering on the lawn around us, waiting to see what was going to unfold. Behind me, someone let off a round of bullets into the air, and Crius whooped. "This is what happens when you fuck with the Othonos!" Tam screamed in terror, and several of Cronus' cooks ran for cover.

I glanced over at Tam, who had a trail of snot sliding down his face as he cried. "Please Styx, gods, please! Please, I didn't mean anything, I'll give you everything I made from it. Every single penny. I'll pay it all back. I promise. I promise." His begging made my ears ring, made my guts cramp up in shame.

Cronus barked, "Get on with it. His whimpering is pathetic."

I jerked Tam once to make sure he was listening as I leaned in close, pretending like I was looking for my weapon. "Whatever happens, do not leave my side. Got that?"

He blubbered, "What?"

There was no time to repeat myself. I gripped the handle of my favorite knife and whipped around, sending my blade in an arc of spinning death towards its target.

It hit its mark, but not perfectly enough. I watched and the world slowed to a crawl as my knife sank into Cronus' chest. His brothers, Ivan, Leon, all of them, turned to their leader in shock. Watched him sink down on one knee. His face became blood red with fury and Cronus screamed, "Do something!" but I was already grabbing every blade on me, tossing them like darts. One, two, three.

"Glorious! Magnificent! Do not let up now!"

Ares howled his praise as two knives found their homes deep inside Hyperion's gut. The third blade managed to slice away Crius' ear, sending him to the ground in a heap of panic while he searched for the missing appendage, blood spurting from the place where it had once been attached.

Ivan stood frozen with indecision, while Leon cowered behind his human shield. Despite having a knife buried in his chest, Cronus reached into his jacket and pulled out his gun. He tried to shoot at me, his aim wildly off with his left hand holding the gun, but it was enough to terrify Tam who sprinted away from my side like a frightened animal sensing imminent danger.

He bolted for the gates and I chased after him, trying to cover his ass. "Tam, get the fuck back!" I threw another knife towards Cronus, but it went wide, landing in the lawn behind him. I grabbed Tam by his shirt collar, shaking him once to try and force him to snap out of his

215

lunacy. Another shot rang out, this one grazing my thigh.

I screeched from the pain, momentarily distracted by it. I'd never been shot before, and it hurt like a motherfucker. Cronus laughed, rising to his feet. "You thought you could get away with this? You stupid piece of shit." He raised his gun, aiming for me.

And then, in a blur of bodies and blood, Ivan rushed his uncle. He threw his arms around Cronus' waist, just as his finger crushed the trigger. Instinctively I went down, bringing Tam crashing to the ground with me. I waited to feel the bullet find its mark.

But I felt nothing. I saw Ivan with his uncle in a chokehold. He wasn't looking back at me. He was looking at Tam. My hand was still twisted in his T-shirt, but it was wet. *No, no, no, no….*

There was a crimson blossom unfurling in the center of Tam's chest. His eyes were glassy. His mouth opened and closed like a fish out of water.

I screamed, "No, you don't get to die, you have to make it."

"There is nothing that can be done for the boy. He is dying."
Shut up. I don't believe that. You promised.

Tears continued to slowly leak from Tam's eyes, he sputtered, and a clot of blood dribbled from his mouth. The words were wet and hard to understand as he said, "Don't tell my mom." Nausea roiled inside me.

"Tam, Tam! Don't." I pleaded with him, throttled him with my hand still clenched in his shirt. It was useless.

He was already dead.

CHAPTER 25

I couldn't release my grip on Tam's shirt. I couldn't move. I couldn't hear the words Ivan was yelling. But then a singular voice came through the ringing between my ears, loud and clear.

"You must flee. Rise. This battle has ended. The only way to find appeasement is to survive another day."

One by one, my fingers uncurled from the marred fabric, and I knew it wasn't *me* that was moving them. I stood mechanically while Ares found his bearings as he pulled my strings. I didn't stop to look at the Othonos family. I ran as fast as my legs could carry me back to Gerty's motorcycle.

The world was distant. I viewed it all from behind a veil as Ares wielded my body for us both. I wondered if it was possible to disappear to the place he always went when I was alone. Maybe I could go there, and never come back to this awful place. I wanted to be done. I wanted all of this bullshit to end.

"You gave your best to Tam."

And he's still dead in the street. What does that say about

217

my best?

    "It was fated. There are things even the gods cannot change."
Fuck fate. Where are you taking us?
"To one who still honors the gods. She'll protect you."

I was too sick with guilt to ask any more questions.
I recoiled further inside myself until all I could feel was
the steady pull of gravity as the motorcycle banked around
curves. That and the slow breaking of my heart.

Ares maintained his hold on my autonomy, but it
didn't feel like an abuse of power. It was more like he truly
was my comrade, carrying my injured carcass away from the
battlefield so that we could fight another day. If he hadn't
been with me, pulling my strings, I'd probably have a bullet
in my skull. The damage I'd left in my wake was sure to
have cataclysmic consequences.

    Lil. I need to get a message to Lil. She's not safe.
    "It shall be done."

The motorcycle slowed to a prowl as we weaved
through the narrow streets of downtown Arcadia into
a place I knew like the back of my hand—Delos Park.
Instead of probing, I just waited to see where exactly Ares
was leading us. In my silence, my assumption of trust, there
was a profoundness. I hoped he recognized it like I did.

We left the motorcycle in a parking spot and
continued on foot towards the dimly glowing lights that
welcomed evening shoppers into the mouth of Delos. The
sensation of floating was intoxicating as Ares navigated
us through the small rows of vendors. I was a kite whose
string had been let out too far, soaring above the chaos that
I'd created.

    Oh gods, what did I do? Ivan.
    "He is a smart man; he'll know how to keep safe."
    Don't be so sure.

Ares halted our stride, and I stood beneath Sylvia's
tent. She emerged from the darkness within, eyes wide,
though it was impossible to tell what she was thinking until

she spoke—

Her tone was curious. Reverent though wary. "You're finding your way quite well after having taken over my favorite girl. Always brave, always brash." Sylvia lowered her chin, curling her spine in a downward arc.

My voice peeled out, but it wasn't *me* who spoke. "She's my champion, and I am her patron. This is not a coup, but a delivery of her person to safety." I felt the muscles working in my jaw, my vocal cords vibrating, but none of it was my own doing.

Can you please never do that again? How do you know Sylvia? How does she know you? What the hell is going on?

Sylvia's head quirked to the side as she studied me—us— then nodded. "If she's in there, let her speak. I want to hear this from her. Styx, darling?"

There was an odd *shifting*, and suddenly I was back in the driver's seat of my own body. I wobbled then buckled to the ground in front of Sylvia. My knees slammed into the pavement, my hands were too slow to brace my fall. They scraped at the ground, further chipping the manicure Lil had given me not three days ago.

"Apologies for the abruptness."

The world spun and nausea roiled inside me. "Sylvia—It's me. I need a place to stay. Hidden."

She squatted across from me, smoothing the hair away from my forehead before letting her hand rest on my shoulder. "I knew it was only a matter of time, kiddo. Come on. Before someone recognizes you." With surprising strength, Sylvia hefted me up then tucked me under her arm as she guided me around the backside of her tent.

The yellow and beige camper was still parked there, complete with a "KEEP OUT- PRIVATE RESIDENCE" sign taped to the front door that I hadn't noticed before. She eyed me. "If I let go of you, are you going to fold like a paper doll again, or can you manage while I open the door?"

"I'm good. Thanks." Sylvia revealed a key hidden beneath the collar of her shirt and unlocked the trailer door. She shifted so that she stood behind me, then began to gently usher me inward. There was a night-light glowing a hazy white in the back, which I assumed was the bathroom. Otherwise, the narrow space was dark, the bustling of Delos Park muted almost entirely. It was like being sealed in a tomb.

"The back room is mine, but this table turns into a bed. Why don't you sit over there while I get it ready for you?" I did as she said, shuffling to a vinyl covered bench nestled against a counter with a sink that had a jumble of bowls and forks stacked inside it. I rushed to it, shoving the dishes aside so I could scrub my hands clean of Tam's blood. Though I knew I'd never be rid of it completely.

My brain was hazy as my adrenaline and Ares' power ebbed within me, but one thought bolted through me, nearly scorching me with panicked curiosity as I soaped and re-soaped. "How did you know that I wasn't—How could you tell?" I trusted Sylvia, obviously. But there was a limit to the insanity I was willing to release into the world. At least not without being sure she wasn't going to call the cops on me.

Sylvia pulled the seat covers off of the breakfast nook and turned the table over before speaking. Once everything was leveled and covered in cushions, she sat down and stared at me. The wrinkles on her face obscured her eyes from me, but I could feel them assessing. "I can see him in you."

Sylvia motioned to a towel hanging off of a cabinet handle. While I dried my fingers I probed, "But *how?*"

Sylvia went around me to a cupboard above the kitchenette, pulling a tangle of sheets from within. "I am an *Epoptai*. A witness to the gods and their deeds in Arcadia. It was no coincidence that you and I found each other, sister."

My spine straightened.

Sister?

"Are you an Oracle too? Why didn't you ever say anything?" A curl of anger stretched inside me, but I was too tired to give it more life, too hollowed out. "When I came to you, why didn't you tell me?"

"You seemed like you had about all you could handle."

I snorted. "That's true. I still don't really understand. It doesn't seem possible."

Sylvia ran a gnarled hand across the sheets, smoothing out all the wrinkles then raised a brow as she said, "It should not be possible. Not the way you came to it. What Cronus has done to our sacred ways is an abomination. The gods will not remain amicable to its use for much longer."

"You mean Ambrosia?"

"Yes. Now stop talking and get some rest." Sylvia stood then pointed to the bed. I frowned.

I wasn't going to sleep. Not now, not when my sister was somewhere totally clueless to the fact that Cronus was angry and ready to destroy anything having to do with me. "Can you get a message out for me?"

Sylvia's brows lowered and she stepped out of the trailer, leaving my question hanging in the air still unanswered. I stood with the intention of chasing her down, but my knees started quaking from beneath me. It was almost like a come-down, but it felt more human—like I'd just finished a marathon. The shivers and cramping that turned my limbs to stone was nowhere to be found. Instead, I was left with a deep ache that permeated all of me.

Sylvia's face appeared at the door again. "Cap's out here, what do you want me to tell him?"

I peered through a bend in the blinds hanging over the bed, and sure enough, there was the hermit king himself. A tiny spark of warmth rekindled inside me. He saw me, raising his hand in a wave.

"Tell him to find the girls, find my sister, find Ivan. Tell them I'm safe, but they need to hide. Tell them I'm here." Sylvia gave the message to Cap who nodded once, then winked at me before turning on his worn soles. The tension in my bones remained. It would stay with me until I knew that all of mine were someplace safe from Cronus' murderous hand.

"You. Sleep. Now." Sylvia pointed to the bed again, then shut the door behind her. I sat blinking into the dim. Now that I was alone, the full weight of this night threw itself into my face. In my mind, I saw Tam's mom. Or what I imagined she looked like. A feminine version of her son, complete with that same idiotic smile.

She wouldn't be smiling when she found out Tam wasn't coming home. She might never smile again.

"To feel is to be human. Embrace it."

Ares' words were a command I could not ignore, and with one shaky exhale I did what he said.

I embraced it.

All of it.

The lie I'd been living for the last three years. The blood on my hands. The lives I'd ruined. And the life that I mourned the most—mine. My freedom.

Tears cascaded down my chin in droplets that burned my eyes and made my skin itch. The fire that fueled every step I'd ever taken was doused in sorrow. My shoulders shook with pent up grief as little by little, I let it escape from that box inside my mind. The one I'd been stuffing full night after night after sullying my soul with blood work. The seams split, and finally it burst open. Now it was all in front of me. Each moment bathed in pain, in fear.

In survival.

"There it is. To survive, one must sometimes become a

monster. But a monster cannot survive under the weight of their fear." His voice was warm with compassion. It was a tone I didn't believe could ever come from the god of war.

What do you mean? I'm not immortal. Neither are my friends. My sister. They could be on the chopping block right now, because of me. Those fears seem pretty logical to me.

"I do not mean for you to abandon your fear. Instead, fight it."

I hiccupped through the ever-flowing river of tears still rolling out of me. *Fight it? Fight the fear of losing my family? Why try to fight something even the gods can't change?* Skepticism burned in me.

There was a long pause but then Ares said, *"It is true. There are things I cannot do. I am fallible. But my fear does not own me. Not even when it has me surrounded. I will fight it along with my foes until I am no more. And you, acolyte—Calliope, shall fight yours."*

But, how?

"Together. We will annihilate everything and everyone holding you captive."

I swallowed, *And what if we fail?*

"Then Elysium will welcome you as a fallen hero, forever to be lauded in paradise."

I had no response. I was no hero. I was a coward. There was no way in hell I deserved a place in Elysium. But if Ares thought I had a chance, then why the hell not try?

CHAPTER 26

My first twenty-four hours in hiding were so tedious I thought I might wither into ash. Sylvia had come into the trailer sometime after I'd passed out. I woke up to the sounds of sizzling as she scrambled up a couple eggs for the both of us. When I asked about Cap, and if he had any news, she said she hadn't seen him in between hurried bites of her breakfast. She made an obscene amount of coffee, poured herself a tall mug and reminded me to stay put as she sidled out of the trailer to open up shop for the day.

My phone was powered off. I didn't want to risk there being any way of Cronus finding my whereabouts. I was completely cut off, even though I was basically in the middle of town. Every time Sylvia came back in to refill her mug, I assaulted her with questions. Had she seen anyone from Olympus? Any news on Cronus? What about Cap? Where was he? After the second time, she didn't even bother to reply. I doubted she would be able to stand me in her home like this for much longer.

Having only Sylvia intermittently and Ares

constantly was getting to me. He asked so many questions about every little thing. He was fascinated by the modern world. Apparently, it had been a *very* long time since Ares had been out on the town. After eight hours of waiting, not knowing, I realized we weren't that different. Being in the dark was zero fun.

"I'd long wondered why the Pantheon had remained severed from humanity. Now I understand. The people have come to see us as fictitious."

Not everyone though. There's plenty of people like Sylvia out there, spreading the word.

Ares pouted, *"There was a time when not a single human dared to question the gods. To disregard our existence as mere lore? It is stunning. What do people believe?"*

I snorted, *They believe in money. Things they can see and touch and taste. I think people would rather believe they have power in their lives, and not some invisible beings pulling the strings out of boredom.*

"I can assure you I am not here out of boredom."

I couldn't stop myself from asking, *Then why are you here?*

There was a brief pause, then he said, *"I thought that was made plain. We are comrades. You are my chosen one. I am here because you and I are bound."*

Yeah, that still sounds like you were just bored.

"How do I make it clear? Your power gives me power. My power gives you power. It is an exchange of gifts."

I frowned, *My power? What, the power of sarcasm?*

"Your humanity is power. Your defiance. The fight in you that never ceases. You have a true penchant for discord."

I couldn't help but sit up a little straighter. I had something a god wanted, even though it didn't seem all that desirable to me. He'd been called to me for a reason, and whether it sounded cool or not, well…

"For what it's worth—I'm grateful."

Night had fallen after an eon of self-sanctioned imprisonment. By this time, the storefronts in Delos Park were closing up one by one as the last shoppers slowly departed the area. Sylvia was outside packing up her wares and I was inside of course, eating what felt like the fiftieth meal she'd fed me since I'd arrived. Clearly, I was too skinny for Sylvia's liking. I would happily eat whatever she put in front of me. The woman had a gift for spices.

I heard muted voices, and then the trailer door inched open. My stomach bottomed out, and all the pain I'd been sorting through over the last hours resurfaced just like it had the night before. Fresh and jagged. Ivan stood on the bottom step, his face hollow, like he'd become part ghost since the last time I saw him.

When our eyes connected, my heart seized and before I knew what I was doing, I was climbing over furniture to get to him. He rushed up the last two steps, his jacket catching on the edge of the counter, forcing him to halt in his advance. While he reached back trying to free himself, I was already stretching my arms out wide, ready to pull him in.

"I was so worried about you—"

"I thought Cronus had found you—" We both spoke over the other, so many words and feelings getting jumbled as we tried to explain ourselves. Ivan pried his jacket free and pulled me into him. My arms locked around his middle, so tightly they ached. There was a long moment of hugging in silence with bated breath.

I refused to feel anything but relief that we were both alive and in one piece. Guilt would arrive soon enough. There was a slight pressure as Ivan's lips made contact with my head, once, twice, then a third time. When

I finally decided to let my arms relax, I looked up at him. There were dark circles ringing his bloodshot eyes.

A part of me didn't want to ask what he'd gone through since I'd escaped, but I needed to know. "What happened?" I took his hand in mine and dragged him further into Sylvia's home, forcing him to sit on the tiny bed beside me.

He squeezed my fingers and looked into my eyes. He swallowed. "Hyperion's in the ICU. They don't think he's gonna make it. Cronus has every cop in town out looking for you with orders to bring you to him."

The air whooshed out of me. It was a lot to take in. "How are you here? I figured Cronus would have at least put you on house arrest or something for turning on him like that."

He shook his head. "Nah. He just disowned me."

My jaw went slack. "*What?*"

He shrugged, as if he was just sharing a bit of ordinary gossip. "Yep. He said he would have killed me if I wasn't his sister's son. Told me never to show my face in Olympus ever again." He looked me over, a half-smile threatening to show itself. "Guess that means I'm off the hook?"

I studied Ivan's face searching for any hint of regret or shame, but there was nothing. Instead, he seemed a little taller. His shoulders were back, his spine straight. The weight of Cronus' control had been dragging him down, making him smaller all these years, inch by inch. And now it was finally gone. He was no longer under anyone's thumb. Except maybe mine.

I threw my arms around his neck. Soaking up the feel and smell of him so close to me. Clean. He'd always been so clean and so good, even when he'd been forced into dealing Cronus' cards. Now, he was entirely free. No more darkness staining the pure soul within.

I wanted to be that free, that clean, too.

"Thank the gods." It was barely more than a breath, but I knew Ivan heard it.

He pulled back, looking hard into my face. Searching like he always did. "I came as soon as Cap found me. We have to leave. I have a bag packed in my car. You and me. Let's get the fuck out of Arcadia." His voice was warm and pleading and *oh*, how I wanted to cave in and say yes. I could practically feel an island breeze caressing my skin.

I swallowed again, hating the voice inside—*my voice*—that said *no*. "I can't."

Ivan balked. "What? Why the hell not? If one cop spots you, that's it. Cronus isn't going to send you to prison. He's going to kill you. Are you seriously that crazy?"

I pinched the bridge of my nose. Every cell in my body wanted to go with Ivan. I was so tired, so done with all of this bullshit. But I had to stay. I had to see this thing through to the end. "I am *fucking* crazy. You know that."

He scoffed, "So what? You're just going to stay and turn yourself in? Just give up like that?"

I smirked, wishing once more that I had fangs to bare, to prove I was vicious, and wild, and bold enough to really do this. "Who said I was giving up?"

"Ah. The plot thickens. Does my acolyte have a plan?"

You'll just have to wait and see.

Ivan took my hands in his, rubbing his thumbs over my skin. His touch was rough, almost frantic. I could feel the anxiety oozing out of him. "Styx—Calliope. I can't sit by and watch you do something that's going to lead to…I won't just let you walk in there."

I flared my nostrils, trying to keep the burning sensation growing behind my eyes from overtaking me. I'd cried enough in the last twenty-four hours to last a lifetime. "I understand what you're saying, but you don't get to decide what I do or don't do. This is my gig, and I'm seeing it through to the end." I clamped my mouth shut, still actively rebelling against any shedding of tears. Why did he have to go and care so much like that? He was so gods-damned dreamy but *so* stupid.

Ivan nodded, rolling his bottom lip between his teeth. "I wasn't telling you not to do this. What I'm trying to say is—You're not doing this *alone*."

I couldn't believe the words coming out of his gorgeous mouth. "Are we about to get into a fight right now? Because what I'm hearing from you sounds like you want to fight."

He cocked his head. "I don't get to decide what you do? Fine, that's great. I have nothing but respect for your autonomy. But you know what that means?"

"Don't you dare."

He saw the realization dawn on me and grinned, and I wanted to hate how cute he was. "*You* don't get to decide what *I* do." He let go of my hand so he could pat my leg. "See how that works? Now we're on the same level." I scowled; his good nature was so intoxicating I wanted to wrap myself around him. So, I did.

I scooted towards him as I put my legs on either side of his waist. Ivan pulled my foot into his lap while I snuggled up closer. I wrapped my arms around him, leaning my head against his shoulder. He put his cheek against my head, and we stayed that way for a while.

I didn't want to destroy the peace of the moment with plans or discussions, or reality. But peace would only arrive when this mess was cleaned up, and I had a *shit ton* of cleaning to do. The words tumbled out from my lips as I rushed to get them out before I lost my nerve. "You know it's my fault. Tam." I couldn't let it remain unspoken any longer. I was to blame. I would not run from that reality.

Ivan kept his head against mine as he spoke. His voice was low, but it somehow managed to crack. "It's not your fault."

Of course, he would turn this into an argument.

"Yes, it is. I gave him the Ambrosia." There was a heavy pause, and I swore my heart didn't beat the entire time.

Then Ivan said, "I know. He told me. He never could keep a secret."

My stomach turned to rot as I pictured Tam's round face, his eyes alight with humor. I wanted to curse him again for his stupidity, but it was wrong to speak ill of the dead. "He was just a kid."

"He was." Ivan reached up to pat my arm as I continued to hold him like my life depended on it. Part of me was afraid that if I let go, he would run for the hills and never want anything to do with me again. The other part was luxuriating in the feeling of someone accepting me and all my shit, just as I was. Ivan's fingers traced circles against my skin. "It's not your fault. You tried to save him. I tried to save you. It was fucked from the beginning."

I moved to look into Ivan's eyes. I needed him to see how serious I was. "And now it's time to end it."

He reached for my face, cradling my jaw between his hands. "There's something I need to tell you. You're not going to like it." He pursed his lips, waiting for me to do or say anything. But I couldn't. I already knew, deep in my bones.

"It's Lil, isn't it?"

Ivan dropped his hands, leaving me feeling cold and anchorless for the terrifying moments between his next words and the billions of ways Cronus had already tortured her in my mind.

"I think he's using her as bait."

My spit turned to acid in my mouth. "Say that again."

"She's locked down in his house. That's all I know. She was there when I was demoted. Handcuffed to a table."

My blood turned molten inside me. "That's it. I'm going to kill him."

The god in my head hissed, "*No. We're going to kill him. It's been a long time coming.*"

CHAPTER 27

For a moment I wanted to leap from my place and charge down to Olympus, but Ares kept me grounded to the spot.

"Do not be a fool. Wait until your plans are final."

I groaned internally, *I hate waiting.*

"I think you would hate to lose what's at stake even more."

Touché.

Instead of running to my death, I leaned into Ivan. There was one more thing he needed to hear. "So, did you know that Ambrosia is actually like…a recipe of poisons that can allow humans and gods to…" Ivan's eyes bulged so far out of his skull I lost my train of thought. His eyebrows got all bunched up. He stared at me like I'd just grown a second head.

"I almost don't want to know what you're going to say next."

I couldn't help but crack a smile. I shook my head. "When someone takes Ambrosia, a god is invited into their bodies—"

Ivan's lips curled in horror. "What the fuck are you

talking about?"

"This reaction is quite entertaining."

Oh, shut up.

I patted Ivan's back in an attempt to reassure him. "I know it sounds insane. I know. Trust me. I thought I was going insane. Or that Ambrosia was cooking my brain. But no—It's just that Ares?" I cleared my throat for the next part. "Yeah. He's…I'm his Oracle."

Ivan peeled himself away from me as he stood. His head almost reached the ceiling of the trailer, his hazel eyes looked down into mine. "You are an *Oracle?* Like in all those old movies?"

I rolled my eyes. "Kind of. Basically, he's in my head and sharing a bit of his power with me."

Ivan hunched over so he could get a closer look at me. He squinted as he examined each of my eyeballs, nearly smashing our foreheads together in the process. "He's in there right now?"

I rolled my eyes. "Yep. He says hi."

"I did not."

Ivan's olive skin paled, as he rose back to his full height. "Is he…Has he always been in there? Do you ever get any *privacy?*"

My eyebrows rose up and I smirked. "Well…" Ivan's Adam's apple bobbed in his throat. "Yeah, he leaves me alone. Sometimes."

"Can he leave you alone now?"

Can you? My heart started thrumming in my chest. Ares said nothing, but I felt his departure. It was like feeling the absence of someone's hand after they'd been pressing it against you for so long you forgot about it until they moved. After that, there was an odd *roominess* in my head.

I pulled Ivan down beside me, and this time he ended up kneeling awkwardly before me. I pulled my fingers through his curly hair. It was so soft, so clean. I didn't want to care about anything else besides the man kneeling in front of me. I definitely didn't want to care about our impending future waiting to pounce from just outside the camper doors.

Because for all I knew, there was no future. Not for me. There was only *now*. I leaned forward.

Ivan closed his eyes. His lips twitched upwards just once at the corner before they parted. He reached both hands up to cradle the back of my head. He pulled me closer, forcing me to curl at the waist so I could reach his mouth with mine. I couldn't stop the giggle that peeled out of me. Ivan grinned, and our teeth clacked together in a moment of painfully awkward joy. He twisted, dragging me so we were laying down the length of the camper floor. Ivan's legs were tangled up beneath mine. I'd somehow managed to get myself under him.

I could feel the pressure of his chest colliding against mine with each breath he took. I laughed, breathless with anticipation. "All this for a measly kiss?"

Ivan scoffed, "I'll show you *measly*." His fingers traced the shell of my ear before he pulled me once more to him. I stared up into his eyes, the amber in them burning bright enough to scorch. I arched my back, pressing harder against him, my own fingers sliding up the back of Ivan's shirt. He brought his lips to my other earlobe, teasing it between his teeth for just a moment before abandoning that bit of flesh for another stretch, a little lower. His lips grazed my jaw and I shivered. His breath whispered against my skin, sending my toes curling up in my socks.

I turned my face into Ivan's, daring him to kiss me. I couldn't take my eyes off his mouth as it spread into a heady grin. I pressed in closer, until my nose brushed against his. He closed the miniscule gap, his lips finding mine in a crush of heat. He wasted no time as he swept his tongue into my mouth. My hands tangled in Ivan's hair once more, pulling him so that he was completely on top of me. Then he started laughing against my lips.

"What? Why're you laughing?" I didn't know whether to be upset or confused. One look at Ivan's stupid smug face was enough to clue me in.

"I think we can both agree here, that kiss was definitely not *measly*. Yeah?"

I shoved him. "Get off me." Ivan stood then helped me up to my feet. Once we were both on the same level, I looked him up and down, marveling at this feeling of supreme lightness. I said, "I bet you can do better." Ivan's eyes flashed as he grinned, melting me further.

I gripped his shirt, yanking him towards me. It was my turn to prove something and I needed a win, badly. Ivan's hands slid to my waist, pulling me against him. He was a magnet that I'd always been drawn to, never once had I successfully pried myself free of him. Now I didn't want to. My hands went to either side of his face, fingers delicate against his skin. The tiny flecks of gold and green in Ivan's eyes swallowed me whole. I rose up on my toes and took his lips. Gently. It was probably the only moment in my life when I had actually succeeded at doing something delicately. I felt Ivan shiver against me, his hands strong against my lower back. I slid my tongue over his bottom lip, my hands still holding his face, keeping him close.

I could have kissed him over and over for the rest of my life. I could have done a lot more than that, too. But Sylvia's trailer was *so* not the place for anything more… intimate. Instead, I slowly lowered my heels and pulled away. Ivan's face was flushed, the bags under his eyes seemed less stark.

He squinted at me. "Not bad, not bad at all."

I raised my eyebrows. "Not bad? That's all you're going to say?"

He shrugged. "We can keep working on it. I have a few pointers."

"Ha-ha. You're hilarious."

The veil of levity was thin, and within minutes

the mood in the trailer had gone from elation to numbed disillusionment. I sighed through my nose, plopping down on the bench across from my makeshift bed.

Ivan watched me, curiosity plain on his face. "What's it like? Having Ares coexisting inside…you." There was another question hiding just beneath the surface, and I knew what Ivan was really after.

"It's like having an extra loud, somewhat heinous conscience. He does what he can to look out for me. I imagine it might be like having a big brother, except he exists solely between my ears."

Ivan sat down across from me, his knees centimeters from my own. "That actually sounds kind of cool."

I'd never thought of it like that. There hadn't been much time to process what being an Oracle meant, let alone the mere fact that I wasn't crazy—just chosen. There were about a million more layers to peel back before I'd be able to wrap my head around this new form of existence and all that came along with it. For now, I could just be happy that Ares hadn't turned me into a human torch. Instead, he'd decided I was worthy of his time, worthy enough to be his vessel. "I'm still acclimating to the idea that I'm not just a drug-addled lunatic. But yeah, I guess it is kind of cool." I scratched at my scalp, fluffing my hair at the same time.

"And that's why you aren't broken to pieces or dead. Because Ares has been keeping you going."

"Pretty much."

"Huh." Ivan tilted his head, considering me from head to toe. "Seems like a handy thing, being a god's-chosen. So how is Ares going to help us storm Olympus? What's your plan?" He leaned forward resting his elbows on his thighs.

I called the god back to me. *Ares? It's safe, you can return now.*

"Safe? From what? Kisses and pretty words?"

Hey, you're getting the hang of that sarcasm pretty nicely! Good for you.

"Are you talking to him now? Is he in there?" Ivan squinted, looking even more closely at my face. I nodded. "Your eyes go kind of distant. I've noticed it for a long time, but I always thought you were just daydreaming or…"

I smirked, sour yet understanding. "Or high? Yeah, I was. But also communicating with Ares."

"Right."

"Well now that we're all present—I'm planning on busting through the gates, storming the palace, and killing Cronus. Then I'm going to burn it all to the ground. The end. Want to help?"

"A masterful strategy."

Really?

"No."

Ivan and Ares were on the same wavelength it seemed. Ivan's eyes were wide as he said, "That's not a plan. That's you walking to your execution. Come on, Styx. Let's at least *try* not to get killed, okay?"

I rolled my eyes. "I hate to break it to you, but it's just the two of us. This is kind of a suicide mission. No, not kind of—it is. I foresee exactly zero chances of leaving Olympus alive."

I could sense his anger rising up, see it as it turned Ivan's skin a shade of crimson. He spat the words at me, "So you're just giving up?"

His fire fed mine and I scowled back at him. "No, I'm not giving up. I'm facing my fear and I'm going to clobber it until I'm dead."

Ares began chastising me the moment I closed my mouth. *"This is not how you conquer your demons. This is how your demons consume you. Think, Acolyte. What are your resources? Where are your allies? You must have some who would aid you."* A lick of warmth threaded its way through me, a reassuring pat on the back from Ares as he continued, *"Though I admire your tenacity, I would like to see you live past this event."*

Duly noted. But I can't ask my friends to do this. It's only going to end in bloodshed and tears. And I think I cried all mine out.

"Can't or won't?"

Ivan sighed, "I can see that there's some internal dialogue happening here, but I'd like to be in on things too. What's he saying? What're you saying? Don't leave me in the dark."

"Ares said I should call on my *allies*. He wants me to try harder."

Ivan chuckled at my scowl. "I'm with Ares. Where are the girls? What about all those seedy contacts you've made over the last three years? You've got to have an edge on Cronus in that regard at least. We both know the man doesn't often get his hands dirty."

I mulled over his ideas. I did have my fair share of "friends" in the underground. But I was pretty sure most of them would turn me in the second I tried to get in contact with them. Fear only works for so long, and not so much in the "I need your help for free" department. I didn't want to admit it but having Gerty with me would be a real asset. I couldn't do that to Eve though. If something happened to her, Eve would never forgive me. There was Sylvia, who obviously loved me. Maybe she could help me. But how?

I sighed. "The real problem is the minute I turn my phone on to get a hold of anyone, Cronus will be able to find me. Nick's been tracking me with it, and I know he'd jump at the chance to hand me over on a silver platter."

Confusion danced across Ivan's face. "What happened between you and Nick? I thought you guys had an understanding."

I snorted. "I thought so too. But then he tried to kill me." Ivan's brows went down, protective boyfriend mode activated. I held up a hand to illustrate my okay-ness. "Don't worry. As you can see, he did not succeed."

"He did succeed in breaking several of your bones and teeth if I remember."

So what? I'm all better now, thanks to you.

Ivan chimed in, breaking up our internal spat. "I had no idea." He frowned, reaching for one of my hands. My heart fluttered as his fingers slid in between mine, squeezing my hand as they curled around it. "You've been through one storm after another, all by yourself. I'm sorry I didn't know."

Ares murmured, *"Tell him you were not alone."*

There was a brief moment when my tears threatened to fall again, but I managed to hold them back. If there was any more sweetness, I was done for.

"Ares wants me to tell you that he was with me." I squeezed Ivan's fingers back, committing every contour of his face to memory. "And I want to tell you that I'm glad you're here now. I was losing my mind with worry."

He raised an eyebrow. "You were worried? About me?"

"Yeah, you. Who else put my boss, slash your uncle, in a headlock to keep me from getting shot to death?"

Ivan held my knuckles up to his lips. He murmured against them, eyes lowered, "I'm sorry I didn't move sooner. I was… afraid. I was so afraid." He continued kissing my hand and my heart split. Everything about that night had been so terribly wrong. There was so much pain in him. If he hadn't moved, it might have been me bleeding out on the pavement instead of Tam.

There was a long aching silence and then Ares piped in, *"Can we please return to our strategy?"*

Why? Are you embarrassed?

"No. Merely bored."

I detected a hint of frustration from Ares, and I knew he was right to be tense. We couldn't hide out in Sylvia's home forever. I cleared my throat, trying to stifle an inappropriate laugh. I shouldn't tease Ares so much. "I told

Cap to find Eve and Gerty, maybe they can—"

Sylvia's front door slammed inward, and a head covered in gorgeous Mycenaean curls shot through the threshold. The trailer wobbled as Eve made her way up the steps and into the tiny living area. Her hips barely cleared the narrow walkway, but she made a smooth entrance, nonetheless. Her eyes were bright. It took me a moment to realize they were shiny with unspent tears.

"Calliope Lawson, don't you ever scare me like that again. You hear me?" Before I could react, she was shoving Ivan out of the way and pulling me up into her arms. I tried to respond, but my face was buried in her chest. All I could do was hug back.

Ares chuckled. "*Some things are fated. You see?*"

CHAPTER 28

We were running on a skeleton crew, but even though it was just us, even though we were going against the Titans, I wasn't afraid. Like Ares said, I needed to fight my fears. So here I was, fighting. I would go all the way down to hell kicking and screaming if I had to.

When Eve showed up, naturally Gerty had been right behind her. The trailer quickly became stifling with the number of bodies in such a tight space. Condensation collected on the windows, sliding down one tiny bead at a time. Eve's perfume had filled the air around us, floral and spice. It was a comfort to be so completely surrounded by my loved ones, even though the heat was slowly starting to melt my brain. There was a lot of explaining going on, and crying, and angry yelling, but all of it was good. Everything was finally out in the open, with everyone. No more hiding. No more fear.

When it came time to explain the plan, I tried my best to sell it as a suicide mission. I tried to make it sound impossible. But they would have none of my bullshit, even though I wasn't trying to bullshit them at all. I was trying to save their dumb asses. But no.

Gerty slammed her fist against her thigh. "Hell yeah, let's take down these sons-a-bitches. I've never been in a fight that actually mattered."

Eve had perched herself on the counter, her legs swinging back and forth. She scoffed, her expression souring. "You think you get to go and risk your life without me? Hell no."

Gerty's eyes went wide. "But babe, you don't really fight…at all. I don't think I've ever seen you kill a bug. It's going to be a no from me."

Eve leaned forward, eyebrows lowered and ready for battle. "Excuse me? I've killed bugs before. I'm not saying I want to go in there with my fist swinging like you idiots. I want to help. And I'm not getting left behind." Her lips pooched outward, as Gerty ran a hand down Eve's leg to comfort her.

Ivan asked, "Did you get an invitation to the Expo?" The four of us exchanged looks.

Eve said, "Yeah. But is that still happening, now that the Othonos family is crumbling from the inside out?"

We all waited to hear Ivan's response. "You bet it is. Cronus wants to look strong, especially now that he's had his world rocked by little Miss Killer Bee over here."

I blushed at his use of Cap's nickname. "Aw shucks."

Eve adjusted the bangles on her wrists as she glanced between all of us. "So…are we going to a party?"

Ivan grimaced at Eve as he threw his arm around my shoulders. "You're going to a party. And you'll be sneaking us in."

"This was a bad idea. Why couldn't you let someone else pick out your knives?"

My body vibrated with anxiety, but I ignored Eve while I perused the merchandise. Before me was a glass display case, scratched and milky from age. Inside that case were piles of shiny, sharp knives and daggers. My favorite knife had been buried in Cronus' chest, and was no doubt being kept hostage, just like my sister.

Sylvia sent me this way with a promise that the vendor would protect my anonymity. This part of Delos Park was sketchy as hell. I hardly ever made it this deep into the maze of stalls, and that was saying something. This was where the really nasty business went down. Where people got rid of their dirty weapons and traded them for clean ones. Among other things.

Ares was charged like a battery, his excitement circuiting through me like it was my own. *"I like the one with the serrated blade. And the long one. And the one that unfolds. And—"*

If it was up to you, we'd buy the whole case. Pick six.

"Only six?"

How many do you think we need?

"At least an armory's worth."

Okay, well I only have two hands and one body to hide all of those knives.

Ares whined, *"A dozen will have to do."*

I danced on my toes, trying to count out twelve nasty looking knives while Eve checked over her shoulder yet again.

The man behind the counter pressed his palms flat against the glass as he waited, watching though much more discreetly than Eve. After he was sure no one was within earshot he muttered, "Whatever you need. On the house. I've also got some pistols." He turned, pulling a duffle bag up from behind him. "A couple of scavengers pawned them and never came back. I've got ammo too."

He unzipped the faded red bag, revealing a pile of guns in a clutter that made me dizzy. *Guns?*

"I say guns. There will be much blood to spill, and in very little time."

We'd literally be bringing knives to a gun fight. Shit.

Eve looked me up and down. Those big doe eyes of hers honed in on me. "Guns? Really?"

I frowned. "Look. I know. But, without them we're all going to end up dead. And this will just be a suicide mission. With them, we have a slightly better chance of surviving to see another day." I stared her down, knowing full well that she was already regretting her decision to go along on this escapade. Normally Eve wouldn't be caught dead in a place like this, but here she was, standing at my side. I didn't deserve her.

I zipped up the bag. "We'll take everything you've got."

The merchant raised his eyebrows, flushing. "When I said it was on the house, I didn't think you'd be cleaning me out…" There was an awkward shifting from side to side on both ends of the counter while we all thought seriously about how much we would pay to have the Othonos family out of the picture. I started digging through my pockets, and Eve followed suit, even going so far as to dump the contents of her purse onto the countertop.

I shoved the crumpled mound of bills towards the man, and he grinned. "That's enough." He then proceeded to scoop out the entirety of his inventory into the duffel bag already mostly filled with guns. Eve started slapping me on the shoulder, making bizarre whining noises like she was an old radiator struggling to get started.

"What?" I whipped around irritated at her persistent smacking. The wall of man meat who'd kidnapped me from the diner. Cirillo's muscle was walking not twenty feet away from the stall. I turned back toward the vendor, tugging my hood further forward. I tried to swallow but my spit had dried.

"Steady."

The constant rumble of chatter and foot traffic became muted. Except for my breath rattling in my lungs, and my heart as it hammered against my ribs. I had no time to deal with a rival boss getting on my ass about things I no longer gave two shits about. Without thinking, I reached out, taking a hold of Eve's fingers and putting a death grip on them. Her hand cradled mine as we stood still, not daring to do anything but wait. The milliseconds stretched on for eons. But he kept walking. His heavy steps echoed in my ears even after we lost his shape in the crowds.

Eve jiggled my hand at the wrist, yanking me out of my spiral. "C'mon. Gerty's probably losing her mind with worry."

I wiped the sweat from my palm onto my thigh as I tossed the heavier than hell duffel bag over one shoulder. I'd set so many things into motion, without thought, without time to consider the billions of complications and now there was no controlling it, no stopping it. What was to ensue in the next few hours was sure to be a kind of chaos Arcadia had never witnessed.

And it was all because of me.

A little help? Ares didn't respond, but the bag felt instantly lighter as he channeled a tiny bit of his immortal strength into my limbs. The familiar sensation had me curling my toes, but without the inebriation. I had a god fueling me, without the aid of Ambrosia. I nodded at the merchant who'd just handed me so much death and for such a deep discount, too. "Thanks for the hook-up."

"A fine specimen of a man. Clearly, he understands the importance of this bloodletting."

He's probably on Cronus' bad side and wouldn't mind seeing him put six feet under.

"Perhaps. Either way, we are indebted to him. I will not soon forget his good deed."

Lucky him.

Eve's fingers squeezed mine. "What the hell are you

going to do with all *that*?"

I adjusted the duffel strap to keep it from digging into my shoulder. "I'm not using all of them. You and everyone else get some goodies too. Otherwise, it wouldn't be fair."

She stopped dead in her tracks. "Uh-uh. No way I'm getting a knife. People who use knives get cut."

I sighed, hating what was already streaming out of my mouth, even though it was the gods-damned truth. "Yeah, well people without them get killed." I continued walking, until my arm was stretched backwards at an annoying angle, still clutching her fingers. When I looked back, the color had drained from Eve's face. I bit the inside of my cheek. "I'm sorry. But I'm not going to pretend this is a good idea. I don't want you to think for one second that I'll save you. Because I can't." The usual steel in my voice was gone, instead a pathetic, whining thing came out of me. "I'll *try*. But no promises."

Eve inched closer to me, then bumped a shoulder into mine. "Fine. But you better teach me some moves. Otherwise, what's the point?"

She smiled, and I tried to return it, but my stomach was all watery, and my eyes threatened to leak again. Instead I said, "We need to get back." hurrying in the direction of Sylvia's camper.

A bolt of electric awareness went through me. Ares hissed, "*No. We're being followed.*"

I veered, letting our joined instincts lead the way. Eve shouted, surprised by my jerking movement. "Just—Shut up and follow me." I held on to her like my life depended on it, feeling her skin grow slick with perspiration. She was afraid. She should be.

I dared a glance behind us, catching sight of Cirillo's goon. He was at least five stalls away, glaring at me while power walking towards us like he stood a chance. I'd been walking these shabby rows since I was a little girl. I stuck my tongue out at him before I jerked Eve to the side, sliding between a makeshift alleyway and a vendor selling knock off sneakers.

Eve snarled under her breath, her jeans snagging on a rough patch of the wall we inched along as we followed the narrow path. "This is fucking nuts. Is he going to kill you?"

I grunted, still holding her hand with every muscle in every digit. "Us. You mean us."

"Fine. Is he going to kill us?" A vendor with sheared off hair that had been dyed green opened their mouth to scold us for going behind stalls, but I caught their eye and held my pointer finger to my lips. Pleading with my eyes the way Lil always did. Eve caught on, and did the same, instead she held up our joined palms as if offering up our very friendship as proof of our worthiness. The vendor's mouth was agape as they took in the sight of us, crouching now to avoid detection.

They nodded, and then turned back to their wares. Neither of us was brave enough to breathe. To even think of breathing would be to tempt fate in a way I didn't have time for. We heard the telltale foot slaps of a behemoth muscle man, hurried, but not overly fast. He had a lot of weight to haul around after all.

His voice was slightly winded as he asked, "You seen two women come through here? Hoods, one a little scrawny thing, and the other one curves for days." One glance at Eve was enough to know she was very conflicted with this description of herself.

I couldn't help it as I mouthed at her, *For days*. And she bared her bottom teeth like an angry animal, erasing all of the very necessary tension from the air.

Our new green-haired friend replied, "It's been dead here all day. Wanna buy something?" The goon grumbled and jogged past, off to waste his time elsewhere. We waited until the vendor broke the silence again. "He's long gone."

The exhales that escaped our lungs were record breaking. I took in a gulp of air, tasting a hint of brine wafting in from the False Sea. I released Eve's hand, feeling instantly freezing after being kept ridiculously warm by her body heat. Eve followed me. She shimmied out from behind the stall, brushing the dust from her knees and ass. I readjusted my jacket, fixing my hood again. Shrugging my shoulders to get those pesky seams to line up with my body.

I went to the vendor who'd stuck their neck out for us and held my hand out. "Thanks."

They slapped my palm, a crooked grin splitting across their face. "What are you two, runaway lovers or something? That's so old school."

"Ha!" I covered my mouth to keep the rest of my guffaw trapped deep inside my chest.

Eve just rolled her eyes. "You think I'm attracted to this mess? Please." I got a painful side-glare that left me slack jawed.

"Ouch. Well, glad to help either way. Urchins like us should always look out for each other."

I swallowed, turned away. "Let's go, Eve, before somebody else who wants to kill me shows up."

CHAPTER 29

There were few things in my life that were so good I'd do bad things to keep them, and Lil was number one on that list. Every time. Once, when we were just little kids, she'd gotten roughed up pretty good by some pain-in-the-ass neighbor kids. They'd taken her favorite doll, destroyed it, then given tiny Lil a smack or two.

The thing is, Lil never came to me screaming and crying. She never begged me to stick up for her or get vengeance for the wrongs she'd suffered. No. She tried to hide it. Tried to hide when she was most weak, when she actually should have talked to someone who could help.

But me? It was instinct. I was her big sister and the *only* person who should be allowed to smack her around. Even when she deserved it, which was most of the time. Anyway, those kids got their asses kicked, and I got grounded for a week. Lil hated that I'd gotten in trouble for her. She was so upset, she didn't talk to me even after my parents' punishment had ended. Making my sister happy wasn't a strong suit of mine. I was best at protecting her, at retribution. That had never changed. I'd done my duty, and

I'd do it a hundred times over.

I was still doing it.

There were just some things a person was born to do. I was a fighter. It had never been pretty. It had never been easy. I was just too stubborn to figure that out.

My jeans cut into my knuckles as I stuffed my hands deeper into my pockets, trying to keep them from freezing completely. Ivan stood before me, facing Olympus' perimeter fence, while I stared in the opposite direction. The churning green of the False Sea was beginning to make me dizzy, but I couldn't look away. We'd found a spot nestled between a stack of empty shipping containers, hidden from view on the docks. The air was thick with bated frenzy, it was like all of Arcadia stood on her toes, waiting to see this new calamity of the gods as it unfolded.

"Hold steady. This night will be unlike any other. Tonight, we shall feast on the souls of your enemies."

I almost choked. *You do what you like, but I'm not eating anyone's anything.*

"It is meant to stay your courage. A figure of speech, clearly. Acolyte, I must tell you—If there lies in my power a way to win this day, for you, my champion, I will try."

An upwelling of emotion had me grinding my teeth together to keep the tears from reemerging. Ivan glanced down at me, noted my expression with muted curiosity before continuing to survey our surroundings. I blinked the moisture back. In my head, I could see the faintest glow of crimson. Ares' color.

Can you really promise me that? I can't fail again. Too many people have died by my hand or by my complicity. No more.

He sighed, and I imagined him as a wizened soldier, scarred and hardened from battle. Once again there was a moment when our joined psyches became further enmeshed. *"There are many who would say I'm neither true nor trustworthy. I myself do not disagree with these judgments. I'm not beloved or revered. To my brethren and even my own parents, I am wretched. But know this, comrade—I am the best at what I do."*

"You two discussing your battle plans?" Ivan's hazel eyes flitted back and forth between my face and the perimeter. We were close enough that his presence threatened to engulf me. There was so much warmth to him that he'd shoved way down deep to cope with being Cronus' plaything. Just like I had. Now our chains were almost completely broken, the ties nearly severed. There was just this one last, terrifying act. One more bout of blood.

"And glory."

"We are. Trying to focus myself. Are you ready for this? You can still back out. Get the hell out of here before…"

Ivan frowned, and his head jerked back in disgust. "It may not seem like it to you, but I've got my own score to settle. All my life I've been groomed to become a new Cronus. Told how to act, how to treat others, and all of it was just a sham. It meant nothing to my uncles. So long as they had an obedient lackey who was willing to do the extra work while they sat on their asses, getting richer off the blood of innocents." He set his jaw, muscles feathering out before he spoke again. "I'm not going anywhere. This is just as much my fight as it is yours."

I tugged my hands from my pockets and checked all of my weapons for the umpteenth time. Ivan had been able to secure us some flak jackets. My body felt off balance with the weight, but I was grateful for the additional layer of protection. We wouldn't make it very far without them.

The sunlight grew faint, casting long shadows in the heavy violet of winter twilight. Soon. This was all coming to a head, very soon now.

I swallowed, finding my courage a bit easier than usual. I tapped Ivan's boot with my toe. "Whatever happens in there…I want you to know that—Well. What I'm trying to say is—"

"You love me." I clamped my mouth shut, face turning an abrupt shade of red.

I looked up, and Ivan was already staring down at me, his eyes practically lighting up the night. If there was a way to hold this moment frozen just as it was, I would have. But life is not so easy. "Yeah. I do."

Ivan hooked his fingers into my belt loops tugging me to him. "I love you too." His mouth claimed mine, and all the anxiety, the fear, the rage, it all bubbled away. If only just for that kiss. It was a tiny slice of paradise. More delicious than any amount of Ambrosia had ever been.

When Ivan pulled away, eyes once again trained on our surroundings, my heart nearly broke. But I forced it back together. It would be okay. I could keep that kiss for all the time I had left, and it would be enough. Ivan loved me. *Me*. The human tornado. The Killer Bee. And I loved him back.

Something was wrong. Eve and Gerty should have found us by now. It was full dark, and if it weren't for the yellow lights lining the docks, I wouldn't be able to see two feet in front of me. My palms had grown slick with anxiety. What if Cronus had recognized them as my friends? What if they were already dead, tossed in Cronus' lake with his other enemies. Ivan had been trying to keep me calm for the better part of the last half hour, but now his own nerves were wearing thin.

"I can't believe I let them go in like this. This was a terrible plan. I'm such an idiot."

Ivan's voice was clipped with worry. "They agreed to do this, Styx. They wanted to help. It's going to be okay." The violent urge to argue with him fought its way up my throat, but I held it back. I would not allow my last words to this man be words of anger.

"How unlike you to be so withholding."

I'm trying to be a better person.

"Anger is neither good nor bad. It is a purely human reaction, and one I rather like."

Yeah well, I'd rather be angry at someone who deserves it. Know what I mean?

"Very well."

My internal sparring with Ares was enough to distract me for a few moments, but then Ivan went rigid. "Flashlights—in the trees. Told you it was going to be okay." I had no time for a retort, because Ivan had gripped my hand in his, pulling me with him as we half-ran while staying crouched low to avoid anyone spotting us. Ivan lurched to a stop as we waited for the security camera to turn just enough away that we could sneak through, undetected by its lens. When he neared the perimeter fence, the flashlights had been turned off leaving us awash in the blue black of night.

"Styx! Ivan!"

"Human eyesight is atrocious. Try this." There was another trickle of energy, but this time instead of feeling stronger, my eyes sharpened, taking in the barest hint of light. I yanked Ivan's arm, silently warning him to stall. There were *three* people moving towards us.

Ares hissed the words I dared not whisper, *"Betrayed? Who is the third?"*

I squinted, further pushing my god-gifted vision. It was a face I'd only glimpsed briefly, and confusion pooled in my gut.

Gerty's voice rasped in the quiet, "Don't be scared—this is Lil's *friend.* Antony."

Antony? The Spaniard's bodyguard? Ivan and I exchanged stymied looks while Antony pulled out a ring of keys from his back pocket.

As he jimmied key after key in and out of the lock on the gates, Eve and Gerty talked over one another in spastic whispers. Eve started, "Okay so we get there, and there are tons of people pouring through the main entrance, so it's like no problem. Hand the gatekeepers our invitation, and waltz right on in. But then, when we get into the palace, which holy shit—You never told me how *ridiculous* that place was—"

Then Gerty piped in, "Yeah, so we're walking around, trying to make an excuse to leave the building, but it's like guarded to the nines. They wanted everyone inside, and they weren't letting people leave. So, we start panicking, and then we almost run into Nick. So, then we really start panicking."

Gerty tossed her braid over her shoulder, wrapping an arm around Eve, who continued, "So we run up some stairs to avoid him, cause I know he knows me at least. And we duck into this room. Guess who we find in there?"

Both women said, "Lil."

Eve went on, "She tells us to wait, and so we do, and she fills us in on this guy—Antony. He and Lil apparently…" Antony stalled in his jimmying to glare at Eve.

His voice was a deep baritone, shocking us all into silence. "Cronus has her imprisoned, it's a disgrace. I couldn't do anything for her on my own, but with you…"

Eve side-eyed Antony, waiting half a breath before continuing to ramble. "Anyway, we had to wait a lot longer than we thought. But we're here. And we have a new recruit. Pretty neat, huh?" A sly grin curled the corners of Eve's mouth. She was enjoying this just a little too much.

"Ah! Got it." The chains slid to the ground with a metallic tinkling as Antony pushed the gate open. As I sidled past him, I couldn't help but glare. The protective sister in me wasn't about to let some random guy sweep Lil off her feet.

I growled, "Where's Lil? Why didn't she come with you?" And I didn't care one bit how mean I sounded.

Antony acknowledged my vehemence with the tuck of his chin. "I thought it best to keep up the ruse, for now. As far as Cronus is aware, I'm taking two lovely ladies out for a bit of moonlit *fun*." Gerty giggled like a schoolgirl, but Eve elbowed her in the gut, sending the remaining laughter out in a whoosh.

My mouth curved in a downward arc, impressed. "Okay, that was actually pretty smart. Let's not waste any more time." Ivan dropped the duffel he'd been hauling, and unzipped it as I squatted beside him, pulling out guns, knives, and two more Kevlar vests. I doled it all out to the three stooges before I helped Gerty and Eve strap their vests around themselves.

There was a moment when all of us stood in a half-formed circle. Antony was imposing in a navy suit with his gold watch barely visible beneath his sleeve. His eyes were dark, but in them I saw only honesty. Gerty stood next to him, lithe yet muscled, her suit cut to fit her figure exactly. Eve looked like she was ready to hit the runway, not a massacre, with glammed hair, cat eye makeup to the nines, and so much glitter it was kaleidoscopic in the starlight. And then Ivan and I, who'd come ready for battle. We'd leaned into the operative look, wearing only black, and covered from head to toe in murderous tools. Everyone glanced around at each other, our eyes connecting us in some profound way that none of us would likely forget.

I grinned, feeling the immortal fires of Ares stoking my adrenaline. Heat filled my veins, boiling my blood, sending me deeper into that place where I was a warrior, a deadly threat to any mortal. "Whatever happens—Get Lilith out. And leave Cronus to me." Each person found their courage and their eyes went steely with it. There was nothing left to say. Only actions mattered now.

We walked in silence, hiding in the shadows behind the rows of empty bungalows lining the streets of Olympus. His whole village of goons was in on tonight's festivities. From the sounds of it, there were likely to be hordes of partygoers. And most of them had at least some part in the shady dealings of the Othonos family business.

I warned Ares, "*Anyone who gets in my way is going down. There are no innocents tonight.*"

This is the very same view I hold. What a night it shall be.

My body thrummed with Ares' power. I'd never felt more honed. I was like a blade, ready to cut the world to ribbons.

CHAPTER 30

The circle driveway in front of Cronus' palace was lined in red carpet. It was truly a gala event. There were twinkling lights and flowers the likes the world had never seen covering every surface. We could hear the band performing from where we stood at the edge of the property. Like Gerty and Eve had said, all the attendees seemed to be packed like sardines inside. There were only a few meatheads at the main entrance, some goons I knew well enough to stay away from, checking invites of the last few stragglers.

Antony whispered, "I'll go in first, try to get Lilith out."

"Hey, only I get to call her that." I threw a scowl his way.

He scowled right back at me. "She told me to call her Lilith, and that's what I'm calling her."

"Give her this—" I hated that I liked him already. I pulled a gun from my back pocket. I had more than enough on me to get the job done and I was not leaving my sister undefended. Antony nodded before taking the gun in his massive hand.

I started moving towards the side entrance. Gerty and Ivan followed but Eve stood motionless behind us. Gerty turned to her. "Babe? Are you okay?"

Eve's shoulders tremored. Her eyes pinned to the ground in front of her. "No. I'm not okay. Are we really doing this? Can't Antony just get Lil and leave? Can't we all just get the fuck out of here?" Gerty looked to me, then back at her girlfriend, begging for me to intervene. Eve had been so insistent, so gung-ho about this idiot operation, but it had been a facade. I couldn't blame her, not in a million years.

I sighed, feeling a tiny bit of relief at my friend's hesitation. "*You* don't have to do this. You have done more than enough. You can go home and wait for us. It's okay Eve. Really." Her eyes welled up with tears when she looked into my face.
Gerty went back to Eve, pulling her into her arms, resting her cheek on Eve's head. She whispered something in her ear, then leaned down to kiss her. I looked away, trying to give them as much privacy as possible.

There was a moment of shuffling awkwardly while we waited. I turned as Eve stepped back, tucking her hands into her coat pockets. "I'll be waiting with Sylvia. You'll come back soon, right?" Her eyes scanned each of our faces. My stomach twisted inside me, reminding me that I was just a puny human with a big mushy heart that didn't want to see the people I loved get hurt.

I opened my mouth to say *no promises*, but Ares commandeered my vocal cords in a move that both infuriated and surprised me. Our voices twined together as they escaped my lips, but I don't think anyone else noticed. *We* said, "Yes."

A promise.

"*Apologies. But I gave my word, and I will not have you sullying my reputation with your doubt.*"

You also gave your word that you would never do that again.
"Did I? I don't think I did. I'd remember that."

I almost laughed, but Eve's warm brown gaze forced me to remember my stoicism. She was about to watch her nearest and dearest walk into a maelstrom of death and chaos. I couldn't handle it anymore, the hurt in Eve's eyes. The fear. So, I turned back towards the palace, leaving her behind.

"This is not a procession of the dead. We shall be victorious."

Instead of voicing my fears, I remained silent. Eve was going to live and that would be fine enough. One less person for me to worry about.

Ares must have lended me a boost to all my senses because as we neared the kitchen entrance, I could hear Ivan and Gerty's breath. They didn't seem panicked, though they both had clearly elevated pulses. The air felt charged. Every single thing had become alive with the anticipation of battle. I felt it down in my very bones.

The band's vocalist started wailing and Gerty perked up. "I know this band! I saw them last month. Let's try not to hurt them, okay?"

I sighed. "Fine. The band gets to live." Ivan pushed ahead of me, brazenly looking through the kitchen door. I hissed, "Are you crazy?"

"What? If Marla's working, she'll let us in. She's like my second grandma." He shrugged.

Gerty and I swapped incredulous glances. "Whatever."

Ivan pressed his face against the glass and his eyes lit up. He waggled his fingers at someone on the other side, then the door was opened for us by a plump woman who had to be in her early sixties. She was rosy faced and perspiring quite heavily. When she saw Ivan had brought friends, her eyes narrowed. "What's going on, Ivan? If Cronus sees you, he's going to lose his marbles. And who are these…"

Our eyes caught and—*Shit*. She recognized me.

My body could hardly contain the surge of adrenaline that arrived with the impending chaos. If I had to go in swinging, I would, but that didn't mean I *wanted* to. Now that I knew this person meant something to Ivan, I had to keep my bloodlust caged…for now.

Marla pointed at me. "*You*. Oh, no. No, no, no. You are in big trouble, Missy. Big trouble. The boss wants your head on a stake. You can't be here. None of you can be here." She started pushing at Ivan, pushing him back out the door and into the dark.

I put my foot down, literally and metaphorically. "Sorry, lady. But we're coming in. And if I was you, I would get the fuck out while you still can."

Marla glanced nervously at Ivan who was now glaring at me for insulting his Nana, or whatever. "She's right, Marla. *Rude*, but right. It's time. Cronus is going down."

Wary understanding filled her ruddy expression. She looked like she might've swallowed a golf ball, but she nodded and started untying the strings of her apron. "Give me two minutes."

"*No. She cannot be trusted.*"

I grunted, moving to stand in her way. "That's not going to work. You're either in or you're out. What's it gonna be?"

Ivan's face went red as he grabbed my arm. "Styx. She just wants to tell the sous chef she's leaving. Can't she do that?"

"You think she's *not* going to go tell her boss we're here? *Really*?"

Gerty stepped forward, silencing us both with her towering presence. "Stop arguing." She stuck a calloused hand out towards the cook. "Marla, is it?" Marla nodded and Gerty went on. "You got thirty seconds. Any funny business and I'll take you down." Marla surveyed Gerty from her toes, up, up, up, and into her icy blue eyes. Then she whipped into the kitchen and out in a flash that would make Hermes jealous.

As she hurried past us, she whispered to Ivan, "Don't drink the champagne. He's done something to it. Cronus is…He's not well right now." There was a mixture of regret and shame mingling in Marla's eyes. I hadn't thought of toasting champagne before annihilating the Othonos mob. Too bad the option was off the table.

With Marla out of the way, I stormed through the doorway into a steamy kitchen that was bustling with line cooks shouting at each other, and bussers rushing back and forth with trays full of dainty food. My mouth watered for a moment as I caught wind of something delicious sailing past us.

"Focus on your battle. We will celebrate the spoils of this night after it is finished. First, we must do what we have intended."

You'd think I would still be full after all the food Sylvia's been stuffing down my throat.

Ares chuckled, and it soothed my rankled nerves just a little. *"You would think."*

I looked to my left and right, realizing I was flanked by Gerty Galantis, the Amazon of Arcadia, and Ivan Diamantis Othonos, the right hand of the Number One Titan. Any fear that lingered in me was quickly dissipating. We were mortals, but we were also legends in our own right.

"Do not forget who they are walking beside."

I imitated a ring announcer in my head, *Oh right, Ares, god of discord and bloodshed. The mightiest of the big twelve!*

"I'm flattered, acolyte. But I meant you. A human who has gone to great lengths for survival, and for justice. An Oracle. Blessed by the gods."

My heart swelled, but I maintained my cool. *Aw, if I wasn't preparing to murder swaths of people just now, I would be* so *emotional. Can you say that to me later?*

"It was meant for now."

So that's a no.

Gerty pulled out a pair of brass knuckles, sliding them over her fingers, and Ivan took a gun in one hand, and a blade in the other.

What do you want to start with?

"Guns. Start with the guns. Save the blades for the second wave."

I did as Ares said, grabbing two pistols. I mentally cursed my dad for never taking me to the shooting range when I was a kid. Training his daughters to defend ourselves with our hands had been his only priority. I'd never actually shot a gun…But I'd seen plenty of other people do it, *and* I was *Makarios,* so that had to count for something. Right?

I raised my foot to kick down the door when a great rumble of applause stopped me in my tracks. The drummer hit their cymbals, and then all was silent.

Cronus' voice rumbled throughout his palace. "It is my great pleasure to welcome you all to my home, Olympus. Tonight, we celebrate *your* dedication, your contribution to the successes of the Othonos family." There was a round of muted cheers and delicate clapping. "Because of you, we own this city *and* the people who live here."

Cronus' tone took on a sour note and I imagined his eyebrows crinkling, eyes icing over with disdain. I'd seen that look so many times. Hated it with all my might. He continued, a shiver running down my spine at his next words. "There are some who think to steal our claim, our glory." Tension began building from the guests. I could almost feel it through the kitchen door. I imagined the look that would be on Cirillo's face. Her red lips curled in a sneer.

Cronus seemed to sense it as well. "But those

people, they forget that because of *me*, the gods walk again. Because *we* are gods. We are the gods of Arcadia. Of all of Mycenae!" There was an awkward beat of heavy silence before the crowd understood that applause was warranted. Cronus' voice boomed once again, "Cheers! To the new Olympus!" People began shouting and cheering over the sound of hundreds of glasses clinking together. The band kicked up again and the din of the party swallowed the strangeness of his speech.

I exhaled, rolled my shoulders. With Ares' full power behind me, I easily thrust my boot through the door, ripping it from its hinges. Ivan and Gerty followed closely beside me. Both held their weapons raised and ready for killing. But then the screaming started.

At first, I thought it was because of us. But the screams came from everywhere. The foyer, staircase, the dining room. Then came shattered glass as people started seizing. Some fell to their knees, their eyes rolling back into their skulls. Others simply froze, squeezing their head with their hands as if trying to stop their brains from coming out of their ears.

The band stopped in a discordant wave as one by one each musician dropped their instrument, falling to the stage. Cronus remained beside them; arms crossed over his chest. The look on his face was disgustingly smug. His eyes were frosted with maniacal glee. Then he saw us.

His smug grin turned acidic, and I imagined his own set of fangs elongating behind his lips. "Nephew, I see you've brought our honored guest. Perfect timing."

Ivan yelled, gesturing with his gun at his uncle, "What did you do? Poison the champagne?"

From the corner of my eye, I saw a man stumble as he rose to his feet. He looked down at his palms like he was trying to see something that wasn't there. Cronus laughed. "Poison? It's only poison if you're weak enough to die from it." The man continued staring at his palms while my instincts began screaming out. I recognized myself in that man, in his stance, the wild gleam in his eye. *Fucking shit.*

"I gave out the ultimate party gift. The gift of power." Cronus held his arms out wide like he was welcoming us in for a hug.

My mouth swung open as the man to the right started vibrating, and then smoke began pouring from between his teeth. Sparks fizzled from his fingertips. All at once blue streaks of lightning shot from his palms, zinging around the room, shorting out the electricity in one violent arc that put us all in darkness for a single terrifying moment when there was nothing but the screams of agony as a drug meant only for communion with the gods tore through their innards.

When the lights shuddered back to life, more and more people began rising up, their eyes alight with the high of Ambrosia. Some were visibly sizzling as the god within them grappled for their very soul.

This is a fucking shit show.

CHAPTER 31

When my mom would put Lil and I to bed, she would tell us stories about the Pantheon. I'd imagine winged beings, blazing swords clashing together during chariot races. Creatures so beautiful and all powerful they couldn't possibly exist anywhere outside my imagination.

I had to blink twice to be sure that what I was seeing now wasn't just some awful dream from the past that I'd somehow fallen into.

There was drug induced chaos all around us, as partygoers became puppets for the gods inside them. I saw several familiar faces, people I'd threatened into working for Cronus. A woman on the staircase howled as she held out her hands, flowers and vines erupting from her palms like she was herself a living plant. Several people below her were quickly engulfed in the swelling greenery, struggling to free themselves from the vines that were wrapping around them faster than they could move.

There were two people tumbling through the air, careening left and right, up and down. Colliding together before slamming down to the floor. A deafening crack told me at least one of them wouldn't be getting up, not anytime soon. I caught a glimpse of crimson, and saw M with that damned Meathead again, but they held no champagne glasses. Instead, he was shielding her from the onslaught as he guided Cirillo towards the front doors to safety.

Cronus cackled, the sound echoing across the room, dragging my attention towards him. He nodded at me. "I'll find my new champion, and you Styx—You will die." He pulled a gun from his pocket, aiming for my heart. I moved, darting away from Ivan and Gerty who had begun to grapple with the hoard of unhinged party guests.

Cronus fired his gun, not caring when one of his stray bullets found a home in a woman's shoulder who was slowly transforming into a bear. His bullet didn't stop her transformation and, in a moment, she was a beast, massive and roaring in pain. The bear woman turned and sprinted on all fours towards Cronus, who looked completely dumbstruck.

That made two of us.

"We can use this to our advantage. Remember what Sylvia said? The gods do not condone this reckless summoning."

How the fuck do I get them to focus enough to do something about it?

"On your left!"

Nick was shoving his way through the crowd, his face swollen and bruised. The gaping hole where his eye should have been hidden with a black patch. He bellowed, "You. You die now."

I aimed my guns at Nick, "I don't think you're seeing the situation clearly enough."

"Less banter, more killing."

Fine.

Nick sneered but wasted no time throwing *my own fucking knife* at me. I narrowly avoided it, sliding to the left just as it flew past my arm. I fired my piece and Ares let out a warrior's whoop. My body absorbed the jolt of power that threatened to push me back. Nick roared, grabbing at his shoulder as it began spurting crimson onto the floor.

"Again! Again! But aim this time!"

I'm trying.

I closed one eye, hoping that would somehow get me the angle I needed, but before I could squeeze the trigger, something—*someone* slammed into me, tossing me to the ground. My gun slipped from my hand, skittering between two people nearby who'd been laid out by Ambrosia. I yelled, "What the fuck?"

It was Gerty. She was holding me down with one arm while she looked around, her eyes bright from the violence. "Cronus was aiming for you, sorry! You said you wanted him. You better go get his ass before he takes you down. Go!" She hauled me up, and immediately raised her fists to Nick, who was stalking toward us. I wasted no time and began forcing my way through the mob to the stage. When I tried to find my mark, he was nowhere to be found. There was Ivan, using his knife against a man who looked like he'd grown three feet taller. I didn't have time to wonder which god was responsible for that.

Ares growled in my head. It was the voice of a commander rising above the melee in order to give orders. *"Use me. Use me to make the gods heed you. Champion of Ares, Oracle of Discord. Now is your time."*

Okay. I got this.

I climbed over several broken bodies still hot from burning out and pulled myself up onto the stage. I looked out at the crowd—a writhing mass of magic and blood. Humans mingling with power they thought was only a myth.

I took the mic in my hands and let our voices meld together. Ares channeled his might through me, and I became a living flame. The Oracle of Ares.

"Listen. Hear me!" I waited until the hoard took notice. Several people locked in combat froze, possibly sensing the divine presence within me. "I speak for Ares. God of war. God of Bloodshed." I held my knife out in front of me, like a torch to light up the dark. "Too long has this man, this *weakling* Cronus, claimed to be a god. No—more than a god. A Titan. He summoned you here as nothing more than a party trick. To mock your true divinity." As I spoke, our voices rumbled out of me. It sounded like the clash of steel, the thick of battle.

I plunged my knife into the air, as if I was stabbing Cronus myself and Ares thundered through me. For an instant, I was his Oracle well and truly. "We must destroy him. The gods can no longer abide by this treachery. Yes. We walk among mortals once more. Let's remind them of our might. Let them never forget the will of the gods is our own." There was a strange pulsing of energy. Like every person and the god dwelling within them seemed to hear, seemed to understand what must be done.

Someone in the crowd shouted, another unearthly voice, another god using a mortal's body as a mouthpiece. "Will you lead us? Where is this human traitor?"

I nodded, feeling a surge of burning ecstasy racing through my veins. "Destroy any who stand in our way. But do not leave this compound. Do not maim an innocent. The Othonos Family are Titans no longer." I held my fists aloft as I screamed a battle cry unlike any other. My blade ignited, burning ruby with the passion of Ares. I leapt from the stage, charging for where I was sure Cronus had barricaded himself. His study.

There were still humans collapsing left and right. Those who remained standing had either had enough of a taste that they weren't in danger of overdosing, or they were like me—*Makarios*.

There was an odd unification among us. It was a kind of agreement that made the hoard more stable as we surged like a battalion through Cronus' palace. "Search every room! Bring him to me!" As I shouted, I scanned the crowd for my companions. Ivan was now walking with the overly large man, and Gerty was with a smaller group, charging up the stairs. We were all still standing, for now.

My blades still burned, but there was no heat to blister my skin. Behind me a growing crowd of Makarios stormed through each doorway, ransacking room after room, destroying all of Cronus' spoils. There were no people hiding, no one trying to escape. Everyone was either already dead, or currently inhabited by a god. Everyone except for Cronus. The crowd behind me thinned out as I directed people to search different areas of the house. Soon, I was left on my own, stalking ever closer to his private study.

"Will you shoot him, or will this be more…interesting?"

I could feel the lust for revenge growing inside me. The urge to do very very bad things to the man who'd forced me to wallow in the blood of his foes.

I'm going to kill him, and then he's going to be dead. That's about as far as I've thought.

"Very well. The man deserves a wicked end."

I could hear stomping feet above me as people stormed room after room on the second floor. There were crashing sounds and whoops from those who were destroying all Cronus held dear. His world of things, his power, was collapsing, one room at a time. I let myself enjoy the realization that brick by brick, it was being torn to pieces. I sprinted the last distance, hating to put off a Titan-free future for any longer. My fingers curled around the doorknob before I wrenched it open and lunged inwards.

Empty. The room was perfectly in order. Quiet, still. I stood for a moment, raging silently at his disappearance. He could *not* get away. What would be the point of this without Cronus' corpse to show for it? I took my flaming dagger, and held it to his desk, carving my name into the ebony wood.

Not *Styx,* my moniker of death, bestowed upon me by my captor, but my real name. The name my mother and father had chosen for me.

CALLIOPE

As I dug each letter into the desk, the wood began

to smolder, and then in moments it was engulfed in flame. I walked out of the room and shut the door behind me.

As the catch clicked shut, I heard Ivan screaming.

And then I was running as though my feet had been turned to wings. His voice echoed my name in a frenzy, and I knew where he was. The receiving room. The throne room.

I tripped over a pile of downed people, nearly tumbling to the ground in my haste, but I quickly righted myself as I continued careening toward Ivan. Toward my fate. I knew that whatever lay in that room, whoever lay in that room—this was it. My moment.

Ivan hollered again, "Styx! Get in here!" and I tried to get to him, but then a burst of pain exploded in my side, sending me sprawling. I slammed into a wall, mere feet from the entrance to the throne room as something metallic clattered to the floor.

My hand went to my hip and came back wet with blood. "Gods-damn it Nick, how many times do I have to kick your ass for you to get it?"

The bastard had thrown another knife at me. Nick looked insane as he pushed his oiled black hair out of his furious eye. He yelled, "You're not leaving here! Tonight, you die. I don't care if I go down with you, but your time is up. *Styx*. The ferryman has called your number."

Ares began channeling strength to my injury, and I seethed through the burning sensation. "Not that I wouldn't love to take you down myself, it's just that I've got bigger fish to fry." I started to walk away to make Nick think I was really dumb enough to turn my back on him, but I twisted, pivoting toward him as I put my whole body into throwing the six-inch blade from my hand. It slid deep inside Nick's gut, right above his belly button. He groaned while his fingers curled around the hilt, yanking it out with one watery squelch.

I curled my lip. "You know they tell you not to do that…"

He slumped to his knees, one hand pressing against his wound while the other searched his pockets for something else to hit me with. He came up wanting. A rasping sound escaped his throat, one that whispered of lungs filling with blood.

That was a killing blow. He'll certainly die now.

Ivan shouted again, "Styx, get the fuck in here!"

I replied, "I'm coming!" and started moving towards his voice. I checked my personal arsenal, still hanging on to my knife in one hand, and the second gun in my left.

You are ready. Face your fear. Fight it to the death.

I'm ready. Let's do this.

Once again, I was submerged in an endless well of fiery power as Ares stoked the flames of my rage, my need for vengeance. I walked through the grand hall, noting the smudges of blood coating the once pristine walls and marble floors. Cronus sat in his favorite seat. His hair was in disarray, but it was the only visible sign that he had lost his edge. I knew him well enough now to see that this man was off. A rat cornered by a fighting dog.

"Hi." For the first time in my life, I was not afraid of this man. I did not cower or avert my gaze. I stood tall like a warrior queen. A wicked grin split my face as I stalked slowly towards my prey. Cronus' eyes flashed, the average person would have missed it; the slight widening, the dilated pupils, but I—with my god's eyes—could see. It was Cronus who was now afraid.

I glanced around the room and saw Ivan, holding a gun aimed at Cronus. But that's when it got sticky. It wasn't just the three of us. My heart dipped low into my stomach. Crius was holding a gun to Ivan with one hand, and in the other hand, he held a knife up to Lil's throat. On the floor behind them was a crumpled pile of what looked like Antony.

No, no no no. It was all the same, I'd been here before, and I'd be here again and again. It would never end.

I was like Sisyphus rolling that gods-damned rock up the hill for eternity.

Ares' voice boomed inside me. *"Silence. You are no coward. No weakling could be immense enough to hold the god of war inside them. This ends tonight, and it ends when you say it does. Now, fight. Fight to the end."*

I exhaled, breathing out the fear, and sucking in a lungful of dogged determination. *This is not my end.*

"Fight!"

Without thought, without a lick of terror, I pointed my gun at Crius and fired, sending a bullet directly between his eyes. Lil screeched as Crius fell, head only partially intact. Ivan yelled as Cronus started running. I began sprinting after him but was knocked flat on my face by a mammoth force from behind.

My chin slammed into the marble floor, cracking several teeth. I spit a pearl of blood out, smiling when I saw how it marred the white marble even more. The weight remained, but I was able to maneuver myself, so I was facing whoever had pummeled me.

"Are you fucking serious? You should be dead, like three times over." I grunted out the words, angry and surprised at Nick's reappearance.

He held a knife to my neck, pushing the blade so that it bit my skin. I knew he was drawing blood. I knew he was going to kill me then. I tried to bring my hand up, the one holding my gun, but his knee was lodged in the crook of my elbow, forcing it to remain on the ground. "I told you, and I meant it. I'm going to kill y—" There was no opportunity for him to continue his sentence. A shot rang out and he flopped on top of me, completely limp. It was only a matter of moments until Ivan started tugging his corpse from me. There was no time for thanks, for anything. We were so close to this being the end. My boot slipped on the blood I'd spit on the floor, and I fell back on my ass.

I looked around, screaming. "Where's Cronus?

Where's Lil?" Ivan looked just as bewildered as I was, but then he pointed out the window. Towards Cronus' lake. A lone spotlight shining on the fountain in the center of it traced the silhouettes of two figures—A man in a fine suit dragging a long-legged blond who was flailing in protest every step of the way. He'd slipped through a back door. Coward.

I shot through the window, shattering the massive panes of glass, and leapt through my new exit. Flashes of our first night in this place danced behind my eyes, but I shoved them out. I needed to be present. All that mattered was now.

I raced through the dewy grass, screaming, "Cronus, you let her go right now and I promise I'll kill you quickly." Cronus said nothing, didn't even acknowledge my presence, only kept dragging my little sister in a semi-head lock towards the icy waters ahead. Lil let out a horrendous yowl. There were no words, nothing but endless rage spewing from her lungs into the night.

"I said, stop!" I shot my gun, too stupid with fury to be afraid of hitting my sister while we were moving, and I managed to clip his right leg. Cronus yelled out but stumbled only a step. It wasn't enough.

As he neared the shore, he whipped around, jerking Lil with him. "You're too much of a coward to end it." He shook Lil while she scratched and clawed at his arm locked around her, like an animal ready to bite its own leg off to be free. "This idiot sister of yours is why I own you. You'll do anything for her. I've seen it. Over and over."

I froze. My gun still pointed at his head. Now terrified to risk Lil's life in the crossfire. "What do you want?" A chill began to weed its way into my bones that had nothing to do with the winter night.

"Do not yield to him. Do not give in to your fears."

I ignored Ares, instead waiting to hear what Cronus had to say. He kept walking backwards, his feet dipping into the water, then his knees. "I promise not to drown her, if you let me live." He hissed as the lake water lapped at his bullet wound.

I looked into Lil's eyes and saw in them something I'd never seen before, never bothered to see until now. Then back at Cronus, who was clearly out of his mind. His face twisted, horror flashing across his once handsome features. "You lit my fucking palace on fire!" I glanced back, and sure enough, the back of the house was beginning to glow, flames slowly eating up every bit of Cronus' worth. "Oops."

He thrashed, squeezing Lil as he pulled her deeper into the lake. Her exposed legs had to be stinging with the frigid water. She didn't cry out, didn't start begging for her life. A curtain of steel had enveloped her.

I swallowed before I shouted, "If you let Lil go, I promise not to kill you."

"What? Is this a ruse?"

Cronus scoffed, his eyes wild, tremors running up and down his body. "Please. Why should I trust a lowlife like you?"

Ideas raced around in my skull, each one more insane than the last. I searched our surroundings, looking to see if Ivan was anywhere nearby. He must not have followed us. Ares was silent in my skull, the lone witness to this last transgression. I inhaled, then pushed my words into the air like a fist, aiming directly for Cronus. "I swear on my family's honor. On the Lawson seal." I held my hand over my heart, in an act of supreme stupidity.

Cronus stared, from my hand to my face, and back. Trying to see the lie. When he saw there was none, he began to laugh. Cackling like an old lunatic. He released Lil, pushing her forward. She stumbled but found her balance. She kept her eyes on me the whole time while Cronus hooted in victory and began splashing in the lake like a child enjoying his own pool party.

"To what end?"

Just watch.

273

I nodded at my baby sister. She nodded back. Lil twisted in a low crouch, pausing to stare up at the man who'd wrought so much humiliation and pain upon her. She swept Cronus' legs out from under him, pinning him beneath the frigid water with her body. Lake water lapped at her chest as she used her full weight to keep him down. She grappled for his neck as he thrashed, sending waves of icy lake water cascading around them. Cronus almost broke free for a single gulp of air. He gasped in shock, flecks of spittle mingling with lake water flew around Lil. But she did not flinch.

Instead, she held him up for a moment in a feat of strength that surprised even me. Her hands wringing around his neck as she spat back in his face. "My name is Lilith, *not* Lily. You fucking piece of shit." Then with every ounce of strength in her, she shoved him beneath the water, holding him there with every muscle, every fiber of her being until his thrashing ceased. She kept her hands submerged beneath the water until it had settled completely. My little sister, a force of reckoning in her own right.

The spell broke and I ran into the lake to help her. Lil wrapped her arms around me as she sobbed, "I did it. I did it. We're free." My own cheeks had grown damp with tears I thought had been rung dry. There was too much to feel, too much to let go of, but here we were, doing our best.

Cronus was dead.

It wasn't the ending I had imagined—it was so much better.

CHAPTER 32

I smoothed Lil's hair away from her face. "You did it, babe. Now let's get the fuck out of here." She nodded, her body vibrating with the exhilaration that comes only after vanquishing one's enemy. I tugged off my coat and threw it around her. She wasn't that scrawny little pain in the ass kid anymore. She'd grown into herself and like it or not, she'd taken after me more than I'd thought possible. I wrapped my younger sister in my arms, feeling for the first time in three years that there was nothing between us.

We shuffled to the front of the mansion that was still ablaze, though firefighters were actively combating against the flames. Dozens of people coming down hard from their forced Ambrosia highs were huddled on the ground, wrapped in coats and emergency blankets. My heart suddenly ached for each and every soul that never made it out of Cronus' palace. They'd come for a party and ended up the victims of a lunatic. No more, no more death would come from this place. Never again.

My eyes scanned the scene, looking for my Amazon and my reformed gangster. Gerty was standing with her phone to her ear, one hand on her hip. She didn't appear to have a single injury. I knew who she was talking to without hearing her conversation. The one person who needed to know she was alright.

Ivan was talking with a firefighter and several police officers, running his hands through his hair again and again as he tried to explain the events of the night. How long had it been? I suddenly found myself itching for a watch. Maybe knowing the time might ground me, bring me back down to the mortal world where I was just a person, nothing more.

"You are more. So much more. Oracle. Miracle of Malice. Deity of devastation."

Oh, come on, I'm no deity. Just your faithful comrade trying to make you proud. There was an awkward breath and then I had to ask, *Did I make you proud? I'm sorry if I had you worried there.*

Ares replied, cool as steel, *"I did not realize your sister could fight. I was worried, yes, but now I am proud. Very proud. Comrade."*

A new kind of warmth filled me from within. It was still Ares, yes, but this time it wasn't rage or discord. It was friendship. And I welcomed it. The feeling faded away quickly however, when Lil's grip around me tightened.

She whispered, "We need to get out of here. Now. Like, right the fuck now." She started leaning against me, pushing me towards our cottage, away from the glare of police lights and flames.

A baritone sounded from behind us, and Lil lit up like a sparkler. "You're alright. Thank the gods."

Even though I didn't want to let her go, I relinquished my grip on Lil so that she could dive into Antony's open arms. Her face was glowing and something I'd never seen before danced across her eyes.

Lil pulled away from him and said, "The cops can't find us. We have to go." Antony looked around, most likely searching for his boss.

Then he nodded. "Right. I've got a car. I'll meet you at your place. Go." He pressed a kiss to my sister's temple before storming towards Leon, who was among those with EMT's rushing around them. I hadn't seen him in the thick of it all, but it looked like he'd been in on the champagne toast just like everyone else.

Lil reclaimed her place by my side, and without another glance, we raced to our cottage. I knew Ivan would understand, after he'd gotten the anger out of his system, anyway. He was too good to be anything but supportive.

The streets of Olympus were deserted, turning slick as the evening dew turned to frost. Lil and I were silent as we hustled towards the place that had been our home for the last three years. The only thing that had felt even remotely ours, or safe. We held hands, both of us gripping the other with all we had in ourselves. There were no thoughts in my mind. For once, it was quiet.

The house was dark, and we kept it that way. Best to avoid any chance of detection when we were so close to freedom. My eyes still held Ares' power within them, making navigating the space easy. But I found myself standing still, absorbing every inch of wall, every nook and cranny. It was just another cell, another prison we'd been forced into, and now this was it. We were leaving.

Lil wasted no time, running to her room to presumably throw her clothes and things in some kind of bag. The sound of drawers slamming and hangers slapping against each other echoed in my ears, but still, I couldn't move. My tongue had gone fat in my mouth. I became stupid with relief.

"You need water. The battle has ended, and you are weary."

I heeded Ares' suggestion and made my way to the kitchen where I chugged a glass of tap water, then another while I leaned against the sink. My eyes traced across the scene of palm trees swaying over a hula girl that had always hung above the stove.

"A warrior deserves to rejoice in the spoils of war. Where are your spoils? How will you rejoice?"

I don't deserve to rejoice, Ares. I'm a wanted criminal. I should be in prison. A couple times over now.

Ares' color bloomed behind my eyes, a hazy scarlet, the color of the ancient soldiers of Mycenae. *"I believe this night you have found your redemption. Are you truly so afraid to claim it?"*

I set my glass on the counter, frowning. *Claim what? What is left for me? What do I even want? I feel…*

"Revenge is a task that is beautiful in the doing, but after the work is finished, we are left wanting."

Yeah, pretty much.

Lil emerged from her room wearing jeans and a wool coat with three duffel bags slung around her shoulders. "Are you ready?"

My brows creased, and I found that I didn't understand. "Ready for what?"

Lil looked me over, a mixture of concern and annoyance danced over her features. She blew a wayward strand of hair out of her face. "To leave. You and me. Just for a little while." She tugged something out of her pocket—the passport I'd had Chester forge for her. I shook my head, feeling a wave of anxiety crest over me. "I can't just leave. I don't have a passport. I still have things…I need to do." Gerty and Eve and Ivan. They deserved a goodbye. At the very least. The old me, the one who was always running—she was gone. I didn't want to be a coward anymore.

A beam of light punched through our front window. It was Antony pulling up in front. Lil squinted as she looked from his headlights to my face. "You have your phone?"

I shook my head. "It's at Sylvia's."

Lil raised an eyebrow. "The old lady from Delos

Park?"

"Yeah, she let me hide out there. I need to go back to get a few things. Figure out how to get out of here."

Lil sighed, then said, "Okay. I'll text you when I know where I'm going. You'll meet me there, right?" Lil set her mouth into a tight line. We exchanged a long look, so many unspoken things passing between us.

"Yes. I promise." Lil threw her arms around me, nearly taking me down with one of her wayward bags. She planted a kiss on my cheek, and I whispered in her ear, "Be careful."

When Lil pulled back, her cheeky grin had replaced all prior seriousness. "I always am." I returned her smile with my own, paired with some solid eye-rolling, of course. Lil took one last look around our shabby, secondhand home, tossed her key onto the couch and bolted through the front door. I was tempted to go outside and lecture Antony on the importance of keeping my sister safe, but something stopped me.

"She's going to be fine." My voice sounded loud, too harsh for such a quiet empty place. But I needed to say it. Needed to hear it to really believe it.

"You will too."

I let Ares' words sink in. I would be fine. Soon.

Then I stalked towards what would soon be just another room, a space for someone else, but not for me. There wasn't much I needed, or even wanted. I grabbed the framed picture of Gerty, Eve, and I, all smiling after Gerty won her first tournament, and stuffed it into my satchel. I opened my dresser drawer and scooped up every last bit of cash that I'd been squirreling away. I'd never thought about this part of my journey. The small steps in between the grand escape and the final destination. It was strange that I was finally attempting to leave this gods-forsaken place. I thought I wasn't going to make it. I believed I was a lost cause. Just another rat going down with the ship. This bungalow was officially a part of my past. It was time to start looking forward.

Before I left, I made sure to take my favorite coat and pulled a warm knit hat over my head. The red and white beams of strobing emergency lights still painted the night with fluorescent colors. I stayed far away from the scene of the crime.

Instead, I meandered through the many side streets of Olympus, reminding myself with every step how much this place had hurt me, had become a part of me. Sunk its teeth so deep I thought it would never come away. With every block I trekked, its grip on me loosened, bit by bit. I walked past the pool, glancing briefly through the panes of glass to see if maybe there was a familiar swimmer doing laps, but I knew Ivan was still hung up with the cops. It was highly unlikely they'd let him slip away so soon.

When I made it through the wide-open metal gates that had once kept the world out and Cronus and his riches tucked safely inside, his palace was no more than a skeleton. No longer a grand home full of opulence. I didn't want to think about the innocent people who'd died there tonight. I wondered if anyone had bothered to look in the lake, or if Cronus' body was still laying at the bottom of it.

It didn't matter. None of it did. The Othonos family, Ambrosia. The deaths I'd dealt on their behalf. My tainted soul. It was only a small sliver in the grand scheme of things. Arcadia would outlive all of this darkness, and perhaps be better for it.

Perhaps the gods would find a way to help humankind once again. To restore this place to a semblance of its past glory. Things would be different from here on out.

"You seem surprisingly optimistic, Calliope. It is rather

strange to witness."

Sorry, am I scaring you?

"I am merely curious. What happens now that the great battle of your life has concluded?"

I'm just trying to get to tomorrow, is that alright?

"Tomorrow. To live in the present is a delicious thing humans do so well. Yes. Tomorrow."

I started walking towards Delos Park. After Sylvia's I would go to the girls' place.

"Styx! Wait!" I turned back toward Olympus to see Ivan loping my way. He was out of breath and seemed to be favoring one leg. Instinct pulled me to him, my feet pounding against the asphalt as I sprinted his way.

We connected like magnets, held together by forces outside our control. His hands were in my hair, on my waist, everywhere. Mine locked around his middle, keeping him as close to me as I could get him. Ivan peppered my cheeks with light kisses, and then my ears, and then my lips. I kissed back, frantic and desperate for all of his affections. His nearness filled me with the euphoria I'd been craving since walking away from Cronus' lake.

He was breathless as he asked, "Where are you going? What's happening?" His eyes searched mine, his large palms moving to cradle my face. They were so warm. He was so marvelously alive and good and handsome, and I wanted nothing more than to take him with me.

"I'm leaving. I have some business to take care of, but then I—I have to get out of here. Just for a little while. I don't know how but…I have to go." A lump had formed in my throat, one that was too big to try and ignore. "I want you to come with me. Forget about all of this."

Ivan's eyes started getting wet, stealing my breath from me. Damn him for his heart, for his love. "Leaving? Why, and I can't, it's just…" His thumb wiped at my cheek, and I realized I'd let a tear escape somehow. Was I really being that selfish? It's not like I could keep the cops at bay forever. One crime did not forgive another.

Ivan cleared his throat, and I knew he was trying to hold it all together, for me. "I understand that you need to go. But I can't. You said you have things to do? So do I. Right here. I need to make things right my own way."

I wanted to hate him for choosing to be noble over choosing me. I wanted to shove him and walk away. But I could never hate him. It was the good in him that had always pulled me in. And it was his goodness that held me captivated still. I put my hands over his, giving them a squeeze. "I won't stay away forever. I'll come back. For you."

Ivan leaned down, pulling my lips to his. We melted into each other, and his tongue mingled with mine, sending me out of Arcadia and up into the heavens. His hands fisted in my jacket, our bodies pushing against one another, wanting so much more than what we had. I pulled back, my lungs needing air, though the rest of me craved only Ivan.

I breathed, "Can we go somewhere?" Ivan's eyes began to smolder, the pale brown in them going molten. He tucked me under his arm and walked me towards his parked car. I hesitated. "Your car? *Really?*"

Ivan blushed furiously. "You think we're going to—Gods no, I just wanted to drive you to my place."

I rolled my eyes. "Shut up and get in."

The drive was fast but not near enough. The fire growing in my belly would not be made patient. Ivan's villa was close to Cronus' palace. It was much nicer than the shitty housing meant for the rest of the grunts like me and Lil. We'd spent most of our nights together here, but it had been so long. My face flushed when I recalled the last time I'd found myself in Ivan's bed. We wasted no time getting out of his car and heading inside.

The place was squeaky clean, every surface polished and shined like Ivan was preparing to host a gathering. I still didn't understand why he'd chosen a mess like me.

Ivan laced his fingers between mine and guided me to his bedroom. I couldn't decide whether to be elated or distraught. I didn't know when I'd be here again. I didn't know if…

As though he'd read my mind, Ivan tugged me to him and murmured against my neck, "I want you to remember this night, remember it so that you won't want anyone else but me." He pressed his lips to my skin, sending a wave of goosebumps to rise up and down my body. "I want you to think of me every day. To think of this." Ivan's hands trailed down my sides, teasing me with the lightest of touches. And then he was taking off my hat. Peeling away my jacket. I sat on the edge of the bed, and he knelt before me to unlace my boots. Tugging each one off with so much care it made me sick with want. My fingers tangled in his dark curls as I tried to memorize the feel and texture of them in my hands.

Ivan remained kneeling while I pulled his shirt from over his head, his eyes gleaming with the same passion that echoed in me. His body was so familiar, so enticing. I couldn't help but devour every inch of bare skin with my eyes. I waited to see what he would do next. I wanted to savor every second of this. Drink it down and sear it into my memory.

He hooked his thumb and finger around my wrist, bringing my palm to his lips. My eyes fluttered closed at the tender sensation. Ivan's voice was low with reverence as he said, "I want you to remember the feel of my lips against you." He rose from his kneeling position and kicked off his boots. Ivan unbuttoned his pants, grinning at me as I watched them slide to the floor. He hadn't been wearing any underwear. Heat rose to my face. He was ready for me. And I was burning up with need for him. I wasted no time ripping off my remaining clothing, throwing my shirt and jeans to the wayside as though they might be on fire.

I laid back on the bed, holding myself up by my

elbows and the two of us drank in every inch of the other. I was afraid to breathe, afraid that one small move would break this delicious fantasy. Ivan made his way for the bed, his eyes locking onto mine.

"I want you to take everything from me, Calliope. Leave me with nothing. Leave me aching for you."

I swallowed. "I don't want to *take* everything from you, Ivan. I want you to *give* it to me." I grinned as I spread my legs, a blatant invitation for him to come closer.

Ivan wet his lips as he leaned over me, resting his hands on either side of my body. His mouth found mine, and this time it was a crescendo of passion that he'd held back from me for so long. It was a reunion, one that I'd wanted desperately but forced myself to abstain from.

No longer.

I pulled him on top of me, bringing our bodies together in a way that set every single inch of me on fire. Ivan pulled away, breathing heavy, eyes dark. "I will give you all of me. Forever. Will you have me?"

I laughed, relief and the crushing agony of longing at war inside me, "I'll have you. And I'll have you now."

CHAPTER 33

Ivan looked down at me, dragging a hand softly against my arm. His hair shrouded his eyes, but I could still see hints of caramel and green peeking out. Begging me to stay. One more day. One more hour. I knew if Ivan voiced his plea, gave life to his wish, I would do just that. I would let Ivan and Arcadia swallow me whole until I was discovered and tossed in a grimy prison cell for the rest of my days.

I was that stupid, and that much in love with him. Ivan knew that. And so, he pressed a kiss to my head, rolled over to find his pants, and I did the same.

I kept my eyes on him, devouring his subtly toned body, that shitty tattoo of a heart on fire atop his bicep. "Will you come with me? Not like—away. But until I leave?" I cleared my throat, embarrassed by the rasping sound of my voice.

Ivan smiled, his lips parting just enough to reveal the glint of his teeth. "Calliope, I'd love to."

I wanted to lean on my anger, get pissed at the lightness in his tone, but I exhaled instead. A tiny spark remained but I knew that would never change. "I don't have a passport or anything, but I can't stay in the city." I grunted as I tugged on one of my boots. Ivan scowled and I smirked back. "I hate that I'm leaving. Well, kind of. I hate that I'm leaving *you*. I can't be sticking around here just waiting to get arrested. You know that." I watched his throat bob up and down with buried emotion.

Ivan tossed me my hat and said, "I know. Remember when I said I was working on a way to help you? I have something for you." He went to the drawer I knew he kept his undershirts in, and lifted something out of the bottom of it. Something red, and gilded in gold letters. *No fucking way.*

He turned, handing me the passport. "I had this made for you. I just got it not two days ago actually."

"Are you serious?"

Ivan nodded, a small smile parting his lips. "I'm not done yet either. I'm going to find a way for you to come back. Without the need for a fake identity." I tried to absorb some of his optimism so that my eyes wouldn't roll all the way into the back of my head. If I knew anything, I knew that Ivan would do his damndest to scrub my records clean.

Fully dressed, Ivan held his hand out towards the door of his room. "Where to?"

I finished securing my coat when I said, "I need you to text Gerty and Eve and have them meet us at Sylvia's. Oh, make sure Eve brings the thumb drive I asked her to make."

Ivan already had his phone out and was plugging away at the text. "Probably let Sylvia know, too."

Ivan's fingers flew over his phone. "Done."

"Good."

I heaved a sigh. Gods, I hadn't realized that I would hate this so damned much. "It's time to say my goodbyes to Arcadia."

Ivan held his car door open for me. "It's only goodbye for now. You promised, remember?"

"Right."

When we got to Sylvia's, Eve and Gerty were already there. Gerty was wearing a clean change of clothes, and her hair looked damp, like maybe she'd gotten in the shower as soon as she'd gotten home. Eve looked like she'd been through the emotional wringer. Her eyes were bloodshot, with globs of mascara tracks running down her cheeks. Sylvia and Gerty were sitting opposite each other in the breakfast nook that had been my bed for the past two days. Eve was leaning against the counter behind Gerty, a hand placed protectively on her shoulder.

I surprisingly still had tears to squeeze out. When Eve lunged for me, pulling me into the tightest hug I'd ever had in my entire life, I burst like a dam breaking. Rivers of tears raced down my face, and I sniffled like a baby against Eve's bosom. My body shook with pent up emotion. As I let go of the weight of this night, more arms found their way around me. The scent of patchouli and cologne filled my nose. My heart stopped racing, and slowly, my tears subsided. When I'd finally regained my composure, Ivan and everyone else slowly stepped away, until only Eve and I remained.

I pressed my forehead to hers. "You saved me."

Confusion pooled in Eve's eyes. "What d—"

The next words rushed out of me, too powerful, too real to keep stymied any longer. "You loved me when I didn't. You made me see the better side of me." Eve's face crumpled. Her own tears further mangling her makeup. There might have been more words exchanged, but my ears were ringing, the tenderness overwhelming my everything.

Gerty reached around and handed me a box

of tissues. I took two and Eve took a couple more as I dabbed at my eyes and nose. I didn't want to drag this out any longer than necessary. I was the kind of person who preferred to rip the bandage off in one go. If it's got to hurt, make it count.

"Eve, I need you to give the thumb drive to Sylvia." Eve pulled the slender device from her bag and handed it to Sylvia who looked incredibly perplexed. "Sylvia—The list of chemicals that make up Ambrosia are on that thumb drive. I'm giving it to you, because I trust you to do the right thing, even though I have no idea what that might be." I shrugged, not wanting to dwell on the fact that I'd openly admitted some smidgen of ignorance to my friends.

Sylvia looked me up and down, her wrinkled face inquisitive as she said, "Have you thought of your place as *Makarios*? What you might do with your status?"

I crinkled my brows. "Sylvia, I don't give a shit about my status. As long as I'm alive, that's good enough for me." She pursed her lips, and I think it was the first time I'd ever seen her disappointed.

"Do you truly not care?"

Life is too precious for all that tedious bullshit.

There was a lengthy pause, but then Ares muttered, *"Some tedium is worthwhile."* I ignored Ares' slight and reached for Sylvia's hand instead. Her expression smoothed, a warm smile replacing her frown. I opened my mouth to speak, but there was nothing in my head, only an immense sensation of love pouring out of my heart. She wrapped her fingers around mine, squeezing them with surprising strength.

She nodded, clearly holding back her own emotions. "I'll always be here for you, my girl."

Ivan looked at his watch, and my mouth ran dry. Every hour I lingered was another hour closer to police detection. "I have to go. I have to leave Arcadia."

Eve winced. Like I'd slapped her. But then she

nodded, grabbing another tissue from her girlfriend. "For how long?"

"Until it's safe for me to come back, I guess." I ran my teeth over my bottom lip. "I need my phone. Lil said she would tell me where to meet her." Sylvia rose, shimmying between everyone to the charging port. She passed my phone to Ivan, who passed it to Gerty, who tossed it to me. The screen was lit up, with one message from Lil. When I read the words, a sweet phantom breeze wafted through the air. For once, my sister had made a pretty decent choice.

"When I get there, I'll be in touch." My words started coming out all mushy and wrong sounding. I felt the pressure of another wave building behind my eyes. I had to get out of there before I melted into a puddle of my own emotions again.

Gerty's mouth hung open, still in shock over everything that had taken place that night. She said, "Promise? Don't you dare say no. Don't you dare." Her face was splotchy, but she held her sorrow at bay…for now.

I nodded, my voice refusing to work at all. And then I started backing away. "This is the last time I'm running away. I promise." And then I burst through the door, stumbling down the steps and into Ivan's car. He wasn't far behind, his face veiled, but still I could see the look of grim determination in his eyes as he ducked into the driver's seat.

Ivan took the scenic route as he drove us through the city. My eyes raked over every building, each alley, the marbled statues of gods dotting the random corners of town. The neon lights of the clubs and bars began fading, and the sun began its rise. As we crested over the hill towards the airport, honeyed sunlight danced across the glassy surfaces of skyscrapers and along the waves of the False Sea.

I needed to distract myself from the mounting

sense of doom that was going to be our goodbye, so I asked, "What are you going to do that's supposed to fix the mess your uncle left?" I traced a heart in the condensation that collected on the passenger window.

Ivan glanced over at me, "I'm going to use all the money he probably left me to do something good. Something right."

I snorted. "Okay. Vague, but I guess it's a start. Like what? What would be so good it would undo Cronus' bullshit?" Clouds dotted the periwinkle sky, tinged yellow from the morning rays.

Ivan asked, "What would you do? What do you think would make Arcadia more bearable?" I sensed a hint of resentment in his comment. He'd never understood my disdain for his city. I thought hard for a moment, tried to summon up some brilliant idea that would show Ivan I was smarter than I actually was. I imagined myself walking through the streets. What did I see? What did I hear?

Suffering.

"What if you give all of that money to the people who are stuck on the streets? Like Cap. What about giving him some of Cronus' riches?"

Ivan's eyebrows furrowed. "That's an interesting idea. What else you got?"

I shrugged, hating the growing frequency of planes overhead. That meant we would be parting soon. "Whatever you do, find a way to give those people a better shot. Arcadia has too many citizens without an actual place to put their roots down." Ivan was quiet, and I wasn't sure if it was because he was considering my idea, or if he too was dreading the nearing moment when we would have to separate for…a while.

All too soon he came to a stop outside of the door that read, DEPARTURES. He dutifully pulled my bag from the back and yanked something else out from under his seat. When he came around the car, I could see what he was holding. It was a book.

He held it out to me, along with my satchel. "I thought you might need something to read, while you're pining for me." I looked down at the cover. The book in question was *Arcadia, City Of 1,000 Joys*. It had a watercolor painting of Delos Park on the cover. Ivan grinned. "So you'll have some good date ideas when you get back."

"Where did you even get this book?" I laughed, slapping him playfully with it.

"It was in my house. I've had it forever. And now you get to borrow it, for a while."

"Just a while. I'll be back." I tucked the small book into my bag, stepping closer to Ivan. "I love you." He snaked an arm around my waist and tugged me closer. I pressed my cheek against his chest and tried to hear his heart beating.

I felt his chin against my head as he said, "I love you too. I expect a full list of date plans. With detailed schedules."

I snorted. "No way, man. You think I'm actually going to read that book? Ha." I stood on my toes, planting my lips on Ivan's. I kissed him the way I'd kissed him for the very first time. Tender, like I might break him if I went too far. He was precious, sacred to me. All the goodness in the world didn't measure up to this man, and he was all mine.

Ivan held me against him for another long moment that went by all too quickly, and then I left. I bought a ticket to a tiny island in the middle of nowhere, and I left Arcadia.

14 MONTHS
LATER

EPILOGUE

The braid Lil had given me was making my scalp itch. She'd pulled too tight, and I'd dealt with the discomfort for too long. I yanked out the elastic and shook my hair free. It hadn't grown as much as I thought it would. Apparently, it liked being short. The relief came immediately, but it did nothing to stop my guts from screaming with anticipation. Lil had opted to stay on Digyo with Antony, who'd been crashing in our tiny bungalow since about March. I was sick of him, and he was sick of me telling him I was sick of him.

After we'd left Arcadia, we'd chosen a place that was warm, beautiful, and unknown to many. Lil started working as a grocery store clerk, painting on the side, and I did a little bit of everything I could to help pay the rent. We'd made up a totally ridiculous story to Mom and Dad about how Lil had an emotional breakdown and needed to take a gap year somewhere else. Of course, I needed to go with her, being the wonderful big sister that I was. Lil and I even offered to have them come visit us, but Mom hated flying, and Dad hated being hot. It worked out pretty

295

perfectly.

Except for the fact that every single gods-damned day, Ares drove me crazy with his relentless tirades about remaining fit until I caved and began an extensive routine to maintain my prowess as a fighter. And then there was the fact that my boyfriend and my best friends were living their best lives in Arcadia while I was stranded on some remote island without them. You know what they say about the grass being greener? It was greener for about two weeks. Then Ares started barking, and I started getting restless.

I thought I would be relieved to finally be out of the city that eats dreams right along with the dreamers who thought them up, but when the daily life of Digyo caught up to me, it was nothing compared to late nights spent wandering downtown Arcadia. Don't get me started on missing the fights.

It was something I'd 100 percent taken for granted. All my life I'd been an avid fan, attending matches whenever my dad had the time to take us to the city. Then bam, no fights. No outlet for the blood thirsty heathen inside me. It grew increasingly more difficult to remain on the island.

Then Ivan came to visit. And he told me that he and Sylvia were working on giving me special immunity because of my status as *Makarios*. I had served the will of the gods; how could I be faulted for their divine intervention? Ares *loved* that.

Unfortunately, bureaucracy sucks, so months and months later, I was finally standing on the sidewalk outside of the Arcadia airport, waiting for my ride. The air was warm. I was grateful I didn't need to wear the coat I'd tucked into my carry-on. Honestly, I'd wear a burlap sack if it meant I could be in Arcadia. I would walk down the streets naked if I had to.

A silver sedan pulled up next to me, and Ivan burst from the driver's side, slid over the hood of his car, and

landed directly in front of me. He wasted no time hoisting
me up in his arms. My legs flew out behind me as he spun
us around. I screeched with delight, so insanely relieved to
be with this person again. My person.

Ivan let out a rich belly laugh, allowing my feet to
find the concrete beneath me again. I wrapped my arms
around his neck, standing on my toes to kiss him. We'd
seen each other a few months ago, but that was just a tease,
promising us the kind of life we never thought we'd have
together, and then taking it all back when he had to fly
home, leaving me safely behind.

He melted against me, and I joined him, letting my
limbs go soft with wanton relief. When we parted, Ivan was
already grinning. He looked more like a schoolboy, excited
to show off his new toy than a man about to take his
girlfriend back to her parents' house for dinner. I couldn't
help the stirring of butterflies in my stomach. Everything
felt surreal. How could any of this actually be my life? Ivan
started dragging me toward the car, toward Arcadia.

I'd been awake going on eighteen hours, thanks to
the ridiculously difficult route I had to take traveling home,
but I was riding on the intense high of disbelief.

*"Will we be visiting the ring before long, as you said we
would?"*

Ares had been badgering me incessantly about a
chance to test my salts once we got back to the city. I'd
given him my word hoping it would shut him up. Instead,
he just continued to bother me about it. Constantly.

*I said we would, so we will. Can you give me some privacy
for a bit?*

"I'll return when it's time to fight."

We cruised into the towering maze of gleaming
steel and glass. My heart slammed against my ribcage and
something like joy started rattling the parts I'd been hiding
away until this exact moment. Delos Park wasn't far ahead,
and as Ivan steered us down the winding streets that would

take us there, I couldn't help but grin. It felt almost as if I had finally proven myself. I'd had my own stupid journey and now the city of Arcadia was welcoming me back as one of her own.

We drove by Jason's, and I almost pressed my nose up against the glass, like a dog excited to chase after squirrels. And then we drove by the club, closed until nightfall thankfully, otherwise Ares would've started howling between my ears.

"How does it feel to be back?" Ivan was considering me, his hazel eyes catching the sunshine in the most dazzling way. I wanted to look at him looking at me like that for the rest of time.

"It feels like a dream. I'm here. I'm *not* dead. And I'm happy? What the hell?" I couldn't help but laugh. It was completely absurd.

Ivan cocked his head to the side. "It *is* a dream. The best dream I've ever had. You know what's really great about it?"

I raised an eyebrow. "What?"

"It's not a dream."

"That is the cheesiest thing you've ever said." I tried not to let him have another smile over such an awful joke, but it came out anyway. I wasn't sure I'd ever be able to stop smiling. "Where are we going anyway? I really don't like surprises."

Ivan turned, taking us past the intersection that would lead us to Delos. I was getting anxious to arrive at our destination, wherever that may be. He said, "We don't have to be at your family's thing until tonight, so I thought we'd throw you a little…welcome home party."

The feeling of love was so acute it was like an arrow shot straight through my heart. For so long I'd been hard, protected by my own cruelty. A year off the job and I was a soft little thing, ready to cry at the drop of a hat. I cleared my throat. "You're throwing me a party?"

"Yep. But don't get all choked up, it's just a small thing. And no matter what Eve says, it was *my* idea."

A few minutes passed, and I realized where we were headed. "You're still at Olympus? I thought you said you'd moved out." I frowned.

Ivan shook his head. "No, I don't live there anymore. I'm not the host of the party."

He'd piqued my interest. "Then who is?" We pulled through the entry, though it no longer had gates keeping the general population out. The buildings and bungalows remained the same, but where Cronus' palace once stood was now just a stretch of green, sprinkled with trails and benches. A park, complete with a lake. There were people walking around, riding bikes, carrying sacks of groceries, strolling along in couples. It was like any other neighborhood in the suburbs, only this was in the heart of Arcadia. "What's going on?"

Ivan parked and we got out before he decided to answer me. "Welcome to the newest subdivision in the city." He hooked his arm through mine, leading me like a tour guide. He pointed at his old villa. "This is where the subdivision director lives. He's hosting us today."

"Hey, Ivan!" An older man with white hair and a snaggled grin I'd know anywhere started walking down the front steps towards us.

I stopped in my tracks, looking back and forth between the two, in complete disbelief. "Cap?" He kept grinning as he went to shake my hand. I pulled his arm, dragging him in for a hug. "I missed you while I was gone. Looks like you've been doing alright for yourself."

Cap elbowed Ivan playfully. "I've had some pretty good comeuppance. It's been quiet without a certain Killer Bee on the streets. Welcome back." He led us around the corner to a small garden bursting with flowers. Sitting at a bistro table were the girls, Sylvia, and Ivan's dad, Tobi. They'd been chatting, cups of coffee steaming in their hands.

When they saw me, all three women rose as one, and proceeded to maul me to death. They sang a chorus of, "You look so good!" and "You're still too skinny!" To all of which I replied, "Mmhphhh" because there was nothing else I could possibly utter while being suffocated with so much love. Tobi rose, standing beside me, laughing.

Eve broke free of our group huddle first and began dragging me towards a table situated further back in the yard. "Come get some food, and some caffeine, I'm sure you want some." When we were a little further from earshot, Eve murmured, "He's turned Olympus into transitional housing. Isn't that great?"

That was the last straw. This heart of mine had become weak with love. I choked out my next words, "He did?"

Eve nodded as she loaded up a plate with berries and scones drizzled with chocolate. "He did. He said it was your idea."

"He did?"

Eve's smile lit up like a beam of pure starlight. "It's a new world. He's been working with the city officials to clean up the last dregs of Ambrosia, too. It's still out there, though." Even a year and some change later, my salivary glands went wild at the thought of that sweet, terrible drug. I curled my fingers into a fist, then released. It didn't have a hold on me. Not anymore. Eve went on, "Cirillo's gone into hiding, no one's talking about where she and her people have holed up. I'd say you're all clear."

I'd long stopped caring about what happened to that conniving woman, but it was comforting to know she was out of the picture. "Good riddance."

Eve handed me the plate, and I took a massive bite out of the chocolate scone. She said, "But now that you're back…I'm sure things will get more entertaining." She bumped my hip with hers and laughed. It was a sound I'd never get tired of.

I meandered toward the group, marveling at the sensation of lightness in my feet. Happiness in Arcadia? I used to think it was impossible. Ivan was eyeing more than just my plate, devouring my figure with one glance that had me feeling completely ablaze with pent up sexual energy. We broke eye contact one heated moment later, after the conversation had gone awkward when everyone noticed the tension roiling off us.

The next hours were spent with the people who'd somehow managed to fill my heart with their very persons. We laughed and gorged ourselves on delicious fresh fruit, enjoying the warm day as it settled against our skin. I started to meld into this strange dream that wasn't a dream. It was too sweet, too beautiful, and I struggled to believe I deserved it. And still, I leaned into it. I forced myself to pretend that yes, yes, I did deserve good things, and yes, I did deserve this wonderful day. It wasn't long until I began to really see it that way.

Gerty and Eve had to leave; they had plans to visit an art gallery on the east side of town. We embraced, and I savored the idea that this would happen all the time. There was no more running for me.

Sylvia stayed longer, wanting to discuss the finer points of my *Makarios* status. She'd said, "Be prepared for strangers to notice you. Be wary of your surroundings. Just because you are no longer a criminal doesn't mean you are off the hook. People know what you are. It's out in the world, and they might come for you." Sylvia took my hand in both of hers. They were so strong, and so soft. "Be careful. We'll be in touch." A whisper of curiosity flitted across my psyche. I knew there was more to what she was saying, but at the moment, I didn't much care. I was busy living in this strange paradise.

Ivan straightened his blue tie for the twentieth time as we neared the front door of my parents' house. I hadn't been home in way too long. More than a year had passed since I'd seen either my mom or dad. Sure, we'd talked, sent letters and that sort of thing, but it wasn't the same. Things were strained and distant. I wanted them to be right again. What better way to start than to bring a boy home?

"It's straight. I promise. They won't even notice."

Ivan gave me a sweltering side eye. "Are you saying they won't notice I'm wearing a tie, or they won't notice that it's crooked?"

I rolled my eyes, tugging my dress down. I didn't want to admit that I was feeling nervous too. They were just my parents; how bad could it be? "This is the least scary thing you've ever had to do. It's going to be fine."

Ivan laughed, and it was fluttery with nerves. "Easy for you to say, you know them. And you're not dating their oldest child."

I snatched Ivan's hand with my own. "That's true. They're probably going to roast you and eat you." It was too much fun to pester him like this. "It's been nice knowing you."

Ivan yanked me closer to him, whispering in my ear, "I'm just messing around. They're going to love me and disown you."

I pretended to bite him. "We'll see about that." I took in a deep breath, then let it out and with it all of my petty anxieties. There were worse things to fear, and none of them were here, not anymore.

The End

Other works by Kait Waterhouse

A Stirring from the Depths, 2024

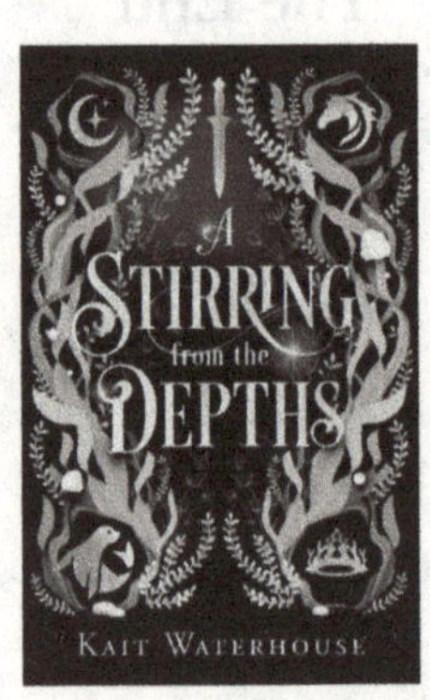

Acknowledgements

Oracle City: The Makarios wouldn't be what it is without the love and support of countless people. This book poured out of me in a fire of obsession, much like Styx's fury. My sister, and critique partner, Mel, helped me find the balance in the mayhem while also managing to encourage me to make it just a little more chaotic. Thank you for always reading every sentence I write, and for cheering me on whenever I need it most.

I came up with this book during a weekly meeting with my AWG writing group. Amelie, Carrie, Andrea, Nicole, and Dareth were there the moment Styx was born, and because they all shouted into their cameras "This needs to be a book!" I kept going. Thank you all for the love you continuously show as I muddle my way through publishing.

The characters Eve and Gerty were deeply inspired by two of my chosen sisters, who've always had my back. They have both loved me completely, and always managed to make me feel like a million bucks. My heart aches that Ashlee will never get to see this finished work, but my deepest gratitude goes to her for being an endless light in my life. I will love you and cherish your memory, always.

Books require lots and lots of attention before they can make it out into the world. These amazing writer friends helped me hone my craft and polish *Oracle City* into what it is today: Michaela Cunningham, you are an incredible beta reader and I will always throw my manuscripts at your feet for your wisdom. Ashley Merdalo, I'm really sorry that Ares isn't into Styx like that, but your feedback fueled my fire to keep honing their storyline.

Sophie Henderson, your excitement for this book was much needed, thank you for believing in me and in Styx. To my Tortured Writer's Department– thank you for gently holding my hand through this journey. To Kay Morton, the amazing editor who absolutely saved the day when I was left high and dry– you are fabulous and I am so grateful for your eye and your speed. Bless you.

My family. Oh, my family. My beloved grandfather, T who suggested the list of characters at the beginning, was able to read an early draft before passing away. I miss calling him for advice, but I know he is proud. Gram, who loved the darkness and the brutality of this book and always loves my stories, I love you dearly. My mom, and step-dad who come to my bookish events, bring copies of my books to sell for me when they travel, and hype me up any other way they can— I am so lucky to have you. My sisters, Mel and Kari who support me and cheer me on with every story I finish— I love you.

And to my dear Marouane, who helped me see that I can do this, that I *should* do this, and that I am only just getting started— I am so glad I found you.

About the Author

Kait Waterhouse is a fantasy and speculative fiction author. You can usually find her reading or obsessively drafting another novel, unless she's busy making a mess of herself crafting or teaching college students.

Kait writes stories for people who are curious about the darkness inside all of us, and for those who know there is good to be found in every corner of the world. She is pursuing her PhD in Youth Literature at the University of Arizona.

Find her at:
kaitwaterhousewrites.com

9 789899 301120